OXFORD WORLD'S CLASSICS

DISCOURSES, FRAGMENTS, HANDBOOK

EPICTETUS (*c*.50–*c*.135) was an influential teacher of Stoic ethical philosophy. He was born a slave in Hierapolis (modern Anatolia), and was owned for a while by Epaphroditus, a powerful freedman (ex-slave) at the court of Nero in Rome. He studied with the Stoic teacher Musonius Rufus and taught philosophy in Rome. When banished, along with other philosophers, from Rome in 89 by the emperor Domitian, he set up a school in Nicopolis in Greece on the Adriatic coast and taught there until his death. He did not marry but adopted an infant child late in life. Epictetus' school was well known and attracted many students and visitors, including Hadrian (emperor 117–38).

Arrian (*c*.86–160), later an important historian, studied with Epictetus in his youth, perhaps in 107–9. Arrian recorded and published Epictetus' informal lectures and conversations on ethics, in eight books, of which four books and some fragments survive. These are the *Discourses*; Arrian also wrote a summary of main themes, the *Handbook* or *Manual* (*Enchiridion*). Epictetus uses these conversations to bring out key principles of Stoic ethics, and conveys these in vivid, accessible language. He aims to show that Stoic ethics can have a transforming influence on the way you live and offers a powerful pathway to human happiness. These writings made Epictetus one of the best-known Stoic teachers in antiquity; they strongly influenced the *Meditations*, a philosophical diary by Marcus Aurelius (emperor 161–80). They have attracted the interest of many readers and thinkers in later antiquity and from the sixteenth century to the present. In the modern world, Epictetus helped to shape the development of cognitive psychotherapy and is becoming more widely used in 'guide-to-life' writings.

ROBIN HARD has translated Apollodorus' *Library of Greek Mythology* and Diogenes the Cynic, *Sayings and Anecdotes*, for Oxford World's Classics, and is the author of *The Routledge Handbook of Greek Mythology*.

CHRISTOPHER GILL is Professor of Ancient Thought at the University of Exeter. He has written extensively on ancient philosophy, especially on Hellenistic and Roman ethics and psychology.

OXFORD WORLD'S CLASSICS

*For over 100 years Oxford World's Classics have brought
readers closer to the world's great literature. Now with over 700
titles—from the 4,000-year-old myths of Mesopotamia to the
twentieth century's greatest novels—the series makes available
lesser-known as well as celebrated writing.*

*The pocket-sized hardbacks of the early years contained
introductions by Virginia Woolf, T. S. Eliot, Graham Greene,
and other literary figures which enriched the experience of reading.
Today the series is recognized for its fine scholarship and
reliability in texts that span world literature, drama and poetry,
religion, philosophy, and politics. Each edition includes perceptive
commentary and essential background information to meet the
changing needs of readers.*

OXFORD WORLD'S CLASSICS

EPICTETUS

Discourses, Fragments, Handbook

Translated by
ROBIN HARD

With an Introduction and Notes by
CHRISTOPHER GILL

OXFORD
UNIVERSITY PRESS

OXFORD
UNIVERSITY PRESS

Great Clarendon Street, Oxford OX2 6DP
United Kingdom

Oxford University Press is a department of the University of Oxford.
It furthers the University's objective of excellence in research, scholarship,
and education by publishing worldwide. Oxford is a registered trade mark of
Oxford University Press in the UK and in certain other countries

Translation © Robin Hard 2014

Editorial material © Christopher Gill 2014

First published as an Oxford World's Classics paperback 2014

Impression 18

Published in the United States of America by Oxford University Press
198 Madison Avenue, New York, NY 10016, United States of America

British Library Cataloguing in Publication Data

Data available

Library of Congress Control Number: 2013938925

ISBN 978–0–19–959518–1

Printed and bound in Great Britain by
Clays Ltd, Elcograf S.p.A.

CONTENTS

INTRODUCTION

EPICTETUS' *Discourses* form one of three compelling statements of
Stoic practical ethics from the early Roman Empire; the other two are
Seneca's *Letters* and Marcus Aurelius' *Meditations*. Epictetus' work is
in some ways the most important. Epictetus, unlike the other two
thinkers, was a formal Stoic teacher and one of the best known of
his age. The *Discourses* and *Handbook* are forceful, direct, and chal-
lenging, and are expressed in a way that is accessible to a very wide
range of people. They set out the core ethical principles of Stoicism
in a form designed to help people put them into practice and to use
them as a basis for leading a good human life. One central message is
that the basis for happiness or well-being is 'up to us' and that we all
have the capacity to move towards this state, regardless of our specific
social context or individual character. A related theme is that making
progress in this direction requires a combination of sustained reflection and hard work, especially in embedding our principles in our
actions and relationships. Epictetus also stresses that this capacity
forms an integral and inalienable part of what makes human beings
distinctive in the natural universe, as well as the prime expression of
what is 'divine' within us. Epictetus' *Discourses* have been the most
widely read and influential of all Stoic writings, from antiquity
onwards. They still speak eloquently to modern readers and have
taken on a new significance in recent years as the basis for 'life-guides'
and cognitive psychotherapy.

Epictetus' Life and the Background to the Writings

We know little about Epictetus' life (*c*.50–*c*.135);[1] and most of what
we know comes from his writings. He was born in Hierapolis, a substantial city about a hundred miles east of Ephesus in what is now
south-western Turkey. He was probably a slave by birth, and moved to
Rome at some point, perhaps when he was acquired by Epaphroditus,
a freedman (ex-slave), who was a secretary and influential figure
during the rule of the emperors Nero (54–69) and Domitian (81–96).

---

[1] All dates are AD unless otherwise indicated.

Epictetus describes himself at one point as a lame old man (1.16.20);[2] his lameness may have been the result of old age. It was probably while with Epaphroditus that Epictetus gained experience of the ambition, jealousy, and capriciousness of life at the imperial court that he evokes vividly in the *Discourses*. Epaphroditus allowed him to study philosophy, while still a slave (1.9.29), with Musonius Rufus (*c*.30–*c*.101), a well-known Stoic, some of whose teachings on practical ethics have been recorded. At some stage, Epictetus was freed by Epaphroditus and set himself up as a teacher at Rome, perhaps supported by Musonius. In 89 the emperor Domitian banished all philosophers from Italy, suspecting them of opposition to his regime. Epictetus settled in Nicopolis in Epirus, in eastern Greece, a large and prosperous city, which was easy for people to visit from Italy as well as Greece. He set up a school of philosophy, which became quite famous, and was visited on one occasion by Hadrian (emperor 117–38). He seems to have remained there, with short visits elsewhere, until his death. He was single, dedicated to his teaching it would seem; but we are told that late in life he adopted an infant who would otherwise have died, and took a wife or partner to look after the child.

Although we normally refer to the *Discourses* and *Handbook* as works by Epictetus, it seems that Epictetus, like Musonius and, more famously, Socrates (469–399 BC), wrote nothing. These works constitute records of his teaching preserved by Arrian, who studied with Epictetus as a young man, probably under Trajan (emperor 105–13), when Epictetus was in his fifties or early sixties. Arrian came from a wealthy Greek family in Nicomedia (on the south-western coast of the Black Sea), and went on to have a distinguished political and military career at Rome under Hadrian. He was also the author of a number of historical works, including an important biography of Alexander the Great. Book 1 of the *Discourses* is prefaced in our manuscripts by a letter in which Arrian presents them as a literal record of Epictetus' teachings, based on the notes he took as a student, and designed to reproduce the powerful effect that Epictetus had on his listeners. Arrian may understate his own role in turning his notes into written discourses, in monologue or dialogue form, of which each has its own coherence and one (4.1) is extremely long. However, the simple

---

[2] All references are to the *Discourses* unless otherwise indicated; references are to Book and Discourse (e.g. 4.8) and sometimes also the paragraph within the Discourse (e.g. 4.8.3).

language (Greek 'common usage', or *koinē*) and forceful directness of style are very different from Arrian's own writings; and so we may indeed be hearing something very close to Epictetus' own voice. It seems that Arrian originally wrote eight books, of which only the first four survive, and that he himself produced the *Handbook* (or *Manual*, *Encheiridion*) which is a summary of key themes from the *Discourses*.[3]

What is the main function of the *Discourses?* Although we often refer to them as Epictetus' teachings, this is at least partly misleading. The writings are not reports of Epictetus' main formal instruction to his students. It is clear from references in the *Discourses* that this took the form of exposition of major Stoic treatises, especially by the third head of the school, Chrysippus (*c*.280–206 BC), written exercises in logic, and probably some dialogues of Plato. Presumably the lessons covered the three main parts of the Stoic curriculum, that is, ethics, logic, and physics (study of nature), though logic seems to have been studied most intensively.[4] The *Discourses* record discussions that are more informal in character, which took place in or around the school, probably in the open air. Most of the discourses are directed, explicitly or by implication, at Epictetus' students, that is, young men in their late teens or early twenties, many of whom were living away from their families. This was a group of people whose experience of practical or social life was often quite limited, but who were already quite sophisticated in their knowledge of philosophy.

A recurrent theme of Epictetus' teachings is that studying philosophy is not just a matter of interpreting texts or developing facility in intellectual activities, notably logical reasoning. It is a matter of learning to give an overall shape and purpose to your life and of using your understanding to inform all aspects of your actions, attitudes, and relationships.[5] This view of the aim of philosophy would have been

---

[3] Although various titles were attached in antiquity to the main writings (*Diatribai* or *Dissertationes*, both meaning 'informal talks'), it seems unlikely that Arrian gave the work any title: the title used here, *Discourses*, is one conventionally used to identify the work. See A. A. Long, *Epictetus: A Stoic and Socratic Guide to Life* (Oxford, 2002), 38–43.

[4] Study of formal logic (valid and invalid forms of reasoning) formed a central part of philosophical training in the early Imperial period, and not only in Stoic schools; Epictetus' works represent an important source for this training: see J. Barnes, *Logic and the Imperial Stoa* (Leiden, 1997), ch. 3; P. Crivelli, 'Epictetus and Logic', in T. Scaltsas and A. S. Mason (eds.), *The Philosophy of Epictetus* (Oxford, 2007).

[5] See e.g. 1.4.6–15, 1.7.1–8, 1.17.13–18, 3.21.7–9. See also Long, *Epictetus*, ch. 4; J. M. Cooper, 'The Relevance of Moral Theory to Moral Improvement in Epictetus', in Scaltsas and Mason (eds.), *Philosophy of Epictetus*.

widely accepted in the Hellenistic era (third to first centuries BC) and
in the first two centuries AD. The distinctive feature of Stoicism is
the claim that, as the Stoics put it, 'virtue is the only good', and that
living virtuously is the only proper overall goal of a human life, in
comparison with which other so-called good things are 'matters of
indifference'.[6] Much of Epictetus' teaching is directed at underlining
the point that the aim of studying philosophy is to give your life an
overall structure and sense of priorities in line with the Stoic view
of happiness, a message sometimes reinforced by criticism of other
ethical approaches, notably, the Epicurean (1.23, 2.20). Also,
Epictetus sets out to offer guidance about the way that this process
should affect one's belief-set, emotions, personal relationships, and
pattern of activities. Typically, the addressees are presumed to be
Epictetus' students; sometimes he is presented as talking to older
men, who visited his school because they lived locally or were
attracted by his reputation (e.g. 2.4, 2.14, 2.24, 3.4, 3.7, 3.9). His
message is essentially the same in both cases, but is sometimes specifically directed to people with more practical experience but with
little previous study.[7]

Distinctive Themes: Relationship to Stoic Theory

If this is Epictetus' overall aim in his teachings, how do the writings
we have reflect this aim? Is there an explicit or implied system of
organization in the *Discourses* and *Handbook*? How far do the topics
covered in Epictetus' works correspond with those recognized as
standard in Stoic theory? Does Epictetus have original or innovative
ideas, within Stoicism, that are put forward in these records of his
discussions? These are rather complex, sometimes debated, questions, but ones that need to be addressed to make full sense of these
suggestive writings.

   First, how far do the topics in the *Discourses* map onto recognized

---

[6] On this conception of philosophy in the Hellenistic–Roman period and the distinctive Stoic thesis on virtue and happiness, see J. Annas, *The Morality of Happiness*
(Oxford, 1993), chs. 1, 19, 22; R. W. Sharples, *Stoics, Epicureans and Sceptics: An
Introduction to Hellenistic Philosophy* (London, 1996), ch. 5; J. Sellars, *Stoicism* (Chesham,
2006), ch. 5. For evidence for the Stoic position, see A. A. Long and D. N. Sedley, *The
Hellenistic Philosophers*, 2 vols. (Cambridge, 1987), 58, 63, hereafter referred to as LS;
references are to sections and passages unless otherwise indicated.

[7] See e.g. 1.11 (also Long, *Epictetus*, 77–9), centred on a father's reaction to his daughter's
illness.

themes in Stoic theory? As noted earlier, Stoic doctrines were, typically, subdivided between logic, ethics, and physics (study of nature), all interpreted quite broadly. At the same time, Stoic thinkers aimed to combine and synthesize the main findings of these branches of knowledge, and certain 'interface' topics, notably on the boundaries between ethics and physics or logic, were regarded as especially important. Ethics is the main area relevant for Epictetus, though also important are topics relating to connections with logic and physics.[8] Here is a standard list of Stoic ethical topics: motivation (*hormē*), good and bad, emotions or passions (*pathē*), virtue, the end or goal of life (*telos*), value and actions, 'appropriate actions' (*kathēkonta*), modes of encouragement or discouragement. Although we have lost all but quotations from the treatises on these subjects from the heads of the Stoic school in the Hellenistic period, we have summaries of Stoic ethics that match these headings.[9] How far do the subjects of Epictetus' writings relate to these summaries?

A simple glance at the titles of the *Discourses*, which seem to go back to Arrian, shows that Epictetus' topics do not map directly onto the standard headings or subheadings of Stoic ethical theory. Epictetus' subjects are more diverse, localized, and repetitious; like the Socratic dialogues in Plato or Xenophon (a significant background influence on the *Discourses*), they often focus on topics that arose in exchanges between Epictetus and his various interlocutors. However, it is also clear that Epictetus presupposes the contents of Stoic ethical doctrines. In formulating an interpretative framework for the *Discourses*, how useful is it to read them as reflecting the full range of those doctrines? In two rather remarkable studies written at the end of the nineteenth century, Adolf Bonhöffer set out to show that the themes of the *Discourses* could be correlated, point for point, with standard topics and specific doctrines in Stoic ethics and cognate

---

[8] See LS 26: topics such as psychology (LS 53), theology (LS 54), and determinism (LS 62) fall in the interface between these branches of knowledge. See also C. Gill, *The Structured Self in Hellenistic and Roman Thought* (Oxford, 2006), 160–6, 197–203.

[9] See LS 56 A; this list forms the basis for the selection of evidence in LS 56–66 (except for 62). The main summaries of Stoic ethics are in Cicero, *On Ends* 3; Diogenes Laertius 7.84–131; Stobaeus 2.5–12 (= 2.57–116 in the edition of C. Wachsmuth and O. Hense (Berlin, 1884–1912; repr. 1958)). For complete translations, see B. Inwood and L. P. Gerson, *Hellenistic Philosophy: Introductory Readings* (Indianapolis, 1997), 190–260; B. Inwood and L. P. Gerson, *The Stoics Reader: Selected Writings and Testimonia* (Indianapolis, 2008), 113–76. See also M. Schofield, 'Stoic Ethics', in B. Inwood (ed.), *The Cambridge Companion to the Stoics* (Cambridge, 2003).

areas, especially psychology.[10] More recent scholars have suggested
that this gives an over-systematic view of the character of Epictetus'
discussions. A. A. Long, for instance, in his monograph on the
Discourses, highlights six broad and partly overlapping types of
topic, namely: theoretical, methodological, and polemical, and psychological, social, and vocational.[11] Other scholars have tended to see
ethical progress or development as the unifying theme, sometimes
using Epictetus' own three-topic programme for this process as an
interpretative key for making sense of the writings.[12]

If we look at this question in more detail, we can identify three
subjects or clusters of subjects that are especially prominent in the
Discourses. All three subjects are also important in other writings on
Stoic ethics, though Epictetus' treatment sometimes has distinctive
emphases. One is our capacity for rational agency, and a second our
capacity for ethical (especially social) development; a third is the idea
that these capacities form key distinctive features of human nature
within the framework of a divinely shaped universe.[13] It is worthwhile
to consider each of these topics, and to see how far Epictetus' treatment
of them fits with typical patterns of Stoic thinking. Subsequently, I
shall discuss how these themes fit together and what overall purpose
they serve within the context of Epictetus' teaching.

A cluster of ideas prominent in the *Discourses* can be linked with
the notion of rational agency. One is the idea that we can and should
distinguish clearly between what is 'up to us' (or 'in our power', *eph'*
hēmin) and what is not 'up to us', and focus our concern and desire on

---

[10] A. Bonhöffer, *Epictet und die Stoa: Untersuchungen zur Stoischen Philosophie*
(Stuttgart, 1890; repr. 1968); *Die Ethik der Stoikers Epictet* (1894; repr. 1968), trans. as *The
Ethics of the Stoic Epictetus* by W. O. Stephens (New York, 1996); also *Epiktet und das Neue
Testament* (Giessen, 1911; repr. 1964), rejecting the idea that Epictetus was influenced by
early Christian ideas.

[11] Long, *Epictetus*, 46–8; see also R. Dobbin, *Epictetus: Discourses Book 1* (Oxford,
1998), pp. xiv–xix.

[12] P. Hadot, *Philosophy as a Way of Life: Spiritual Exercises from Socrates to Foucault*
(Oxford, 1995), 191–5; P. Hadot, *The Inner Citadel: The Meditations of Marcus Aurelius*,
trans. M. Chase (Cambridge, Mass., 1998), ch. 5; J. Sellars, *The Art of Living: The Stoics on
the Nature and Function of Philosophy* (Aldershot, 2003), 134–42; G. Roskam, *On the Path to
Virtue: The Stoic Doctrine of Moral Progress and its Reception in (Middle-) Platonism*
(Leuven, 2005), ch. 6. For the three-topic programme, see 3.2.1–5 and references in nn.
26, 38–9.

[13] These three topics correspond broadly with those identified as central for Epictetus
in Long, *Epictetus*, ch. 8 (on autonomy), chs. 7 and 9 (on ethics and ethical development),
and ch. 6 (on human nature and theology).

the first group, rather than the second. The first group consists of psychological states and responses such as beliefs and motives, and the second of our bodily condition, property, or social standing. This theme is sometimes linked with the idea that we can and should 'examine our impressions' (perceptions and thoughts) before 'assenting' to them. In particular, we should be careful not to attach the notion of 'good' or 'bad' inappropriately, that is, to 'externals' such as our bodily condition or property. Doing so produces (negative and misguided) emotions such as disappointment or resentment. These two themes are often expressed in terms of our use of *prohairesis*. This is a standard Greek term meaning 'decision' or 'choice', and one that plays a major role in Aristotle's ethical writings. Epictetus uses it to mean the kind of rational agency that is expressed in focusing on what is 'up to us' and in 'examining impressions'.[14]

Although some features of Epictetus' terminology on this topic are rather non-standard within Stoicism,[15] in general his treatment fits well with certain well-known and characteristic features of Stoic thinking about human psychology. In the Stoic theory of action, both human and non-human animals are motivated by 'impressions' or 'appearances' (*phantasiai*), a broad category including perceptions and thoughts. But the reactions of humans, or 'rational animals', differ in two ways from those of non-human animals. A rational impression has what we call 'propositional content', that is, meaning that can be expressed in the form of a statement, such as 'this act or object is right or good'. Also, human beings need to 'assent' (or 'say yes') to the content of the impression before this stimulates motivation to action (*hormē*) or other such reactions, including emotions or feelings. Epictetus' themes seem to assume this pattern of thinking about human motivation. As rational animals, we are able to 'examine' the content of our 'impressions' before we 'assent' (or 'say yes') to them. We can determine in this way whether the things concerned are or are not 'up to us', and do or do not fall within the scope for choice or decision (*prohairesis*). This, in turn, can shape our motives and emotional reactions. Hence, to take a simple example, if we 'assent' to the idea

[14] See e.g. *Handbook* 1, 2, 5; also 1.1.7–12, 1.4.1–3, 1.12. See also Long, *Epictetus*, ch. 8; R. Sorabji, 'Epictetus on *Proairesis* and Self', in Scaltsas and Mason (eds.), *Philosophy of Epictetus*.

[15] See B. Inwood, *Ethics and Human Action in Early Stoicism* (Oxford, 1985), 115–25 and app. 2.

that an object is good that falls outside our control (a shiny new car, or a good-looking and congenial girlfriend or boyfriend), this can generate an emotion of disappointment when we do not actually obtain it.[16]

More broadly, Epictetus uses this theme to suggest an idea that is fundamental for much of the content of the *Discourses*, and Stoic ethics more generally. This is the idea that the capacity to achieve happiness is 'up to us' (or 'in our power') and does not depend on external factors, as is often supposed in conventional thinking. To some degree, this idea is common ground to much Hellenistic and Roman thought. But the Stoics make this claim in a particularly strong form, which is linked with their view that happiness is constituted by virtue; more precisely, that virtue is both necessary and sufficient for happiness.[17] Epictetus does not present this idea in expository form, which would, in any case, not fit the informal and practical aim of the discussions recorded in the *Discourses*.[18] But this idea is presupposed throughout the work and underlies a theme that Epictetus does accentuate strongly, namely, ethical development or progress.

A distinctive and fundamental feature of Stoic ethics is the idea that all human beings are constitutively capable of carrying out two kinds of ethical development, one relating to the progressive understanding of categories of value, the other to forms of relationship. In the first kind, human beings move from instinctive attraction to natural goods, such as health, to 'selecting' between such things in a rational way. Finally, if they progress properly, they will come to understand that what matters, ultimately, is not obtaining these natural goods but doing so *in the right way*, that is, in a way that expresses the qualities fundamental to a good human life, or the virtues. At this point, anything other than virtue comes to seem 'a matter of indifference', though it is also natural for us to find some things, such as health or property, 'preferable', rather than 'dispreferable'.[19]

---

[16] See LS 33 C, I, 53 Q(1); 65 A–K (on emotions); *Handbook* 5, 20, 42; 1.18.1, 3.2.1–5. See also T. Brennan, 'Stoic Moral Psychology', in Inwood (ed.), *Cambridge Companion to the Stoics*; Gill, *Structured Self in Hellenistic and Roman Thought*, 139–45; M. R. Graver, *Stoicism and Emotion* (Chicago, 2007), ch. 2.

[17] See references in n. 6.

[18] Contrast Cicero, *On Ends* 3–4, where this Stoic thesis is examined and debated in depth. On the character and aim of Epictetus' discussions, see text to nn. 4–7.

[19] See Cicero, *On Ends* 3.17–22 (= LS 59 D); LS 57 A, 58; see also Inwood, *Ethics and Human Action in Early Stoicism*, ch. 6; Annas, *Morality of Happiness*, ch. 5; Gill, *Structured Self in Hellenistic and Roman Thought*, 129–66.

The second kind of ethical development also consists in a movement from an instinctive or primitive state to a more rational (and virtuous) one. Human beings, like non-human animals, are naturally disposed to want to benefit at least some others of our kind; parental love for offspring is a clear example of this. But in humans, unlike other animals, this instinct can be developed as part of our developing rationality, and this can lead to various kinds of other-benefiting motivation. One is engaging in our own neighbourhood, community, or state in a way that enables us to benefit others. Another—a more unusual and striking feature of Stoic thought—is coming to regard all human beings (as fellow rational animals) as members of the brotherhood of humanity or fellow citizens of a world community.[20] Although we have no explicit analysis in Stoic theory of the relationship between these two strands of ethical development (personal and social), it seems clear that, ideally, the two kinds of development are combined and become mutually supporting.[21] Taken together, they enable us to move towards the ideal of virtue that also constitutes human happiness. Even if few or perhaps none of us carry out this programme in full, undertaking this project of development, and doing so on a life-long basis, forms the core of ethical life for any committed Stoic.

Although Epictetus does not make much use of the technical Stoic term for this process, that is, *oikeiōsis* ('appropriation', or 'familiarization'), it is clear that it is central for his *Discourses*, even though his treatment of it is rather partial. He gives rather little attention, for instance, to the idea that we progress towards understanding the value of virtue by 'selection' between 'preferable' and 'dispreferable indifferents'.[22] He focuses more on the desired outcome of the first type of development, that is, our recognition of the absolute value of virtue, and, especially the kind of character-state associated with this recognition, that of whole-hearted ethical engagement or

[20] See Cicero, *On Ends* 3.62–8 (= LS 57 F); LS 57 G–H; see also Annas, *Morality of Happiness*, 262–75; M. Schofield, 'Social and Political Thought', in K. Algra *et al.* (eds.), *The Cambridge History of Hellenistic Philosophy* (Cambridge, 1999), 760–8.

[21] On the two kinds and their possible linkage, see LS 57 D–E; Annas, *Morality of Happiness*, 275–6. On the relationship between the two kinds in Roman philosophy, see G. Reydams-Schils, *The Roman Stoics: Self, Responsibility, and Affection* (Chicago, 2005), ch. 2.

[22] This is sometimes seen as reflecting the influence of the early Stoic thinker Aristo (on whom, see LS 58 F–G): see Long, *Epictetus*, 184–5, 201–2; Roskam, *On the Path to Virtue*, 112–14. But it may reflect, instead, a pedagogic focus on the moral ideal towards which he urges his students.

complete integrity. But he gives more prominence again to the second, social strand of development, especially the later, rational stages. He accentuates both possible aspects of social development, that is, well-reasoned involvement with our social roles and connections, and a benevolent concern for humanity as a whole. He also explores, in various ways, the interplay between the two strands, and the way in which our developing understanding of the absolute value of virtue, by contrast with other so-called goods, can and should inform our attitudes to, and feelings about, other people. Some of the most striking and memorable features of the *Discourses* derive from Epictetus' exploration of this interplay, as illustrated later.[23]

A third distinctive cluster of themes in the *Discourses* falls into the interface between ethics and logic or physics, which are, as noted earlier, important spheres in Stoic thought. In the first area, one important theme is the idea that the state of mind of the normative wise person is marked by a consistency and structured understanding that is informed by mastery of logic and ethical principles. This idea is sometimes characterized as 'dialectical virtue', as Stoic logic was also described as 'dialectic'.[24] Epictetus does not refer often to the wise person as a norm for aspiration. More often, he cites as his ideals Socrates or Diogenes the Cynic.[25] But he does present the state of mind linked with 'dialectical virtue' as a goal to aim at, for instance, as the outcome of the third phase of his three-phase programme of ethical progress.[26] He also stresses—very often—a related theme, that logic should not be pursued solely for its own sake, as an intellectual pastime, but as something that should promote our ethical development.[27]

The interface between ethics and physics provides a number of important Stoic ideas, centring on the idea that the natural universe provides an informing framework for ethical life. The universe, or its shaping, or 'divine', element, does so either as a paradigm of order, structure, and rationality or as a source of providential care for the

---

[23] See the illustrative readings of 1.1 and 1.2, pp. xxii–xxiv. See also C. Gill, 'Stoic Writers of the Imperial Era', in C. Rowe and M. Schofield (eds.), *The Cambridge History of Greek and Roman Political Thought* (Cambridge, 2000); Long, *Epictetus*, 230–44.

[24] See LS 31 B; see also A. A. Long, *Stoic Studies* (Cambridge, 1996), 91–4, 104–6.

[25] See e.g. 4.1.159–66 (Socrates), 3.22 (Diogenes the Cynic). On the significance of Socrates and Diogenes for Epictetus, see also n. 37.

[26] See 3.2.2, 5; see also 1.4.11, 3.12.14–15, 4.10.13.

[27] See references in n. 5.

component parts of the universe, especially human beings, who share its 'divine' rationality. A related idea is that for human beings to exercise their capacity for rational agency is to act in line with the rational (divine) direction of the universe as well as with one's own inner, rational 'guardian spirit' (*daimōn*).[28] This complex of ideas has a prominent place in the *Discourses*, as also in some other writings on Stoic practical ethics, notably, Marcus Aurelius' *Meditations*.[29] Epictetus stresses especially the last idea, accentuating the idea of God as director of the universe and as the source of the divine rationality in us. Another theme stressed is that the capacity to exercise rational agency in developing towards virtue (expressed as our *prohairesis*) is a fundamental, or inalienable, human capacity, which is built into the natural, divinely shaped universe. He stresses less than Marcus the idea that one aspect of virtue consists in conceiving ourselves as an integral part of the whole universe, and accepting the course of events within this whole as inherently good, even if they seem disadvantageous to us personally. Similarly, he lays less emphasis than Marcus on the idea of universal causal determinism, or Fate, as an expression of divine, providential agency.[30]

Philosophical Innovation or Pedagogic Style?

Can we find an overall explanation for the Stoic themes emphasized or de-emphasized by Epictetus? If so, does this derive from philosophical innovation and originality or from the nature of the kind of practical ethical encouragement offered in the *Discourses*?

It has sometimes been suggested that Epictetus was introducing new ideas into Stoicism. For instance, close attention has been given to his focus on rational agency (the first theme noted here) and the idea that this is an inalienable human capacity (the third theme). His lack of emphasis on determinism has sometimes been coupled with this. It has been suggested that Epictetus is aiming to define in a new way the scope for autonomy and responsibility that is normally seen by Stoics as a fundamental human capacity, and one that is compatible with the idea of universal causal determinism. Epictetus has been

[28] See LS 54 C(6), H, L–M, 60 A, 63 C.

[29] Cf. Marcus Aurelius, *Meditations* 3.6, 4.4, 5.21.

[30] See e.g. 1.1.7–13, 1.14.11–14, 1.17.15–27, 2.8.12–13, 4.12.11–12; see also (unusually), on accepting things as fated, 2.6.9. Contrast Marcus Aurelius, *Meditations* 2.3, 2.17, 4.45, 5.8.

thought to be aiming to define an area, that of our capacity to control our thoughts and motives, especially by 'examining our impressions' before giving 'assent', which is immune from the broader pattern of causal determinism.[31] Epictetus sometimes characterizes this capacity in terms of 'freedom' (e.g. 3.22.42, *Handbook* 1.2–3), although he does not himself present this move as constituting a theory about 'free will'. However, it has been claimed, his move was a crucial influence on the development of the idea of 'freedom of the will', which was expressed in those terms in Christian writers influenced by Epictetus.[32] Most of the ideas Epictetus puts forward about God are recognizable strands of Stoic thinking in this area. But it has been thought that Epictetus presents these in a new or distinctive way, with a more personal view of God and of divine care for humanity than is generally found in Stoic thinking.[33]

Given the loss of the main Hellenistic Stoic treatises, and our dependence on later summaries of doctrines, it is difficult for us to track with any certainty moves towards innovation in later Stoic writers. Also, in works such as the *Discourses*, it is not easy to distinguish between original ideas and striking formulations of key features of existing Stoic theory, designed to be effective in the context of practical ethics. As regards Epictetus' treatment of rational agency, it has been argued that, although his formulations are unusual, he is simply defining in his own way human capacities already well recognized by Chrysippus. The earlier Stoic theorist had already maintained that the fact that human beings need to 'assent' to 'impressions' makes them causal agents of a different kind from other animals (or objects), and this capacity is compatible with universal causal determinism. So Epictetus' call to 'examine impressions' before giving 'assent' to them, along with his stress on the 'inalienable' character of human rational agency (or *prohairesis*), can be seen simply as a striking restatement of this theory. The demand for an 'indeterminist' conception of human agency (incompatible with determinism) belongs, it has been claimed, to a later phase of ancient debate on this subject.[34] As regards Epictetus' presentation of God, it has been

---

[31] See R. Dobbin, '*Prohairesis* in Epictetus', *Ancient Philosophy*, 11 (1991), 111–35.

[32] M. Frede, *A Free Will: Origins of the Notion in Ancient Thought* (Berkeley, 2011), 44–8, 76–83, 113, 157–8.

[33] See e.g. Long, *Epictetus*, 142–7.

[34] S. Bobzien, *Determinism and Freedom in Stoic Philosophy* (Oxford, 1998), 331–8,

questioned whether this is actually more personal in approach or tone than can be found in earlier Stoic thought.[35]

An alternative, and perhaps more promising, approach may be to explain Epictetus' distinctive emphases, and gaps (or unstressed elements) by reference to his practical or pedagogic aims in the discussions recorded by Arrian. It is worth underlining again that these discussions are mainly directed at young students or at visitors to the school, and seem to be especially designed to bring home to students the idea that Stoicism is not simply an academic exercise but is intended to shape or reshape one's whole way of life. This is not a context in which one would, on the face of it, expect Epictetus to put forward innovative ideas within Stoic thinking, even if he did so in his formal classes (of which we have no records).

It may be useful here to keep in mind some of the typologies used to characterize methods of practical ethics in this period. One typology subdivides practically oriented ethical discourse into protreptic, therapy, and advice. The aim of protreptic is to induce the listener to engage with philosophy at all, or to do so more deeply; that of therapy is to use philosophy to help him get rid of false beliefs, affecting his motives, emotions, and actions; advice aims to replace the rejected beliefs with better-grounded guides to action.[36] Epictetus, while not using this typology in a systematic way, alludes to the idea of philosophy as protreptic and therapy, and also uses his discourses extensively to offer advice about how to live a life based on Stoic principles. He also uses the category of *elenchus*, or 'elenctic' discourse, adopting the language and, to some extent, the methodology of Socrates, as depicted in the early Platonic dialogues. Epictetus, like Socrates, sets out to show his interlocutor that he is living his life on the basis of beliefs that are inconsistent with each other, or at least with beliefs that he induces his interlocutor to accept, and so reforms his belief-set. Epictetus also uses Zeno, founder of Stoicism, and Diogenes, founder of Cynicism,

341–5 (on 'indeterminism' in later debate, see her ch. 8). For Chrysippus' theory of agency (conceived as compatible with determinism), see Cicero, *On Fate* 39–43 (= LS 62 C).

[35] K. Algra, 'Epictetus and Stoic Theology', in Scaltsas and Mason (eds.), *Philosophy of Epictetus*.

[36] This typology is especially associated with the Academic (Platonic) philosopher Philo of Larisa (158–84); see Stobaeus 2.39–41 (ed. Wachsmuth and Hense). But it matches Hellenistic–Roman philosophical practice more generally. On typologies of practical ethics in this period, see C. Gill, 'The School in the Roman Imperial Period', in Inwood (ed.), *Cambridge Companion to the Stoics*, esp. 40–4.

as symbols for two contrasting, but compatible, styles of discourse, one more 'doctrinal' or instructive, and the other 'reproving', or critical of the listener's convictions or pattern of life (or both).[37] Epictetus' use of terminology of this kind, along with references to his three-topic programme for ethics, brings out the point that his central concern in the discourses is a practical one, intended by criticism and constructive methods to take forward his listeners' engagement and progress in the project of leading a Stoic life.[38]

If we return to the three distinctive themes or clusters of themes in the *Discourses* with this background in mind, we can interpret them, taken together, as forming material for a progressive programme of ethical engagement conducted on Stoic lines. The emphasis on the human capacity for rational agency (*prohairesis*), especially agency as regards achieving happiness (or starting to do so), can be seen as a protreptic device, prodding his listeners to engage more fully with the ethical content of Stoicism. It may be significant that this theme is signalled as being a primary or preliminary one by placing it first in Epictetus' three-topic programme. Underlining our capacity for rational agency, and urging us to focus on what is 'up to us' (as well as to 'examine our impressions' before 'assenting to them'), is perhaps designed to serve as the first step towards translating philosophical ideas into a programme for living.[39]

The next step may be provided by Epictetus' many allusions to Stoic ideas about ethical development as 'appropriation'; significantly perhaps, the social strand of this is presented as the second stage in Epictetus' three-topic programme (3.2.4). As noted earlier, Epictetus' focus, in the personal side of development, falls on the desired outcome of the process, that is, coming to see other so-called 'good things' as 'matters of indifference' compared with virtue, rather than on the process of distinguishing between 'preferable' and 'dispreferable indifferents', which is normally presented as instrumental

[37] See 2.26.4, 3.21.19, 3.23.33–7; see also 1.11, 1.28.6–8, for Socratic-style *elenchus* in Epictetus' *Discourses*. See further Long, *Epictetus*, 52–66, 74–9. On the significance attached to Cynicism, esp. Diogenes, in Epictetus, see K. Ierodiakonou, 'The Philosopher as God's Messenger', and M. Schofield, 'Epictetus on Cynicism', both in Scaltsas and Mason (eds.), *Philosophy of Epictetus*.

[38] On the three-topic or three-stage programme for ethical development or progress, see 3.2.1–5 and references in n. 26; see also Long, *Epictetus*, 112–18; Gill, *Structured Self in Hellenistic and Roman Thought*, 380–9; references in n. 12.

[39] See p. xiii and n. 14; 3.2.1, 3; see also Gill, *Structured Self in Hellenistic and Roman Thought*, 382–4.

towards that recognition. This emphasis can be seen as 'protreptic' in a different sense, that of pointing the listener towards the end-point of ethical development even if they are themselves a long way from this outcome. Epictetus' advice on how to conduct the social strand in development, similarly, stresses the desired end-point of this process: committed ethical engagement with a specific social role or taking up the mission of helping humanity more generally. He also accentuates the interplay between the two strands, and the significance for our relationships with others of recognizing the absolute priority of virtue (or 'the good') as distinct from securing indifferents (or 'externals', as he tends to call them). Although Epictetus directs his listeners' attention and aspiration towards high ideals or advanced ethical attitudes or states of character, he does so in a very vivid way, with a combination of plain language and dramatic characterization. This reminds us again that, even if he is describing levels of ethical understanding that go well beyond that reached by his interlocutors, he wants them to grasp and feel the force of these ideals.[40]

The third cluster of themes highlighted earlier, falling in the interface of ethics with logic or physics, can be seen as defining aspects of the more intellectual or reflective aspects of virtue (or 'wisdom', in Stoic terms). One aspect of this is the ideal of consistent ethical understanding, or 'dialectical virtue', which figures, perhaps significantly, as the third stage of Epictetus' three-topic programme (3.2.1, 5). Another aspect is conceiving rational agency, or *prohairesis*, as an inalienable human capacity in a divinely shaped universe. Although these motifs concern intellectual states of mind or understanding, they are also closely linked with the other two, more practically oriented, distinctive themes (rational agency and ethical development).[41] They can be seen as constituting another dimension of virtue, whose force and value as an ideal for living Epictetus aims to convey. Hence, taken as a whole, Epictetus' most characteristic motifs can be understood as reflecting what seems to be the main aim of his discussions with his students and others. This is bringing home to them, as forcefully as possible, what it means to engage, sincerely and deeply, with the ethical project of living out one's commitment to Stoic philosophy.[42]

[40] See pp. xv–xvi and nn. 22–3; Gill, *Structured Self in Hellenistic and Roman Thought*, 384–6 and discussion of 1.2.

[41] See pp. xvi–xvii and nn. 24–30.

[42] See p. ix and n. 5.

Illustrative Readings: Discourses 1.1–2

To illustrate some of these themes and the way Epictetus brings out
their force, let us consider the first two discourses in Book 1. In both
cases, Epictetus begins by identifying a theme in general terms, before
exploring its implications for trying to live a good life. He combines
general, expository statements with vividly realized imagined dialogue,
especially in bringing out the implications for practical ethics. In
terms that Epictetus himself sometimes uses, he combines a doctrinal
mode with protreptic and elenctic (refuting) modes, the latter two
sometimes fused with each other.

In 1.1 Epictetus begins by presenting the reasoning faculty as the
one which, unlike other arts and faculties, comprehends both itself and
the other faculties. He then isolates one salient aspect of this faculty,
'which enables us to make right use of our impressions' (7), which
encapsulates this combination of self-management and management
of other things. The latter capacity is described, by contrast with our
bodily condition, possessions, and personal relationships, as the only
thing that is wholly 'up to us' or 'within our power' (*eph' hēmin*). This
idea is presented by saying that this capacity (which is 'a portion' of
divinity) is the only one that Zeus, king of the gods, could place wholly
within our power (10–13, expressed as a speech by Zeus). Epictetus
goes on to maintain that, typically, we misuse this capacity; we concern
ourselves with the things that are not 'up to us' (possessions and so
on). Instead, we should 'make the best of what lies within our power
and deal with everything else as it comes' (17). This recommendation
is then illustrated by a series of imagined dialogues, some of them
involving historical figures, including famous Stoicism-inspired
examples of resistance to tyrannical attitudes or actions by Roman
emperors.[43] Each of these is designed to show what is involved in
'making the best of what lies within our power', and at the same time
'dealing with everything else' as regards our body or continued life—'as
it comes'. These examples show, as he points out, 'what it means to
train oneself in the matters in which one ought to train oneself' (31).

The discourse focuses on distinctive themes that fall in the first
and third groups discussed earlier. It is sometimes taken, along
with other discourses, such as 1.17, as marking a new or innovative
contribution to Stoic thinking on psychological agency, or 'free will'.

---

[43] See, further, Explanatory Note to 1.1.

However, the capacity identified (rational agency) can also be seen as part of long-standing Stoic ideas about the distinctive character of human rationality and the capacity for ethical progress.[44] The second half of the discussion concentrates wholly on two features that are presented as aspects of virtuous action (or at least that show progress towards virtue). The figures depicted 'make the best of what lies within our power', acting courageously, for instance, while also 'dealing with everything else', including the imprisonment, exile, or death that follows from this courageous act 'as it comes' (17; cf. 18–32). Epictetus' conclusion, that this is 'what it means to train oneself in the matters in which one ought to train oneself' (31), indicates that his concern here is as much with the proper use of rational agency as a basis for ethical action and development as with the idea that this capacity is a distinctive and fundamental property of human beings.

Discourse 1.2 has a similar overall structure and style; but the focus on ethical attitudes and actions, which emerges in the latter half of 1.1, is dominant throughout 1.2. The discourse presupposes a theory that we find more fully presented in Cicero, *On Duties* 1. 107–21. This is the idea that, in our ethical life, we should see ourselves as bearing four 'roles', or 'characters' (*prosōpa* in Greek and *personae* in Latin): our overall human role as rational ethical agents, our individual character, and the specific social roles that are the results of our background or choice. Achieving virtue, or making progress towards it, is in part at least a matter of trying to reconcile these roles.[45]

Epictetus begins by asserting that, 'For a rational creature, only what is contrary to nature is unendurable, but everything that is reasonable can be endured.' But people have different views about what is or is not reasonable to endure; and to advance our education in this respect, we need to get better in judging both 'the value of external things' and 'how they stand in relation to our specific character' (7). Epictetus' initial presentation may suggest that he takes a quite neutral view about how different people carry out this process of evaluation; but this is far from the case. Epictetus goes on to present

[44] See pp. xviii–xix and nn. 31–4.
[45] On this theory, see C. Gill, 'Personhood and Personality: The Four-*Personae* Theory in Cicero, *De Officiis* 1', *Oxford Studies in Ancient Philosophy*, 6 (1988), 169–99; J. Annas, 'Epictetus on Moral Perspectives', and M. Frede, 'A Notion of Person in Epictetus', both in Scaltsas and Mason (eds.), *Philosophy of Epictetus*; B. E. Johnson, 'Socrates, Heracles and the Deflation of Roles in Epictetus', *Ancient Philosophy*, 32 (2012), 125–45.

a series of exemplary figures, all of whom believe that expressing their particular character and the social role they have undertaken requires them to place a high value on courageous action and a very low value on 'external things', including their continued life.[46] He also characterizes such people as setting a high value on themselves and their rational agency (*prohairesis*), by contrast with 'selling it cheap' (33), and explicitly associates himself with their stance (11, 29, 33). He acknowledges that not everyone may feel ready to take this stand, or ready to do so now, at any rate. But he urges his listeners to 'undergo hard winter training' to prepare themselves for doing so (32), and, like Epictetus himself, not to 'cease to make any effort . . . merely because I despair of achieving perfection' (37).[47]

This discourse, clearly, relates to the second cluster of ideas discussed earlier, on ethical development, especially the practice of social roles linked with the second topic in Epictetus' three-topic programme (3.2.2, 4). More precisely, it is linked with the interplay between the two strands in ethical development between engagement with one's specific social role and recognizing that, in comparison with acting virtuously, other so-called goods (even continued life) are 'matters of indifference'. This rather complex area is one that Epictetus explores repeatedly in the *Discourses*, highlighting the potential conflict, for instance, between acting out one's family role (as conventionally understood, at any rate) and choosing to act virtuously. He also stresses, for similar reasons, that we should remain aware of the mortality of those we love (as well as our own mortality), and yet view this fact with an appropriate moral perspective.[48] The latter comments have often struck readers as cold and unfeeling, and as bringing out an inhuman side in Stoic ethics. But they are better seen as drawing out the implications for interpersonal relationships of an ethical standpoint that, taken as a whole, has a high degree of credibility as well as coherence.

Reception of Epictetus

The *Handbook* and *Discourses* of Epictetus have been probably the most widely read and influential of all Stoic texts from their first

---

[46] On these figures, see, further, Explanatory Note to 1.2.

[47] See Gill, 'Personhood and Personality', 187–91.

[48] See 3.3.5–8, 3.24.84–8; *Handbook* 3; see also Long, *Epictetus*, 233–44, 248–9; Gill, *Structured Self in Hellenistic and Roman Thought*, 385–6.

appearance until now. The combination of ethical idealism with directness and accessibility has given these works a remarkable impact, extending far beyond the boundaries of those committed to Stoicism. Although the nature of the responses has varied, it has focused on the features singled out here as distinctive, especially the stress on our own moral agency and mastery of our happiness, and the constructive and practical guidance on ethical self-improvement.

In the second century Epictetus was a major influence on the thought and style of Marcus Aurelius' philosophical diary (*Meditations*), and was seen as a significant thinker by (non-Stoic) intellectuals such as Galen, Gellius, and Lucian. His uncompromising moral stance made him attractive to early Christians such as Clement, Origen, and John Chrysostom. His thinking on rational agency and decision (*pro-hairesis*) has been seen as helping to shape the emergence of Christian thinking on the will and freedom of the will, especially in Origen and Augustine (third and fourth centuries).[49] In the sixth century Simplicius wrote a substantial commentary on the *Handbook*, treating it as an introductory text to the Neoplatonist philosophy and way of life. The *Handbook* was also adopted, with some modifications (including replacing the name of 'Socrates' with 'St Paul'), by Christian monks, and used for centuries by the Eastern (Greek Orthodox) Church. Through Syriac Christian scholars, Epictetus' thought spread to the Islamic East, influencing, for instance, the teaching on 'dispelling sorrow' by al-Kindī, a major figure in the study of Greek texts in ninth-century Baghdad.[50]

From the late fifteenth century onwards, translations and editions of Epictetus' works became widely available in most European countries. This promoted the emergence of Neostoic philosophy, which selectively adopted key Stoic themes, by Justus Lipsius (the Netherlands, 1547–1606) and Guillaume de Vair (France, 1556–1621). Epictetus also exercised a significant influence on two major thinkers in the early seventeenth century, Pascal (1623–62) and Descartes (1596–1650). Both responded to Epictetus' presentation of rational agency as fundamental to human nature and his call to emotional

---

[49] See Frede, *Free Will*, 113, 157–8. On influence on Christianity more generally, see M. Spanneut, 'Epiktet', in T. Klauser (ed.), *Reallexikon für Antike und Christentum*, 24 vols. to date (Stuttgart, 1950–), vol. v.

[50] See R. Dobbin, *Epictetus: Discourses and Selected Writings*, with introd. and notes (London, 2008), pp. xv–xvi.

endurance. However, Pascal, like other Christian writers in this period, had reservations about Epictetus' Stoic 'arrogance', that is, the belief that our perfection depends on our own efforts rather than God's grace. Descartes, in his methodology of systematic sceptical enquiry, responds to Epictetus' stress on 'examining impressions' before 'assenting' to them.

In Britain, Epictetus' influence is more evident in the eighteenth century. The first English translation of the *Discourses* was published by Elizabeth Carter in 1758 and remained the standard English version until the twentieth century. English thinkers influenced by Epictetus in this period include the third earl of Shaftesbury (Anthony Ashley Cooper, 1671–1713) and Bishop Joseph Butler (1692–1750). These thinkers also responded to Epictetus' emphasis on the human capacity for independent rational and moral agency ('conscience' or 'moral reason', in Butler's terms).[51]

Epictetus has had a long-standing resonance in the United States; his uncompromising moral rigour chimed in well with Protestant Christian beliefs and the ethical individualism that has been a persistent vein in American culture. His admirers ranged from John Harvard and Thomas Jefferson in the seventeenth and eighteenth centuries to Ralph Waldo Emerson and Henry David Thoreau in the nineteenth. More recently, Vice-Admiral James Stockdale wrote movingly of how his study of Epictetus at Stanford University enabled him to survive the psychological pressure of prolonged torture as a prisoner of war in Vietnam between 1965 and 1973. Stockdale's story formed the basis for a light-hearted treatment of the moral power of Stoicism in Tom Wolfe's novel *A Man in Full* (1998).[52]

In recent times, Epictetus' writings, along with other works of Stoic practical ethics, have been important in providing material for the upsurge of writings offering a 'guide to life' or pathway to happiness.[53] Stoicism, especially as presented by Epictetus, was also an important influence on the emergence of the cognitive approach to

---

[51] See Long, *Epictetus*, 261–8. On editions of the text of Epictetus, see W. A. Oldfather, *Epictetus: The Discourses as Reported by Arrian, the Manual, and Fragments*, with trans. and notes, 2 vols. (London, 1926), pp. xxxi–xxxiii; Dobbin, *Epictetus: Discourses Book 1*, pp. xxiii–xxiv.

[52] See Long, *Epictetus*, 268–70; see also J. Stockdale, *Thoughts of a Philosophical Fighter Pilot* (Stanford, 1995).

[53] See e.g. J. Evans, *Philosophy for Life: And Other Dangerous Situations* (London, 2012), 25–38.

psychotherapy, which focuses on deliberate attempts by the patient
to address emotional disturbance and depression, rather than aiming
to uncover their unconscious roots, as Freudian analysis does.
Epictetus helped to shape the evolution of this approach by Albert
Ellis and Aaron Beck, and is potentially yet more relevant to some
current versions of this approach, which lay increasing stress on
inviting the patient to reflect on her values and life-choices as well as
modifying her beliefs and behaviour.[54] In these and other ways,
Epictetus' forceful appeal to understand the crucial role of recognizing
what is 'up to us' still resonates with modern readers.

[54] See D. Robertson, *The Philosophy of Cognitive–Behavioural Therapy (CBT): Stoic
Philosophy as Rational and Cognitive Psychotherapy* (London, 2010); T. Le Bon, *Wise
Therapy* (London, 2001).

NOTE ON THE TEXT AND TRANSLATION

THIS is not my first approach to this material, since I have previously revised Elizabeth Carter's eighteenth-century translation of Epictetus' *Discourses* for an edition published by Everyman (London, 1995). I should like to stress, however, that this is not a revision of that revision, but a completely new translation. In the main, the translation follows the Greek text in the Loeb Classical Library edition prepared by W. A. Oldfather (London, 1926; largely based on the text in the Teubner edition by Heinrich Schenkl, 2nd edition, Leipzig, 1916), although I have also consulted the text prepared by Joseph Souilhé for the Budé series (Paris, 1948–65). I have benefited by being able to refer to the excellent translations by Oldfather and Souilhé; I am also familiar with the older English translations by George Long (London, 1877) and P. E. Matheson (Oxford, 1916) and the Italian translation by Renato Laurenti (Bari, 1960). I am indebted to Christopher Gill for many valuable suggestions.

As can be seen in the Prefatory Letter, these discourses were presented by their editor, Arrian, as being direct transcriptions of conversations in Epictetus' school. Irrespective of how much of their content really was recorded on the occasion, and how much was recreated by Arrian from his notes and memory, they provide a vivid impression, in relatively colloquial Greek, of how Epictetus conducted his teaching and strove to convey his message. In making these translations, I have tried to preserve that feeling of spontaneity, and I hope that readers will come to feel that they are overhearing living conversation about matters of urgent practical concern, even if there is inevitably a certain amount of philosophical jargon and the discussion can get quite technical at times.

Epictetus is naturally the main speaker, and in many of the discourses he speaks for most of the time, with an occasional question or interjection from others who are present; but there are also passages in which there are series of short interchanges. To try to make clear who is speaking at any one time, I have generally not enclosed Epictetus' contributions in inverted commas, reserving those for the questions and remarks of his interlocutors. Verse quotations, mostly from Homer and Greek tragedy, have been put in italics.

R.H.

SELECT BIBLIOGRAPHY

Greek Editions of the Discourses, Fragments, and Handbook

Oldfather, W. A. (ed.), *Epictetus: The Discourses as Reported by Arrian, the Manual, and Fragments*, with trans. and notes, 2 vols. (London, 1926) (Loeb Classical Library).

Schenkl, H. (ed.), *Epicteti Dissertationes ab Arriano digestae*, 2nd edn. (Leipzig, 1916) (Teubner).

Souilhé, J. (ed.), *Epictète: Entretiens*, with French trans. and notes, 4 vols. (Paris, 1948–65) (Budé).

English Translations of the Discourses, Fragments, and Handbook

Boter, G., *The Encheiridion of Epictetus and its Three Christian Adaptations* (Leiden, 1999).

Carter, E., *Epictetus: Moral Discourses* (London, 1758; often reprinted).

Dobbin, R., *Epictetus: Discourses and Selected Writings*, with introd. and notes (London, 2008) (Penguin Classics; a selection from the *Discourses* and other writings).

Hard, R., *The Discourses of Epictetus*, with introd. and notes by C. Gill (London, 1995) (Everyman).

Matheson, P. E., *Epictetus: The Discourses and Manual*, with introd. and notes, 2 vols. (Oxford, 1916).

White, N., *The Handbook of Epictetus*, trans. with introd. and annotations (Indianapolis, 1983) (Hackett).

Epictetus' Philosophical Context

Algra, K., Barnes, J., Mansfeld, J., and Schofield, M. (eds.), *The Cambridge History of Hellenistic Philosophy* (Cambridge, 1999).

Annas, J., *The Morality of Happiness* (Oxford, 1993).

Barnes, J., *Logic and the Imperial Stoa* (Leiden, 1997).

Bobzien, S., *Determinism and Freedom in Stoic Philosophy* (Oxford, 1998).

Braund, S. M., and Gill, C. (eds.), *The Passions in Roman Thought and Literature* (Cambridge, 1997).

Brennan, T., *The Stoic Life: Emotions, Duties, and Fate* (Oxford, 2005).

Colish, M., *The Stoic Tradition from Antiquity to the Early Middle Ages*, 2 vols. (Leiden, 1990).

De Lacy, P., 'Stoic Views of Poetry', *American Journal of Philology*, 69 (1948), 241–71.

Desmond, W., *Cynics* (Stocksfield, 2008).

Dudley, D. R., *A History of Cynicism from Diogenes to the Sixth Century* (London, 1937).

Frede, M., *A Free Will: Origins of the Notion in Ancient Thought* (Berkeley, 2011).

Gill, C., 'Personhood and Personality: The Four-*Personae* Theory in Cicero, *De Officiis* 1', *Oxford Studies in Ancient Philosophy*, 6 (1988), 169–99.

—— *The Structured Self in Hellenistic and Roman Thought* (Oxford, 2006).

—— 'Stoicism and Epicureanism', in P. Goldie (ed.), *Oxford Handbook of Philosophy of Emotion* (Oxford, 2009).

—— *Naturalistic Psychology in Galen and Stoicism* (Oxford, 2010).

—— 'Cynicism and Stoicism', in R. Crisp (ed.), *Oxford Handbook of the History of Ethics* (Oxford, 2013).

Graver, M. R., *Stoicism and Emotion* (Chicago, 2007).

Hadot, P., *Philosophy as a Way of Life: Spiritual Exercises from Socrates to Foucault*, trans. M. Chase (Oxford, 1995).

Inwood, B., *Ethics and Human Action in Early Stoicism* (Oxford, 1985).

—— (ed.), *The Cambridge Companion to the Stoics* (Oxford, 2003).

Long, A. A., *Hellenistic Philosophy* (London, 1974; 2nd edn., Berkeley, 1986).

—— *Stoic Studies* (Cambridge, 1996).

—— *From Epicurus to Epictetus: Studies in Hellenistic and Roman Philosophy* (Oxford, 2006).

—— and Sedley, D. N., *The Hellenistic Philosophers*, 2 vols. (Cambridge, 1987).

Moles, J. L., 'Cynicism', in C. J. Rowe and M. Schofield (eds.), *The Cambridge History of Greek and Roman Political Thought* (Cambridge, 2000).

Morford, M., *The Roman Philosophers from the Time of Cato the Censor to the Death of Marcus Aurelius* (London, 2002).

Nussbaum, M. C., *The Therapy of Desire: Theory and Practice in Hellenistic Ethics* (Princeton, 1994).

Reydams-Schils, G., *The Roman Stoics: Self, Responsibility, and Affection* (Chicago, 2005).

Rist, J. M., *Stoic Philosophy* (Cambridge, 1969).

Roskam, G., *On the Path to Virtue: The Stoic Doctrine of Moral Progress and its Reception in (Middle-) Platonism* (Leuven, 2005).

Salles, R. (ed.), *God and Cosmos in Stoicism* (Oxford, 2009).

Sandbach, F. H., *The Stoics* (London, 1975).

Schofield, M., *The Stoic Idea of the City* (Cambridge, 1991; 2nd edn., Chicago, 1999).

Sellars, J., *Stoicism* (Chesham, 2006).

Sharples, R. W., *Stoics, Epicureans and Sceptics: An Introduction to Hellenistic Philosophy* (London, 1996).

—— and Sorabji, R. (eds.), *Greek and Roman Philosophy (100 BC to 200 AD)*, *Bulletin of the Institute of Classical Studies*, suppl. 94, 2 vols. (London, 2007).

Sorabji, R., *Emotion and Peace of Mind: From Stoic Agitation to Christian Temptation* (Oxford, 2000).

——*Self: Ancient and Modern Insights about Individuality, Life, and Death* (Oxford, 2006).

Stadter, P. A., *Arrian of Nicomedia* (Chapel Hill, NC, 1980).

Trapp, M., *Philosophy in the Roman Empire: Ethics, Politics and Society* (Aldershot, 2007).

Vogt, K. M., *Law, Reason, and the Cosmic City: Political Philosophy in the Early Stoa* (Oxford, 2008).

Epictetus' Philosophical Teachings

Three very useful recent books on this topic:

Dobbin, R., *Epictetus: Discourses Book 1*, trans. with introd. and comm., Clarendon Later Ancient Philosophers (Oxford, 1998).

Long, A. A., *Epictetus: A Stoic and Socratic Guide to Life* (Oxford, 2002).

Scaltsas, T., and Mason, A. S. (eds.), *The Philosophy of Epictetus* (Oxford, 2007).

See also:

Bonhöffer, D., *Epictet und die Stoa: Untersuchungen zur Stoischen Philosophie* (Stuttgart, 1890; repr. 1968).

——*Die Ethik der Stoikers Epictet* (Stuttgart, 1894; repr. 1968), trans. as *The Ethics of the Stoic Epictetus* by W. O. Stephens (New York, 1996).

——*Epiktet und das Neue Testament* (Giessen, 1911; repr. 1964).

Brennan, T., and Brittain, C., *Simplicius: On Epictetus' Handbook*, trans. with introd. and notes, 2 vols. (London, 2002).

Brunt, P. A., 'From Epictetus to Arrian', *Athenaeum*, 55 (1977), 19–48.

De Lacy, P., 'The Logical Structure of the Ethics of Epictetus', *Classical Philology*, 38 (1943), 112–25.

Gill, C., 'Stoic Writers of the Imperial Era', in C. J. Rowe and M. Schofield (eds.), *The Cambridge History of Greek and Roman Political Thought* (Cambridge, 2000).

Herschbell, J., 'The Stoicism of Epictetus: Twentieth Century Perspectives', *Aufstieg und Niedergang der römischen Welt*, II.36.3, ed. W. Haase and H. Temporini (Berlin, 1989).

Hijmans, B. L., *Askēsis: Notes on Epictetus' Educational System* (Assen, 1959).

Johnson, B. E., 'Ethical Roles in Epictetus', *Epoché*, 16/2 (2012), 287–316.

——'Socrates, Heracles and the Deflation of Roles in Epictetus', *Ancient Philosophy*, 32 (2012), 125–45.

Kamtekar, R. '*Aidōs* in Epictetus', *Classical Philology*, 93 (1998), 136–60.

Long, A. A., 'Epictetus and Marcus Aurelius', in J. Luce (ed.), *Ancient Writers: Greece and Rome*, 2 vols. (New York, 1982), ii.

—— 'Epictetus as Socratic Mentor', *Proceedings of the Cambridge Philological Society*, 46 (2000), 79–98.

—— 'The Socratic Imprint on Epictetus' Philosophy', in S. K. Strange and J. Zupko (eds.), *Stoicism: Traditions and Transformations* (Cambridge, 2004).

Sellars, J., *The Art of Living: The Stoics on the Nature and Function of Philosophy* (Aldershot, 2003).

Spanneut, M., 'Epiktet', in T. Klauser (ed.), *Reallexikon für Antike und Christentum*, 24 vols. to date (Stuttgart, 1950–), vol. v.

Stanton, G. R., 'The Cosmopolitan Ideas of Epictetus and Marcus Aurelius', *Phronesis*, 13 (1968), 183–95.

Stephens, W. O., 'Epictetus on how the Stoic Sage Loves', *Oxford Studies in Ancient Philosophy*, 14 (1996), 193–210.

Xenakis, J., *Epictetus: Philosopher–Therapist* (The Hague, 1969).

Putting Epictetus into Practice

Evans, J., *Philosophy for Life and Other Dangerous Situations* (London, 2012), ch. 2.

Robertson, D., *The Philosophy of Cognitive–Behavioural Therapy (CBT): Stoic Philosophy as Rational and Cognitive Psychotherapy* (London, 2010).

Seddon, K., *Epictetus' Handbook and the Tablet of Cebes: Guides to Stoic Living* (London, 2005).

Sherman, N., *Stoic Warriors: The Ancient Philosophy behind the Military Mind* (Oxford, 2005).

Stockdale, J., *Thoughts of a Philosophical Fighter Pilot* (Stanford, 1995).

Further Reading in Oxford World's Classics

Cicero, *On Obligations*, trans. P. G. Walsh.

Diogenes the Cynic, *Sayings and Anecdotes, with Other Popular Moralists*, trans. R. Hard.

Marcus Aurelius, *Meditations*, trans. R. Hard, with introd. and notes by C. Gill.

Seneca, *Dialogues and Essays*, trans. J. Davie, with introd. and notes by T. Reinhardt.

—— *Selected Letters*, trans. E. Fantham.

A CHRONOLOGY OF EPICTETUS

(All dates are AD)

c.50	Epictetus born in Hierapolis (in Phrygia).
54	Nero becomes emperor.
57	Nero orders senators and knights to participate in his Games.
59	Nero murders his mother, Agrippina.
c.60	Musonius Rufus goes into exile in Asia Minor.
Date unknown	Epictetus comes to Rome; becomes a slave of Epaphroditus, a powerful freedman of Nero.
62	Musonius Rufus returns to Rome; Seneca loses his position as Nero's adviser. Nero banishes his former wife, Octavia (then murdered), and marries Poppaea Sabina.
65	Musonius Rufus exiled to Gyara; conspiracy of Piso against Nero; Plautius Lateranus executed; Seneca forced to commit suicide.
66	Thrasea Paetus forced to commit suicide.
68	Nero deposed and commits suicide; Galba becomes emperor; Musonius Rufus returns to Rome.
Between 68 and 69	Epictetus studies with Musonius Rufus; he is freed by Epaphroditus and sets himself up as a philosophy teacher at Rome.
69	Year of the four emperors (Galba, Otho, Vitellius, Vespasian).
70–9	Musonius Rufus exiled again at some point.
75	Helvidius Priscus exiled and executed.
79	Vespasian dies; Titus becomes emperor.
After 79	Musonius Rufus returns to Rome.
81	Titus dies; Domitian becomes emperor.
c.86	Arrian born.
89	Domitian banishes philosophers from Rome; Epictetus goes to Nicopolis in Greece and sets up philosophical school.
96	Domitian assassinated; Nerva becomes emperor.

98	Trajan becomes emperor.
c.100	Musonius Rufus dies.
c.107–9	Arrian studies with Epictetus.
117	Trajan dies; Hadrian becomes emperor.
Date unknown	Hadrian visits Epictetus' school.
121	Marcus Aurelius born.
Date unknown	Epictetus adopts a child.
c.135	Epictetus dies.
138	Hadrian dies; Antoninus Pius, father of Marcus Aurelius, becomes emperor.

DISCOURSES

PREFATORY LETTER

Arrian to Lucius Gellius, greeting

[1] I did not write these discourses of Epictetus as one might normally write books of this kind, nor did I myself release them to the public, since I can in fact declare that I did not even write them. [2] But rather, I tried to note down whatever I heard him say, in his own words as far as possible, so as to preserve memoranda for myself in the future of his manner of thought and frankness of speech. [3] These are, then, as one might expect, the kind of things that one person would say to another on the spur of the moment, and not such as he would write to find a readership in later times. [4] Being such as they are, they have fallen somehow or other, without my consent or knowledge, into the hands of the public. [5] But to me it is of no great matter if I shall be thought incapable of writing a book, and to Epictetus it will not matter in the slightest if anyone views his discourses with disdain, because even when he was speaking, he plainly had no other aim than to move the minds of those who were listening towards what is best. [6] If these discourses should achieve that same effect, they would be producing the result, I think, that the words of a philosopher ought to produce; [7] but if they fail to do so, those who read them should understand that when Epictetus himself was speaking, the listener was compelled to feel just what Epictetus wanted him to feel. [8] If the words on their own, however, do not accomplish that effect, it may be that I am to blame, or perhaps it could hardly be otherwise. Farewell.

BOOK 1

1.1 *About things that are within our power and those that are not*

[1] Among all the arts and faculties, you'll find none that can take itself as an object of study, and consequently none that can pass judgement of approval or disapproval upon itself. [2] In the case of grammar, how far does its power of observation extend? Only as far as to pass judgement on what is written. And in the case of music? Only as far as to pass judgement on the melody. [3] Does either of them, then, make itself an object of study? Not at all. If you're writing to a friend, grammar will tell you what letters you ought to choose, but as to whether or not you ought to write to your friend, grammar won't tell you that. And the same is true of music with regard to melodies; as to whether or not you should sing or play the lyre at this time, that is something that music won't tell you. [4] What will tell you, then? The faculty that takes both itself and everything else as an object of study. And what is that? The faculty of reason. For that alone of all the faculties that we've been granted is capable of understanding both itself—what it is, what it is capable of, and what value it contributes—and all the other faculties too. [5] For what else is it that tells us that gold is beautiful? For the gold itself doesn't tell us. It is clear, then, that this is the faculty that has the capacity to deal with impressions. [6] What else can judge music, grammar, and the other arts and faculties, and assess the use that we make of them, and indicate the proper occasions for their use? None other than this.

[7] It was fitting, then, that the gods have placed in our power only the best faculty of all, the one that rules over all the others, that which enables us to make right use of our impressions; but everything else they haven't placed within our power. [8] Was it that they didn't want to? I think for my part that, if they could, they would have entrusted those other powers to us too; but that was something that they just couldn't do. [9] For in view of the fact that we're here on earth, and are shackled to a body like our own, and to such companions as we have, how could it be possible that, in view of all that, we shouldn't be hampered by external things?

[10] But what does Zeus* have to say about this? 'If it had been possible, Epictetus, I would have ensured that your poor body and

petty possessions were free and immune from hindrance. [11] But as
things are, you mustn't forget that this body isn't truly your own, but
is nothing more than cleverly moulded clay. [12] But since I couldn't
give you that, I've given you a certain portion of myself, this faculty
of motivation to act and not to act, of desire and aversion, and, in a
word, the power to make proper use of impressions; if you pay good
heed to this, and entrust all that you have to its keeping, you'll never
be hindered, never obstructed, and you'll never groan, never find
fault, and never flatter anyone at all. [13] What, does all of that strike
you as being of small account?' Certainly not. 'So you're content with
that?' I pray so to the gods.

[14] But as things are, although we have it in our power to apply
ourselves to one thing alone, and devote ourselves to that, we choose
instead to apply ourselves to many things, and attach ourselves to
many, to our body, and our possessions, and our brother, and friend,
and child, and slave. [15] And so, being attached in this way to any
number of things, we're weighed down by them and dragged down.
[16] That is why, if the weather prevents us from sailing, we sit there
in a state of anxiety, constantly peering around. 'What wind is this?'
The North Wind. And what does it matter to us and to him? 'When
will the West Wind blow?' When it so chooses, my good friend, or
rather, when Aeolus chooses; for God hasn't appointed you to be con-
troller of the winds, he has appointed Aeolus. [17] What are we to do,
then? To make the best of what lies within our power, and deal with
everything else as it comes. 'How does it come, then?' As God wills.

[18] 'What, am I to be beheaded now, and I alone?'

Why, would you want everyone to be beheaded for your consolation? [19] Aren't you willing to stretch out your neck as Lateranus*
did at Rome when Nero ordered that he should be beheaded? For he
stretched out his neck, received the blow, and when it proved to be
too weak, shrank back for an instant, but then stretched out his neck
again. [20] And moreover, on an earlier occasion, when Epaphroditus*
came to him and asked him why he had fallen out with the emperor,
he replied, 'If I care to, I'll explain that to your master.'

[21] What, then, should we have at hand to help us in such emergen-
cies? Why, what else than to know what is mine and what isn't mine,
and what is in my power and what isn't? [22] I must die; so must I die
groaning too? I must be imprisoned; so must I grieve at that too? I must
depart into exile; so can anyone prevent me from setting off with a

smile, cheerfully and serenely? 'Tell me the secrets.' [23] I won't reveal them; for that lies within my power. 'Then I'll have you chained up.' What are you saying, man, chain *me* up? You can chain my leg, but not even Zeus can overcome my power of choice. [24] 'I'll throw you into prison.' You mean my poor body. 'I'll have you beheaded.' Why, did I ever tell you that I'm the only man to have a neck that can't be severed? [25] These are the thoughts that those who embark on philosophy ought to reflect upon; it is these that they should write about day after day, and it is in these that they should train themselves.

[26] Thrasea* was in the habit of saying, 'I'd rather be killed today than be sent into exile tomorrow.' [27] So what did Rufus* say in reply? 'If you choose death as being the heavier misfortune, what a foolish choice that is; if you choose it as being the lighter, who has granted you that choice? Aren't you willing to be content with what is granted to you?'

[28] So what was it that Agrippinus* used to say? 'I won't become an obstacle to myself.' The news was brought to him that 'your case is being tried in the Senate'. [29] —'May everything go well! But the fifth hour has arrived'—this was the hour in which he was in the habit of taking his exercise and then having a cold bath—'so let's go off and take some exercise.' [30] When he had completed his exercise, someone came and told him, 'You've been convicted.'—'To exile,' he asked, 'or to death?'—'To exile.'—'What about my property?'—'It hasn't been confiscated.'—'Then let's go away to Aricia and eat our meal there.' [31] This is what it means to train oneself in the matters in which one ought to train oneself, to have rendered one's desires incapable of being frustrated, and one's aversions incapable of falling into what they want to avoid. [32] I'm bound to die. If at once, I'll go to my death; if somewhat later, I'll eat my meal, since the hour has arrived for me to do so, and then die afterwards. And how? As suits someone who is giving back that which is not his own.

1.2 *How one may preserve one's proper character in everything*

[1] For a rational being, only what is contrary to nature is unendurable, while anything that is reasonable can be endured. [2] Blows are not by nature unendurable.—'How so?'—Look at it in this way: Spartans will put up with a beating in the knowledge that it is a reasonable punishment. [3] —'But to be hanged, isn't that past bearing?'—When

someone feels it to be reasonable, though, he'll go off and hang himself. [4] In short, if we look with due care, we'll find that there is nothing by which the rational creature is so distressed as by that which is contrary to reason, and that, conversely, there is nothing to which he is so attracted as that which is reasonable.

[5] But these concepts of the reasonable and unreasonable mean different things to different people, as do those of good and bad, and the profitable and unprofitable. [6] It is for that reason above all that we have need of education, so as to be able to apply our preconceptions of what is reasonable and unreasonable to particular cases in accordance with nature. [7] Now, to determine what is reasonable or unreasonable, not only do we have to form a judgement about the value of external things, but we also have to judge how they stand in relation to our own specific character. [8] It is thus reasonable for one person to hold out a chamber pot for another simply in view of the fact that, if he fails to do so, he'll get a beating and no food, but will suffer no rough or painful treatment if he does hold it; [9] whereas, for another person, it won't just seem intolerable to hold out a pot himself, but even to allow someone else to do so for him. [10] If you ask me, then, 'Shall I hold out the pot or not?', I'll reply that it is of greater value to get food than not to get it, and a worse thing to be beaten than not to be beaten, so if you measure your interests by these standards, you should go and hold out the pot. [11] 'Yes, but that would be beneath me.' It is for you to take that further point into consideration, not me, since you're the one who knows yourself, and knows what value you set on yourself, and at what price you'll sell yourself; for different people sell themselves at different prices.

[12] That's why, when Florus was considering whether he should attend Nero's show to perform some part in it himself, Agrippinus* said to him, 'Go!'; [13] and when Florus asked him, 'Then why aren't you going yourself?', he replied, 'Because I've never even considered it.' [14] For as soon as anyone begins to consider such questions, assessing and comparing the values of external things, he comes near to being one of those people who have lost all sense of their proper character. [15] What are you asking me, then? 'Is death or life to be regarded as preferable?' I answer: Life. [16] 'Pain or pleasure?' I answer: Pleasure. 'But if I don't agree to play a role in the tragedy, I'll lose my head.' [17] Go and play that role then, but I won't play one. 'Why?' Because you regard yourself as being just one thread

among all the threads in the tunic. 'So what follows?' You should
consider how you can be like other people, just as one thread doesn't
want to be marked out from all the other threads. [18] But for my
part, I want to be the purple,* the small gleaming band that makes all
the rest appear splendid and beautiful. Why do you tell me, then, to
'be like everything else'? In that case, how shall I still be the purple?

[19] Helvidius Priscus* saw this too, and having seen it, acted
upon it. When Vespasian sent word to him to tell him not to attend
a meeting of the Senate, he replied, 'It lies in your power not
to allow me to be a senator, but as long as I remain one, I have to
attend its meetings.' [20] —'Well, if you do attend, hold your
tongue.'—'If you don't ask for my opinion, I'll hold my
tongue.'—'But I'm bound to ask you.'—'And I for my part must
reply as I think fit.' [21] —'But if you do, I'll have you executed.'—'Well, when have I ever claimed to you that I'm immortal?
You fulfil your role, and I'll fulfil mine. It is yours to have me killed,
and mine to die without a tremor; it is yours to send me into exile,
and mine to depart without a qualm.'

[22] What good, you ask, did Priscus achieve, then, being just a
single individual? And what does the purple achieve for the tunic?
What else than standing out in it as purple, and setting a fine example
for all the rest? [23] Another man, if he'd been told by Caesar to stay
away from the Senate in such circumstances, would have replied,
'Thank you for excusing me.' [24] But Caesar wouldn't have tried to
stop such a man from going to the Senate in the first place, knowing
that he would either sit there like a jug, or else, if he did speak, would
say exactly what he knew Caesar would want him to say, piling on
plenty more in addition.

[25] It is in this way that a certain athlete behaved too, when he was
in danger of dying if his genitals* weren't cut off. His brother (who
was a philosopher) came to him and said, 'Well brother, what are
you planning to do? Are we to cut off this part of you and go to the
gymnasium as usual?' But the athlete wouldn't submit to that, but set
his mind against it and died. [26] When someone asked, 'How did he
do that? Was it as an athlete or as a philosopher?', Epictetus replied:
As a man, and as a man who had been proclaimed as victor at Olympia,
and had fought his corner there, and had passed his life in such places,
rather than merely having oil smeared over him at Baton's training
ground. [27] But another man would be willing even to have his head

cut off, if it were possible for him to live without a head. [28] This is what is meant by acting according to one's character, and such is the weight that this consideration acquires among those who make a habit of introducing it into their deliberations. [29] 'Come now, Epictetus, shave off your beard.'* If I'm a philosopher, I'll reply: I won't shave it off. 'Then I'll have you beheaded.' If it pleases you to do so, have me beheaded.

[30] Someone asked, 'Then how will each of us come to recognize what is appropriate to his own character?' How is it, replied Epictetus, that when a lion attacks, the bull alone is aware of its own might, and hurls itself forward on behalf of the entire herd? Isn't it clear that the possession of such power is accompanied at the same time by an awareness of that power? [31] And in our case too, if someone possesses such power, he won't fail to be aware of it. [32] And yet a bull doesn't become a bull all at once, any more than a man acquires nobility of mind all at once; no, he must undergo hard winter training, and so make himself ready, rather than hurl himself without proper thought into what is inappropriate for him.

[33] Only, consider at what price you're willing to sell your power of choice. If nothing else, make sure, man, that you don't sell it cheap. But what is great and exceptional is perhaps the province of others, of Socrates* and people of that kind.

[34] 'Why is it, then, if we are fitted by nature to act in such a way, all or many of us don't behave like that?'

What, do all horses become swift-running, or all dogs quick on the scent? [35] And then, because I'm not naturally gifted, shall I therefore abandon all effort to do my best? Heaven forbid. [36] Epictetus won't be better than Socrates; but even if I'm not too bad,* that is good enough for me. [37] For I won't ever be a Milo* either, and yet I don't neglect my body; nor a Croesus, and I don't neglect my property; nor in general do I cease to make any effort in any regard whatever merely because I despair of achieving perfection.

1.3 *How, from the idea that God is the father of human beings, one may proceed to what follows*

[1] If only one could be properly convinced of this truth, that we're all first and foremost children of God,* and that God is the father of

both human beings and gods, I think one would never harbour any mean or ignoble thought about oneself. [2] Why, if Caesar were to adopt you, no one would be able to endure your conceit; so if you know that you're a son of God, won't you be filled with pride? [3] As things stand, however, we don't react in that way, but since these two elements* have been mixed together in us from our conception, the body, which we have in common with the animals, and reason and intelligence, which we share with the gods, some of us incline towards the kinship that is wretched and mortal, and only a few of us towards that which is divine and blessed. [4] Now since everyone, whoever he may be, is bound to deal with each matter in accordance with the belief that he holds about it, those few who think they were born for fidelity, for self-respect, and for the sound use of impressions will never harbour any mean or ignoble thought about themselves, whereas the majority of people will do exactly the opposite. [5] 'For what am I? A poor wretched man,' they say, or 'This miserable flesh of mine'. [6] Miserable, to be sure, but you also have something better in you than that poor flesh. Why do you neglect that, then, and attach yourself to what is mortal?

[7] It is because of this kinship with the flesh that some of us who incline towards it become like wolves, perfidious, treacherous, noxious creatures; or others like lions, wild, savage, and untamed creatures; or in most cases like foxes, or something even more ignominious and base. [8] For what else is a slanderous and ill-natured person than a fox, or something even more unfortunate and base. [9] Watch out, then, and take care that you don't end as one of these wretched creatures!

1.4 *On progress*

[1] One who is making progress, having learned from the philosophers that desire has good things for its object, and aversion bad things, and having also learned that serenity and freedom from passion can be achieved only by one who is neither frustrated in his desires nor falls into what he wants to avoid—such a person, then, has rid himself of desire* altogether and put it aside for the present, and feels aversion only towards those things that lie within the sphere of choice. [2] For if he tries to avoid anything that lies outside the sphere of choice, he

knows that he'll run into some such thing one day, in spite of the aversion that he feels for it, and so be unhappy. [3] Now, if virtue promises to enable us to achieve happiness, freedom from passion, and serenity, then progress towards virtue is surely also progress towards each of these states. For it is invariably the case that, [4] whatever the end may be towards which perfection in anything definitively leads, progress marks an approach towards that end.

[5] How does it come about, then, that when we agree that virtue is something of this kind, we seek and display progress elsewhere? What does virtue achieve for us? Serenity. [6] Who is making progress, then? Someone who has read many treatises by Chrysippus?* [7] For if that is the case, virtue assuredly consists in nothing else than in having gained a knowledge of Chrysippus. [8] As things are, then, while acknowledging that virtue achieves one result, we're yet declaring that the approach to virtue, namely progress, produces another. [9] 'That person', someone says, 'is already able to read Chrysippus on his own.' By the gods, man, you're making excellent progress, what wonderful progress! [10] 'Why are you making fun of him?' And you, why are you diverting him from an awareness of his own failings? Aren't you willing to show him what virtue achieves, so that he may learn where to look for progress? [11] Look for it, wretch, where your proper task lies. And where is that? In desire and aversion, so that you may neither fail to attain what you desire, nor fall into what you want to avoid; in motivation to act or not to act, so that you may not go wrong in that; and in assent and the withholding of assent, so that you may not be deceived. [12] The first two areas of study come first, as the most essential. But if you're still afraid and trembling as you seek to avoid falling into what you want to avoid, how, I ask, can you make any progress?

[13] Come now, show me what progress you're making in this regard. Suppose I were talking with an athlete and said, Show me your shoulders, and he were to reply, 'Look at my jumping-weights.'* That's quite enough of you and your weights! What I want to see is what you've achieved by use of those jumping-weights. [14] 'Take the treatise *On Motivation* and see how thoroughly I've read it.' That's not what I'm seeking to know, slave, but how you're exercising your motives to act and not to act, and how you're managing your desires and aversions, and how you're approaching all of this, and how you're applying yourself to it, and preparing for it, and whether in

harmony with nature or out of harmony with it. [15] If in harmony, give me evidence of that, and I'll tell you whether you're making progress; but if out of harmony, go away, and don't be satisfied merely to interpret those books, but also write some books of that kind yourself. And what good will that do you? [16] Don't you know that the whole book costs only five denarii?* So do you suppose that someone who interprets it is worth more than five denarii? [17] Never look for your work in one place, then, and your progress in another.

[18] So where is progress to be found? If any of you turns away from external things to concentrate his efforts on his own power of choice, to cultivate it and perfect it, so as to bring it into harmony with nature, raising it up and rendering it free, unhindered, unobstructed, trustworthy, and self-respecting; [19] and if he has come to understand that whoever longs for things that are not within his power, or seeks to avoid them, can neither be trustworthy nor free, but must necessarily be subject to change, and be tossed in all directions along with those things, and is inevitably placing himself under the domination of other people, namely, those who can secure or prevent such things; [20] and if, finally, when he gets up in the morning, he holds in mind what he has learned and keeps true to it, if he bathes as a trustworthy person, and eats as a self-respecting person, putting his guiding principles into action in relation to anything that he has to deal with, just as a runner does in the practice of running, or a voice trainer in the training of voices [21] —this, then, is the person who is truly making progress; this is the person who hasn't travelled in vain!

[22] But if he has directed his efforts to what is contained in books, and that is what he toils away at, and it was for that that he has travelled abroad, I would ask him to return home at once and no longer neglect his affairs there, [23] because he has made his journey for no purpose; no, what is truly worthwhile is to study how to rid one's life of distress and lamentation, and of cries of 'Ah, what sorrow is mine!' and 'Poor wretch that I am!', and of misfortune and adversity; [24] and to learn what death, banishment, prison, and hemlock really are, so that one may be able to say in prison like Socrates, 'My dear Crito,* if it pleases the gods that this should come about, so be it!', rather than, 'Alas, poor old man that I am, this is what was kept in store for my grey hairs!' [25] Who speaks in such terms? Do you think

that I'll mention some obscure man of humble origin? Doesn't Priam talk like that? Doesn't Oedipus? Is there, indeed, any king who doesn't? [26] For what else is tragedy than the portrayal in tragic verse of the sufferings of men who have attached high value to external things? [27] If one has to be deceived into learning that external things that lie outside the sphere of choice are nothing to us, I for my part would willingly undergo such deception, if it would enable me to live a life of undisturbed serenity from that time onward; but as to what you wish for, it is for you to look to that.

[28] What does Chrysippus offer us, then? 'So that you may know', he says, 'that those thoughts are not false from which serenity comes to us and freedom from passion, [29] take my books and you will know that they are true and in harmony with nature, the thoughts that render me free from passion.' Oh, what great good fortune! And how great is the benefactor* who shows us the way! [30] People everywhere have raised shrines and altars to Triptolemus* for having given us cultivated crops for our nourishment; [31] but to him who discovered, and brought to light and communicated to all, the truth that enables us not merely to keep alive, but to live a good life—who among you has ever raised an altar in his honour, or a temple or statue, or bows down to God to thank him for this benefaction? [32] For having granted us corn or the vine, we offer up sacrifices to the gods, and yet when they have brought forth such a wonderful fruit in the human mind, by setting out to reveal to us the truth about happiness, shall we fail to offer thanks to God for that?

1.5 *Against the Academics*

[1] If someone, says Epictetus, refuses to accept what is patently obvious, it is not easy to find arguments to use against him that could cause him to change his mind. [2] And the reason for this lies neither in his own strength, nor in the weakness of the one who is trying to instruct him; but the fact is that when someone who has been driven into a corner turns to stone, how can one hope to deal with him any further through argument?

[3] Petrifaction of this kind takes two forms, the one being a petrifaction of the intellect, and the other of moral feeling, when someone who is in the line of battle is willing neither to grant assent

to what is plainly obvious nor to withdraw from the fray. [4] Most of us fear the deadening of the body and would resort to every means to avoid falling into such a state, but when it comes to the deadening of the soul, we're not in the least concerned. [5] And if, by Zeus, with regard to the soul itself, someone falls into such a state as to be incapable of following or understanding any argument, we think that he is in a bad way; but if someone's moral feeling and sense of shame are deadened, we even go so far as to call that strength of mind!

[6] Do you recognize that you're awake? 'No', replies the Academic, 'no more than when, in my dreams, I have the impression of being awake.' Is there no difference at all, then, between the one impression and the other? 'None.' [7] How can I argue with this man any further? What fire, what steel, can I apply to him to make him realize that he has become deadened? If he does realize, he pretends not to; he is even worse than a corpse. [8] One man doesn't see the contradiction; he is in a bad state. This man, by contrast, sees it, but isn't moved and doesn't improve; he is in an even worse state. [9] His sense of shame and moral feeling have been completely excised, and his faculty of reason, if not excised, has been brutalized at any rate. Am I to call this strength of mind? Heaven forbid, unless I am also to apply that description to the quality that enables degenerates to do and say in public whatever comes into their heads.

1.6 *On providence*

[1] From everything that comes about in the universe one may easily find cause to praise providence* if one possesses these two qualities, the capacity to view each particular event in relation to the whole, and a sense of gratitude. [2] For, otherwise, one will either fail to recognize the usefulness of what has come about, or else fail to be truly grateful if one does in fact recognize it.

[3] If God had created colours without also having created the faculty of vision, what good would that have served?—'None at all.' [4] —Conversely, if he had created the faculty of vision without causing objects to be of such a nature as to be visible to it, what good would have been served in that case too?—'None.' [5] —Or again, if he had brought about these two things, but hadn't created light? [6] —'In that case, too, no good would have been served.'—Who is it,

then, who has adapted one thing to another? Who has adapted the sword to the scabbard and the scabbard to the sword? Can it be no one? [7] And yet from the very structure of such artefacts, we're accustomed to recognize that they're undoubtedly the work of some maker, rather than being mere products of chance. [8] Does each of these works reveal its maker, then, while visible objects and vision and light do not? [9] And male and female, and the desire that they have for intercourse with one another, and the power that they have to make use of the organs that have been constructed for that purpose, do these things not reveal their maker either? Surely they do. [10] This remarkable constitution* of our mind, which enables us not only to receive impressions from sensible objects when they act upon us, but also to choose certain impressions from among them, and subtract from them, and add to them, and so make various combinations, and also, by Zeus, substitute some for others which are in some way related to them—can it really be the case that even this isn't enough to move some people, and make them change their ideas so as to make allowance for the maker? [11] Or otherwise, let them explain what it is that brings all of this about, or how it is possible that such wonders that bear all the signs of workmanship could come into being by chance and of their own accord.

[12] Well now, is it in us human beings alone that these things come about? Many, indeed, in us alone, those of which the rational animal has a special need, but you'll find that we share many of them with the irrational animals too. [13] Is it the case, then, that they too understand how things come about? No, not at all, since use is one thing and understanding is another. God had need both of these creatures, which merely make use of impressions, and of ourselves, who understand the use of them. [14] For them, it is enough merely to eat, drink, take rest and procreate, and perform such other functions as are appropriate to each, whereas for ourselves, who have been further endowed with the faculty of understanding, [15] that is no longer enough, but unless we act in a methodical and orderly fashion, and in accordance with our own specific nature and constitution, we shall no longer attain our proper end. [16] For in so far as beings have different constitutions, their works and their ends will differ too. [17] So where a being's constitution is adapted for use alone, mere use suffices; but where a being also has the capacity to understand that use, unless that capacity be properly exercised in addition, he will never attain his

end. [18] What of the animals? God has constituted each according to its intended purpose, one to be eaten, another to be used in the fields, another to produce cheese, and another for some comparable use; and to be able to perform these functions, how is it necessary for them to be able to understand impressions and be capable of distinguishing between them? [19] But God has brought the human race into the world to be a spectator of himself and of his works, and not merely to observe them, but also to interpret them. [20] It is thus shameful for a human being to begin and end where the irrational animals do. Rather, he should start off where they do and end where nature ended with regard to ourselves. [21] Now it ended with contemplation, and understanding, and a way of life that is in harmony with nature. [22] Take care, then, that you don't die without having contemplated these realities.

[23] You travel all the way to Olympia to look at the work of Phidias,* and all of you regard it as a misfortune to die without having seen such sights; [24] and yet, where no journey is required and you already have the works in front of you, have you no desire, then, to view them and to understand them? [25] Will you never come to recognize, then, who you are and what you were born for, or what is the nature of this spectacle to which you have been admitted?

[26] 'But unpleasant and distressing things come about in this life.'

And don't such things come about at Olympia? Aren't you scorched by the heat? Aren't you crowded and jostled? Don't you find it difficult to wash? Don't you get soaked when it rains? Aren't you exposed to no end of uproar and shouting and other irritations? [27] But by balancing all these things off against the remarkable nature of the spectacle, I imagine that you're able to accept and endure them. [28] Come now, haven't you been endowed with faculties that enable you to bear whatever may come about? Haven't you been endowed with greatness of soul? And with courage? And with endurance? [29] If only I have greatness of soul, what reason is left for me to be worried about anything that may come to pass? What can disconcert or trouble me, or seem in any way distressing? Shall I fail to apply my capacities to the end for which I have received them, but instead groan and lament about things that come about?

[30] 'Yes, but my nose is running.' Then what do you have hands for, you slave? Isn't it to be able to wipe your nose? [31] 'But is there any good reason why there should be runny noses in the world?' [32]

How much better it would be for you to wipe your nose than to find fault. What kind of a man do you suppose Heracles* would have become if it hadn't been for the famous lion, and the hydra, the stag, the boar, and the wicked and brutal men whom he drove away and cleared from the earth? [33] What would he have turned his hand to if nothing like that had existed? Isn't it plain that he would have wrapped himself up in a blanket and gone to sleep? First of all, then, he would surely never have become a Heracles if he had slumbered the whole of his life away in such luxury and tranquillity; and even if he had, what good would that have been to him? [34] What would have been the use of his arms and of all his strength, endurance, and nobility of mind if such circumstances and opportunities hadn't been there to rouse him and exercise him?

[35] 'What, should he have secured such opportunities for himself, then, and have sought to introduce a lion into his land from somewhere else, and a boar, and a hydra?'

[36] That would be sheer stupidity and madness. But since they did in fact exist and were to be found, they served a useful purpose in revealing and exercising Heracles.

[37] So come on, then, now that you recognize these things, and consider the faculties that you possess, and after having done so, say, 'Bring on me now, Zeus, whatever trouble you may wish, since I have the equipment that you granted to me and such resources as will enable me to distinguish myself through whatever may happen.'* [38] No, but you sit there trembling at the thought that certain things may come about, and wailing, grieving, and groaning at others that do come about; and then you cast blame on the gods. [39] For what else than impiety can result from such meanness of spirit? [40] And yet God has not only granted us these faculties that enable us to endure whatever may happen without being debased or crushed by it, but has also granted them to us—as befits a good king and, in truth, father—free from all hindrance, compulsion, and restraint, placing them entirely within our own power, without reserving any power even for himself to hinder or restrain them. [41] Possessing these faculties as you do, free and as your own, you fail to make use of them, however, and fail to perceive what it is that you have received, and from whom, [42] but sit there grieving and groaning, some of you blinded towards the giver and not even recognizing your benefactor, while others are led astray by their

meanness of spirit into making reproaches and complaints against
God. [43] And yet I can show you that you have the resources and
equipment that are needed to be noble-minded and courageous,
while it is for you to show me what occasion you have for complaint
and reproach!

1.7 *On the use of equivocal and hypothetical arguments and the like*

[1] Most people fail to realize that the study of equivocal and
hypothetical arguments, and of those that are developed through
questioning, and, in a word, all such arguments, has some relevance
to the duties of life. [2] For in every area of study, we're seeking to
learn how a good and virtuous person may discover the path that
he should follow in life and the way in which he should conduct
himself. [3] So it must be said, then, either that a virtuous person
won't engage in question and answer, [4] or that if he does, he will
make no effort to approach such arguments in anything other than
a random and careless manner; or else, if one accepts neither of
these assertions, it must be conceded that one should make some
study of those topics with which question and answer are principally
concerned.

[5] For what is required in reasoning? To establish the truth, reject
what is false, and suspend judgement in doubtful cases. [6] Is it
enough, then, to learn that alone?

'Yes, it's enough,' someone replies.

Is it also enough, then, for someone who wants to avoid any mistake in the use of coinage merely to hear it said, 'Accept good drachmas and reject those that are counterfeit'?

[7] 'No, that's not enough.'

So what is required in addition? Why, what else than the capacity
to test the coinage and distinguish the good drachmas from the counterfeit? [8] And likewise, in reasoning too, the words that are spoken
are surely not sufficient, but it is necessary too to know how to test
them and distinguish the true from the false and the uncertain?

'That is indeed necessary.'

[9] Apart from that, what else is required in reasoning? You must
accept what follows from the premises that have rightly been
granted by you. [10] Come now, is it enough in this area, too, merely

to know this specific thing? No, it is not enough, one must also learn how one thing follows as a consequence from certain other things, and how one thing is sometimes derived from a single thing, and sometimes from several in conjunction. [11] Isn't it necessary, then, to acquire this skill in addition if one is to conduct oneself intelligently in argument, and be able to prove each of one's points, and to follow other people's demonstrations, without being misled by those who put forward sophistic arguments by way of proof? [12] This has given rise among us to the study and practice of inferential arguments and logical figures, and it has become clear that these are necessary.

[13] But it sometimes comes about that, when we have properly granted certain premises, certain conclusions are derived from them that, though false, nonetheless follow from them. [14] What am I to do, then? Accept the false conclusion? [15] And how is that possible? Then should I say that I was wrong to accept the premises? No, this isn't permissible either. Or say: That doesn't follow from the premisses? But that again isn't permissible. [16] So what is one to do in such circumstances? Isn't it the same as with debts? Just as having borrowed on some occasion isn't enough to make somebody a debtor, but it is necessary in addition that he continues to owe the money and hasn't paid off the loan; likewise, our having accepted the premises isn't enough to make it necessary for us to accept the inference, but we have to continue to accept the premises. [17] If the premises remain* to the end such as they were when they were granted, it is altogether necessary that we continue to hold to them, and admit the conclusions that follow from them; [18] [or if the contrary applies, that we shouldn't]. [19] For us, in that case, and from our present point of view, that conclusion no longer follows, since we've renounced our acceptance of the premises. [20] This, then, is what we need to examine with regard to premises, changes of this kind and modifications in them, because if in the course of question and answer, or in drawing conclusions, or at any other stage of the argument, the premises undergo these modifications, they will become a cause of trouble for the inexperienced if they cannot see what follows. Why do we need to do this? [21] So that in this regard, we should not act inappropriately, or at random, or in a confused manner.

[22] And the same is true of hypotheses and hypothetical arguments. For it is sometimes necessary to postulate some hypothesis as a basis for

the approach to the argument that follows. [23] So should we grant every hypothesis that is proposed, or not all of them? And if not all, then which? [24] And once one has granted a hypothesis, should one hold to it for ever and continue to maintain it, or are there occasions when one should abandon it? And as regards the conclusions that follow from it, should one accept them, and reject those that conflict with it?

'Yes.'

[25] But someone says, 'If you grant a possible hypothesis, I'll force you through argument to accept an impossibility.' Would a wise person refuse to engage with someone such as this, and avoid all enquiry and discussion? [26] And yet who would be more capable than he of conducting an argument, and more adept in question and answer, and less liable, by Zeus, to be deceived and fall victim to sophisms? [27] Well then, will he agree to engage in discussion, but without taking care not to proceed carelessly and haphazardly in the argument? If so, how could he still be the kind of person we imagine him to be? [28] Without some such practice and preparation, however, how will it be possible for him to reason conclusively? [29] Show that he will be able to do this, and all these studies will be superfluous and absurd, and inconsistent with the idea that we have formed of the good person. [30] Why do we still remain indolent, careless, and sluggish; why do we look for excuses to avoid hard work, or avoid staying awake to cultivate our reason?

[31] 'But after all, if I go astray in these matters, it's not as if I've killed my father, is it?'

Tell me, slave, where was your father present here for you to kill him? So what have you actually done? Committed the only fault that it was possible for you to commit in the present context. [32] I myself made the very same remark to Rufus* when he once criticized me for not having discovered the missing step in a syllogism: Why, I said, it's not as if I've burned down the Capitol! To which he retorted, 'In this case, slave, that missing step is indeed the Capitol!' [33] Or are there no other faults than burning down the Capitol or killing one's father? Whereas to deal with our impressions in a random, ill-considered, and haphazard fashion, to be unable to follow an argument or demonstration or sophism, and, in a word, to be unable to make out, in question and answer, what is consistent with one's position and what is not—is none of this is to be regarded as a fault?

1.8 *That our reasoning faculties are not free of danger for the uneducated*

[1] In as many ways as we can vary the forms of equivalent terms with one another, in so many ways also may the forms of logical proofs and enthymemes* be varied in reasoning. [2] Take this form of argument, for instance: 'If you have borrowed and have not repaid, you owe me the money.' This is equivalent to 'You have not borrowed and have not repaid, so you do not owe me the money.' [3] And no one is better fitted than a philosopher to vary the forms of argument with skill. For if an enthymeme is indeed an incomplete syllogism, it is clear that someone who has had practice in handling the complete syllogism will be no less capable of handling the incomplete one.

[4] Why is it, then, that we fail to train ourselves and one another in this way? [5] Because even now, when we aren't training ourselves in these matters, and aren't being diverted by me at least from the study of moral questions, we're making no progress all the same towards the right and the good. [6] So what should we expect if we undertake this work in addition? And especially because this would not only be a further activity that would distract us from more essential studies, but it would also give occasion for vanity and conceit, and in no small way. [7] For logical and persuasive reasoning can exercise a powerful effect, especially if they're developed through training and are lent further plausibility through the skilful use of language. [8] The fact is that, as a general rule, every capacity that is acquired by uneducated people of weak character tends to be dangerous for them, in so far as it makes them conceited and presumptuous in that regard. [9] For how on earth can one persuade a young man who excels in these studies that he should not become an appendage to them, but rather make them an appendage to himself? [10] Won't he trample all these appeals underfoot, and walk about among us full of pride and puffed up with conceit, never being willing to allow that anyone should try to remind him of his shortcomings, and of where he has gone astray?

[11] 'What, wasn't Plato* a philosopher?'

Yes, and wasn't Hippocrates* a doctor? And yet you can see how well Hippocrates expresses himself. [12] But is it by virtue of being a doctor that he expresses himself so well? Why, then, do you confuse things that come to be found together by accident in the same

individual? [13] If Plato was strong and handsome, is it necessary that
I too, sitting here, should toil to become strong or handsome, as
though that were essential to philosophy just because a certain
philosopher happened to be strong and handsome as well as being a
philosopher? [14] Don't you want to understand and distinguish
what qualities people require in order to become philosophers, and
what other qualities may be present in them accidentally? Come now,
if I could be counted* as a philosopher, would you need to become
lame like me?

Now, do I want to deny you these capacities? [15] Heaven forbid! No
more than I would wish to deny you the capacity to see. [16] All the
same, if you ask me what the human good is, I can offer you no other
reply than to say that it lies in a certain quality of choice.

1.9 *How, from the idea that we are akin to God,* *one may proceed to what follows*

[1] If there is any truth in what the philosophers say about the kinship
between God and humanity, what course is left for human beings
than to follow the example of Socrates, and when one is asked where
one is from, never to reply, 'I'm an Athenian' or 'I'm a Corinthian',
but rather, 'I'm a citizen of the universe'? [2] For why say, in fact, that
you're an Athenian rather than just a citizen of that corner in which
your poor body was thrown down at the time of your birth? [3] Isn't it
obvious that you choose the place that is more sovereign, and not
merely that little corner, but also your whole household, and, in a
word, the source that your entire race of ancestors has come down to
you, and on that basis you call yourself an 'Athenian' or a 'Corinthian'?

[4] Now, suppose that one has studied the organization of the universe, and has come to understand that, 'of all things, the greatest,
and most important, and most all-embracing, is this society in which
human beings and God are associated together. From this are derived
the generative forces to which not only my father and grandfather
owe their origin, but also all beings that are born and grow on the
earth, and especially rational beings, [5] since they alone are fitted by
nature to enter into communion with the divine, being bound to God
through reason.' [6] Why shouldn't one who understands this
call himself a citizen of the universe? Why should he fear anything
that comes about for human beings? [7] What, shall kinship with

Caesar, or some other man of great power at Rome, be enough to ensure that one will be able to live in safety, and be secure against contempt and free from all fear, whereas having God as our maker, our father, and our protector won't be enough to deliver us from fear and suffering?

[8] 'And how am I to feed myself', someone asks, 'if I have nothing?' And how do slaves do so, how do runaways; what do they rely on when they flee from their masters? On their fields, their servants, their silverware? No, on nothing but themselves, and yet all the same they don't fail to find food for themselves. [9] And must our philosopher, when he ventures abroad, place his confidence in others and rely on them, instead of taking care of himself, and so show himself to be worse and more cowardly than the irrational animals, every one of which is self-sufficient, and lacks neither its proper food nor the way of life that is appropriate to it and in accord with nature?

[10] I think for my part that your old master shouldn't need to be sitting here working out how to prevent you from having a mean view of yourselves, or from developing mean and ignoble ideas about yourselves in the course of discussion. [11] No, he should rather be seeking to ensure that there may not be among you any young men who, when they've become aware of their kinship with the gods, and have come to know that we have, so to speak, these chains attached to us—the body and its possessions, and all that is necessary in that regard for the maintenance and continuance of our life—may wish to cast all of this aside as being burdensome, distressing, and useless, and depart to their own kin. [12] That is the struggle that your master and educator, if he could properly be described as such, should be engaging in.

You for your part would come to him and say, 'Epictetus, we can no longer bear to be chained to this poor body of ours, having to give it food and drink, and provide it with rest, and keep it clean, and then having to associate with all manner of people because of it. [13] Isn't it true that these things are indifferent and nothing to us, and that death is no evil? And that we are in some sense related to God, and draw our origin from him? [14] Allow us to go back to where we came from; allow us to be delivered at last from these chains that are fastened to us and weigh us down. [15] Down here thieves and brigands, and law-courts, and those who are known as tyrants, imagine that they hold some power over us because of our poor body and its possessions. Allow us to show them that they don't really hold power over anyone.'

[16] It would be for me to reply as follows: You must wait for God,* my friends. When he gives the signal and sets you free from your service here, then you may depart to him. But for the present, you must resign yourselves to remaining in this post in which he has stationed you. [17] It is short, in truth, the time of your stay in this world, and easy to bear for people who are of such a mind as you. For what tyrant, or what thief, or what law-courts, can still inspire fear in those who no longer attach any importance to the body and its possessions? So wait, and don't make your departure without proper reason.

[18] Such is the stance that a teacher should adopt towards gifted young men. [19] But what happens at present? Your teacher is a mere corpse, and you yourselves are corpses. As soon as you've eaten your fill today, you sit and moan about what tomorrow may bring, worrying about how you'll be able to feed yourselves. [20] If you manage to get any food, slave, you'll have it, and if you don't, you'll leave this world; the door stands open. Why grieve? What place is left for tears? What occasion is left for flattery? Why should one person envy another? Why should one let oneself be dazzled by those who have great possessions and hold powerful positions, especially if they're both strong and bad-tempered? [21] For what can they do to us? The things that they have the power to do are of no concern to us, and when it comes to the things that matter to us, they have no power over those. Who can still exert any power, then, over people who think in this way?

[22] What attitude did Socrates hold with regard to these matters? Why, what other than that which someone is bound to hold if he is convinced that he is akin to the gods? [23] 'If you were to say to me now,' he tells his judges, '"We will acquit you on these conditions, that you no longer conduct the discussions that you have conducted hitherto, and no longer pester any of us, young or old,"' [24] I would reply, 'How absurd of you to think that if one of your generals had stationed me in a post, I should hold it, and defend it, preferring to die a thousand deaths rather than abandon it, but if God has stationed us in some position and laid down rules of conduct, we should abandon it!'* [25] This is what it means for a man to be truly akin to

the gods. [26] As for us, however, we think of ourselves as being mere bodies, entrails and sexual organs, because we give way to our fears and desires; and we flatter those who might be able to help us in this regard, while fearing those same people.

[27] Someone once asked me to write to Rome on his behalf, because he had suffered what would commonly be regarded as a misfortune; for after having been a man of position and wealth, he had lost everything and ended up here. And I wrote on his behalf in a very humble tone. [28] After reading the letter, however, he gave it back, saying, 'It was your help that I was asking for, not your pity; it isn't as if anything bad has happened to me.'* [29] In the same way, Rufus would say to me by way of a test, 'Your master is going to do this or that to you,' [30] and when I responded by saying, Such is the way of human life, he replied, 'What use would it serve, then, for me to intercede with your master when I can get the same result from you?' [31] For it is indeed pointless and foolish to seek to get from another what one can get from oneself. [32] Since I can get greatness of soul and nobility of mind from myself, shall I seek to get a patch of land from you, or a bit of money, or some public post? Heaven forbid! I won't overlook my own resources in such a manner. [33] But if someone is abject and cowardly, what on earth can one do for him except write letters for him as though on behalf of a corpse, 'Do please grant us the corpse of this man and a pint of his miserable blood'; [34] for in truth such a person is merely a corpse and a pint of blood, and nothing more. If he amounted to anything more, he would realize that no one suffers misfortune because of the actions of another.

1.10 *To those who have set their hearts on advancement at Rome*

[1] If we had devoted the same unsparing effort to our own work as the senators at Rome have in achieving what they have set their mind on, perhaps we too might have achieved something. [2] I know a man older than myself who is now the official who superintends the grain supply at Rome; while he was passing through this town on his journey back from exile, I recall what things he said to me as he denounced his former way of life, and declared that from now on, after he got back, he would concern himself with nothing other than living the rest of his life in peace and calm—'For how little time is

now left to me!' [3] To which I replied, No, you won't do that, but as soon as you get the slightest whiff of Rome, you'll forget every word of it. I added that if he were granted the least access to the palace, he would push his way in, with a joyful heart and offering up thanks to the gods. [4] 'If you ever find me putting one foot inside the palace, Epictetus,' he replied, 'then think what you like of me.'

[5] And what do you suppose he did? Before he even arrived in Rome, he was met with dispatches from Caesar; on receiving them, he forgot all that he had previously intended, and from that moment on he never ceased from heaping one activity on top of another. [6] How I wish that I could be standing beside him now to remind him of what he said while he was passing through, and tell him, I've proved to be a much shrewder prophet than you!

[7] So what am I saying, then? That man is an animal who ought to remain inactive? Heaven forbid! But how is it that we philosophers fail to keep active? [8] To start with me, as soon as day arrives, I recall briefly what I am due to read over in my lessons,* and then say all at once to myself, But what does it really matter to me how So-and-so expounds his text? The main thing is that I should get some sleep. [9] Even so, how are the activities of those people at Rome comparable to ours? If you look at what they spend their time doing, you'll see. For what else do they do all day than reach decisions, discuss things together, consult about a bit of grain, a patch of land, and other matters of that kind? [10] Does it come to the same, then, to receive a little petition from someone reading, 'I request your permission to export a little grain,' and this, 'I request you to examine what Chrysippus has to say about the administration of the universe, and the place that a rational animal occupies within it; and to consider also what you are, and what is good for you, and what is bad'? [11] What does the one petition have in common with the other? Do both deserve equal attention? [12] And is it equally shameful to neglect the one and the other?

What, then, are we old philosophers the only ones who are indolent and are inclined to nod off? [13] No, that's much more the case with you young men. To be sure, we old men, when we see the young at play, feel a desire on our part, too, to join them in their play. How much more, then, if I saw them wide awake and eager to join us in our endeavours, would I be eager to combine my efforts with theirs.

1.11 *On family affection*

[1] Epictetus once received a visit from a government official, and after questioning him about various specific points, he asked him whether he had a wife and children; [2] and when the man replied that he had, he went on to ask, How do you find family life, then? 'Miserable,' the man said. How so? [3] For it's surely not for this that people marry and have children, to be miserable, but rather in the hope of being happy. [4] 'Well, for my part,' the man said, 'my little children are such a source of distress to me that, not long ago, when my little daughter was ill, I couldn't bear even to be in the room with her during her illness, but fled and stayed away until someone told me that she was well again.'—Well then, do you think you were right to have acted in that way? [5] —'I was behaving naturally,' he said. But that is the very thing that you must convince me of, replied Epictetus, that you were behaving in accordance with nature, and I will then convince you that whatever is done in accordance with nature is rightly done. [6] —'That's how all fathers feel,' said the man, 'or at least most do.'—I don't dispute that, said Epictetus, but the point at issue between us is whether it's right to feel like that. [7] For in that case, one would have to say that tumours develop for the good of the body just because they do in fact develop, and, in a word, that to fall into error is natural just because almost all of us, or at least most of us, do fall into error. [8] What you must show me, then, is how your behaviour is in accordance with nature.—'I can't,' the man replied, 'but rather, you should show me how it isn't in accordance with nature and how it isn't right.' [9] —Well, suppose we were enquiring about black and white: what criterion would we call upon to distinguish between them?—'Sight,' the man replied.—And if it were a matter of hot and cold, or hard and soft, what would be the criterion?—'Touch.' [10] —Well then, since our present debate is about whether things are in accordance with nature and rightly done, or the opposite, what criterion would you have us take?—'I don't know,' he said. [11] —When it comes to colours and smells, to be sure, and flavours too, to have no knowledge of the criterion will perhaps cause no great harm, but when it comes to the nature of good and evil, and whether or not our actions are in accordance with nature, do you suppose that someone suffers no great harm if he has no knowledge of that?—'On the contrary, the greatest harm.' [12] —Come, tell me now, is everything

that is thought by certain people to be good and fitting rightly thought to be so? Is it possible, for instance, that all the opinions that the Jews, Syrians, Egyptians, and Romans currently hold with regard to food are rightly held?—'And how is that possible?' [13] —I imagine, on the contrary, that if the opinions of the Egyptians are right, it must necessarily follow that the opinions of the others aren't right; or if those of the Jews are right, those of the others aren't.—'Without a doubt.' [14] —Now where there is ignorance, there is lack of knowledge and instruction with regard to essential matters. The man agreed. [15] Now that you recognize this, continued Epictetus, you will have no greater concern henceforth, and set your mind on nothing else, than to come to know the criterion by which one can judge whether things are in accordance with nature, and then to apply that knowledge in judging each particular case.

[16] But for the present, this is all the assistance that I can give you in helping you to achieve your desire. [17] Does love of one's family strike you as being natural and good?—'How could it not be?'— Well then, love of one's family is natural and good, and isn't what is reasonable also good?—'Without a doubt.' [18] —So there is thus no conflict between love of one's family and what is reasonable?—'I think not.'—Otherwise it would follow that if one of the conflicting things was in accordance with nature, the other would be contrary to nature. Isn't that so?—'Absolutely.' [19] —So it follows that wherever we find family affection accompanied by reason, we can confidently declare it to be right and good?—'Yes, indeed,' the man replied. [20] —Well then, I imagine that you won't deny that to abandon a child when it is ill and go off is an unreasonable thing to do. It remains for us to consider whether that is consistent with love of one's family.—'Let's consider the matter, then.'

[21] Since you had such affection for your child, then, was it right for you to rush off and leave it? And its mother, has she no affection for the child? [22] —'Of course she does.'—Should its mother too have abandoned it, then, or not?—'She shouldn't have.'—And its nurse, does she love it?—'She does,' he said.—Should she too have abandoned it?—'In no way.'—And its attendant, does he love it?—'He does.' [23] —Should he too have abandoned it, then, and gone off, so that the child would have been left on its own without help as a result of the great affection in which it was held by you, its parents, and all who had charge of it, and would quite possibly have

died in the hands of people who had no love or care for it?—'Heaven forbid!' [24] —And in truth, wouldn't it be unfair and unreasonable that actions that one considers proper for oneself, because one feels such affection, should not also be permitted to others who feel no less affection?—'It would be absurd.' [25] —Tell me now, if it had been you who were ill, would you have wanted all your relations, down even to your children and wife, to prove their affection by leaving you all on your own and deserted?—'In no way.'

[26] Would you wish to be loved by those around you to such a degree that, because of their all-too-great affection, you would always be left on your own when ill? Or rather, for that very reason, wouldn't you have wished to be loved by your enemies instead, if that were possible, so that it would be they who left you alone? If so, it can only be concluded that your actions were in no way prompted by affection. [27] Well then, was it nothing at all that stirred and impelled you to abandon your child? How could that be possible? No, it was a motive like the one that impelled a man at Rome to cover his face when the horse that he had backed was running, so that when the horse did in fact win, against all expectation, they had to apply sponges to revive him from his faint. What motive is that, then? [28] This is perhaps not the right moment for a precise explanation,* but it is enough for us to be convinced that, if what the philosophers say is correct, we shouldn't look for the motive anywhere outside ourselves, but rather accept that it is one and the same cause that moves us in every case to do something or not do it, or to say something or not say it, or to avoid something or pursue it, [29] the very same cause, in fact, that has motivated my present action too and your own, yours to have come to me and be sitting here to listen, and mine to be speaking as I am. And what cause is that? [30] Is it anything other than this, that we thought fit to do so?

'Nothing other.'

And if we had thought fit to act otherwise, what else would we have been doing than that which seemed good to us? [31] Isn't it true, then, that in the case of Achilles, too, it wasn't the death of Patroclus* that was the cause of his grief (for not everyone reacts in that way to the death of a comrade), but rather that he thought fit to grieve. [32] And in your case the other day, when you ran off, the reason was that you thought fit to do so; and if, on the contrary, you were to stay, that too would be because you thought fit. And now you're going off to Rome because you think fit to do so; and if you were to decide otherwise, you wouldn't go. [33] In a word, it is neither death, nor exile, nor distress, nor anything else of that kind, that causes us to do something or not to do it, but rather our judgements and opinions. [34] Have I convinced you of that, or not?

'You've convinced me.'

So in each case, as the causes are, so also are the effects. [35] From this day forth, then, whenever we fail to act rightly, we'll ascribe the blame to nothing other than the judgement that led us to act as we did, and will endeavour to destroy it and cut it out, even more than with the tumours and abscesses of our body. [36] In like fashion, we will also ascribe what we do rightly to the same cause. [37] And no longer will we blame slave, or neighbour, or wife, or children as being responsible for any of our ills, since we're now convinced that unless we judge things to be of a certain nature, we don't carry out the actions that follow from that judgement. Now when it comes to forming a judgement, or not forming one, we're the masters of that, and not things outside ourselves.

'Quite so', the man said.

[38] So accordingly, from this day onward, we'll investigate and examine the nature and condition of nothing else at all—be it land or slaves or horses or dogs—but only of our judgements.—'That's my wish,' he said. [39] —You can see, then, that it is necessary for you to become a student, that creature who is the butt of everyone's laughter, if you really want to subject your opinions to proper examination. And that, as you are fully aware, is not the work of a single hour or day.

I.12 *On contentment*

[1] With regard to the gods,* there are some who say that the divine doesn't even exist, while others say that it does exist, but that it is inactive and indifferent, and exercises no providential care; [2] while a third set of people maintain that it both exists and exercises providential care, but only with regard to important matters relating to the heavens, and in no way to affairs on earth; a fourth set declare that it does take thought for earthly and human affairs, but only in a general fashion, without showing concern for each particular individual; [3] while a fifth set, to which both Odysseus and Socrates belonged, say, '*Not a movement of mine escapes you.*'*

[4] We must thus start off by examining each of these positions, to see whether or not it is soundly argued. [5] For if the gods don't exist, how can it be our goal in life to follow the gods? And if they do exist, but show concern for nothing whatever, how again can that be our goal? [6] If, on the other hand, they both exist and exercise care, but there is no communication between them and human beings, and indeed, by Zeus, between them and me specifically, how even in that case can this idea still be sound?

[7] One who has achieved virtue and excellence, after having examined all these questions, submits his will to the one who governs the universe just as good citizens submit to the law of their city. [8] And one who is still being educated should approach his education with this aim in view: 'How may I follow the gods in everything, and how can I act in a way that is acceptable to the divine administration, and how may I become free?' [9] For someone is free if all that happens to him comes about in accordance with his choice and no one else is able to impede him.

[10] 'What, is freedom madness, then?'

Heaven forbid! For freedom and madness are hardly compatible with one another.

[11] 'But I want whatever I wish to happen indeed to happen, regardless of how I arrive at that wish.'

[12] You're crazy, you're out of your mind! Don't you know that freedom is a precious and admirable thing? But for me to desire arbitrarily that things should happen as I arbitrarily decide risks being not merely far from admirable, but even exceedingly reprehensible. Consider, now, how do we proceed when it comes to writing? [13] Do I write the name 'Dion'* just as I wish? Of course not, I'm taught to want to write it as it ought to be written. And when it comes to music? The same applies. [14] And in general, with regard to any of the arts and sciences? The same applies. Otherwise there would be no point in trying to gain knowledge of anything, if it could be adapted to fit everyone's individual wishes. [15] Is it, then, only in this most grave and important matter, that of freedom, that it is possible for me to desire according to my whim? In no way, but rather true education consists precisely in this, in learning to wish that everything should come about just as it does. And how do things come about? As the one who ordains them has ordained. [16] And he has ordained that there be summer and winter, and abundance and shortage, and virtue

and vice, and all other opposites of that kind, and he has granted to each of us a body, and the parts that make up that body, and objects for us to possess, and companions to share our life.

[17] It is with this order of things in mind that we should approach our education, and not so as to change the existing order of things (for that has not been permitted to us, nor would it be better that it should be), but rather, things around us being as they are and as their nature dictates, so that we for our part may keep our will in harmony with whatever comes to pass.

[18] Well then, is it possible to flee from human society? And how could that be possible for us? Is it possible to change people, then, if we do associate with them? And who has granted me such a power? [19] What remains to be done, then; what method can we discover to apply in dealing with them? A method that will ensure that, while they for their part act as they think fit, we for our part will remain nonetheless in accord with nature. [20] But you're weak-spirited and discontented, and if you're alone, you call it desolation, and if you're in the company of others, you call them cheats and robbers, and you find fault even with your parents and children, your brothers and neighbours. [21] Whereas in fact, if you're living alone, you should call that peace and freedom, and view yourself as being like the gods; and if you find yourself in the company of a mass of people, you should call that not a mob and a source of uproar and vexation, but rather a feast and a public festival, and so accept everything with contentment. What is the punishment, then, of those who fail to accept things in that spirit? To be just as they are. [22] Is someone discontented to find himself on his own? Then let him be all alone. He is discontented with his parents? Then let him be a bad son and grieve. He is discontented with his children? Then let him be a bad father.

[23] 'Throw him into prison.'

What sort of prison? That in which he already finds himself. For he is there against his will, and whenever someone is in any place against his will, that is a prison for him. Just as Socrates* for his part was not in prison because he was there willingly.

[24] 'So I had to have a crippled leg, then?'

So because of one miserable leg, slave, you're going to cast reproaches against the universe? Aren't you willing to make a gift of it to the whole? Won't you give it up? Won't you happily surrender it to the one who gave it to you? [25] And will you be angry and displeased at the ordinances of Zeus, which he has prescribed and ordained together with the Fates, who attended your birth and spun the thread of your destiny? [26] Don't you know how small a part you are by comparison to the whole? With regard to your body, I mean; for when it comes to your reason, you're not inferior to the gods nor do you fall short of them, because the greatness of reason is measured not by height or length, but by the quality of its judgements.

[27] Aren't you willing to place your good, then, in that which renders you equal to the gods? [28] 'Oh how miserable I am to have such a father and mother!' What, was it granted to you to choose your parents in advance and say, 'May this man have intercourse with this woman at this hour so that I may come into this world'? [29] No, that wasn't granted to you, but your parents had to exist before you, and then you had to be born in the way that you were. And from parents of what kind? From parents of such a kind as they were.

[30] What, then, considering that they were such as they were, is no remedy available to you? Now, if you were ignorant of the purpose for which you possess the power of sight, you'd be unfortunate and in a bad way if you closed your eyes when colours were presenting themselves; so when you have nobility and greatness of mind to enable you to deal with every circumstance, and yet are ignorant of that, aren't you even more unfortunate and even worse off? [31] Things that the faculty in your possession is well fitted to deal with present themselves to you, and yet you renounce the use of it at the very moment when you should be keeping it open for use and fully attentive. [32] Shouldn't you be giving thanks, rather, to the gods for having enabled you to rise above everything that they have placed within your power, and having rendered you accountable only for what is subject to your control? [33] With regard to your parents, they have discharged you from all accountability; and likewise with regard to your brothers and sisters, and to your body, and to your property, and life and death. [34] Well then, what have they made you accountable for? Only for what lies within your power, the right use of your impressions. [35] Why do you charge yourself, then, with things for which you're not accountable? You're merely creating trouble for yourself.

1.13 *How may everything be done in a way that is pleasing to the gods?*

[1] When someone asked him how one can eat in a manner that is pleasing to the gods, he replied: If one eats as one ought and politely, and indeed with temperance and restraint, won't one also be doing so in a manner that is pleasing to the gods? [2] And when one has called for hot water and the slave-boy fails to respond, or if he does, brings it merely lukewarm, or if he isn't even to be found in the house, and one doesn't get angry or lose one's temper, is that not pleasing to the gods?

[3] 'But how can one put up with such people?'

Slave, can't you put up with your own brother, who has Zeus for his father, and is, so to speak, born of the same seed as you, and is of the same heavenly descent? [4] Or because you've been stationed in a somewhat more eminent position, will you set yourself up all at once as a tyrant? Won't you keep in mind who you are, and who these people are whom you are ruling over? That they belong to the same family, that they are by nature brothers of yours, that they are offspring of Zeus?

[5] 'But I have right of purchase over them, and they don't have any such right over me.'

But don't you see to where it is that you're directing your view? That it is to the earth, to the pit, to these miserable laws of ours, the laws of the dead,* so that you fail to have any regard for the laws of the gods?

1.14 *That the divine watches over all of us*

[1] Someone asked him how one might be convinced that everything that one does is carried out under the eye of God. Don't you think, he replied, that all things are bound together in a unity? 'Indeed I do,' the man said. [2] Well then, don't you think that things here on earth are subject to the influence of those in the heavens? 'I do,' he said.

[3] For how else could it come about with such regularity, as though at God's express command, that when he tells the plants to flower, they flower, when he tells them to bud, they bud, and to bear their fruit, they bear it, and to bring it to ripeness, they bring it to ripeness, and when again he tells them to strip themselves and shed their leaves,

and drawn in on themselves, remain inactive, and take their rest, they remain so and take their rest? [4] And how else could it come about that, in accord with the waxing and waning of the moon, and the approach and recession of the sun, we observe things on the earth undergoing such great transformations and changing into their opposites? [5] Now, if plants and our bodies are so intimately bound up with the whole and subject to its influence, won't the same be true of our souls in much higher degree? [6] But if our souls are closely bound and united to God in this way as portions and fragments of himself, surely God will be aware of their every movement, as being a movement of his own that is grounded in his own nature?

[7] Consider, now, you're able to reflect upon the divine governing order and every operation of the divine, as well as upon human affairs; and you have the capacity to be moved by countless things all at once, both in your senses and in your intelligence, and in such a way as to give your assent to some, and to reject others, or to suspend judgement; [8] and to preserve in your mind so many impressions from so many diverse objects, in such a way that when moved by them, your mind comes to conceive ideas that correspond to the impressions that were originally made on it, and so from these countless objects, you derive and preserve the arts, one after another, and also memories.

[9] If you're capable of all of that, can it be that God isn't capable of overseeing all things, and of being present throughout, and having some communication with all that is? [10] When the sun is able to illuminate so large a part of the universe, leaving unlit only that very small part that is covered by the shadow of the earth,* can it really be the case that he who created the sun—which is only a small part of him by comparison with the whole—and directs it on its way, could lack the power to perceive all that exists?

[11] 'But for my part,' someone says, 'I'm not capable of following all these things at one time.'

Why, did anyone ever tell you that you have powers to rival those of Zeus? [12] But all the same, he has assigned to each of us, as an overseer, his own personal guardian spirit, and has entrusted each of us to its protection, as a guardian that never sleeps and is never open to deception. [13] To what other guardian could he have entrusted us that would have been better and more vigilant than this? And so, when you close your doors and create darkness within, remember never to say that you're on your own, [14] for in fact, you're not alone, because God is within you, and your guardian spirit too. And what need do they have of light to see what you're doing?

[15] To this god you too should swear allegiance, as soldiers do to Caesar. For they, on receiving their wages, swear to put the safety of Caesar above all else; so will you, who have been judged worthy of so many gifts of such a valuable nature, be unwilling to swear your oath, and having sworn it, hold true to it? [16] And what is it that you must swear? Never to disobey, never to find fault with, never to complain about, anything that has been granted to you by God, and never be unwilling to do what you have to do, or to undergo what you're bound to undergo. [17] Now is the one oath truly comparable to the other? The soldiers swear never to hold anyone in higher honour than Caesar, whereas we for our part swear to hold ourselves in higher honour than all else.

1.15 *What does philosophy promise?*

[1] When someone consulted Epictetus about how he could persuade his brother to stop being ill-disposed towards him, he said: [2] Philosophy doesn't promise to secure any external good for man, since it would then be embarking on something that lies outside its proper subject matter. For just as wood is the material of the carpenter, and bronze that of the sculptor, the art of living has each individual's own life as its material.

[3] 'What about my brother's life, then?'

That again is the material for his own art of living, but with regard to yours, it belongs among external things, like the owning of land, like health, like good reputation. Now, philosophy promises none of these things, [4] but says instead, 'In every circumstance I'll keep the ruling centre in accordance with nature.'—Whose ruling centre?—'That of the individual in whom I am.'

[5] 'But how, in that case, am I to prevent my brother from being angry with me?'

Bring him to me and I'll tell him, but I have nothing to say to you about his anger.

[6] When the man who was seeking his advice then said, 'What I'd like to know is how, even if my brother is unwilling to be reconciled with me, I may remain in accordance with nature,' Epictetus replied: [7] Nothing great comes into being all at once, for that is not the case

even with a bunch of grapes or a fig. If you tell me now, 'I want a fig,'
I'll reply, 'That takes time.' Let the fig tree first come into blossom
and then bring forth its fruit, and then let the fruit grow to ripeness.
[8] So if even the fruit of a fig tree doesn't come to maturity all at once
and in a single hour, would you seek to gather the fruit of a human
mind in such a short time and with such ease? Even if I were to promise you that myself, it is more than you can expect.

1.16　*On providence*

[1] Don't be surprised that the other animals have all that is required
for their bodily needs provided for them, not only their food and
drink but also beds to lie on, and that they have no need of shoes, or
clothes, or bedding, while we have need of all those things. [2] For
since those creatures don't exist for their own sake, but to be of service, it would have brought no advantage to have created them with
those additional needs. [3] Just think what it would mean for us to
have to worry not only about our own needs, but about those of our
sheep and donkeys too, and to think how they are to be provided
with clothes and shoes, and with food and drink! [4] But as with
soldiers who report to their generals ready for service, already
equipped with shoes, clothes, and armour—for it would be a sorry
state of affairs if the commander had to go around seeing to
the clothes and shoes of all the troops of his regiment—so nature
likewise has created the animals, which are born for service, ready
prepared and ready equipped, so that they require no further care.
[5] So accordingly, one small boy with nothing more than a stick can
drive a flock of sheep.

　[6] But as it is, instead of giving thanks for this order of things,
which saves us from having to take as much care of our animals as we
do of ourselves, we go so far as to complain to God about our own lot!
[7] And yet, by Zeus and all the gods, a single one of these blessings of
nature would suffice to make anyone recognize that there is a divine
providence, if he were duly reverent and grateful. [8] And I'm not
thinking for the moment of anything grand, but the mere fact that
milk is produced from grass, and cheese from milk, and wool from an
animal's hide; who brought these things to be, who conceived the idea
of them? 'No one,' someone says. Oh what amazing imperceptiveness,
what impudence!

[9] Well now, let's put aside the main works of nature, and consider those of a more incidental character. [10] Could anything be more useless than the hairs on one's chin? And yet, hasn't nature put these, too, to the most appropriate use that she could? Hasn't she distinguished the male from the female by this means? [11] With regard to each of us, doesn't nature cry out aloud from afar, 'I'm a man, and it's with that in mind that you should approach me—no need to enquire any further, the signs are plain to see.' [12] And again, in the case of women, just as nature has mixed a gentler note into their voices, she has likewise deprived them of facial hair. Oh no, the human animal should rather have been left without any distinguishing signs, so that each of us would have had to proclaim, 'I'm a man!' [13] But what a fine sign this is, how fitting and how distinguished! How much finer than a cock's comb, and more majestic than a lion's mane! [14] It is thus only right to preserve the signs that have been conferred on us by God; we should neither cast them aside nor, so far as possible, confuse the sexes that he has distinguished.

[15] Are these the only works of providence from which we benefit? No, what words could be enough to praise or proclaim them as they deserve! For if we had any sense, what else should we do, both in public and in private, than sing hymns and praise the deity, and recount all the favours that he has conferred! [16] As we dig and plough and sow, oughtn't we to sing this hymn of praise to God: [17] 'Great is God, for having provided us with these implements with which we till the earth; great is God for having given us hands, and the power to swallow, and a stomach, and enabling us to grow without being conscious of it, and to breathe while we're asleep.' [18] This is what we should sing on every occasion, and also the most solemn and divine hymn to thank God for having given us the power to understand these things, and to make methodical use of them.

[19] Well then, since most of you have become blind, isn't it necessary that there should be somebody to take your place, and sing the hymn of praise to God on behalf of one and all? [20] And what else can I do, lame old man that I am, than sing the praise of God? If I were a nightingale, I would perform the work of a nightingale, and if I were a swan, that of a swan. But as it is, I am a rational being, and I must sing the praise of God. [21] This is my work, and I accomplish it, and I will never abandon my post for as long as it is granted to me to remain in it; and I invite all of you to join me in this same song.

1.17 *That logic is indispensable*

[1] Since it is reason that analyses and elucidates everything else, and reason itself shouldn't remain unanalysed, by what means can it be analysed? [2] Evidently either by reason or by something else. Now the latter must surely be a form of reason, or else be something superior to reason, which is impossible. [3] If it is a form of reason, who again will analyse that? For if it is to analyse itself, the first form of reason could achieve that equally well. If we have to take recourse to another form of reason at each stage, the process will be endless and never come to a stop.

[4] 'Very well, but to take care of our soul is a more urgent necessity,' and other similar objections.

So you want to hear something about that? Then attend. [5] Suppose you said to me, 'I don't know whether your argument is true or false,' and when I made use of some ambiguous term, you said, 'Draw the distinction,' I would lose patience with you and reply, 'But there is a more urgent need.' [6] That is the reason, I fancy, why philosophers begin with logic,* just as, when measuring grain, one begins by examining the measure. [7] For unless we start off by establishing what a unit of measurement is, and what a balance is, how shall we ever be able to weigh or measure anything? [8] So also in the present case, if we have failed to acquire full and accurate knowledge of the standard of judgement that we apply in gaining a knowledge of everything else, how are we to be able to acquire any full and accurate knowledge of those things? How could that be possible?

[9] 'Yes, but the measuring bowl is just a piece of wood and is barren.'

But it serves for the measuring of grain.

[10] 'And logic, too, is barren.'

We'll see about that later. Even if one should grant that, however, it is enough that it should give us the power to distinguish and examine all other things, and, so to speak, measure and weigh them. [11] Now who says that? Is it only Chrysippus, Zeno, and Cleanthes?* [12] Doesn't Antisthenes* say so too? And who was it that wrote, 'The beginning of education is the examination of terms'? Wasn't it Socrates* who said that? And who is Xenophon writing about when he says that he began with the investigation of terms, seeking out the meaning of each?

[13] Is this what is important, then, and admirable: to be able to understand Chrysippus and interpret him? Who says that it is? [14] So what is in fact admirable? To understand the will of nature. What, then, are you able to understand that by yourself? If so, what need do you have of anyone else? For if it is true that all who do wrong do so against their will,* and you for your part have come to know the truth, it necessarily follows that you must already be acting rightly.

[15] 'No, by Zeus, I don't understand the will of nature.'

Who can interpret it, then? Chrysippus, so it is said. [16] I go to him to find out what this interpreter of nature has to say. To begin with, I don't understand the meaning of his words, and look for someone who can interpret him. 'Come, consider what this means, just as if it were in Latin.'* [17] Is there anything here to justify the interpreter in feeling proud of himself? Nor does Chrysippus have just reason to be proud if he confines himself to interpreting the will of nature and doesn't follow it himself. [18] For we don't need Chrysippus for his own sake, but only to enable us to understand nature, just as we don't need a diviner for his own sake, but because we expect to be able to understand the future through him, and the meaning of the signs sent by the gods; [19] nor do we need the entrails of the sacrificial victim for their own sake, but because of the signs that are transmitted through them, nor do we attach any value to the crow or raven itself, but to the god who sends omens through the bird.

[20] I thus approach the interpreter and diviner, and say, 'Examine the entrails* for me, and tell me what signs they provide for me.' [21] The man takes the entrails, spreads them out, and interprets them as follows: 'You have a power of choice, man, which is secure by nature from hindrance and compulsion. That is written here in the entrails. [22] I'll demonstrate that to you first of all in the sphere of assent. Can anyone prevent you from assenting to the truth? No one at all. Can anyone constrain you to accept what is false? No one at all. [23] Do you see that, in this area, you have a power of choice that is immune from hindrance, constraint, and obstruction? [24] Well then, are things any different in the sphere of desire and motivation? What can overpower a motive except another motive, and that alone? And what can overpower a desire or aversion except another desire or aversion?'

[25] 'But what if someone threatens me with death,' someone says, 'for he is constraining me then.'

No, it isn't what you're threatened with that compels you, but your own judgement that it is better to do this or that than to die. [26] So once again, it is your judgement that has constrained you, or in other words, your choice has constrained itself. [27] For if God had so created that portion of his being that he has detached from himself and given to us that it would be subject to hindrance or compulsion, whether from himself or from another, he would no longer be God, nor would he be taking care of us as he ought. [28] 'This is what I find in the sacrifice,' says the diviner, 'these are the signs that have been sent to you. If you wish it, you are free; if you wish it, you'll find fault with no one, you'll cast blame on no one, and everything that comes about will do so in accordance with your own will and that of God.'

[29] It is for this prophecy that I go to the diviner and philosopher, and I don't admire him because of the interpretation that he offers, but rather because of the very truths that are revealed in that interpretation.

1.18   *That we should not be angry with those who do wrong*

[1] If it is true, as the philosophers say, that it is for one and the same reason that all people give their assent, namely, because they feel that something is the case, or refuse their assent, namely, because they feel that something is not the case, or, by Zeus, that they suspend judgement, because they feel that the matter is uncertain, [2] and so also, regarding motivation towards something, because I feel that it conduces to my advantage, and that it is impossible to judge one thing to be advantageous and yet desire another—if all of this is in fact true, why is it that we're still angry with so many people?

[3] 'They're thieves', someone says, 'and robbers.'

What does that mean, thieves and robbers? That they've fallen into error with regard to what is good and bad. Should we be angry with them, then, or merely feel pity for them? [4] Just show them where they've gone wrong, and you'll see how they desist from their faults; but if they fail to see it, they have nothing better to depend upon than their own personal opinion.

[5] 'So this thief here and this adulterer shouldn't be put to death?' Not at all, but what you should be asking instead is this: [6] 'This man who has fallen into error and is mistaken about the most important matters, and thus has gone blind, not with regard to the eyesight that

distinguishes white from black, but with regard to the judgement that
distinguishes good from bad—should someone like this be put to
death?' [7] If you put the question in that way, you'll recognize the
inhumanity of the thought that you're expressing, and see that it is
equivalent to saying, 'Should this blind man, then, or that deaf one,
be put to death?' [8] For if the greatest harm that a person can suffer
is the loss of the most valuable goods, and the most valuable thing
that anyone can possess is correct choice, then if someone is deprived
of that, what reason is left for you to be angry with him? [9] Why,
man, if in an unnatural fashion you really must harbour feelings with
regard to another person's misfortunes, you ought to pity him rather
than hate* him. Put aside this inclination to take offence and give
vent to hatred; [10] who are you, man, to make use of these expressions that are favoured by the mob—'Away with these accursed
wretches!' [11] Very well, but how is it that you've suddenly become
converted to wisdom, and are now in a position to be severe towards
other people?

Why, then, are we angry? Because we attach value to the things
that these people steal from us. Well, stop attaching such value to
your clothes, and you won't be angry with the man who steals them.
Don't attach value to the beauty of your wife and you won't be angry
with the adulterer. [12] Recognize that a thief and adulterer belong
not among the things that are your own, but only among those that
are someone else's and aren't within your power. If you give these
things up and count them as nothing, with whom can you still feel
angry? But as long as you attach value to these things, you should be
angry with yourself rather than with those people. [13] For consider
this, you have fine clothes and your neighbour doesn't, you have a
window and want to air them. Your neighbour doesn't know where
our human good truly lies, but supposes that it lies in having fine
clothing, which is exactly what you think too. [14] Won't he come
along, then, and steal those clothes? Why, if you display a cake to
gluttons and then gobble it down all for yourself, aren't you just
asking them to snatch it away from you? Don't provoke them, don't
have a window, don't air your clothes.

[15] Something like that happened to me the other day. I had an
iron lamp* in front of my household gods, and hearing a noise in
front of my window, I rushed down, only to find that the lamp had
been stolen. I thought to myself that the thief had been driven by a

quite persuasive motive. So what of it? Tomorrow, I told myself, you'll find an earthenware lamp. [16] After all, one can only lose what one has. 'I've lost my cloak.' Yes, because you had a cloak. 'I've got a pain in my head.' Well, you don't have a pain in your horns, do you? Why are you annoyed, then? For our losses and our pains only affect things that are in our possession.

[17] 'But the tyrant will chain . . .' What? Your legs. 'But he'll cut off . . .' What? Your head. What is he incapable, then, of chaining up or cutting off? Your power of choice. It was for that reason that the ancients urged us to follow this precept: Know yourself. [18] So what follows? That we should practise, by heaven, with little things, and after beginning with those, pass on to greater things. [19] 'I've got a headache.' Don't give expression to grief. 'I've got an earache.' Don't give expression to grief. And I'm not saying that you shouldn't groan at such things, but that you shouldn't groan in your inmost self. And if your slave is slow in bringing you the bandage, don't cry out and pull a face and exclaim, 'Everyone hates me!' For in truth, who wouldn't hate such a person? [20] From now on, placing your faith in these principles, you should proceed on your way upright and free, not trusting in the strength of your body like an athlete; for you're not meant to be invincible in the way that a donkey is.

[21] Who, then, is the invincible human being? One who can be disconcerted by nothing that lies outside the sphere of choice. I will go on, then, to consider the various circumstances in turn, as one would do in the case of an athlete: 'This man has carried off the victory in the first bout; so what about the second? [22] How will he do if it is baking hot? How will he do at Olympia?' So likewise in the present case. If you offer him a bit of money, he'll view it with contempt. But what if it is a nice young girl? And if it is in the dark? And what if it is a touch of glory? What if it is a dose of abuse? Or some praise, what then? Or if it is death, what then? He is capable of overcoming all these things. [23] What, then, if it is baking hot, or in other words, if he is drunk? What if he is feeling depressed, what if he is asleep? Now that is what I really mean by an invincible athlete.

1.19 *How should we behave towards tyrants?*

[1] If someone is superior in some respect, or at least fancies that he is when that isn't in fact the case, it is altogether inevitable that, if he is

uneducated, he'll become puffed up with pride because of it. [2] A tyrant, for instance, thus exclaims, 'I'm the most powerful man in the world!' Well then, what can you offer me? Can you ensure that my desire will never be impeded? How could you? For can you achieve that for yourself? Can you ensure that my aversion never falls into what it wants to avoid? Why, can you achieve that for yourself? Or that my motive should never fail to be satisfied? [3] And how could you claim to do that? Come now, when you're on board a ship, do you place confidence in yourself or in the man who has expert knowledge? Or when you're in a chariot, do you place trust in yourself or in the man who knows how to drive it? [4] And likewise with regard to the other arts? Just the same. How far does your power extend, then?

'Everyone pays me every attention.'

Yes, and I attend to my little plate, washing it and drying it off, and I knock a peg into the wall for the sake of my oil flask. What are we to conclude from that? That these things are superior to me? No, rather that they're of some use to me. That's why I attend to them. And again, don't I attend to my donkey? [5] Don't I wash his feet and clean him down? Don't you know that everyone attends to himself, and to you too, as he does to his donkey? For in truth, who pays attention to you as a man? Please point him out. [6] Who wants to resemble you; who wants to emulate you as people sought to emulate Socrates?

'But I can have you beheaded.'

Well said! I'd forgotten that one needs to attend to you as one attends to a fever or the cholera; one should doubtless set up an altar to you, just as Fever* has his altar at Rome.

[7] What is it, then, that disturbs and frightens the majority of people? The tyrant or his guards? How so? In no way at all. It is impossible that that which is by nature free should be disturbed or impeded by anything other than itself. [8] No indeed, it is our own judgements that disturb us. For when the tyrant says to someone, 'I'll have your leg shackled,' one who attaches value to his legs will reply, 'No, have pity on me,' while one who attaches value, by contrast, to his choice will say, 'If you think that will do you any good, chain it up.'—'You don't care?'—Not in the least.—'I'll show you that I'm master.' [9] —How will you do that? Zeus has set me free. Do you really suppose that he would allow his own son to be turned into a slave? You're master of my carcase, take that. [10] —'So you mean to say that, when you enter my presence, you'll pay no attention to

me?'—No, but rather to myself. But if you want me to say that I'll attend to you too, I'll reply that I'll do so in the same way as I do to my cooking pot.

[11] This isn't a matter of mere self-regard, because it lies in the nature of every living creature that it does everything for its own sake. Why, even the sun does everything for its own sake,* and so indeed does Zeus himself. [12] But when Zeus wishes to be the Rain-giver and Fruit-bringer* and father of gods and men, you can see that he can't achieve such things or earn such titles unless he contributes to the common benefit. [13] And in general, he has constituted the rational animal to have such a nature that he cannot attain any of his own particular goods without contributing to the common benefit. [14] And so in the end it isn't antisocial to do everything for one's own sake. [15] After all, what do you expect? That one should show no concern for oneself and one's benefit? How, in that case, could all living creatures have one and the same principle of action, namely attachment to themselves?

[16] What follows, then? When people come to hold absurd opinions about things that lie outside the sphere of choice, taking them to be good or bad, it is altogether inevitable that they'll end up paying court to tyrants. [17] And if only it were the tyrants alone, and not their flunkeys too! How is it that someone becomes wise all of a sudden when Caesar appoints him to take care of his chamber pot? How is it that we at once find ourselves saying, 'Felicio* made such wise remarks to me'? [18] How I'd like to see him pushed off his dunghill so that you'd come to regard him as a fool again! [19] Epaphroditus owned a slave who was a cobbler, but sold him because he was utterly useless; and then, as chance would have it, he was bought by a member of Caesar's household, and became Caesar's shoemaker. You should have seen what respect Epaphroditus showed to him then! [20] 'How are things with you, my good Felicio, tell me do.' [21] And then if someone asked us, 'What is your master doing?', he would be told, 'He's consulting with Felicio about some matter.' [22] But all the same, hadn't he sold him as being utterly useless? [23] So what had turned him into a wise man all of a sudden? This is what it means to value anything other than what lies within the sphere of our choice.

[24] 'He's been honoured with a tribune's* post.' Everyone who meets him offers his congratulations; one kisses him on the eyes, another on the neck, while his slaves kiss his hands. He arrives home

to find lamps being lit. [25] He climbs up the Capitol and offers a sacrifice. Yet who has ever offered up a sacrifice because his desires are rightly directed? Or because his motives are in accord with nature? For we offer up thanks to the gods for those things in which we place our good.

[26] Someone was talking to me today about the priesthood of Augustus.* 'Leave that well alone, my friend,' I told him; 'you'll be incurring no end of expense to no purpose.' [27] —'But when contracts are drawn up, they'll be inscribed with my name.'—Do you suppose, then, that you'll be present when people read those contracts so as to be able to say, 'That's my name written there'? [28] And even if it would be possible for you to be present on every occasion now, what will you do when you come to die?—'My name will remain.'—Carve it onto a stone and it will remain just as well. Come now, who will remember you outside Nicopolis? [29] —'But I'll wear a crown of gold.'—If you wish to wear a crown at all, take a crown of roses and put that on your head; you'd look much more elegant in that.

1.20 *How reason is able to examine itself*

[1] Every art and faculty makes certain things its special objects of examination. [2] When that art or faculty is of the same nature as what it examines, it will necessarily be capable of taking itself as an object of examination, but when it is of a different nature, it won't be capable of doing so. [3] The art of leather-working, for instance, concerns itself with hides, but the art itself is altogether different from its material, the hides, and for that reason can't take itself as an object of examination. [4] Or again, the art of grammar concerns itself with the written word, but that doesn't mean, does it, that the art itself is written speech? Not at all. For that reason, it can't take itself as an object of examination. [5] Well then, why is it that we have received reason from nature? To be able to make use of impressions as we ought. And what is reason itself? A collection of impressions of various kinds. It is accordingly fitted by nature to take itself as an object of examination. [6] And wisdom, in turn, has been granted to us for the examination of what? Of what is good, and what is bad, and what is neither the one nor the other. What is wisdom itself, then? A good thing. And foolishness? A bad thing. You can thus see that

wisdom can necessarily take itself, and likewise its opposite, as an object of examination.

[7] For that reason, the most important task of a philosopher, and his first task, is to test out impressions and distinguish between them, and not to accept any impression unless it has been duly tested. [8] When it comes to coinage, where we think our interests are affected, you see how we have devised an art, and what procedures the assayer applies to test out the coinage, through sight, touch, and finally hearing; [9] when he throws the denarius down and listens to hear how it rings, he isn't satisfied to hear that only once, but by attending to the sound repeatedly, develops a musician's ear. [10] And so likewise, in matters where we think it makes a notable difference whether or not we go astray, we apply considerable attention to judging things that are liable to lead us astray; [11] but when it comes to this poor ruling centre of ours, we yawn and slumber, and accept any impression that comes along. For it doesn't occur to us that we'll suffer any damage as a result.

[12] So if you want to know how little concerned you are about what is good and bad, and how seriously you take things that are indifferent, consider what attitude you hold towards physical blindness on the one hand and error of mind on the other; and you'll recognize that you're far from having the feelings that you ought to have with regard to matters of good and evil.

[13] 'Yes, but that requires long preparation, and no end of effort and study.'

What of that? Do you really expect to master the most important of the arts with little effort? [14] All the same, what is most essential in the teaching of the philosophers can be stated very briefly. If you want to know, read Zeno's works, and you'll see. [15] For does it in fact take long to say that 'our end lies in following the gods, and the essence of the good in the correct use of impressions'? [16] If you ask, 'What, then, is God, and what is an impression? And what is nature in the individual and nature in the universe?', the discussion is already beginning to drag out. [17] If Epicurus should come along and say that the good must lie in our flesh, it again grows long, and you need to learn what the principal part of us is, and what our substantial nature is and our essential nature. Since it is hardly probable that the good of a snail should lie in its shell, is that probable, then, in the case of a human being? [18] What do you yourself possess that is superior

to that, Epicurus? What is there within you that deliberates, that
examines everything, and that decides with regard to the flesh itself
that it is our principal part? [19] And why do you light your lamp and
toil away on our behalf, writing so many books? Is it so that we may
not be ignorant of the truth? Who are we? And what are we to you?
And so the argument becomes a lengthy one.

1.21   *To those who want to be admired*

[1] When someone has taken up the position that he ought to hold in
life, he doesn't hanker after anything beyond it. [2] What is it that you
would wish to have happen to you, man? For my part, I'm satisfied if
I exercise my desires and aversions in accordance with nature, and
apply my motives to act and not to act as my nature requires, and
likewise my purposes, designs, and acts of assent. So why are you
walking around in front of us as though you'd swallowed a spit?
[3] 'What I've always wanted is to be admired by those who meet me,
and that they'll follow me exclaiming, "What a great philosopher!"'
[4] Who are they, these people whose admiration you want to win?
Aren't they the very people whom you're in the habit of describing as
mad?* What, do you want to be admired by madmen?

1.22   *On preconceptions*

[1] Preconceptions are common to all people, and one preconception
doesn't contradict another. For who among us doesn't assume that
the good is beneficial and desirable, and that we should seek and
pursue it in every circumstance? And who among us doesn't assume
that what is just is honourable and appropriate? When does contradiction arise, then? [2] It comes about when we apply our preconceptions to particular cases, [3] as when one person says, 'He acted well,
he's a brave man,' while another says, 'No, he's out of his mind.' That
is how people come to fall into disagreement. [4] Hence the Jews,
Syrians, Egyptians, and Romans hold conflicting views, not about
whether holiness should be valued above all else and pursued in all
circumstances, but whether the specific action of eating pork is holy
or unholy. [5] You'll find that the quarrel between Agamemnon and
Achilles also arose* in that way. Let them be summoned to appear in
front of us:

'What do you say, Agamemnon, shouldn't one do what is right and proper?'

'Indeed one should.'

[6] 'And what do you say, Achilles, don't you agree that one should do what is right and proper?'

'Of course, I'd agree absolutely.'

So now apply these preconceptions to the particular cases. [7] It is there that the contradiction arises. One says, 'I need not return Chryseis to her father,' while the other says, 'Oh yes, you ought to.' One or the other of them is assuredly making a bad application of the preconception of what one ought to do. [8] And again, one of them says, 'Very well, if I ought to hand over Chryseis, I ought to get someone else's prize of war,' to which the other man replies, 'So you want to take away this woman of mine whom I love?' 'Yes, that woman of yours,' he says, 'or am I to be the only one who has nothing?' 'Then shall I for my part be the only one who has nothing?' And so a conflict arises.

[9] What does it mean, then, to become properly educated? It is to learn to apply our natural preconceptions to particular cases in accord with nature; and further, to draw the distinction that some things lie within our power while others do not; [10] within our power lie moral choice and all actions that depend on that choice, whereas our body and every part of it are not in our power, and likewise our possessions, parents, brothers and sisters, children, country, and, in short, everyone with whom we associate. [11] Where, then, are we to place our good? To what kind of reality are we to apply that name? To what lies within our power.

[12] 'Then isn't health a good thing, and having an unimpaired body, and life? No, and not even our children, parents, and country? And who could accept that from you?'

[13] Well, let's transfer the designation of good to those things. Is it possible, in that case, to be happy if one suffers injury and fails to acquire good things?

'No, it's not possible.'

And to live as we ought with those with whom we associate? And how is that possible? For I'm moved by nature to look to my own benefit. [14] If it is to my benefit to have a piece of land, it is also to my benefit to take it from my neighbour. If it is to my benefit to have a cloak, it is also to my benefit to steal one at the baths. Hence the origin of wars, revolts, tyrannies, and plots. [15] And how, moreover, shall I still be able to accomplish my duties towards Zeus? For if I suffer injury and misfortune, he pays no attention to me. And people say, 'What business do I have with him if he can do nothing to help me?', or again, 'What business do I have with him if he wishes me to be in the difficulties in which I find myself?' In the end, I begin to hate him. [16] Why, then, do we build temples, why do we raise statues, as though in honour of evil spirits, and in honour of Zeus as god of fever? How in that case can he still be the Saviour, the Rain-bringer, the Fruit-giver? Yes, in truth, if we place the essence of the good somewhere here, all these conclusions necessarily follow.

[17] So what are we to do? This is the object of enquiry for someone who is truly a philosopher and whose mind is pregnant with thoughts. 'At present,' he says, 'I can't see what's good and what's bad, so surely I'm mad?' [18] Yes, but what if I place the good somewhere here, among things that lie within the sphere of choice? Everyone will laugh at me. Some white-haired old man, with many rings on his fingers, will come along and shake his head, and say to me, 'Listen to me, child, yes, one ought to practise philosophy, but one should also keep one's head. This is sheer stupidity. [19] It's all very well for you to learn syllogisms from the philosophers, but when it comes to how you should act in life, you know that far better than they do.' [20] Then why are you finding fault with me, man, if I know that? What am I to say to this slave? If I keep silent, he loses his temper. [21] So I can only reply, 'You must forgive me as one forgives lovers; I've lost control of myself, I'm out of my mind!'

1.23 *Against Epicurus*

[1] Even Epicurus recognizes that we're social beings by nature, but once he has placed our good in our bodily shell, he is no longer in a position to say anything that conflicts with that. [2] For he maintains forcefully, besides, that we should neither admire nor accept anything that is cut off from the nature of the good, and rightly so.

[3] How can we still be social beings, then, if we have no natural affection for our offspring? And why is it, Epicurus, that you seek to dissuade the wise person from rearing children? Why are you afraid that he'll suffer distress as a consequence? [4] What does it matter to him, then, if a little mouse cries out in his house? [5] No, Epicurus

was well aware that as soon as one has a small child, it's no longer in our power not to love it and take care of it. [6] For the same reason, he says, anyone who has any sense won't engage in public affairs either, because he knows what a man in public life has to do. And in truth, if you want to live among human beings as though among flies, who is to prevent you? [7] Yet even though he is well aware of this, he has the audacity to say that 'we shouldn't rear children'. But when a sheep doesn't abandon its own offspring, and neither does a wolf, will a human being abandon his? What do you want? That we should be as stupid as sheep? [8] And yet they don't abandon their young. As savage as wolves? And yet they don't abandon their young. [9] Come, who could be persuaded by what you say when he sees his little child in tears after having fallen to the ground? [10] For my part, I think that even if your mother and father could have foreseen that you would say such things, they wouldn't have exposed* you!

1.24 *How should we contend with difficulties?*

[1] It is difficulties that reveal what men amount to; and so, whenever you're struck by a difficulty, remember that God, like a trainer in the gymnasium, has matched you against a tough young opponent.

[2] 'For what purpose?', someone asks.

So that you may become an Olympic victor; and that is something that can't be achieved without sweat. It seems to me that no one has had a difficulty that gives a better opportunity than the one you now have, if only you're willing to tackle it as an athlete tackles his young adversary. [3] We're now sending you off to Rome as a spy, and no one sends a coward on such a mission, someone who, if he hears the slightest rustle and sees a patch of shadow somewhere, will come rushing back in a panic to warn us that the enemy is already at hand. [4] So too in the present case, if you should come back to us and say, 'The situation at Rome is desperate, death is a terrible thing, banishment is terrible, abuse is terrible, poverty is terrible—take to your heels, everyone, the enemy is at hand!', [5] we'll reply, 'Be off with you, and address your prophecies to your own ears alone. Our one mistake was to send out someone like you to spy out the ground.'

[6] Diogenes, who was sent out before you as a spy, has brought entirely different news. He says that 'Death is no evil, since there is nothing dishonourable in it.' He says that 'Bad reputation is an empty

noise made by madmen.' [7] And what reports this spy has brought to us about pain and pleasure and poverty! 'Nakedness', he says, 'is preferable to any purple robe, and it is better to sleep on the bare ground than on the softest of couches.' [8] And as proof of his various claims, he offers his own courage, his imperturbability, his freedom, and, moreover, his gleaming robust body. [9] 'No enemy close at hand,' he says; 'peace prevails everywhere.' How can that be, Diogenes? 'Just look at me,' he replies; 'have I been hit, am I wounded, have I fled from anyone?' [10] That is what a true spy should be, but as for you, you come back and tell us all kinds of nonsense. Won't you go away again and observe more accurately, without giving way to cowardice?

[11] 'What should I do, then?' What do you do when you step ashore from a boat? You don't walk off with the rudder, do you, or the oars? So what do you take? What belongs to you, your oil flask, your knapsack.* So, too, in the present case, if you remain mindful of what is your own, you won't ever lay claim to what belongs to another. [12] He tells you, 'Take off that senator's robe.' Look, an equestrian robe. 'Take off that as well.' Look, a plain toga.* 'That too.' Look, I'm naked. [13] 'But you still make me feel envious.' Then take my whole miserable body. If I can toss my body to this man, what further reason do I have to be afraid of him?

[14] 'But So-and-so won't make me his heir.'

What of it? Have I forgotten that none of these things is my own? In what sense, then, can we call them our own? In the sense that we say that of our bed in an inn. If the innkeeper leaves you the beds when he dies, well and good; but if he leaves them to someone else, they'll belong to him, and you'll have to look for another. [15] And if you can't find a bed, you'll end up sleeping on the ground; only, be of good heart and snore away, remembering that it is among the wealthy, among kings and tyrants, that tragedies play out, and that no one who is poor has any role in a tragedy except as a member of the chorus. [16] The kings begin in prosperity—'*Hang the palace with garlands*'—but then, in around the third or fourth act, '*Alas Cithaeron, why did you receive me?*'* [17] Slave, where are your crowns, where is your diadem? Are your guards of no use to you? [18] So henceforth, when you approach any of these great men, keep this in mind, that you're meeting a figure from tragedy, and no mere actor either, but Oedipus in person.

[19] 'But So-and-so is blessed by fortune, to walk around with such a large retinue.'

Yes, and I too only have to mingle with the crowd to find myself walking around with a large retinue.

[20] But this is the essential point: remember that the door stands open.* Don't be more cowardly than a young child, but just as children say, 'I won't play any longer' when the game no longer amuses them, you should say likewise, when things seem that way to you, 'I won't play any longer', and so depart; but if you stay, stop moaning.

1.25 *On the same theme*

[1] If all of this is true, and we're not merely being silly and putting on an act when we say that the good of man, and likewise his ill, lies in how he exercises his choice, while everything else is nothing to us, why do we still allow ourselves to be troubled or afraid? [2] No one else has any power over the things that really matter to us; so what is left for us to worry about?

[3] 'Give me some specific instructions.'

But what instructions should I give you? Has Zeus failed to provide you with any? Hasn't he granted to you that what is your own should be free from hindrance and restraint, while that which is not your own should be subject to hindrance and restraint? [4] And with what orders did you come from that other world into this, with what commands? You should guard what is your own by every means, but shouldn't desire what is another's. Your good faith is your own, your self-respect is your own; for who can take those away from you? Who apart from yourself can prevent you from making use of them? But for your own part, how do you behave? Whenever you devote your attention to what is not your own, you lose what is truly your own. [5] Since you have already received such orders and instructions from Zeus, what is it that you still want from me? Am I better than he, or more trustworthy? [6] And if you follow those orders of his, do you have need of any more? Bring out your preconceptions, bring forth the demonstrations of the philosophers, bring out what you've often heard, or what you yourself have said, bring out what you've read, and what you've studied and reflected upon.

[7] How long, then, should we hold to these rules and not break up the game? [8] As long as the game is going nicely. At the Saturnalia* a

king is selected by lot (for they have decided to play that game). He orders, 'You there, drink, you mix the wine, you sing, you go, you come.' I obey, so as not to be the one who spoils the game. [9] 'But as for you, suppose that you're in the grip of misfortune.' That I don't accept; for who can compel me to suppose such a thing?

[10] Or again, we have agreed to act out the story of Agamemnon and Achilles. The man who has been chosen to play Agamemnon tells me, 'Go to Achilles and take Briseis* away from him.' [11] I go. He says, 'Come,' and I come. For in point of fact, just as we proceed with regard to hypothetical arguments, so we should proceed in life too. [12] 'Let's suppose that it's night.' All right. 'Very well then, is it day?' No, because I've accepted the assumption that it's night. 'Let's accept, then, that you're thinking it is night.' All right. 'Not only that, but think that it really *is* night.' [13] But that doesn't follow from the hypothesis. So likewise with regard to life. 'Let's suppose that you're unhappy.' All right. 'You're in a bad way, then?' Yes. 'So you're in misfortune?' Yes. 'But now make the further assumption that you really *are* in a bad way.' That doesn't follow from the hypothesis; and there is, moreover, another* who prevents me from believing that.

[14] How long, then, should we obey such rules of conduct? As long as it continues to be profitable, that is to say, as long as I can preserve what is fitting and appropriate. [15] Some people are cantankerous and oversensitive, and say, 'For my part, I can't bear to dine with such a man, and put up with him recounting the story of his military exploits in Mysia day after day—'I've told you, my dear fellow, how I made my way up to the top of the hill, but then I came under siege again . . .' [16] But another person will say, 'As for me, I'd rather have the dinner and listen to whatever chatter he cares to come up with.' [17] It is for you to judge between these different points of view. Only, don't do anything with a heavy heart or sense of affliction, thinking that you're in a bad situation; for no one is forcing you to do that. [18] Has someone made smoke in the house? If there isn't too much, I'll stay; if it's excessive, I'll leave the house. For one should remember this fact and keep it firmly in mind, that the door stands open.

[19] But someone says, 'Don't live in Nicopolis.' I won't live there. 'Nor in Athens.' Nor there. 'Nor in Rome.' Nor there. [20] 'You must live in Gyara.'* I'll go and live there. But living in Gyara strikes me as being like living in a smoke-filled house. So I'll go away to a place that

no one can prevent me from making my home, since it is a dwelling that is open to everyone. [21] And beyond my final garment, that is to say, my poor body, no one has any power at all over me. [22] That is why Demetrius said to Nero, 'You're threatening me with death, but nature threatens you with it.' [23] If I attach value to my poor body, I have given myself up to slavery; if I attach value to my miserable possessions, I'm likewise a slave; [24] for by doing so, I'm at once showing to my own detriment by what means I may be caught. Just as when the snake draws in its head, I say, 'Strike at the part that it's trying to protect!', you too should be aware that it is at the very point that you most want to protect that you'll be attacked by your master. [25] If you keep all of this in mind, whom will you flatter any longer, whom will you fear?

[26] 'But I want to sit where the senators do.'

Can't you see that you're merely crowding yourself in, creating aggravation for yourself?

[27] 'How else, then, can I get a proper view in the amphitheatre?'

Don't go to watch, man, and you won't be exposing yourself to aggravation. Why create trouble for yourself? Or else, wait a while, until the show is over, and then go and sit where the senators* do, and bask in the sun. [28] But as a general rule keep this in mind, that it is we who cause aggravation to ourselves; that is to say, it is our own judgements that aggravate us and crowd us in this way. What does it mean, for instance, to be abused? [29] Go up to a stone and subject it to abuse; what effect will you produce? Well then, if you listen like a stone, what will anyone who abuses you be able to achieve? But if he is able to use the weakness of the victim of his abuse as a handhold, then he can achieve something. [30] 'Strip him.' What do you mean, 'him'? Take his cloak and strip that off. 'I've subjected you to insulting treatment.' Much good may it do you!

[31] These are the principles that Socrates practised, and that is why he always bore the same expression on his face. But we for our part want to study and practise anything other than to become unrestrained and free. [32] 'The philosophers talk in paradoxes.' And are there no paradoxes in the other arts? What is more paradoxical than to poke a lancet into a man's eyes to restore his sight? If anyone mentioned that to someone who had no knowledge of medicine, wouldn't he laugh at the person who said it? [33] Is it at all surprising, then, if in philosophy, too, many things that are true seem paradoxical to the ignorant?

1.26 *What is the law of life?*

[1] As someone was reading out hypothetical arguments, Epictetus said, 'It is also a law of hypothetical arguments that one must accept what follows from the hypothesis. But far more important is the law of life that states that we must do what follows from nature. [2] Because if, in regard to every matter and in every circumstance, we wish to hold to what is in accordance with nature, it is clear that we should make it our aim in everything neither to shrink from what is in accord with nature, nor to accept what is in conflict with nature. [3] And so the philosophers must train us first in theory, which is the easier task, and then lead us on to more difficult matters; for in theory, there is nothing to restrain us from drawing the consequences of what we have been taught, whereas in life there are many things that pull us off course. [4] It would be absurd for anyone to say that he wanted to start off with the latter, since it is not at all easy to begin with what is more difficult.

[5] And this is the defence that should be offered to those parents* who are angry to see their children studying philosophy: 'I've doubtless gone wrong, father, and don't know where my duty lies or what is right for me. But if this can neither be learned nor taught, what reason do you have to criticize me? Or if it can be taught, teach me. If you're unable to do so, however, allow me to learn from those who claim to know. [6] Come, what do you suppose? That I willingly fall into evil and miss what is good? Heaven forbid! What is it, then, that causes me to go astray? Ignorance. [7] So don't you want me to deliver myself from that ignorance? To whom has anger ever taught the art of navigation or music? When it comes to the art of life, do you suppose, then, that your anger will teach me what I need to know?'

[8] All of this can only properly be said, however, by one who has made a serious effort to embark on that path. [9] But if someone reads up about these matters and frequents the philosophers merely because he wants to show off his knowledge of hypothetical arguments at a dinner, what else is he doing than simply trying to win the admiration of some senator who is sitting beside him at the table? [10] It is there at Rome, in truth, that the great fortunes are to be found, and the wealth here would look there as being no more than child's play. It is thus by no means easy to keep control of one's impressions there, since the disturbing forces are so great. [11] I know someone who once grasped the knees of Epaphroditus with tears in his eyes, telling

him that he was in a terrible state because he was left with nothing more than a million and a half sesterces! [12] And what do you suppose Epaphroditus did? Laugh as you're laughing now? Not a bit of it, he exclaimed in astonishment, 'Oh you poor man, how have you been able to keep quiet about it, how have you been able to endure it?'

[13] The student* who was reading out the hypothetical arguments was thus thrown into confusion, and when the man who had set him the task burst into laughter, Epictetus said, You're laughing at yourself; for you didn't give this young man any preliminary instruction, nor did you find out whether he is capable of following these arguments, but merely made use of him as a reader. [14] Why is it, he continued, that when a mind is incapable of grasping the conclusions of a complex argument, we yet place trust in what the person has to say in praise or blame, or his judgements as to whether things are well or badly done? Now if such a person should speak ill of another, will that other person care, or if he should praise someone, will that other person feel any pride, when even in such slight matters such a person cannot work out the logical consequences? [15] This, then, is the first step in philosophy, to become aware of the condition of one's ruling centre. For when a person comes to know that it is in a weak state, he will no longer wish to employ it on matters of importance. [16] But as things are, people who are incapable of swallowing down a small morsel go and buy a whole treatise and set out to devour it. With the result that they vomit it up or suffer from indigestion; and then come bowel upsets, diarrhoeas, and fevers. [17] They ought to have begun by considering whether they had the capacity. Yes, in matters of theory it is easy to refute the ignorant, but in the affairs of life no one willingly exposes himself to refutation, and we hate anyone who has refuted us. [18] But as Socrates used to say, the unexamined life* isn't worth living.

1.27 *In how many ways do impressions arise, and what should we have at hand to help us to deal with them?*

[1] Impressions come to us in four ways. Either things are, and appear so to be; or else they are not, and do not appear to be; or else they are, and do not appear to be; or else they are not, and yet appear to be. [2] It is thus the task of an educated person to hit the mark in each case.

Whatever difficulty may trouble us, we must bring forward the appropriate remedy to apply against it. If it is the sophisms of the Pyrrhonists and Academics* that trouble us, let us bring forward our remedies against them; [3] if things have a specious appeal that makes them appear good when they're not, we must seek the remedy that is applicable in that area. If it is a habit that troubles us, we must endeavour to find a remedy to use against it. [4] What remedy can be found, then, to use against a habit? The contrary habit. [5] You hear uneducated people saying, 'Oh dear, the poor fellow's dead, his father's heartbroken, and his mother too; he's been struck down before his time, and in a foreign land!' [6] Listen to the opposing arguments, pull yourself away from these expressions, counter a habit by setting a contrary habit against it. Against sophistic arguments we should apply logical reasoning, and train ourselves in such reasoning so as to become familiar with it. Against specious appearances, we should apply clear preconceptions, keeping them well polished and ready for use.

[7] When death appears to be an evil, we should have at hand this thought, that it is our duty to avoid evils, and yet death is something that is inescapable. [8] So what can I do? Where can I flee to escape it? Let's suppose that I'm Sarpedon,* son of Zeus, so that I may declare in the same noble spirit, 'I set off with the desire either to distinguish myself in battle or to give someone else an opportunity to do so; for if I can't succeed in something myself, I shan't grudge another the honour of performing some noble deed.' Granted that such nobility is beyond us, doesn't it fall within our power to accept this line of thought? [9] And where can we go to escape from death? Point me to the place, show me to what people I should go who lie beyond the reach of death, show me a charm that is effective against it. Otherwise, what would you have me do? I can't escape death; [10] but is it beyond my power to escape the fear of death, and must I die grieving and trembling? For this is the origin of passion, to wish for something that cannot come about. [11] So if I can change external circumstances according to my wish, I change them; if not, I want to rip out the eyes of whoever is standing in my way. [12] For such is human nature, we cannot bear to be deprived of the good, and cannot bear to fall into what is bad. [13] And so in the end, when I can neither alter things nor rip out the eyes of the man who is standing in my way, I sit down and groan, and hurl abuse where I can, at Zeus and the rest of the gods.

For if they fail to take care of me, what are they to me? [14] 'Yes, you'll fall into impiety.'

Can things get any worse for me, then, than they already are? In brief, one must keep this point in mind, that unless piety and self-interest go hand in hand, piety cannot be safeguarded by anyone. Doesn't this line of argument seem conclusive? [15] May a follower of Pyrrho or an Academician step forward to oppose it. For my part, I have no leisure for such disputes, nor can I offer myself as an advocate of common sense. [16] Even if I had a case to pursue about a bit of land, I would call in someone else to plead my cause. With what argument should I be satisfied, then? With such as is appropriate to the matter in question. [17] As to how sensation is produced, whether through the mind as a whole or just a part of it, I'm unable to defend one position rather than the other, and both perplex me. But that you and I are not one and the same person, that I know with full certainty. [18] And how so? Why, when I want to swallow a piece of food, I never carry it to your mouth, but to my own. When I want to get some bread, I never pick up a broom, but go straight to the bread as though to a target. [19] And do you yourselves, who deny the evidence of the senses, do anything different? Which of you, when he wants to go to a bath house, goes to a mill instead?

[20] 'Well then, shouldn't we devote every effort to defending this position or safeguarding common sense, while shoring ourselves up against the arguments that would seek to oppose it?'

[21] And who says any different? But only one who has the capacity and the leisure should make this his concern; as for one who trembles with fear, who is troubled, whose heart is broken within him, he should devote his time to something else.

1.28 *That we should not be angry with others; and what things are small, and what are great, among human beings?*

[1] For what reason do we give our assent to something? Because it appears to us to be the case. [2] If something appears not to be the case, it is impossible for us to give our assent. And why so? Because that is the nature of our mind, that it should agree to things that are true, not accept things that are false, and suspend its judgement with regard to things that are uncertain. [3] What is the proof of that? 'Form the impression, if you can, that it is night at present.' That is

impossible. 'Put aside the impression that it is day.' That is impossible. [4] So whenever anyone assents to what is false, one may be sure
that he does not willingly give his assent to falsehood ('for every mind
is deprived of the truth against its will', as Plato observes), [5] but
rather that what is false seemed to him to be true. Well then, in
the realm of action, have we anything that corresponds to truth and
falsehood in the realm of perception? What is fitting and not fitting,
beneficial and not beneficial, appropriate for me and not appropriate
for me, and so on.

[6] 'A person can't think something to be of benefit to him, then,
and yet not choose it?

He can't.

[7] 'So how can Medea say,

> *I know that what I intend to do is bad,*
> *But anger is master of my plans?'* *

Because she regarded this very thing, the gratification of her anger
and exacting of vengeance against her husband, as being more beneficial than keeping her children safe.

[8] 'Yes, but she is mistaken.'

Show her clearly that she is mistaken and she won't follow that
course; but as long as you haven't shown it, what else can she do than
follow what seems best to her? Nothing else. [9] Why should you be
angry with her, then, because, poor wretch, she has gone astray on
matters of the highest importance, and has changed from a human
being into a viper? Shouldn't you, if anything, take pity on her
instead? And just as we pity the blind and the lame, shouldn't we also
take pity on those who have become blinded and crippled in their
governing faculties?

[10] Whoever keeps this fact clearly in mind, then, that for human
beings the present impression is the measure of every action—an
impression that may, besides, be well or badly formed; if well, that
person is beyond reproach; if badly, he himself pays the penalty,
since it is impossible that one person should go astray and another
pay the penalty for it—whoever keeps this in mind, then, will never
be angry with anyone, and will never abuse, never criticize, never
hate, and never offend anyone.

[11] 'Do such great and terrible deeds also have their origin in this,
in appearances?'

[12] Yes, in that and nothing else. The *Iliad* consists of nothing more than impressions and the use of impressions. An impression prompted Paris to carry off the wife of Menelaus, and an impression prompted Helen to go with him. [13] If an impression, then, had prompted Menelaus to feel that it was a gain to be deprived of such a wife, what would have come about? Not only the *Iliad* would have been lost, but the *Odyssey* too!*

[14] 'Can such great issues depend on such small causes?'

What do you mean by great issues? Wars and civil strife, the loss of many human lives, the destruction of cities? And what is great in all of that?

'You call that nothing?'

[15] Why, what is great in the death of a multitude of sheep and cattle, and in the burning and destruction of countless nests of storks and swallows?

[16] 'But are the two cases at all similar?'

Perfectly similar. In one case, the bodies of human beings are destroyed, and in the other, the bodies of sheep and cattle. In the one case the little dwellings of human beings are destroyed, and in the other, the nests of storks. [17] What is great or terrible in that? Or show me how a human house differs from a stork's nest. Except that we build our houses from planks, tiles, and bricks, while storks build theirs from twigs and clay?

[18] 'Are a stork and a human being similar in nature?'

How do you mean? At a bodily level, entirely similar.

[19] 'So a human being is no different from a stork?'

Far from it, but they're no different in this respect.

'In what respect do they differ, then?'

[20] Enquire, and you'll find that the difference lies elsewhere. See whether it doesn't lie in the fact that a human being understands what he is doing; see whether it doesn't lie in his sense of fellowship, in his fidelity, in his sense of shame, his steadfastness, his intelligence. [21] So where in human beings is the great good and evil to be found? In that which distinguishes them as human; and if that is preserved and kept well fortified, and if one's self-respect, and fidelity, and intelligence are kept unimpaired, then the human being himself is safeguarded; but if any of these are destroyed or taken by storm, then he himself is destroyed. [22] All that is great in human affairs turns on this. Did Paris suffer his great disaster when the Greeks arrived and ravaged Troy, and when his brothers perished? [23] Not

at all, since no one comes to grief as the result of another person's actions; no, that amounted to nothing more than the laying waste of storks' nests. His true undoing was when he lost his sense of shame, his loyalty, his respect for the laws of hospitality, his decency. [24] And when did Achilles come to grief? When Patroclus died? Far from it. But rather, when he himself yielded to anger, when he wept over a young girl, when he forgot that he was there, not to acquire mistresses, but to make war.* [25] These are the ways in which human beings are brought to grief, this is the siege, this the razing of the citadel, when right judgements are overturned, when they are destroyed.

[26] 'But when women are led away and children are reduced to slavery, when the men themselves are slaughtered, is it really the case that these are not evils?'

[27] Where did you acquire this further notion? Please tell me.

'No, it's for you to explain how you can say that they're not evils.'

[28] Let's take recourse to our standard, bring forth your preconceptions. This is why one cannot be sufficiently amazed at how people act in this regard. When we want to make a judgement with regard to weights, we don't judge at random; when we want to judge whether things are straight or crooked, we don't do so at random; [29] in short, when it is important to know the truth in any case, none of us ever does anything at random. [30] But when it comes to the first and only cause of acting rightly or in error, of succeeding or failing, of being unfortunate or fortunate, there alone we act in a random and precipitate way. Nowhere anything like a balance, nowhere anything like a standard, but no sooner does some impression strike me than I immediately act upon it. [31] Am I any better than Agamemnon and Achilles, to be satisfied by impressions alone, when they caused and suffered such evils by following their impressions? [32] What tragedy has had any other origin than this? What is the *Atreus* of Euripides? All a matter of impressions. The *Oedipus* of Sophocles? Impressions. The *Phoenix*? Impressions. The *Hippolytus*?* Impressions. [33] What do you call those who follow every impression that strikes them? Madmen! What about us, then; do we act any differently?

1.29 *On steadfastness*

[1] The essence of the good is a certain disposition of our choice, and that of the bad likewise. [2] What are externals, then? Materials for our

choice, which attains its own good or ill through the way in which it deals with them. [3] How can it attain the good? By not overvaluing the materials. For if its judgements about the materials are correct, that makes the choice good, whereas if they are twisted and perverse, that makes it bad. [4] Such is the law that God has laid down, saying, 'If you want anything good, you must get it from yourself,' while you for your part say, 'No, get it from elsewhere.' [5] So when a tyrant makes threats and summons me, I ask, 'What is he threatening?' If he says, 'I'll throw you into chains,' I'll reply, 'Then it is my hands and feet that he is threatening.' [6] If he says, 'I'll have you beheaded,' I'll reply, 'Then it is my head that he is threatening.' If he says, 'I'll throw you into prison,' I'll reply, 'Then it is my whole miserable carcase,' and if he threatens me with exile, I'll say the same.

[7] 'Then he isn't really threatening you in any way.'

In no way at all, if I feel that all these things are nothing to me; [8] but if I'm afraid about any of this, it is me whom he is threatening. Who is left for me to fear? He who holds mastery over what? Over things that are within my power? But there is no such man. Over things that aren't within my power? And what do I care about things like that?

[9] 'Do you philosophers teach us, then, to hold kings in contempt?'

Heaven forbid! Who of us teaches you to oppose them over things that are subject to their authority? [10] Take my poor body, take my possessions, take my reputation, take the people around me. If I'm urging anyone to offer resistance with regard to any of that, may someone please accuse me!

[11] 'Yes, but I also want to exercise control over your judgements.'

And who has given you that power? How can you control another person's judgement?

[12] 'By striking him with fear, I'll overpower him.'

You fail to understand that a judgement can only overpower itself, and cannot be overpowered by another person. And nothing can overpower our choice, apart from choice itself. [13] That is why this law of God is most excellent and just: 'Let that which is stronger always prevail over that which is weaker.'

[14] 'Ten men are stronger than one,' someone says.

In what respect? In throwing people into chains, taking their life, dragging them off wherever they want, stripping them of their property. Yes, ten men can assuredly prevail over one in that in which they are stronger!

[15] 'In what, then, are they weaker?'

If the one person has correct judgements, and the others don't. Well then, how can they prevail over him in that? How could they? If we are weighed in the balance, isn't it the case that that which is heavier must always carry down the scales?

[16] 'So that Socrates may suffer what he did at the hands of the Athenians?'

Why do you say 'Socrates' here, you slave? State the matter as it really is, and say, 'So that the poor body of Socrates may be arrested and dragged off to prison by those who were stronger than he, so that someone may administer hemlock to the poor body of Socrates, and that body of his may grow cold and die.' [17] Does that seem strange to you, does that seem unjust, is it because of that that you criticize God? Did Socrates gain nothing in exchange? [18] In what, for him, did the essence of the good consist? Who should we listen to on this point, to you or to him? Now what does he say? 'Anytus and Meletus can kill me, but they cannot harm me,' and again, 'If this is what God wills, so be it.'* [19] 'But you prove to me that someone who holds inferior judgements can prevail over one who is superior in his judgements. You'll never prove that, or even come close to doing so. For it is a law of nature and of God that "what is stronger must always prevail over what is weaker".' In what? In that in which it is stronger. [20] One body is stronger than another, several people are stronger than a single person, a thief is stronger than someone who is not a thief. [21] That is why I lost my lamp,* because the thief was better than me at keeping awake. But he has paid a high price for the lamp, since in return for a lamp he has become a thief, in return for a lamp, a man of bad faith, in return for a lamp, a wild beast. That struck him as being a good bargain!

[22] Very well; but someone has now seized me by my cloak and is dragging me into the marketplace, while others call out to me, 'Tell me, philosopher, what good have your judgements done you? For look, you're being dragged off to prison; look, you're going to lose your head!'

[23] And what kind of induction into philosophy could I have acquired that would have saved me from being dragged off in that way if a stronger man than me seized me by the cloak, or have saved me from being thrown into prison if there were ten men to seize me and throw me in? [24] But have I learned nothing else, then? I have

learned to see that whatever comes about is nothing to me if it lies beyond the sphere of choice. [25] So have I gained no benefit in that? Why look for your benefit, then, in anything other than what you've learned? [26] As I sit in prison, I'll say accordingly, 'The person who shouts this at me neither understands the explanation that is offered to him, nor follows what is said to him, nor, in short, has he made any effort to know what the philosophers say, or what they do. Send him away.

[27] 'But you may come out of prison now.'

If it is of no further use to you that I should be in prison, I'll leave; if it is of use to you again, I'll return.

[28] 'For how long?'

For as long as reason may choose that I remain attached to my poor body; but when reason chooses otherwise, take it, and much good may it do you! [29] Only, let me not surrender it in an unreasonable manner, or out of cowardice, or on some arbitrary pretext. For that would again be contrary to the will of God, since he has need of such a world as ours, and beings such as us to go and live on the earth. But if he sounds the signal for retreat, as he did to Socrates, then I must obey the one who gives the signal as I would a general.

[30] 'What, should one say this to all and sundry?'

[31] To what end? Isn't it sufficient to be convinced in one's own mind? When children come to us clapping their hands and saying, 'Today's the Saturnalia,* rejoice!', do we reply to them, 'There's nothing to rejoice at in that'? Of course not, we clap in return. [32] Well then, you should do the same—when you're unable to make someone change his views, recognize that he is a child, and clap as he does. Or if you don't care to act in such a way, you have only to keep quiet.

[33] We should keep all of this in mind, then, and when we're summoned to confront any difficulty of this kind, we should know that the moment has come to show whether we have received a proper philosophical education. [34] For a young man who leaves his studies to confront such a difficulty is like one who has studied how to resolve syllogisms, and if someone offers him one that is easily solved, will say, 'No, please give me a complicated one instead, to enable me to gain some practice.' Athletes likewise are none too happy to be matched against young lightweights. [35] 'He can't lift me off the ground,' they'll say. Such is the attitude of a gifted young man. But no, when

the moment calls, you have to burst into tears and say, 'I want to continue my studies.' Study what? If you didn't learn these things so as to be able to put them into practice, why did you learn them in the first place? [36] I imagine that there must be someone among those who are sitting here who feels the labour pains within his mind and says, 'Why is it that a difficulty does not fall upon me now such as that man had to face? Must I be wasting my time sitting in a corner when I might have been crowned at Olympia? When will anyone ever bring me news of such a contest?' Such is the spirit that all of you ought to show. [37] Even among Caesar's gladiators, there are some who take it amiss that no one is bringing them out or matching them against an opponent, and they pray to God, and go to their manager to beg to be sent out into combat. So will none of you show yourselves to be like them? [38] I wanted to sail off to view that very spectacle, and see how my athlete is doing, and how he is carrying out the task that is set for him. [39] 'I don't want a task of that kind,' he says. Is it, then, within your power to choose whatever task you want? You have been given such a body, such parents, such brothers, such a country, and such a post within it, and then you come to me and say, 'Change my task.' What, don't you have the resources to able to deal with that which has been given to you? [40] What you should say is, 'It's for you to set the task, and for me to attend to it well.' But no, you say, 'Don't propose this kind of hypothetical argument to me but rather that kind.' [41] The time will soon be coming when the actors think that their masks, and high boots, and robes* are their very selves. Man, you have all of that only as your subject matter, your task. [42] Speak out so that we may know whether you're a tragic actor or a buffoon; for in other respects, both are just alike. [43] Thus, if one deprives a tragic actor of his high boots and mask, and brings him on the stage like a ghost, has the actor disappeared or does he remain? If he has his voice, he remains.

[44] So also in life. 'Take a governorship.' I take it, and in doing so, show how a properly educated man conducts himself. [45] 'Take off your senatorial robe, dress in rags, and step forward in that role.' What, then, hasn't it been granted to me to display a fine voice? [46] 'In what role, then, are you coming on the stage now?' As a witness summoned by God: [47] 'You there, come forward and bear witness for me; for you're worthy of being produced by me. Is anything that lies outside the sphere of choice either good or bad? Do I cause harm

to anyone? Have I placed each person's advantage under the control of anyone other than himself?' What witness will you offer up to God? [48] 'I'm in a terrible way, Lord, and suffer nothing but misfortune; no one cares for me, no one gives me anything, everyone finds fault with me, everyone speaks badly of me.' [49] Is that the sort of witness that you'll offer? Is that the way in which you'll disgrace the appeal that he has made to you, conferring such honour on you, and judging you worthy of being brought forward to bear witness in such a cause?

[50] But the one who holds power has declared, 'I pronounce you to be impious and unholy.' What has happened to you? 'I've been judged to be impious and unholy.' [51] Nothing more than that? 'Nothing more.'

Suppose he had passed judgement on some hypothetical proposition, declaring, 'I judge the proposition "if it is day, there is light" to be false'; how would that affect the hypothetical proposition? Who has been condemned? The proposition itself or the man who is mistaken about it? [52] Now who is this man who has power to pass judgement upon you? Does he know what piety or impiety really is? Has he studied the matter? Has he learned about it? Where, and from whom? [53] A musician would surely pay no heed to him if he declared the string that sounds the lowest note to be that which sounds the highest, nor would a geometer if he declared that the lines that pass from the centre of a circle to its circumference are not of equal length. [54] So should a properly educated person pay any attention to an uneducated one when he passes judgement about what is holy and unholy, or what is just and unjust?

How very unjust that would be on the part of the educated! Is that what you have learned here, then? [55] Aren't you willing to leave quibbles about such matters to other people, silly little men with no energy, so that they can sit in a corner and collect their small fee, or else grumble that nobody is giving them anything? And for your part, won't you come forward and put into practice what you've learned? [56] For it is not fine arguments that are lacking nowadays; no indeed, the books of the Stoics are brimming with them. What is it that is lacking, then? Someone to put them into practice, someone to bear witness to the arguments in his actions. [57] Take up this task for me, so that in the school we may no longer have to appeal to examples from long ago, but may also have some example from our own time.

[58] To whom does it fall, then, to examine these theoretical questions? To someone who has the leisure. For man is a creature who loves to engage in contemplation; [59] but it is shameful to contemplate such questions in a state of distraction like runaway slaves. No, we should settle down free from all distraction, and listen now to a tragic actor, now to a lyre player, rather than behaving as such slaves do. He is very attentive and full of praise for the actor, but peers around nervously at the same time, and if anyone comes to mention the word 'master', is immediately thrown into agitation and alarm. [60] It is shameful likewise for philosophers to contemplate the works of nature in such a state of mind. For what exactly is a master? One person is not master of another, but it is rather life and death, pleasure and pain, that are his masters. Bring Caesar to me without those, and you will see how calm I am; [61] but when he arrives with all of that, to the accompaniment of thunder and lightning, and I allow myself to be intimidated by that, what else am I doing than recognizing my master, like a runaway slave? [62] As long as I have, as it were, some relief from those things, I too am like a runaway slave who is watching in the theatre; I take a bath, I drink, I sing, yet do so in fear and misery. [63] But if I free myself from my masters, that is to say, from all those things that render masters terrifying, what further worry do I have; what master do I have?

[64] What, then, are we to announce these truths to all and sundry? No, we must accommodate ourselves to laymen and say, 'What this man thinks good for himself, he also recommends to me, so I excuse him for that.' [65] Socrates excused the jailer who wept when he was about to drink the poison, and said, 'How gracious of him to shed those tears for me.' [66] Was it to him that Socrates said, 'That is why we sent the women away'? No, but to his friends, to those who were capable of understanding. As for the jailer, he accommodated himself to him, as one would to a child.*

1.30 *What should we have at hand the help us in difficult circumstances?*

[1] When you enter the presence of some powerful man, remember that there is another who is looking down from above on what is happening here, and that it is him whom you need to please rather than this man. [2] That other asks you, then, 'What did you call exile,

imprisonment, chains, death, and dishonour in your school?'—'These I called matters of indifference.' [3] —'So what do you call them on the present occasion? Have they changed in any way?'—'No they haven't.'—'And have you yourself changed?'—'No.'—'Tell me, then, what is meant by matters of indifference, and what follows from that?'—'They're things that lie outside the sphere of choice, and they're nothing to me.' [4] —'Tell me further, what were the things that you regarded as being "goods"?'—'The right exercise of choice and right use of impressions.'—'And what is the end?'—'To follow God.' [5] —'And do you say the same on the present occasion too?'—'Yes, I say the same even now.'

Then make your way in with confidence, keeping all of this in mind, and you will see what it means for a young man who has undertaken proper philosophical training to appear among people who haven't. [6] I for my part am inclined to suppose, by the gods, that you will have some such feelings as these: 'Why have we made such great and elaborate preparations for nothing whatever? [7] Is this what power amounted to? Is that all that the antechamber, chamberlains, and armed guards meant? Was it for this that I listened to so many lectures? It is really nothing at all, and yet I prepared for it as though it were something of great consequence.'

BOOK 2

2.1 *That confidence does not conflict with caution*

[1] The following assertion of the philosophers may perhaps seem paradoxical to some people, but let us examine nonetheless, as best we can, whether it is true that 'we ought to combine caution with confidence in all that we do'. [2] For caution seems in some sense contrary to confidence, and contraries cannot coexist in any way. [3] What strikes many people as being paradoxical in this matter rests, I think, in some such thought as this: if we were to demand that people should exercise caution and confidence at the same time with regard to the same things, we could be justly accused of wanting to combine qualities that are incompatible. [4] And yet, is it really the case that there is anything objectionable in this saying? For if what has often been stated, and often demonstrated, is sound, namely, that 'the essence of the good lies in the use of impressions, as does that of the bad likewise, but things that lie outside the sphere of choice participate neither in the nature of the good nor in that of the bad', [5] what is paradoxical in the contention of philosophers who say, 'Where things that lie outside the sphere of choice are concerned, there you should act with confidence, but when it comes to things within the sphere of choice, there you should act with caution'? [6] For if the bad lies in the bad exercise of choice, it is with regard to objects within the sphere of choice alone that caution needs to be exercised; and if those that lie outside the sphere of choice, and which are not within our power, are nothing to us, it is with regard to those that confidence needs to be exercised. [7] And thus we will be at once cautious and confident, and, by Zeus, confident by virtue of our caution; for by exercising caution with regard to things that are truly bad, we will gain confidence with regard to those that are not.

[8] Yet we behave like deer; when the hinds are scared by the feathers and run away from them, where do they turn and where do they retreat to in the hope of finding safety? To the nets;* and it is thus that they meet their end, because they have mistaken what should inspire fear for a source of confidence. [9] And likewise with us too, where is it that we show fear? With regard to things that lie outside

the sphere of choice. And where, on the other hand, do we behave with confidence, as if there were nothing to fear? With regard to things that lie within the sphere of choice. [10] To be deceived, then, or to act rashly, or to carry out some shameful act or harbour some shameful desire, we regard as being of no importance, provided only that we achieve our aim with regard to matters that lie outside the sphere of choice. Where we're faced with death, or banishment, or pain, or ignominy, it is there that we try to retreat, there that we grow agitated. [11] And so, as might be expected of those who are mistaken on matters of the highest importance, we transform our natural confidence into rashness, recklessness, foolhardiness, impudence, and our natural caution and reserve into cowardice and servility, full of fears and alarms. [12] For if one transfers caution to the sphere of choice, then along with the wish to act cautiously, one will at the same time have it within one's power to avoid what one wishes to avoid; whereas if one transfers caution to things that are not within our power and lie outside the sphere of choice, since our will to avoid will then be directed towards things that are within the power of others, one will necessarily be subject to fear, instability, and agitation. [13] For it isn't death or pain that is frightening, but the fear that we feel in the face of death or pain. That is why we praise the man who said, '*To die is not dreadful, but to die with dishonour.*'*

[14] It is towards death, then, that our confidence should be directed, and towards the fear of death our caution; whereas in fact we do the opposite, taking flight in the face of death, while showing carelessness, neglect, and indifference in forming a judgement about it. [15] Socrates rightly referred to such fears as bogeys.* For just as masks seem horrible and frightening to children because of their lack of experience, we allow ourselves to be affected like that too by events, for just the same reason as children are frightened by bogeys, and in the same fashion. [16] For what is a child? Ignorance. What is a child? Lack of knowledge. For in those areas in which he does have some knowledge, he is in no way inferior to us. [17] What is death? A bogey. Turn it round and you'll find out; look, it doesn't bite! Sooner or later, your poor body must be separated from its scrap of vital spirit, just as it was formerly. Why be upset, then, if it should come about now? If it is not separated now, it assuredly will be. [18] For what reason? So that the cycle of the universe may be accomplished; for it has need of what is presently in existence, and what will come to be,

and what has completed its course. [19] And what is pain? A bogey; turn it round and you'll find out. Your poor flesh sometimes undergoes rough treatment, and sometimes gentle. If you don't find that to be to your profit, the door stands open;* if you see some profit in it, you must put up with it. [20] For the door stands open for every eventuality, and we thus have no cause for worry.

[21] What is the fruit, then, of these teachings? Precisely what must be finest and most fitting for those who have received a true philosophical education, namely, peace of mind, fearlessness, and freedom. [22] For on these questions we should put our trust not in the crowd, who say that only free men can be educated, but rather in the philosophers, who say that none but the educated can be free.

[23] 'How do you mean?'

This is what I mean; nowadays is freedom anything other than the ability to live as we wish?

'Nothing other than that.'

Tell me now, my friends, do you want to live in error?

'Surely not.'

Then no one who lives in error can be free. [24] Do you want to live in fear, distress, or agitation?

'Not at all.'

No one who lives in fear, then, or distress or agitation, can be free, but anyone who is released from fear, distress, and agitation is released by the very same course from slavery too. [25] So how can we trust you any longer, beloved lawgivers? Do you allow none but the free to gain an education? For according to the philosophers, we don't allow any but the educated to be free, or rather, the gods don't allow it.

[26] 'So if someone has turned his slave around* in front of the praetor, has he done nothing at all?'

He has indeed done something.

'What?'

He has turned his slave around in front of the praetor.

'Nothing more?'

Something more, since he also has to pay over a twentieth of the slave's value.

[27] 'What, hasn't the slave become free by going through this procedure?'

He has no more become free than he has gained peace of mind. [28] Tell me, those of you who are able to put others through that procedure, do you have no master of your own? Don't you have money as your master, or some girl or boy, or a tyrant or some friend of that tyrant? If not, why do you tremble when you have to have dealings with any of these? [29] That's why I'm forever repeating: You must study these teachings and keep them constantly at hand, to know what you should face with confidence, and what you should approach with caution; that is to say, that you should be confident with regard to things that lie outside the sphere of choice, and exercise caution with regard to those that lie within it.

[30] 'But haven't I read my exercises to you; don't you know what I'm doing?'

[31] In what? In fine phrases? You can keep your fine phrases! No, show me how you are in relation to desire and aversion, and whether you never fail to get what you want, and never fall into what you want to avoid. But as for those elegantly constructed sentences of yours, you'll take them away and wipe them out.

[32] 'What, didn't Socrates write?'*

Yes, who wrote as much as he? But how did he go about it? Since he couldn't always have someone at his side to subject his judgements to examination, or to be cross-examined by him in turn, he used to subject himself to examination, and test himself out, and was always trying out the practical application of some specific preconception. [33] That is the kind of thing that a philosopher writes. But as for fine phrases and the approach that I was speaking about, he leaves those to others, to the foolish or the blessed, to those who live a life of leisure because they are free from passion, or to those who in their folly take no account of logical consequences.

[34] And now, when the moment calls, will you go off and give a reading to show off your compositions, and boast about them, saying, 'Look how well I can put dialogues together'? [35] No, that's not what you should be boasting about, man, but this: 'See how I never fail to attain what I desire, see how I never fall into what I want to avoid. Bring death before me and you'll know. Bring hardships, bring imprisonment, bring ignominy, bring condemnation.' [36] Such should be the display that a young man offers when he leaves school. Leave all the rest to others; let no one ever hear you utter a word about such things, nor should you ever accept praise from anyone in that regard, but let it be thought that you're a nobody and an ignoramus. [37] Show that you know this alone, how

never to fail to attain what you desire, and never to fall into what you want to avoid. [38] Let others study how to plead in the courts, or how to deal with problems, or with syllogisms, while you study how to face death, imprisonment, torture, and exile. [39] Do all of this with confidence, placing your trust in the one who has called you to this task, and has judged you worthy of this position, in which, once you have taken it up, you'll show what can be achieved by a rational ruling centre when it is ranged against forces that lie outside the sphere of choice.

[40] And so the paradox that I referred to will no longer seem either impossible or paradoxical, namely, that we ought to be at once confident and cautious, being confident with regard to things that lie outside the sphere of choice, and cautious with regard to those that lie within it.

2.2 *On calmness of mind*

[1] Consider now, you who are going into court, what you want to preserve and what you want to accomplish. [2] If you want to preserve your choice and keep it in accord with nature, you'll be entirely safe; all will go smoothly; you'll have no trouble. [3] If you want to safeguard those things that lie within your own power and are free by nature, and remain satisfied with those, what is left for you to worry about? For who holds power over them; who can take them away from you? [4] If you want to be self-respecting and trustworthy, who can prevent you? If you want to be subject to no hindrance and constraint, who can constrain you to desire things that you don't think that one should desire, or to avoid things that you don't think that one should avoid? [5] Well then, the judge may take measures against you that are commonly regarded as being frightening, but unless you accept them as such by seeking to avoid them, how can he do that? [6] Since desire and aversion are within your own power, then, what else do you need to worry about? [7] Let this be your introductory statement, your exposition, your proof, your victory, your peroration, and your source of renown.

[8] That is why, when someone reminded Socrates* that he ought to be preparing for his trial, he replied, 'Don't you think that I've been preparing for this my whole life through?' [9] —'By what kind of preparation?'—'I've safeguarded what lies within my power,' he

said.—'How do you mean?'—'I've never committed any wrong, whether in my private life or my public life.'

[10] But if you want to safeguard what is external too, your poor body, your petty possessions, any slight reputation that you have, I can only say to you, begin to make every possible preparation from this time onward, and study the character, furthermore, of your judge and your opponent in the case. [11] If you need to clasp his knees, clasp them, or to weep, then weep, or to groan, then groan. [12] For as soon as you subordinate what is truly your own to external things, you must be a slave ever afterwards, and don't allow yourself to be drawn in different directions, so that you're willing to act the slave at one moment and unwilling to do so at the next, [13] but choose unequivocally and wholeheartedly to be either the one thing or the other, either free or a slave, either educated or uneducated, either a fighting cock of true spirit or one without spirit, either one who will endure a rain of blows until death or one who'll immediately give up the fight. But for heaven's sake, don't accept a large number of blows only to give up in the end! [14] If that is shameful, decide without further delay where the nature of good and bad is to be found, which is where truth is to be found also.

[15] Do you suppose that, if Socrates had wanted to safeguard external goods, he would have stepped forward in court and said, 'Anytus and Meletus* can kill me, but they cannot harm me'? [16] Would he have been so stupid as not to see that this course would have taken him not to the desired end, but elsewhere? Why is it, then, that he takes no account of the judges and even provokes them? [17] Take the case of my friend Heraclitus in a minor lawsuit in Rhodes about a small patch of land. After demonstrating to the judges that his claim was just, he then went on to say in the peroration, 'But I won't plead with you, nor do I care what verdict you pronounce; for it is you who are being judged rather than I.' By speaking in such a way, he ruined his case. [18] And what good did it serve? Be satisfied merely to avoid making any entreaties, without going on to add, 'And I'll make no entreaties,' unless the time has come for you, as in the case of Socrates, to provoke the judges with deliberate intent. [19] If you're preparing a peroration of that kind, why rise to speak; why obey the summons? [20] For if you want to be crucified, you only have to wait and the cross will come to you. But if reason prescribes that you should obey the summons and do your best to speak persuasively,

you should act accordingly, though doing your best to safeguard your own good.

[21] For the same reason, it is also ridiculous to say, 'Give me some advice.' What advice should I give you? No, this is what you should say: 'Ensure that my mind will be able to adapt itself to whatever comes about.' [22] For the former request amounts to the same as an illiterate person asking, 'Tell me what to write when some name is set for me to write.' [23] Suppose I tell him to write 'Dion', and the teacher comes along and sets him not that name, but 'Theon', what will come of it? What is he to write? [24] But if you've studied how to write, you'll be ready for everything that may be dictated to you; and if not, what advice should I give you now? If the circumstances should dictate something different, what will you say, what will you do? [25] Keep this general principle in mind, then, and you'll never be in need of advice. But if you're constantly hankering after external things, you're sure to be tested this way and that in accordance with your master's will. [26] And who is your master? Whoever has authority over anything that you're anxious to gain or avoid.

2.3 *To those who recommend people to philosophers*

[1] Diogenes* made an excellent reply to someone who asked him for a letter of recommendation. 'That you are a human being', said Diogenes, 'he will know as soon as he sees you; whether you are a good or a bad one, he will know if he has learned to distinguish between the good and the bad; and if he hasn't learned that, it would make no difference if I were to write him thousands of letters.' [2] It is just as if a drachma piece were to ask to be recommended to someone to make itself accepted. If that person is an assayer of silver, you'll recommend yourself. [3] We ought to have something in everyday life, then, that is comparable to what we have for silver coinage, so that we might be able to say, as the assayer does, 'Bring whatever drachma you wish and I'll test it out.' [4] When it comes to the testing of syllogisms, I can say, 'Bring whichever you want and I'll distinguish between that which works out properly and that which doesn't.' Why? Because I know how to analyse syllogisms; I have the skill that is required if one is to judge whether syllogisms are rightly constructed. [5] But when it comes to ordinary life, what do I do? On one occasion I call something good, and on another I call the same thing bad.

For what reason? The opposite of that which applies in the case of syllogisms, namely, ignorance and inexperience.

2.4 *To a man who had once been caught in adultery*

[1] As Epictetus was remarking that human beings are born for fidelity, and that anyone who damages it is damaging the distinctive quality of man, there happened to enter someone who passed for a scholar and had once been caught in adultery in the city. [2] But if we lay aside this fidelity, continued Epictetus, to which we are born, and set out to seduce our neighbour's wife, what exactly are we doing? What else, to be sure, than ruining and destroying? Destroying what? The person of fidelity, integrity, piety. [3] Nothing more than that? Aren't we destroying good feeling between neighbours, aren't we undermining friendship and the state? And what position are we placing ourselves in? How am I to treat you, man? As a neighbour, as a friend? And of what kind? As a fellow citizen? How am I to place any trust in you? [4] If you were an old pot that was so cracked as to be good for nothing, you would be thrown out on a dung-heap, and no one would bother to pick you up again. [5] But if, as a human being, you're unable to fulfil any human function, what are we to do with you? Well then, since you can't hold the position of friend, can you hold that of a slave? And who will trust you? Aren't you willing, then, to be thrown out in your turn onto a dung-heap somewhere, like a useless pot, like a piece of shit? [6] And then you'll exclaim, 'No one cares for me, scholar though I am.' Naturally, since you're of bad character and useless. It's just as if wasps were to complain that nobody cares for them, but everyone runs away instead, and strikes them dead if possible. [7] You too have a sting of such a kind as to bring trouble and distress to those whom you strike. There's nowhere to put you.

[8] 'What, aren't women common property* by nature?'

Yes, I'd agree; and a little pig is the common property of those who have been invited to the meal. But when the portions have been handed out, go and grab the share of the person sitting next to you, steal it surreptitiously, or reach out your hand to satisfy your greed; and if you can't tear off a piece of the meat, grease your fingers with the fat and lick them. A fine table companion you'd make, a dinner guest worthy of Socrates!*

[9] 'Come now, isn't the theatre the common property of all the citizens?'*

Very well, come along when everyone has sat down, and, if you have a mind to, chase someone out of his seat. [10] In the same way, women, too, are common property by nature; but when the lawgiver, like the host at a feast, has apportioned them, aren't you willing, then, like everyone else, to seek out your own portion, rather than grab some-one else's in addition to satisfy your greed?

'But I'm a scholar and know how to interpret Archedemus.'*

[11] Understanding Archedemus as you do, then go ahead and be an adulterer and a cheat, and a wolf or ape, rather than a human being. For who can stop you?

2.5 *How greatness of mind may coexist with carefulness*

[1] Materials are indifferent, but the use that one makes of them is by no means indifferent. [2] How, then, can one preserve firmness and calmness of mind, and at the same time the attentiveness that saves us from careless and thoughtless action? By following the example of those who play at dice. [3] The counters are indifferent, the dice are indifferent. How can I know in what way the throw will fall? But to be attentive and skilful in making use of whatever does fall, that is now my task. [4] And so likewise, my principal task in life is this: to distin-guish between things, and establish a division between them and say, 'External things are not within my power; choice is within my power. [5] Where am I to seek the good and the bad? Within myself, in that which is my own.' But with regard to what is not my own, never apply the words good or bad, and benefit or harm, and any other word of that kind.

[6] 'What, then, are we to use these externals in a careless fashion?'

Not at all; for that is again bad for our faculty of choice, and thus contrary to nature. [7] Rather, they should be used with care, because their use is not a matter of indifference, and at the same time with composure and calmness of mind, because the material being used is indifferent. [8] For wherever anything is truly important to me, there no one can hinder or compel me. Where I'm capable of being hindered or compelled, it is in relation to things that are not within my power to obtain, and that are neither good nor bad; whereas the use that I make of them is either good or bad, and that does lie within my power.

[9] It is difficult, to be sure, to unite and combine these two states of mind, the vigilance of one who feels attracted by outside objects, and the composure of one who feels indifferent to them; but all the same it is not impossible. For otherwise it would be impossible for us to be happy. [10] It is rather as if we had to set off on a sea-voyage. What lies within my power? To choose the helmsman, the sailors, the day, the moment. [11] Then a storm descends on us. Now why should that be of any concern to me? For my role has been completed. This is now somebody else's business, that of the helmsman. [12] But now the ship begins to sink. So what can I do? What I can and that alone, namely, to drown without fear, without crying out, without hurling accusations against God, as one who well knows that what is born is also fated to perish. [13] For I am not everlasting, but a human being, a part of the whole as an hour is a part of the day. Like an hour I must come, and like an hour pass away. [14] So what difference does it make to me how I pass away, whether it be by drowning or a fever? For in some way or other, pass away I must.

[15] Experienced ball players can also be seen to act in such a way. None of them is concerned about whether the ball is good or bad, but solely about how to throw and catch it. [16] It is there accordingly that the player's agility, and skill, and speed, and good judgement are demonstrated; so where I for my part can't catch the ball even if I spread out my cloak to do so, an expert will catch it whenever I make a throw. [17] But if we're anxious or nervous when we make the catch or throw, what will become of the game, and how can one maintain one's composure; how can one see what is coming next? But rather, one player will be saying, 'Throw!', and another, 'Don't!', and another again, 'Don't throw so high!' In truth, that is a brawl and not a game.

[18] Now Socrates* certainly knew how to play ball. 'How do you mean?' He knew how to play when on trial in court. 'Tell me, Anytus,' he said, 'how can you claim that I don't believe in God? What do you suppose daemons are? Aren't they either offspring of gods, or a hybrid race born from human beings and gods?' [19] And when Anytus agreed, he continued, 'Do you think, then, that it is possible for mules to exist, but not donkeys?' It was as though he was playing ball. And there in court, what ball was in play? Life, imprisonment, exile, a draught of poison, the loss of his wife, and having to leave his children behind as orphans. [20] That was what was involved, that

was what he was playing with, but play he did nonetheless and threw the ball with dexterity. That is how we too should act, with the close attention of the cleverest of ball players, while showing the same indifference to what we are playing with, as being no more than a ball. [21] For we should do our best to show our skill with regard to any external material, yet without becoming attached to it, but merely displaying our skill with regard to it, whatever it might be. In just the same way, a weaver doesn't make wool, but employs his skill on whatever wool he may receive. [22] Another provides you with nourishment and possessions, and he can take them away again likewise, along with your body too. For your part, you should accept the material and work on it. [23] And then, if you take your leave without having suffered any harm, all who meet you will congratulate you on your escape; but one who has a better insight into these matters, if he sees that you've conducted yourself with honesty, will praise you and rejoice with you, but will do the opposite if he sees that you've escaped through some act of dishonesty.

[24] How can one say, then, that some externals are in accordance with nature, and others contrary to it? It is as if we are asking the question in isolation. Thus, I will say that it is natural for the foot* to be clean, taken in isolation, but if you consider it as a foot and not in isolation, it will be appropriate for it also to step into mud, and trample on thorns, and sometimes even to be cut off for the sake of the body as a whole; for otherwise, it will no longer be a foot. [25] We should think in some such way about ourselves also. What are you? A human being. Now, if you consider yourself in isolation, it is natural for you to live to an advanced age, to be rich, and to enjoy good health; but if you consider yourself as a human being and as part of some whole, it may be in the interest of the whole that you should now fall ill, now embark on a voyage and be exposed to danger, now suffer poverty, and perhaps even die before your time. [26] Why do you resent this, then? Don't you know that in isolation a foot is no longer a foot, and that you likewise will no longer be a human being? What, then, is a human being? A part of a city, first of all that which is made up of gods and human beings, then that which is closest to us and which we call a city, which is a microcosm of the universal city.

[27] 'Must I be brought to trial, then?'

What, would you have someone else fall ill with a fever, someone else sail out to sea, someone else die, someone else be condemned?

For it is impossible, while we are in a body such as ours, and in this universe that contains us, and among such companions as we have, that such things should not happen to us, some to one person and some to another. [28] It is thus your role to step forward and say what you ought, and to deal with these things as they turn out. If the judge then proclaims, 'I judge you to be guilty,' you may reply, 'I wish you well. [29] I have fulfilled my role, it is for you to see whether you have fulfilled yours.' For he too runs some risk: don't forget that.

2.6 *About indifference*

[1] A hypothetical syllogism is something that is indifferent; the judgement that one makes about it is not indifferent, however, but is either knowledge, or opinion, or delusion. And likewise, life is indifferent, but the use that one makes of it is not. [2] So when someone tells you that these things, too, are indifferent, don't become careless, and when someone encourages you, on the other hand, to be careful, don't become submissive and allow yourself to be overawed by material things.

[3] It is also good to know how well prepared one is and be aware of one's capacity, so that if you aren't properly prepared, you may keep silent and not be upset if others show themselves to be superior to you in those matters. [4] For you in turn may regard yourself as being superior to them when it comes to syllogisms, and if they're upset by that, you can console them by saying, 'I've learned this and you haven't.' [5] And likewise, in areas in which practice is required, don't seek the advantage that practice alone can provide, but leave the matter to those who have the benefit of long experience, and be content for your part to preserve your composure.

[6] 'Go and pay your respects to So-and-so.'—'I do so.' —'How?'—'In no submissive fashion.'—'But you had the door shut in your face.'—'Yes, since I haven't learned to climb in through the window.' [7] —'Go and speak to him though.'—'I do so.'—'In what way?'—'In no submissive fashion.'

[8] But you didn't get what you wanted. For that wasn't your business, was it? No, it was his. So why should you want to lay claim to what is another's? Always remember what is your own and what is not, and you'll never be troubled. [9] So Chrysippus* did well to say, 'As long as the consequences remain unclear to me, I always hold to

what is best fitted to secure such things as are in accordance with nature; for God himself, in creating me, granted me the freedom to choose them. [10] But if I in fact knew that illness had been decreed for me at this moment by destiny, I would welcome even that; for the foot, too, if it had understanding, would be eager to get spattered with mud.'

[11] Why, for instance, do ears of corn grow? Isn't it so that they may ripen? If they ripen, isn't it so that they may be harvested? For they don't exist independently. [12] If they had any awareness, wouldn't they be bound to pray that they should never be harvested? Yet it would be a curse for ears of corn never to be harvested. [13] You should know that for human beings likewise, it would be a curse for them never to die; it is the same as not coming to ripeness, as not being harvested. [14] But since we're beings who must both be harvested and be aware at the same time that we're being harvested, we become aggrieved at this. For neither do we know who we are, nor have we studied what it means to be human in the same way as horsemen study everything that relates to horses. [15] Now when Chrysantas* was about to strike down an enemy and heard the trumpet sounding the recall, he held back, thinking it better to fulfil his general's order than his own will. [16] And yet none of us, even when necessity calls, is at all happy to obey, but we suffer our lot with tears and groans, referring to it as force of circumstance. [17] What do you mean by 'circumstance', man? If by that you mean what surrounds you, why, all things are circumstances; but if you use the term as implying something disagreeable, what is disagreeable in the fact that whatever is born must pass away? [18] The instrument of destruction may be a sword, or a wheel, or the sea, or a roof tile, or a tyrant. What does it matter by which road we have to make the descent to Hades? All roads are equal. [19] But if you'd like to know the truth, the shortest is that on which you're sent by a tyrant. It never took a tyrant six months to cut someone's throat, while a fever can often take as much as a year to achieve the same result! All of these things are mere noise, the vain sounding of empty words.

[20] 'I'm at risk of losing my life when I'm with Caesar.'

And don't I have to face the same risk myself, living as I do in Nicopolis, where there are so many earthquakes? And when you for your part have to sail across the Adriatic, what is it that you're risking? Aren't you risking your life?

[21] 'But I'm also put at risk by opinion.'

Your own opinion? How so? Can anyone compel you to think any-thing other than what you want to think? The opinions of others? What sort of risk does it present to you if other people have false opinions?

[22] 'But I'm at risk of being exiled.'

What does it mean to be exiled? To have to live somewhere else than in Rome?

'Indeed, but what if I'm sent to Gyara?'

If it suits you, you'll go there; if not, there is somewhere else you can go instead of Gyara, to that place where he who's banishing you to Gyara will have to go in his turn, whether he wants to or not. [23] Why, then, are you going off as if you were going to have to face great dangers? It is nothing much when compared to the preparations that you've made, so that a gifted young man might say, 'It was hardly worth the trouble of listening to so many lectures, of writing so many exercises, and sitting for all this time with a little old man who was of no great worth.' [24] Just remember the distinction that must be drawn between what is yours and what is not yours. Never lay claim to anything that is not your own. [25] An orator's platform and a prison are two different places, one high and the other low; but your choice can be kept the same in either place, if you want to keep it so. [26] And then we'll be emulating Socrates,* once we're able to write hymns of praise in prison. [27] But as we've been up until now, con-sider whether we would be able to endure it if someone came to us in prison and said, 'Would you like me to read you some hymns of praise?' 'Why are you pestering me in this way? Don't you know what trouble I'm in? Is that possible for me in these circumstances?'—'What circumstances, then?'—'I'm about to die.'—'And is everyone else going to be immortal?'

2.7 *How we should make use of divination*

[1] Because we resort to divination on the wrong occasions, many of us fail to carry out many appropriate actions, [2] for what is a diviner able to see that extends beyond death, danger, or illness, or, in general, things of that kind? [3] If one should be obliged, then, to run a risk on behalf of a friend, or if it is appropriate for me even to die for him, what occasion is left for me to resort to divination? Don't I have a diviner within me who has taught me the true nature of good and bad,

and can interpret the signs that indicate the one and the other? [4] So what further need do I have of entrails or birds? And if a diviner says to me, 'That is what will be of benefit to you,' will I put up with it? Why, does he know what is beneficial? Does he know what is good? [5] In learning to read the signs in the entrails, has he also learned the signs that are indicative of good and bad? For if he has knowledge of those, he also knows those that indicate what is right or wrong, and what is just or unjust. [6] Man, it is your part to tell me whether the signs point to life or death, riches or penury; but to know whether these would be beneficial or harmful, is it really you whom I should be consulting? [7] Why is it that you don't speak out on points of grammar? And yet you do speak out on those matters on which all of us go astray and can never reach agreement? [8] It was thus an excellent reply that the woman made when she wanted to send a boatload of provisions to the exiled Gratilla;* for when someone said to her, 'Domitian will merely confiscate them,' she replied, 'Better that he should take them away than that I should fail to send them.'

[9] What is it, then, that drives us to make such frequent use of divination? Simply cowardice, our fear of what may come about. That is why we flatter the diviners. 'Please, sir, will I get that inheritance from my father?'—'Let me see now, we must offer up a sacrifice.'—'Yes, sir, as fortune wishes.' He then goes on to say, 'You'll get the inheritance,' and we thank him as though we had got the inheritance from the diviner himself.

[10] What is the proper course, then? To go to them with neither desire nor aversion, as a traveller might ask a passer-by which road will take him to his destination, without having any particular desire to go to the right rather than the left; for he has no wish to pass along either of them specifically, but along the one that will take him to where he wants to go. [11] It is in the same spirit, too, that we should ask God to guide us on our way, making use of him as we make use of our eyes; for we don't ask our eyes to show us some things as against others, but are willing to accept the images of everything that they reveal to us.

[12] As things are, though, we tremble in front of the augur, and grasp his hand and appeal to him as though he were a god, imploring him, 'Have pity on me, sir, do please grant that I may come off well.' [13] What, slave, do you wish for anything other than what is best for you? And is anything better for you than what God pleases? Why are

you then making every possible effort to corrupt your judge, to mislead your counsellor?

2.8 *What is the essence of the good?*

[1] God brings benefit; but the good also brings benefit. It would seem,
therefore, that where the true nature of God is to be found, there too
will be that of the good. [2] Then what is the nature of God? Flesh? In
no way whatever. Land? In no way. Fame? In no way. He is intelligence, knowledge, right reason. [3] So it is there alone that one should
seek the true nature of the good. For do you perhaps want to look for
it in a plant? No. Or in an irrational being? No. If you're seeking it in
that which is rational, why do you continue to look for it anywhere else
than in what distinguishes the rational from the irrational? [4] Plants
don't even have the capacity to make use of impressions, and for that
reason you don't speak of the good in relation to them. It requires the
capacity, then, to make use of impressions. [5] That alone? For if that
is all that is required, one might say that the other animals are capable
of the good, and of happiness and unhappiness. [6] But you don't
claim any such thing, and rightly so. For even if they're entirely capable
of dealing with impressions, they have no understanding of the use
that they make of them. And with good reason, since they're born to
serve others, and aren't of primary value.

[7] A donkey, for instance, surely isn't born to be of primary
value? No, but because we had need of a back that is able to carry
our burdens. But we also required, by Zeus, that it should be able to
walk around; so for that reason, it has received in addition the
capacity to make use of impressions, since it would otherwise have
been incapable of walking around. [8] But there its endowment ends.
For if it had also been granted the power to understand its use of
those impressions, it is clear that it would consequently no longer
have been subject to us, nor would it render us the services that
it does, but would be our equal and like ourselves. [9] Aren't you
willing, therefore, to seek the essence of the good in that quality
whose absence from other creatures prevents us from speaking of
the good in relation to them?

[10] 'What, isn't it the case that these creatures, too, are works of God?'

Indeed they are, but they're not of primary value, nor are they portions of the divine. [11] But you for your part are of primary value;

you're a fragment of God. Why are you ignorant, then, of your high birth? Why is it that you don't know where you came from? [12] Don't you want to keep in mind, when you eat, who it is that is doing the eating, and whom it is that you're feeding? And when you engage in sexual intercourse, who it is that is doing so? In your social relationships, in your physical exercises, in your conversations, aren't you aware that it's a god whom you're feeding, a god whom you're exercising? You carry God around with you, poor wretch, and yet have no knowledge of it. [13] Do you suppose that I mean some external god of gold or silver? It is within yourself that you carry him, and you fail to realize that you're defiling him through your impure thoughts and unclean actions. [14] Yet in front of a divine image, you wouldn't dare to do any of the things that you do; but when God himself is present within you, and he sees and hears everything, aren't you ashamed to think and act as you do, you who are ignorant of your own nature and are an object of divine anger?

[15] After all, when we send a young man out of school into the affairs of life, why are we afraid that he'll do something wrong, in the way in which he eats, or in his sexual relationships, or that he may be abased if he's dressed in rags, or be puffed up with pride if he has fine robes? [16] This young man has no knowledge of the god whom he has within him, and doesn't know in whose company he is setting out into the world. But can we allow him to say, 'I wish you were coming with me'? [17] Wherever you may be, won't you have God with you? And having him, do you seek some other companion? [18] And would he have anything different to say to you? Why, if you were one of the statues of Phidias,* his Athena or his Zeus, you would have remembered both yourself and the artist who made you, and if you had any power of perception, you would have tried to do nothing unworthy of the one who made you, or of yourself, and never to display yourself to human eyes in any unsuitable attitude; [19] but as it is, since it was Zeus who made you, are you therefore unconcerned about what manner of person you show yourself to be? And yet what comparison is there between the one artist and the other, between the one work of art and the other? [20] And what work of any human artist contains within itself the very faculties that are displayed in its making? Is such a work anything other than marble, or bronze, or gold, or ivory? And the Athena of Phidias, once she has stretched out her hand to receive the Victory upon it, remains fixed

in that attitude for ever, whereas the works of the gods move and breathe, and are capable of making use of impressions and passing judgements about them. [21] When you yourself are the work of such a maker, will you dishonour him? Not only has he created you, but he has also entrusted you to your own sole charge, [22] and yet will you not only fail to remember that, but also dishonour the charge that he has entrusted to you? If God had entrusted an orphan to your care, would you have neglected him in such a fashion? [23] Yet he has delivered you yourself into your own keeping, and says, 'I had no one in whom I could put more confidence than you. Keep this person as he was born by nature to be; keep him modest, trustworthy, high-minded, unshakeable, free from passion, imperturbable.' And after that, don't you want to keep him so?

[24] But people will say, 'Where did that man get his haughty air and solemn expression?' To be sure, my bearing isn't yet what it should be. For I have yet to place full confidence in what I've learned and agreed to; I'm still afraid of my own weakness. [25] Let me gain some additional confidence, and then you'll see the right look in my eye and right bearing; then I'll show you what the statue is like when it is completed and fully polished. [26] What do you think of it? A haughty air? Heaven forbid! The Zeus at Olympia doesn't display a haughty air, surely? No, he maintains a steady gaze, as befits one who is about to proclaim, 'My word is irrevocable and never deceives.'* [27] That is how I'd like to show myself to you: faithful, modest, noble-minded, imperturbable. [28] What, and immortal too, and eternally young, and immune from disease? No, but as one who can die in a god-like way, who can endure disease in a god-like way. That lies in my power, that I can do, but the rest is not in my power, nor can I do it. [29] I'll show you the sinews of a philosopher. And what sinews are those? Desire that never fails in its aim, aversion that never falls into what it wants to avoid, motivation that accords with one's duty, purpose that is carefully weighed, and assent that is not over-hasty. That is what you'll see.

2.9 *That although we are unable to fulfil our human calling, we adopt that of a philosopher*

[1] Merely to fulfil the role of a human being is no simple matter. [2] For what is a human being? 'A rational and mortal creature,' someone

says. First of all, what does the rational element serve to distinguish us from? 'From wild beasts.' And from what else? 'From sheep and the like.' [3] Take care, then, never to be like a wild beast; otherwise you will have destroyed what is human in you, and will have failed to fulfil your part as a human being. Take care that you never act like a sheep; or else in that way, too, you will have destroyed what is human in you.

[4] 'When is it, then, that we act like sheep?'

When we act for the sake of our belly or genitals, when we act at random, or in a filthy manner, or without proper care, to what level have we sunk? To that of sheep. What have we destroyed? What is rational in us. [5] And when we behave aggressively, and harmfully, and angrily, and forcefully, to what level have we sunk? To that of wild beasts. [6] There are, besides, some among us who are large ferocious beasts, while others are little ones, small and evil-natured, which prompt us to say, 'I'd rather be eaten by a lion!' [7] By all such behaviour, the human calling is destroyed.

[8] When is a complex proposition* preserved as valid? When it fulfils its function, so that its validity is founded on the truth of the propositions of which it is composed. And a disjunctive proposition? When it fulfils its function. And when are flutes, a lyre, a horse, a dog preserved? [9] Is it surprising, then, that a human being, too, should be preserved in the same way, and destroyed in the same way? [10] Each person is strengthened and preserved by actions that are appropriate to his nature; the carpenter by those that accord with the art of carpentry, the grammarian by those that accord with the art of grammar. But if the latter gets into the habit of writing ungrammatically, his skill will necessarily be destroyed and perish. [11] A modest character is preserved likewise by modest actions, while shameless actions will destroy it; and a faithful character is preserved by acts of fidelity, while acts of a contrary nature will destroy it. [12] And the opposing characters are destroyed in turn by behaviour of the opposite kind, the shameless by shamelessness, the disloyal by disloyalty, the slanderous by slanders, the irascible by anger, and the miser by the disproportion between what he takes in and what he gives out.

[13] That is why philosophers recommend that we shouldn't be contented merely to learn, but should add practice too, and then training. [14] For over a long period of time, we have got into the

habit of doing the opposite of what we have learned, and the opinions that we hold and apply are the opposite of the correct ones. So
unless we put the opposite opinions into use, we'll be nothing more
than interpreters of other people's judgements. [15] For who is there
among us at this present time who cannot give a systematic account
of what is good and bad? That some things are good, others bad,
and others again indifferent; that the virtues and what partakes in
the virtues are good, while things of the opposite nature are bad;
and that wealth, health, and reputation are indifferent. [16] Then,
while we're speaking, if some rather loud noise occurs, or someone
in the audience begins to laugh at us, we become disconcerted. [17]
Tell me, philosopher, what has become of the fine things that you
were saying? Where did you get them from? Your lips, and that's
all. Why do you spoil helpful thoughts, then, that are not your own?
Why do you play around with matters of the highest importance?
[18] It is one thing to put bread and wine away in a store-room, and
quite another to eat them. What is eaten is digested and distributed
around the body, to become sinews, flesh, bones, blood, a good
complexion, sound breathing. What is stored away is ready at hand,
to be sure, to be taken out and displayed whenever you wish, but
you derive no benefit from it, except that of having the reputation
of possessing it. [19] What difference does it make, in fact, whether
you expound these teachings or those of another school? Sit down
and give a technical account of the teachings of Epicurus, and perhaps you'll give a better account than Epicurus himself! Why call
yourself a Stoic, then; why mislead the crowd; why act the part of a
Jew when you're Greek? [20] Don't you know why it is that a person
is called a Jew, Syrian, or Egyptian? And when we see someone
hesitating between two creeds, we're accustomed to say, 'He is no
Jew, but is merely acting the part.' But when he assumes the frame
of mind of one who has been baptized* and has made his choice,
then he really is a Jew, and is called by that name. [21] And so we too
are baptized in pretence only, and are Jews in name alone, while in
fact being someone quite different, since we're not in sympathy
with our own doctrines, and are far from making any practical
application of the principles that we express, even though we take
pride in knowing them. [22] And so it is, that when we're not even
able to fulfil the function of a human being, we want to assume that
of a philosopher too, massive burden though that is. It is as though

a man who is incapable of lifting ten pounds wanted to lift up the rock of Ajax!*

2.10 *How may the actions that are appropriate to a person be discovered from the names applied to him?*

[1] Consider who you are. First of all, a human being, that is to say, one who has no faculty more authoritative than choice, but subordinates everything else to that, keeping choice itself free from enslavement and subjection. [2] Consider, then, what you're distinguished from through the possession of reason: you're distinguished from wild beasts; you're distinguished from sheep. [3] What is more, you're a citizen of the world and a part of it, and moreover no subordinate part, but one of the leading parts in so far as you're capable of understanding the divine governing order of the world, and of reflecting about all that follows from it. [4] Now what is the calling of a citizen? Never to approach anything with a view to personal advantage, never to deliberate about anything as though detached from the whole, but to act as one's hand or foot would act if it had the power of reason and could understand the order of nature, and so would never exercise any desire or motive other than by reference to the whole. [5] The philosophers are thus right to say that if a wise and good person could foresee the future, he would cooperate with nature even if it came to illness, death, or mutilation, because he would recognize that these are allotted as a contribution to the ordering of the whole, and that the whole is more important than the part, and the city than the citizen. [6] But since we can't in fact foretell what will come about, it is our duty to hold to what is naturally more fit to be chosen, since that is what we were born for.

[7] Remember next that you are a son. What is required of a person in this role? To regard all that he owns as belonging to his father, to obey him in all things, never to speak badly of him to others, never to do or say anything that might cause him harm, and to defer and yield to him in everything, helping him to the best of his ability.

[8] Know next that you are also a brother. In this role, too, you're obliged to show deference, obedience, and restraint in your language, and never to contend with your brother for anything that lies outside the sphere of choice, but to be happy to give it up, so as to have a better share of the things that lie within the sphere of choice. [9] For

consider what it is to acquire his good will at the price of a lettuce, perhaps, or a chair: what a bargain that is!

[10] And next, if you're sitting on the council of some city, remember that you're a councillor; if you're young, remember that you're young; if an old man, remember that you're an old man; if a father, remember that you're a father. [11] For each of these names, if carefully considered, indicates the actions that are appropriate to it. [12] But if you go off and disparage your brother, I'll tell you that you've forgotten who you are and what name you bear. [13] Now if you were a smith and made poor use of your hammer, you'd have forgotten what you are as a smith; so if you forget what you are as a brother, and become an enemy instead, do you really suppose that you haven't exchanged one thing for another? [14] And if instead of being a man, a civilized and sociable creature, you've become a wild beast that is harmful, treacherous, and liable to kill, have you lost nothing at all? What, must you lose a bit of money to suffer any damage, and does the loss of nothing else cause damage to a human being? [15] If you were to lose your knowledge of grammar and music, you'd regard that loss as being damaging; and yet if you lose your sense of shame, and dignity, and kindliness, you count that as being of no importance? [16] And yet those other losses are brought about through some external cause, beyond the power of our will, whereas these latter qualities are lost through our own fault; and to possess the former qualities is no source of honour, nor is it shameful to lose them, whereas it is shameful not to possess the latter, and to lose them is a stain on one's honour and a true misfortune. [17] If a man submits to being an invert, what is it that he loses? The man in him. And the one who makes use of him? Along with many other things, he loses the man in him no less than the other does. [18] And what does the adulterer lose? The man who has self-respect and self-control, the gentleman, the citizen, the neighbour. Someone who gives way to anger, what does he lose? Something else. One who falls prey to fear? Something else. [19] No one becomes bad without suffering loss and damage. To be sure, if you regard loss of money as being the only loss, all such people remain unharmed and suffer no loss; they may even make some gain and profit if they earn any money from such actions. [20] But consider now, if you bring everything back to money, even someone who loses his nose will have suffered no damage in your view.

'Yes, he has,' someone says, 'because his body is mutilated.'

[21] Come, does a man who loses all sense of smell lose nothing at all? Does there exist no faculty of the mind, then, that brings benefit to one who possesses it, and damage if he loses it?

[22] 'Which do you mean?'

Don't we have a natural sense of shame?

'We do indeed.'

Does someone who destroys it suffer no damage or deprivation; does he lose nothing that properly belongs to him? [23] Don't we possess a natural sense of fidelity, a natural sense of affection, a natural sense of helpfulness, a natural sense of restraint? And if someone carelessly allows himself to suffer the loss of any of these, is it really the case, then, that he suffers no harm or loss?

[24] 'What, then, if someone injures me, won't I injure him in return?'

Consider first what an injury is, and recall what you have heard from the philosophers. [25] If it is the case, then, that the good lies in choice, and the bad likewise, see whether what you've just said amounts to this: [26] 'Since the person in question has injured himself by inflicting some wrong on me, shouldn't I injure myself by inflicting some wrong on him?' [27] Why don't we picture the matter in some such way as that, instead of counting it as an injury when we suffer some loss with regard to our body or possessions, while counting it as no injury at all where our choice is affected? [28] It is that when one is deceived or commits an injustice, one suffers no pain in one's head, or one's eye, or one's hip, nor does one lose any land; [29] and we're concerned about nothing other than things of that kind. As to whether our choice is kept honest and trustworthy, or will on the contrary be shameful and unreliable, that doesn't cause us the slightest concern, except when it comes to making fine speeches in the classroom. [30] And so the progress that we make extends only to speechifying, and apart from that we advance not a step further.

2.11 *What is the point of departure in philosophy?*

[1] The point of departure in philosophy, at least for those who embark on it in the proper way and enter by the front door, is a consciousness of our own weakness and incapacity with regard to essential matters. [2] For we come into the world without having an innate conception of

a right-angled triangle, or of a quarter-tone or half-tone in music, but learn what these are through some kind of systematic instruction, so that, for that reason, those who have no knowledge of them don't suppose that they know anything about them; [3] but who among us enters the world without having an innate conception of what is good and bad, right and wrong, appropriate and inappropriate, and of happiness, and of what is proper for us and falls to our lot, and of what we ought to do and ought not to do? [4] And so it comes about that all of us make use of these terms, and try to apply our preconceptions to individual cases. [5] 'He acted well, he did as he ought or ought not to have done; he has been unfortunate, or was fortunate; he is unjust, or is just'; who among us fails to use such expressions? Who defers the use of them until he has been properly instructed, as with those who are ignorant about lines or musical notes? [6] The reason is that, in this area, we come into the world ready-instructed, as it were, to some degree by nature, and starting from that, we go on to add our personal opinion.

[7] 'But why is it', someone says, 'that I don't know what is right or wrong? Is it that I have no preconception in this regard?'

No, you do have one.

'Is it that I fail to apply it to particular cases?'

No, you do apply it.

'So I don't apply it properly?'

[8] The whole question turns on that, and it is here that opinion enters in. For people start from these generally acknowledged principles, but then get involved in disputes because they fail to apply them in an appropriate way to particular cases. [9] If, in addition to these general principles, they also possessed the knowledge that is required to apply them correctly, what could keep them from being perfect? [10] But now, since you think that you can also apply your preconceptions in an appropriate fashion to particular cases, tell me, how did you come to draw that conclusion?

'Because I think it to be so.'

And yet another person doesn't think the same on the matter, and he too thinks that he's applying the principles properly; or doesn't he?

'Indeed he does.'

[11] Can it be possible, then, that both of you are applying your preconceptions appropriately with regard to matters on which you hold conflicting opinions?

'No, we can't be.'

[12] Do you have anything to show us, then, over and above your personal opinion, that would enable you to make a better application of your preconceptions? But does a madman do anything other than what seems good to him? And would that be a sufficient criterion for him too?

'Of course it wouldn't.'

Pass on, then, to something that stands higher than mere opinion. What could that be? [13] Look now, this is the starting point of philosophy: the recognition that different people have conflicting opinions, the rejection of mere opinion so that it comes to be viewed with mistrust, an investigation of opinion to determine whether it is rightly held, and the discovery of a standard of judgement, comparable to the balance that we have devised for the determining of weights, or the carpenter's rule for determining whether things are straight or crooked.

[14] Is this the starting point of philosophy? Is everything right that appears right to each person? And how could it be possible for conflicting opinions to be right? So they can't be right in every case. But perhaps those that appear right to us specifically? [15] Why to us rather than to the Syrians, or to the Egyptians? Or rather than what strikes me personally, or some other person, as being right? There's no reason to think that some are more likely to be right than others. [16] And so the opinion that each person holds is not a sufficient criterion for determining the truth.

When it comes to weights and measures, too, we aren't satisfied with mere appearances, but have devised a standard to test them out in each case. In the present area, then, is there a higher standard than mere opinion? And how is it possible that that which is most vital for human beings should lie beyond determination, beyond discovery?

[17] 'There surely must be a standard.'

Why don't we seek it out, then, and discover it, and after having discovered it, put it to use without fail ever afterwards, never departing from it by so much as a finger's breadth? [18] For that is something, I think, which, when found, will rescue from madness those who use opinion as their sole measure in everything, so that from that time onward, setting out from known and clearly defined principles, we can judge particular cases through the application of systematically examined preconceptions. [19] What is the subject of our present enquiry?

'Pleasure.'

[20] Submit it to the standard, put it on the scales. For something to be good, must it be something that we can properly place confidence and trust in?

'Indeed it must.'

Can we properly place confidence, then, in something that is unstable?

'No.'

[21] Is pleasure stable?

'No, it isn't.'

Away with it, then; take it out of the scales, and drive it away from the realm of good things. [22] But if your sight is none too keen and one set of scales isn't enough for you, bring another. Is the good something that can properly inspire us with pride?

'It is indeed.'

Is the pleasure of the moment, then, something that can properly inspire us with pride? Take care not to say that it is, or I'll no longer regard you as being worthy of even using the scales! [23] It is thus that things are judged and weighed when one has the standards at hand; [24] and the task of philosophy lies in this, in examining and establishing those standards. [25] As for the use of them, once they are known, that is the business of the virtuous and good person.

2.12 *About the art of argument*

[1] What one needs to learn if one is to know how to conduct an argument is something that has been accurately determined by philosophers of our school; but when it comes to the proper application of that knowledge, we're altogether unpractised. [2] If you get any of us to engage in an argument with a layman, we won't find a way to deal with him. After shifting him a bit, if he then proves uncooperative, we can no longer handle him, and then either abuse him or make fun of him, saying, 'He's only an ignorant amateur; one can't do anything with him.' [3] But a good guide, when he sees someone wandering astray, doesn't abandon him with a dose of mockery or abuse, but leads him back to the proper path. [4] So you too should show him the truth and you'll see how he follows. As long as you fail to make it clear

to him, though, you shouldn't make fun of him, but should recognize your own incapacity instead.

[5] How did Socrates act, then? He forced his interlocutor to bear witness for him and had no need of any other witness. He was thus able to say, 'I can do without everyone else; it is always enough for me to have my interlocutor as witness; as for the rest, I don't seek their vote, but that of my interlocutor alone.' [6] For he would bring the consequences of our preconceptions so clearly to light that everyone, no matter who, recognized the contradiction involved and so abandoned it. [7] 'Does an envious man take pleasure in his envy?'—'Not at all, but quite the reverse, he is pained by it.' Through the contradiction he has shaken his partner. 'Well then, does envy seem to you to be a feeling of pain provoked by the sight of bad things?' [8] And so he has made him say that envy is a feeling of pain provoked by the sight of good things. 'Well now, can anyone envy things that mean nothing to him?' 'In no way.' [9] And so, once he had filled out the concept and systematically examined it, he went off; he didn't say to the other man, 'Define envy for me,' and then, when the man had defined it, go on to say, 'That is a bad definition because the terms of it don't correspond to the object defined,' [10] introducing technical terms, which are tiresome for laymen as a consequence and hard for them to follow, even if we for our part can't manage without them. [11] But as to terms that the layman himself could follow and that would enable him, through recourse to his own impressions, to accept some proposition or reject it—we're altogether incapable of moving him by use of terms such as those. [12] And consequently, being aware as we are of this incapacity, we naturally abandon the attempt, or at least those of us who have some measure of good sense do. [13] But the mass of people, when they stumble into debates of this kind, get thoroughly confused and confuse everyone else, and finally take their leave after an exchange of abuse. [14] Now it was the principal and most distinctive characteristic of Socrates that he never got overheated in an argument, and never resorted to abuse or any form of insolence, but would patiently endure abuse from others and put an end to any conflict. [15] If you want to know what great abilities he possessed in that regard, read Xenophon's *Symposium*, and you'll see how many disputes he settled. [16] Hence among the poets too, this is a quality that is rightly spoken of in terms of the highest praise; '*With sure skill he would soon end even a great quarrel.*'*

[17] Well now, this activity is none too safe these days, especially at Rome. For those who engage in it clearly mustn't set to work in a corner, but must go and find some rich man of consular rank, and ask him, 'You there, can you tell me who you've entrusted your horses to?' [18] —'Yes, of course.'—'Is it to someone who just happened to come along, and knows nothing at all about horses?'—'In no way.'—'Well then, who have you entrusted your gold and silver to, or your clothes?'—'In the case of these, too, not to the first man who came along.' [19] —'And your body, have you ever thought of entrusting that to someone's care?'—'Indeed I have.'—'Doubtless to someone with expert knowledge, in physical training or medicine?'—'Absolutely.' [20] —'Are these your most valuable possessions, or do you have something that is better than all of them?'—'What do you mean?'—'Something, by Zeus, that makes use of those other things, and puts each of them to the test, and deliberates about them?'—'You're presumably referring to the mind?' [21] —'You suppose rightly; that is exactly what I'm thinking of.'—'By Zeus, I really do regard it as being much superior to anything else that I possess.' [22] —'Can you tell me, then, how you look after your mind? For it is hardly possible that a man as wise as yourself, who is so highly respected in the city, will have been so careless as to neglect his most valuable possession and let it go to ruin.' [23] —'Certainly not.'—'But have you indeed taken care of it? [24] And did you learn how to do so from somebody else, or did you discover it for yourself?' At this point the danger arises that he may first exclaim, 'Is that any business of yours, sir? Who are you to me?', and then, if you continue to pester him, he may raise his fist and land a blow on you. [25] This is an enterprise that I too was once very keen to pursue, until I fell into such difficulties.

2.13 *About anxiety*

[1] When I see someone in a state of anxiety, I say, 'What is it that he wants?' For unless he wanted something that was not within his power, how could he still be anxious? [2] That is why a lyre-player* feels no anxiety when singing on his own, but becomes anxious when he enters the theatre, even if he has a fine voice and plays his instrument well. For he wants not only to sing well, but also to win the approval of his audience, and that is something that lies beyond his

control. [3] Where he has skill, then, he has self-assurance too; bring any layman you please in front of him and he won't be concerned; but where it is a case of something that he doesn't know and has never studied, there he feels anxious. [4] So what does this mean? That he doesn't know what a crowd is, or the applause of a crowd. He has learned, to be sure, how to strike the low and high notes, but what the praise of the mass of people is, and what value it holds in life, these are things that he neither knows nor has ever studied. [5] So here he is bound to tremble and turn pale.

I cannot say that someone isn't a lyre-player when I see him in a state of fear, but I can say something else about him, and not just one thing alone, but a number of things. [6] First of all, I call him a stranger and say: this man doesn't know where on earth he is, but although he has been living here all this time, he has no knowledge of the laws of the city and its customs, and of what is permitted and what is not. And, moreover, he has never consulted a lawyer who could tell him and explain what the laws allow. [7] And yet he'd never write a will without knowing how it ought to be written, or else consulting an expert, nor does he act any differently when setting his seal on a bond or signing a guarantee. He exercises his desires and aversions, however, without any advice from a lawyer, and so too his motives and intentions and purposes. [8] And what do I mean by saying, 'Without advice from a lawyer'? Why, that he doesn't know that he wants things that he's not allowed to have, and doesn't want things that he's bound to have, and doesn't know, moreover, what rightly belongs to him or what belongs to others. For if he knew that, he'd never feel hindered, and never feel constrained, and wouldn't fall prey to anxiety. [9] How could it be otherwise? Does anyone feel afraid of things that aren't bad?

'No.'

Well, is one afraid of things that are bad, but that one is in a position to prevent?

'Not at all.'

[10] If the things, then, that lie outside the sphere of choice are neither good nor bad, and those that lie within the sphere of choice are subject to our control, and no one can either take those away from us or impose them on us unless we wish it, what room is left for anxiety? [11] But we're anxious about this poor body of ours, or our petty possessions, or about what Caesar will think, and not in the

least about the things that lie within us. Are we ever anxious about coming to accept a false opinion?

'No, because that is subject to my control.'

Or about coming to have motives that are contrary to nature?

'No again.'

[12] Whenever you see someone who is pale from anxiety, then, just as a doctor infers from somebody's complexion, 'That man is suffering in his spleen, and that one in his liver,' you should declare likewise, 'That man is suffering in his desire and aversion; he is not at all well; he is feverish.' [13] For there is nothing else that changes a man's complexion in that way, or makes him shiver, or sets his teeth chattering, or makes him '*Shift from leg to leg and squat on one foot and then the other.*'*

[14] Zeno was thus in no way anxious when he was about to meet Antigonus;* for Antigonus had no power over the things that he valued, and the things that Antigonus did have power over were of no concern to him. [15] Antigonus for his part did feel anxious when he was about to meet Zeno, and with good reason, since he wanted to please him, and that lay beyond his control. But Zeno had no desire to please Antigonus, any more than any other expert wants to please a layman. [16] For my own part, do I want to please you? What would I gain by it? Do you have any knowledge of the standards by which one person can judge another? Have you made any effort to understand what a good person is, and a bad one, and how each comes to be as he is? Why is it, then, that you yourself are not a good man?

[17] 'And how am I not so,' he says.

Because no good man grieves or groans or laments, no good man turns pale and trembles and says, 'How will he receive me, what sort of a hearing will he give me?' [18] He'll act, you slave, as he thinks fit. Why should you be concerned about other people's business? Now isn't it his own fault if he responds badly to what you have to say?—'Surely so.'—Is it possible for one person to make an error and another to suffer the harm?—'No.'—Why are you anxious, then, about other people's business? [19] —'Yes, but I'm anxious about how I'll speak to him.'—What, isn't it in your power to speak to him just as you wish?—'But I'm afraid that I'll lose my composure.'
[20] —If you were going to write the name 'Dion', would you have that fear?—'Not at all.'—Why not? Isn't it because you have studied how to write?—'Exactly.'—What, then, if you're going to read,

won't you be in the same position?—'Just the same.'—What is the
reason, then? Why, it is because every art brings a certain strength
and confidence within its own field. [21] Haven't you studied how to
speak? And what else did you study at school?

'Syllogisms and equivocal arguments.'

With what end in view? Wasn't it to enable you to conduct an
argument with skill? Which means being able to do so at the right
time, in an assured and intelligent manner, without making mistakes
or being caught out, and in addition to all this, with confidence?

'Yes indeed.'

[22] Now if you're a horseman who has ridden down onto level
ground to confront a foot-soldier, will you feel any anxiety, if you've
practised this form of warfare and he hasn't?

'Perhaps not, but Caesar has the power to take my life.'

[23] Then tell the truth, you wretch, and instead of bragging as you
do, don't claim to be a philosopher, and don't fail to recognize who
your masters are, but as long as you let them have this hold on you
through your body, place yourself at the beck and call of everyone
who is stronger than you. [24] Now Socrates had learned to speak as
one ought, to be able to speak as he did to the tyrants, to his judges,
and in prison. Diogenes had learned to speak as one ought, to be able
to speak as he did to Alexander, to Philip, to the pirates, to the man
who bought him as a slave.* [25] Leave these matters to those who are
properly prepared for them, to those with courage. [26] As for you,
turn to your own affairs and never depart from them. Go and sit in
a corner, and construct syllogisms, and propose them to others—
'*In you assuredly there is no captain of a state.*'*

2.14 *To Naso*

[1] One day, when a certain Roman had come in with his son and was
listening to one of his lectures, Epictetus said, This is the character of
my teaching, but then fell silent. [2] But when the man asked him to
continue, he went on: When one is trying to pass on knowledge of any
art, it is tiresome for a layman who is unacquainted with it. [3] The
products of the arts, however, immediately reveal what use they are in
relation to the end that they have been made to serve, and in most
cases, moreover, they have a certain appeal and charm. [4] Although
it is none too enjoyable, for instance, to stand by and watch how a

shoemaker learns his art, the shoe that he makes is useful, and is, besides, not unattractive to look at. [5] And the way in which a carpenter learns his work is altogether tiresome to observe for a layman who happens to be there, but the products of his work reveal the usefulness of his art. [6] You will find this even more apparent in the case of music. If you're present when someone is being taught that art, the process will strike you as the most unpleasant of all to observe, and yet the products of the art of music are most appealing to laymen, and a delight to hear.

[7] So also in our case, we picture the work of the philosopher as being something like this, that he should adapt his own will to what comes about so that nothing happens against our will, and so that nothing fails to happen when we want it to happen. [8] It follows that those who have engaged properly in this task will never be disappointed in their desires, or fall into what they want to avoid, but will live a life free from pain, fear, and distress, and will maintain, furthermore, in their social dealings, both their natural and their required relationships, as son, father, brother, citizen, man, woman, neighbour, fellow-traveller, ruler, and subject.

[9] The task of the philosopher we picture, then, as being something of that kind. The next thing that we need to examine is how this may be accomplished. [10] Now, we see that a carpenter becomes a carpenter by acquiring a certain kind of knowledge, and that a pilot becomes a pilot by acquiring a certain kind of knowledge. In view of that, isn't it likely that in our case too, it can't be sufficient merely to want to become a virtuous and good person, but that it is also necessary to acquire some kind of knowledge? So we must try to find out which. [11] The philosophers say that the first thing that needs to be learned is the following, that there is a God, and a God who exercises providential care for the universe, and that it is impossible to conceal from him not only our actions, but even our thoughts and intentions. The next thing to be considered is what the gods are like; [12] for whatever they're discovered to be, one who wishes to please and obey them must try to resemble them as far as possible. [13] If the deity is trustworthy, he too must be trustworthy; if free, he too must be free; if beneficent, he too must be beneficent; if magnanimous, he too must be magnanimous. And so thenceforth, in all that he says and does, he must act in imitation of God.

[14] 'Where are we to start, then?'

If you'll agree, I'll tell you that you must start by understanding the meaning of terms.

[15] 'So you mean to say that I don't understand them at present?' Indeed you don't.

'Then how is it that I can make use of them?'

You use them in the same way as illiterate people use written speech, and cattle use sense-impressions; for use is one thing, and understanding is another. [16] If you imagine, however, that you have the necessary understanding, take any term you wish, and let's put ourselves to the test to see if we understand it.

[17] 'But it's tiresome to be subjected to such an examination when one's already of quite an age, and, as it happens, one has served in three campaigns.'

[18] I know that very well, since you came to me just now like a man who doesn't stand in need of anything. After all, what could you even suppose that you have need of? You're wealthy, you quite possibly have a wife and children and any number of servants. Caesar knows you, you have plenty of friends in Rome, you fulfil your duties, you know how to repay a favour and avenge an injury. [19] What is it that you lack? So if I show you that you lack what is most essential and important for happiness, and that up until now you have occupied yourself with everything other than what is proper for you, and I should add, to cap it all, that you know neither what God is, nor what a human being is, nor what is good, nor what is bad [20] —if I say that you're ignorant of these other matters, you may perhaps be able to put up with that, but if I say that you don't even know yourself, how will you be able to bear with me and submit to my questioning, and stay in this room? [21] In no way, you'd immediately take offence and leave. And yet, what wrong have I done you? None, unless a mirror also wrongs an ugly man by showing him what he looks like; and unless a doctor can be thought to be insulting a patient when he says to him, 'You think there's nothing wrong with you, my friend, but you have a fever. Eat nothing today, and drink water alone.' No one would think fit to cry out here, 'What insufferable impertinence!'; [22] yet if you say to somebody, 'Your desires are inflamed, your aversions are low, your purposes are inconsistent, your motives are out of harmony with nature, your opinions are ill-considered and mistaken,' he immediately walks out, exclaiming, 'You've insulted me!'

[23] Our situation is like that at a festival.* Sheep and cattle are driven to it to be sold, and most people come either to buy or to sell, while only a few come to look at the spectacle of the festival, to see how it is proceeding and why, and who is organizing it, and for what purpose. [24] So also in this festival of the world. Some people are like sheep and cattle and are interested in nothing but their fodder; for in the case of those of you who are interested in nothing but your property, and land, and slaves, and public posts, all of that is nothing more than fodder. [25] Few indeed are those who attend the fair for love of the spectacle, asking, 'What is the universe, then, and who governs it? No one at all? [26] And yet when a city or household cannot survive for even a very short time without someone to govern it and watch over it, how could it be that such a vast and beautiful structure could be kept so well ordered by mere chance and good luck? [27] So there must be someone governing it. What sort of being is he, and how does he govern it? And we who have been created by him, who are we, and what were we created for? Are we bound together with him in some kind of union and interrelationship, or is that not the case?'

[28] Such are the thoughts that are aroused in this small collection of people; and from then on, they devote their leisure to this one thing alone, to finding out about the festival before they have to take their leave. [29] What comes about, then? They become an object of mockery for the crowd, just as the spectators at an ordinary festival are mocked by the traders; and even the sheep and cattle, if they had sufficient intelligence, would laugh at those who attach value to anything other than fodder!

2.15 *To those who hold stubbornly to certain decisions that they have reached*

[1] Some people, when they hear such arguments as these, that one should be steadfast, that choice is free by nature and not subject to constraint, whereas everything else is subject to hindrance and constraint, and in bondage and subject to others, imagine that they must always adhere unswervingly to every judgement that they have formed. [2] But it is necessary first of all that the judgement should be a sound one. Yes, I want the body to be strong, but with a vigour of the kind that is found in a healthy man, an athlete; [3] but if you show me that you have the vigour of a madman and boast about that, I'll tell

you, 'Find someone to cure you, man, this isn't vigour but just another kind of enervation.'

[4] It is something of this kind that people feel in their mind when they misinterpret these arguments. Thus, a friend of mine decided, for no proper reason, to starve himself to death. [5] I heard of this when he was already in that third day of his fast, and went and asked him what had happened. [6] 'I've decided to take this course,' he said. Yes, but all the same, what was it that moved you to do so? If your decision is justified, look, here we are at your side and ready to help you on your way; but if your decision is unreasonable, you ought to change it. [7] —'We ought to hold to our decisions.'—What are you up to, man? Not to every decision, but to those that are justified. If you now arrive at the notion, for instance, that night has come, don't change your opinion if it pleases you to think that, but hold to it and say that one ought to hold to what one has decided! [8] Don't you wish to lay a firm foundation at the beginning, by examining whether or not your decision is sound, and then go on to establish your firm and unwavering resolve on that foundation? [9] But if you lay down a rotten and crumbling foundation, you shouldn't try to build on that, but the bigger and stronger the edifice that you heap upon it, the sooner it will come tumbling down. [10] Without any reason at all, you're removing from the world a friend, a companion, a fellow citizen of the great city and the small. [11] What is more, while carrying out a murder and destroying a man who has committed no wrong, you say that you must hold to your decisions! [12] If the idea happened to enter your head to kill me, would you still have to hold to your decision?

[13] With some difficulty, it proved possible to change this man's mind; but there are some people nowadays who aren't open to persuasion. So I think that I can now understand, as formerly I couldn't, the meaning of the proverb 'A fool can be neither bent nor broken'. [14] May heaven preserve me from having for a friend a 'sage' who is no better than a fool! Nothing could be more difficult to deal with. 'I've made my decision.' Why, so have madmen too, and the more firmly they hold to their baseless decisions, the more they stand in need of a dose of medication! [15] Why won't you act like someone who is ill and call for a doctor? 'I'm ill, sir, come to my aid; look and see what I ought to do; it's for me to obey you.'

[16] So also in the present case. 'I don't know what I ought to do

and I've come to find out.' But no, he says instead, 'Talk to me about other things, I've made up my mind about this.' [17] About what other things? What could be more important and valuable than to persuade you that it is not enough to make a decision and refuse to change it. That is the strength of a madman and not of a healthy man. [18] 'I'm willing to die, if you compel me to it.' Why, man? What has happened? 'I've made up my mind.' It's lucky you haven't decided to put *me* to death! [19] 'I won't accept any pay.' Why? 'I've made up my mind.' You may be sure of this, that there is nothing to prevent you from yielding to an irrational inclination one day to accept the money, and then with the same strength that you're now applying in refusing to accept it, you'll say once again, 'I've made up my mind'; [20] for just as in a sick body that is suffering from a flux of humours, the flux will incline now in one direction, now in another, so also in the case of an enfeebled mind, one can never be sure in what direction it is tending; but if strength is added to this inclination and flux, the evil will become fixed beyond help and cure.

2.16 *That we fail to practise the application of our judgements about things that are good and bad*

[1] Where does the good lie? 'In choice.' Where does the bad lie? 'In choice.' And that which is neither good nor bad? 'In things that lie outside the sphere of choice.'

[2] Well then, who of us remembers these principles outside this room? Who of us practises of his own accord to respond to facts in the same way as he would respond to these questions: 'It is day, isn't it?'—'Yes.'—'Well, is it night?'—'No.'—'Or again, are the stars even in number?'—'I can't say.'

[3] When you're shown some money, have you trained yourself to make the right response, that 'It is not a good thing'? Have you trained yourself in replies of this kind, or merely in replying to sophistic arguments? [4] Why should you be surprised, then, that you excel in the areas in which you have practised, while you remain exactly the same in those in which you haven't? [5] Why is it, for instance, that an orator who knows that he has written a good speech, and has fixed it in his memory, and is bringing an attractive voice to the task, still feels anxious nonetheless? Because he is not content merely to practise his art. [6] What else does he want, then? To receive

praise from his audience. Now the matter in which he has trained himself is to be able to practise his art, and he has never trained himself to deal with praise and censure. [7] For when has he heard anything from anyone about what praise is, and what censure is, and what is the nature of each? And what kinds of praise are worth seeking, and what kinds of disapproval are to be avoided? When has he ever undergone any course of training with regard to these principles? [8] Why are you still surprised, then, that he excels other people in the areas in which he has studied and learned, but is no different from the multitude in those in which he has not? [9] He is rather like a lyre-player who knows how to play his instrument, and sings well and has fine robes to wear, but trembles nonetheless when he has to come on stage. Yes, he knows all of that, but he doesn't know what a crowd is, or understand the nature of its shouts and jeers. [10] He doesn't know, indeed, what this anxiety itself is, and whether we ourselves are responsible for it or other people are, and whether or not it lies in our power to put a stop to it. And so he leaves the stage puffed up with pride if he receives applause, but his conceit is soon pricked and deflated if he meets with jeers.

[11] We too experience something of this kind. What do we admire? Externals. What do we make the prime object of our concern? Externals. And then we're unable to grasp how it is that we fall prey to fear, or fall prey to anxiety. [12] What else could possibly come about when we regard things that bear down on us as being bad? We can't fail to be afraid, we can't fail to be anxious. [13] And then we say, 'Lord God, how can I break free of anxiety?' Can it be that you have no hands, fool? Perhaps God didn't make any for you? Then sit down and pray that your nose doesn't run! Or rather, wipe your nose and stop making accusations.

What, has God given you nothing to help you in this predicament? [14] Hasn't he given you endurance? Hasn't he given you greatness of soul? Hasn't he given you courage? And yet, being equipped with the hands that you have, do you still look for someone else to wipe your nose? [15] But we devote no effort to any of this, we pay no attention to it.

Come now, show me a single person who cares how he does what he does, and is concerned not about the result that he can achieve, but about the action itself. Who, when walking around, is concerned about the action itself? Who, when deliberating, is concerned about the deliberation itself, rather than the result that he is hoping to attain through it? [16] If he attains that result, he is full of pride and says, 'Our deliberations have turned out well!' Didn't I tell you, brother, that it is impossible for something not to turn out well when we've properly considered it? But if the matter turns out differently than he'd wanted, the poor wretch is cast into dejection, and can find no possible explanation for what has come about. Who of you has never called on the help of a diviner in cases such as this? [17] Who of you has never slept in a temple* to find out the right course of action? Who? Show me just a single man, so that I may see that man whom I've been seeking for so long, one who is truly noble-minded and gifted; whether he be young or old, show him to me.

[18] Why are we still surprised, then, that if we're engrossed with material things, we're mean, disgraceful, worthless, cowardly, and listless in our actions, and turn out to be complete failures? For we've never paid any attention to these matters and don't take any trouble over them. [19] If it hadn't been death or banishment that we were afraid of, but fear itself, we would have trained ourselves not to fall into those states of mind that seem bad to us. [20] But as things are, we're animated and glib in the schoolroom, and if the smallest question arises about any of these matters, we're able to work out the logical consequences; but drag us into any practical action, and you'll find us to be miserably shipwrecked. Only let a disturbing impression assail us and you'll know what we've been studying, and what we've been training for! [21] And thus, because of our lack of practice, we're always piling up difficulties for ourselves and imagining them to be greater than they really are. [22] So, when I sail out to sea, and I peer down into the depths, or look at the waters all around and see no sign of land, I immediately lose my composure, and imagine that I'll have to swallow all that sea-water if the ship goes down; it never occurs to me that three pints would be enough! What is it, then, that is troubling my mind? The sea? No, my own judgement. [23] Or again, when there is an earthquake, I imagine that the whole town is about to crash down on me. And yet, wouldn't one small stone be enough to knock my brains out?

[24] What is it, then, that weighs down on us and makes us lose our minds? What else than our judgements? For when someone leaves his country and becomes separated from everything that he is accustomed to, comrades, places, and social relationships, what else

weighs down on him than his judgement? [25] When infants begin to
cry because their nurse has gone some small distance away, they
have only to receive a piece of honey-cake to forget their distress.
[26] Do you wish, then, that we too should be like little children? No,
by Zeus. For it is not a cake that should have this effect on us, I
think, but true judgements. [27] And what are they? Those that a
person should reflect upon all day long, so that, feeling no attachment to anything that is not his own, whether comrade, or place, or
gymnasium, or indeed his own body, he may keep the law constantly
in mind and have it forever before his eyes. [28] What law? That of
God; to preserve what is his own, and not lay claim to what is not his
own, but to make use of what is granted to him, and not long for
what is not granted; if anything is taken away from him, to surrender it willingly, and be grateful for the time in which he has enjoyed
the use of it—if you don't want to be crying after your nurse and
mummy! [29] For what difference does it make what we become subjected to and come to depend on? How are you superior to a man
who weeps over a girl if you weep for a wretched gymnasium, or
colonnade, or bunch of young men, and other such things to take up
your time? [30] Someone else comes along and laments that he can no
longer drink the waters of Dirce. And yet, is the water of the Marcian
aqueduct* any worse than that of the Dircean spring?

   'But I was used to that.'

   And you'll get used to this water in turn; [31] and then, if you allow
yourself to get attached to something like that, weep for that in turn,
and try to compose a verse like that of Euripides, '*The baths of Nero
and the Marcian water.*'* See how a tragedy arises when fools are
affected by everyday events! [32] 'Ah, when shall I see Athens and the
Acropolis once again!' Poor wretch, aren't you contented with what
you see every day? Can you see anything better or greater than the
sun, the moon, the stars, the entire earth, the sea? [33] And if you
understand the one who governs the universe, and carry him around
within you, why should you still yearn for some pieces of stone and a
pretty rock?* What will you do, then, when you have to leave even
the sun and the moon? Will you sit down and weep like a small child?
[34] What did you do at school, then; what did you hear; what did you
learn? Why do you mark yourself down as a philosopher when you
might have recorded the truth by writing, 'I've studied a few introductory works and I've read a bit of Chrysippus, but I haven't even

passed through the door of philosophy. [35] What part could I indeed play in that enterprise in which Socrates played such a part, to die as he died and live as he lived? And in which Diogenes played such a part?' [36] Can you imagine either of them weeping or becoming aggravated because he'll no longer be seeing someone or other, or because he'll no longer be living at Athens or Corinth but at Susa, perhaps, or Ecbatana? [37] If he is free to leave the banquet whenever he pleases and abandon the game, will such a man lament while he remains? Won't he stay as one does in a game, only as long as it continues to amuse him? [38] Such a man could surely face up to permanent exile, or to death, if he were to be condemned to that. [39] Aren't you willing to be weaned at last, as children are, and take in more solid food, without crying out for their mummies and nurses.

[40] 'But if I go away, I'll distress them.'

What, you'll cause distress to them? In no way, but rather, as in your own case, it will be their own judgement that brings that about. What is to be done, then? You must get rid of this judgement, and they for their part, if they so wish, would do well to get rid of theirs; or otherwise, it will be their fault if they grieve. [41] As the expression goes, be ready to lose your head, man, for the sake of happiness, for the sake of freedom, for the sake of greatness of soul. Raise up your head at last as one who has been freed from slavery; [42] dare to raise up your eyes towards God and say to him, 'Use me just as you will from this time onward; I'm of one mind with you; I'm yours. I refuse nothing that seems good to you. Lead me where you will, wrap me in whatever clothes you wish. Is it your wish that I should hold office, or remain a private citizen, that I should stay here, or go into exile, that I should be poor, or rich? I'll defend you before my fellow men in every case; [43] I'll show what the true nature of each thing is.'

[44] No, but rather, go and sit inside like a girl, and wait for your mummy to come and feed you. If Heracles* had sat around at home with his family, what would he have been? A Eurystheus, and in no way a Heracles. Come now, as he travelled through the world, how many comrades did he have with him, how many friends? But he had no dearer friend than God; and for that reason, he was believed to be a son of God, as indeed he was. It was accordingly in obedience to him that he travelled around the world purging it of injustice and lawlessness. [45] But you're no Heracles and you can't purge others of

their ills; indeed, you're not even a Theseus to be able to purge Attica of its ills. So purge yourself of your own, and instead of casting out a Procrustes or Sciron,* cast fear and distress from your mind, along with desire, envy, malice, avarice, effeminacy, and intemperance. [46] These you cannot cast out in any other way than by lifting up your eyes to God alone, and devoting yourself to him alone, and faithfully carrying out his commands. [47] If you wish for anything else, though, you'll end up following, with groans and laments, whatever is stronger than you are, because you'll always be seeking your happiness in things outside yourself, without ever being able to find it; for you're looking for happiness where it is not to be found, and are failing to search for it where it actually lies.

2.17 *How we should adapt our preconceptions to particular cases*

[1] What is the first task for someone who is practising philosophy? To rid himself of presumption: for it is impossible for anyone to set out to learn what he thinks he already knows. [2] When we go to visit philosophers, we all chatter freely about what one should do or not do, about good and bad, or about what is right or wrong, and so apportion praise and blame, criticism and reproach, and distinguish some actions as being admirable and others as shameful. [3] But what is it that we go to philosophers for? To learn what we don't suppose that we know. And what is that? General principles. Some like to learn what philosophers are saying because they expect it to be sharp and witty, and others because they hope to gain some profit from it. [4] Now it is ridiculous to suppose that when somebody wants to learn one thing, he will in fact learn something else, or, moreover, that he will make progress in things that he doesn't learn. [5] But most people make the same mistake as the orator Theopompus, who criticized Plato for wanting to define each particular term. [6] What did he say, then? 'Before you came along, did no one ever use the words "good" or "just"? Or did we merely utter them as empty sounds devoid of meaning, without understanding what each of them meant?' [7] Why, who has ever told you, Theopompus, that we don't have natural ideas and preconceptions relating to each of these terms? But it is impossible for us to adapt these preconceptions to the corresponding realities unless we have subjected them to systematic examination, to determine which reality should be ranged under which preconception.

[8] One could, for instance, say the same kind of thing to doctors too: 'Did none of us talk about being "healthy" or "diseased" before Hippocrates came along? Or were we merely uttering empty sounds when doing so?' [9] The fact is that we have a certain preconception of what it means to be 'healthy' too, but aren't able to apply it properly. That is why one person says, 'Continue with the diet,' while another says, 'Give him some food now,' or one says, 'Bleed him,' while another says, 'Apply a cupping-glass.' And what is the reason? Is it anything other than the fact that we're unable to apply our preconceived idea of the 'healthy' to particular cases?

[10] The same also applies to the affairs of life. Who among us doesn't talk about 'good' and 'bad', and about what is 'advantageous' or 'disadvantageous'? For who among us doesn't have a preconception of each of these things? Is it properly understood, however, and complete? Show me that it is. [11] How am I to show that? By applying it properly to particular cases. Plato, for instance, classifies his definitions under the preconception of the 'useful', but you under that of the 'useless'. [12] Now is it possible that both of you could be right? How could it be? Or again, with regard to wealth, doesn't one person apply the preconception of the 'good' to it, while another doesn't? And likewise with regard to pleasure, and likewise with regard to health? [13] In general, then, if all who utter these terms possessed more than an empty knowledge of each, and we didn't need to set to work to make a systematic examination of our preconceptions, why do we disagree, why do we come into conflict, why do we criticize one another?

[14] And yet why do I need to point to this mutual conflict and call that to mind? For in your own case, if you know how to apply your preconceptions properly, why is it that you are troubled, that you are frustrated? [15] For the present, let's leave aside the second field of study, relating to motives and how they may be appropriately regulated; and let's also leave aside the third, relating to assent. [16] I'll let you off all of that. Let's concentrate on the first field,* which will provide us with almost palpable proof that you don't know how to apply your preconceptions properly. [17] Do you presently desire what is possible, and what is possible for you in particular? Why, then, are you frustrated? Why are you troubled? Aren't you presently trying to avoid what is inevitable? Why do you fall, then, into difficulties of any kind, why do you suffer misfortune? Why is it that when you want

something, it doesn't come about, and when you don't want it, it comes about? [18] For that is a very strong proof that you're in a troubled and unfortunate state. I want something and it doesn't come about: who could be more wretched than I? I don't want something and it comes about: who could be more wretched than I? [19] It was because she was unable to endure this that Medea murdered her children. And in this regard at least, she showed a certain greatness of mind, in having a due conception of what it means to be disappointed in one's desire. [20] 'Well then, I'll exact vengeance in this way on the man who has wronged and insulted me. And what shall I gain from putting him into such a miserable plight? How can it be achieved? I'll kill my children. By doing that, I'll also be punishing myself. But what do I care?'* [21] This is the error of a mind that was endowed with great inner strength. For she didn't know where the power lies to do what we wish, that it can't be acquired from outside ourselves, or through the alteration and rearranging of things. [22] Have no desire for that man, and nothing that you desire will fail to come about. Don't wish at any price that he should continue to live with you, don't wish that you'll be able to remain in Corinth, and, in a word, don't wish for anything other than what God wishes. And who will be able to obstruct you then, who will be able to constrain you? No one at all, any more than he could obstruct or compel Zeus.

[23] When you have such a leader, and conform your will and desires to his, what reason do you still have to fear that you may not succeed? [24] Attach your desire and aversion to wealth and property, and you'll fail to get what you desire, and you'll fall into what you want to avoid. Attach them to health, and you'll fall into misfortune, and likewise if you attach them to public office, honours, your country, friends, children, and, in a word, to anything that lies outside the sphere of choice. [25] No, you should attach them, rather, to Zeus, and the other gods. Consign them to their care, for them to govern, and to be ordered in accordance with their will; [26] and how will you then be troubled any longer? But if you continue to feel envy, poor wretch, and pity, jealousy, and fear, and never let a day pass by without lamenting within yourself and before the gods, how can you still claim to have received a proper education? [27] What sort of education, man? Because you've handled syllogisms and equivocal arguments? Aren't you willing to unlearn all of that, if it is possible, and start afresh from the beginning, in the realization that as yet you

haven't even scratched the surface; [28] and then, starting off from this point, build everything up in due order, so that nothing may come about against your wish, and nothing that you wish may fail to come about?

[29] Give me just one young man who has come to the school with this aim in mind, who has become an athlete in this field of action, and declares, 'I for my part bid farewell to all the rest; it is enough for me to live my life free from hindrance and distress, and to be able to hold my head high in the face of events, like a free person, and to look up to heaven like a friend of God, showing no fear of anything that could come about. [30] May one of you show himself to be such a person, so that I can say, 'Enter, young man, into what is your own, for you are destined to become an adornment to philosophy; yours are these goods, yours these books, yours these discourses.' [31] And then, when he has laboured in this fine field of study and proved his mastery, let him come back to me and say, 'I want indeed to be free from passion and disturbance of mind, but I also want, as a pious person, a philosopher, and a diligent student, to know what my duty is towards the gods, towards my parents, towards my brother, towards my country, and towards strangers.' [32] Pass on now to the second field of study; for that too is yours.

[33] 'But I've already studied this second field. What I wanted was to be secure and unshakeable in my knowledge of it, and not only when I'm awake, but when I'm asleep, when I'm drunk, and even when I'm thoroughly depressed.'

Man. You're a god, to harbour such ambitions!

[34] No, one hears nothing like that, but rather, 'I want to know what Chrysippus has to say in his treatise about "the Liar".'* Why don't you go off and hang yourself, you wretch, if that is really what you want? And what good will it do you to know it? You'll read the whole book from one end to the other while grieving all the while, and you'll be trembling when you expound it to others. [35] And the rest of you behave like that too. 'Would you like me to read something out, brother, and you can do so for me in turn?'—'My friend, you write astoundingly well.'—'And so do you, splendidly, quite in the style of Xenophon.' [36] —'And you in the style of Plato.'—'And you in the style of Antisthenes.'* And then, when you've recounted your dreams to one another, you fall back into the same old faults; you have the same desires as before, the same aversions, the same

motives, plans, and intentions, you ask for the same things in your prayers, and have the same preoccupations. [37] And furthermore, instead of looking around for someone who could offer you some advice, you get annoyed if you hear such advice as this. 'What a mean-minded old man,' you say; 'he didn't shed a tear when I left, nor did he say, "That's an awkward situation you're going off to face, my son; I'll light some candles if you come through safely."' [38] Is that the language of a kind-hearted man? It will be a wonderfully good thing for someone like you to come through safely, and one that would truly deserve to be greeted with candles! You surely ought to be absolved from death and disease!

[39] We really must put aside this presumption that we know something worthwhile, as I've already said, before proceeding to philosophy, as we do when we're approaching the study of geometry or music, [40] otherwise we'll not even come close to making any progress, even if we read through all the introductions and treatise of Chrysippus, together with those of Antipater and Archedemus* too!

2.18 *How we should struggle against impressions*

[1] Every habit and capacity is supported and strengthened by the corresponding actions, that of walking by walking, that of running by running. [2] If you want to be a good reader, read, or a good writer, write. But if you pass thirty days without reading and turn to something else, you'll notice the consequences. [3] So also if you lie in bed for ten days, and then get up and try to walk a fair distance, you'll see how weak your legs are. [4] In general, then, if you want to do something, make a habit of doing it; and if you don't want to do something, don't do it, but get into the habit of doing something else instead. [5] The same also applies to states of mind. When you lose your temper, you should recognize not only that something has happened to you at present, but also that you've reinforced a bad habit, and you have, so to speak, added fresh fuel to the fire. [6] When you've yielded to sexual desire, don't count that as being just a slight defeat, but recognize that you've fortified your incontinence, you've given it added strength. [7] For it cannot fail to come about that, as a result of the corresponding actions, some habits and capacities will be developed if they didn't previously exist, while others that were already present will be reinforced and strengthened.

[8] It is in this way, of course, that moral infirmities grow up in the mind, as the philosophers explain. For once you've come to feel a desire for money, if reason is brought to bear in such a way as to make us become aware of the evil, the desire will be suppressed and our ruling centre will be restored to its original authority; [9] but if you apply no remedy, it won't return to its original state, but when it comes to be aroused again by the corresponding impression, it will become inflamed by desire more rapidly than before. And if this happens repeatedly, a callus will finally be formed, and the infirmity will cause the avarice to become entrenched. [10] For if someone has had a fever and then recovered, he is not in the same state as he was before having the fever, unless he is completely cured; [11] and something similar happens with affections of the mind too. Scars and bruises are left behind on it, and if one doesn't erase them completely, it will no longer be bruises that are found there when one receives further blows on that spot, but wounds. [12] If you don't want to be bad-tempered, then don't feed the habit, throw nothing before it on which it can feed and grow. First of all, keep calm, and count the days in which you haven't lost your temper [13] —'I used to lose my temper every day, and after that, every other day, then every third day, then every fourth'—and if you continue in that way for thirty days, offer a sacrifice to God. For the habit is first weakened, and then completely destroyed. [14] 'Today I didn't allow myself to feel any distress, nor on the following day, nor successively for two or three months, but kept on my guard when anything happened that might excite distress in me.' You should know that things are going nicely for you. [15] 'Today, when I saw an attractive boy or woman, I didn't say to myself, "Oh if only one could sleep with her," or, "Her husband's a happy man"; for someone who says that might as well say, "Happy is the adulterer." [16] I didn't even go on to picture what follows next, the woman being with me, and undressing, and lying down beside me. [17] I pat myself on the head and say, "Well done, Epictetus, you've found a solution to a clever sophism, even cleverer than the one they call 'the Master'."* [18] But if the girl is willing, and gives me the nod and sends for me, and also grabs me, and presses herself against me, and I still hold off and prevail, I would then have resolved a sophism even cleverer that that of "the Liar" or "the Silent One"!* Now that is something that one could rightly take pride in, rather than in having posed the problem of "the Master".'

[19] How is this to be achieved, then? Make it your wish finally to be contented with yourself, make it your wish to appear beautiful in the sight of God; you must aspire to become pure in accord with what is pure in yourself and in accord with God. [20] 'Then whenever an impression of that kind assails you,' says Plato, 'go and offer an expiatory sacrifice; go as a suppliant to the temples of the gods who avert evil; [21] it is indeed sufficient merely to withdraw to the company of wise and virtuous men,'* and to examine their life by comparison with theirs, whether you choose your model from among the living or from among the dead. [22] Go to Socrates and watch him as he lies down beside Alcibiades and makes fun of his youthful beauty; consider what a victory it was that he won,* as he himself recognized, a victory worthy of Olympia, and how he thus ranked among the successors of Heracles!* So that, by the gods, one could rightly greet him with the words, 'Hail wondrous man!', rather than those ghastly boxers and pancratiasts,* and the gladiators who resemble them. [23] If you muster these thoughts against it, you'll overpower your impression and not be swept away by it. [24] But first of all, don't allow yourself to be dazed by the rapidity of the impact, but say, 'Wait a while for me, my impression, let me see what you are, and what you're an impression of; let me test you out.' [25] And then don't allow it to lead you on by making you picture all that may follow, or else it will take possession of you and conduct you wherever it wants. But rather, introduce some fine and noble impression in place of it, and cast out this impure one. [26] If you get into the habit of carrying out such exercises, you'll see what shoulders you'll develop, and what muscles, and what strength. But for the present, all of this is empty talk and nothing more.

[27] Here is the true athlete, one who trains himself to confront such impressions! Hold firm, poor man, don't allow yourself to be carried away. [28] Great is the struggle, and divine the enterprise, to win a kingdom, to win freedom, to win happiness, to win peace of mind. [29] Remember God, call upon his aid and support, as sailors call upon the Dioscuri* in a storm. For what storm is mightier than that aroused by powerful impressions that drive out reason? What else, indeed, is the storm itself than an impression? [30] For take away the fear of death, and then bring on as much thunder and lightning as you wish, and you'll see what peace and serenity will prevail in your ruling centre. [31] But if you're defeated on one occasion and say that

you'll win at some future time, and then allow yourself to be defeated again, you can be sure that you'll finally find yourself in such a wretched and feeble state that, in due course, you won't even be aware that you're acting wrongly, but will begin to put forward arguments to justify your behaviour; at which point, you'll be confirming the truth of Hesiod's saying that *'One who delays his work is always wrestling with ruin.'**

2.19 *To those who take up the teachings of the philosophers for the sake of talk alone*

[1] The 'Master' argument seems to have been put forward on the basis of some such principles as the following. These three propositions are irreconcilable in so far as any two contradict the one that is left over: (1) that everything that has come about in the past is necessarily the case, (2) that the impossible cannot follow from the possible, and (3) that something can be possible that is not true at present nor ever will be in the future.

Recognizing this contradiction, Diodorus* relied on the plausibility of the first two propositions to establish that 'nothing is possible that neither is nor ever will be the case'.

[2] Now, of the propositions to be selected, there are some who keep these two, (3) that something can be possible that is not true at present nor ever will be in the future, and (2) that the impossible cannot follow from the possible, but reject this one, (1) that everything that has come about in the past is necessarily the case. This seems to have been the opinion held by the school of Cleanthes, with which Antipater* was in full agreement.

[3] Others, by contrast, keep another pair of propositions, (3) that something can be possible that is not true at present nor ever will be in the future, and (1) that everything that has come about in the past is necessarily the case, and then assert that the possible can indeed follow from the possible. [4] But there is no way in which all three propositions can be maintained at the same time, because they contradict one another in the manner described.

[5] If someone asks me, then, 'For your part, which of the propositions will you keep?', I'll reply that I don't know, but I've found that Diodorus kept one pair, while the school of Panthoides,* I think, and Cleanthes kept another, the school of Chrysippus another again.

[6] 'Yes, but what's your own view?'

I wasn't made for this, to test my own impression, and then compare what is said by others and reach my own judgement about the matter. So I'm no different here from a literary scholar: [7] 'Who was the father of Hector?'—'Priam.'—'Who were his brothers?'—'Paris and Deiphobus.'—'And their mother, who was she?'—'Hecuba. Such is the account that I've received.'—'From whom?'—'From Homer.* And I think that Hellanicus* has written about these matters too, and perhaps other authors of that kind.'

[8] So likewise with me when it comes to the 'Master' argument, what more can I say about it? But if I had vanity enough, I might astonish my companions, especially at a dinner party, by enumerating all the authors who have written about the subject: [9] 'Chrysippus has written a wonderful account in the first book of his treatise *On Possibles*. And Cleanthes has written a special work on the subject, as has Archedemus.* Antipater has written about it too, not only in his treatise *On Possibles*, but also in a special discourse about "the Master". [10] Haven't you read that work?'—'No, I haven't'—'Do read it, then.' And what good will it do him? He'll have an even bigger store of empty talk and be more tedious than he is at present. For have you yourself gained anything other than that by reading it? What judgement have you formed on the subject? Yes, you'll talk to us about Helen and Priam and the island of Calypso,* which never existed and never will exist. [11] In these literary matters, to be sure, it doesn't matter greatly if one merely gains a knowledge of the recorded information without forming any judgement of one's own. But when it comes to moral questions, we're even more inclined to suffer from this fault than with regard to those literary ones. [12] 'Talk to me about what is good and bad.'—'Listen: *A wind bore me far from Ilion to the Cicyonians.*'—'How do you know?'—'Hellanicus says so in his *History of Egypt*.'

[13] 'Of things that exist, some are good, others bad, and others indifferent. Now the virtues and everything that partakes in them are good, the vices and everything that partakes in them are bad, while everything that lies between these is indifferent, that is to say, riches, health, life, death, pleasure, pain.'* [14] —'How did you come to know that?'—'Hellanicus says so in his *History of Egypt*.' What difference does it make whether you offer that reply or say that Diogenes* says so in his *Ethics*, or Chrysippus does, or Cleanthes? For have you

tested any of these ideas for yourself, and formed a judgement of your own? [15] Show me how you're accustomed to behave in a ship when confronted with a storm. Do you remember these theoretical distinctions when the sails are rattling and some mischievous bystander hears your cries of terror and says, 'Tell me, by the gods, what was it that you were saying the other day?' Is it a vice to suffer a shipwreck, surely there's nothing bad in that? [16] Won't you pick up a piece of wood to give him a beating? 'What do you have to do with me, man? We're facing death and you come and make jokes!' [17] And if Caesar sends for you to respond to an accusation, and you remember these distinctions if, as you're entering the room pale and trembling, someone comes up to you and says, 'Why are you trembling, man? What does this matter to you? Is it perhaps that in the palace here Caesar is distributing virtue and vice to those who appear before him?' [18] —'Why are you making fun of me and adding to my troubles?' —'But all the same, philosopher, tell me why you're trembling. Isn't it that you're in danger of death, or imprisonment, or bodily pain, or exile, or disgrace? Why, what else could it be? Now is any of this a vice, or anything that partakes of vice? Tell me now, what did you call these things?' [19] —'What do I have to do with you, man? My own ills are quite enough for me.' And then you're speaking rightly, for your own ills are indeed enough for you, your base character, your cowardice, and the way in which you would bluster when sitting in the schoolroom. Why do you pride yourself on qualities that you don't possess? Why do you call yourself a Stoic?

[20] Observe in this way how you conduct yourselves in all that you do, and you'll find out what philosophical school you belong to. For the most part you'll discover that you're Epicureans, or a few of you that you're Peripatetics,* and pretty feeble ones at that. [21] For where do you in fact demonstrate that you consider virtue to be of equal value, or even superior, to everything else? Show me a Stoic, if you have one among you. Where, or how? [22] Oh yes, you can show me any number who can recite all the arguments of the Stoics. But can they recite the Epicurean arguments any less well? And those of the Peripatetics, can't they explain those, too, just as accurately? [23] Who, then, is a Stoic? As we call a statue Phidian if it has been fashioned in accordance with the art of Phidias,* show me someone who has been fashioned in accordance with the judgements that he professes. [24] Show someone who is ill and yet happy, in danger and yet happy,

dying and yet happy, exiled and yet happy. Show me such a person; by the gods, how greatly I long to see a Stoic! But you can't show me anyone who has been fashioned in such a way. [25] Show me, at least, one who is in the process of formation, one who is tending in that direction. Do me that favour. Don't grudge an old man the opportunity to see a sight that he's never yet seen. [26] Do you imagine that you're going to show me the Zeus or Athena of Phidias, a work of ivory and gold? It is a human soul that one of you should show me, the soul of a man who wants to be of one mind with God, and never find fault with God or man again, and to fail in none of his desires, to fall into nothing that he wants to avoid, never to be angry, never to be envious, never to be jealous, and who—for why must one resort to circumlocution? [27] —wishes to become a god instead of a human being, and though enclosed in this poor body, this corpse, aspires to achieve communion with Zeus. Show me such a person. But you can't. Why, then, do you deceive yourselves and cheat everyone else? [28] And why do you dress in a costume that isn't your own and walk around in it, as thieves and robbers who have filched titles and properties that in no way belong to them?

[29] So here I am, your teacher, and you're here to be taught by me. And this is the task that I've laid down for myself, to set you free from every obstacle, compulsion, and restraint, to make you free, prosperous, and happy, as one who looks to God in everything, great or small. And you for your part are with me to learn these things and put them into practice. [30] Why is it, then, that you don't complete this work, if you on your side have the proper resolve, and I on mine, in addition to that resolve, have the right qualifications for the task? What is lacking? [31] When I see a craftsman who has his material ready at hand, I wait to see the final product. Now here is the craftsman, here is the material: what is it that we lack? [32] Is this something that can't be taught? No, it can be taught. Is it that it lies beyond our power, then? No, this alone of all things lies within our power. To have wealth is not within our power, nor to be healthy, nor to be of good repute, nor, in short, anything other than to make right use of impressions. This alone is by nature immune to hindrance and restraint. [33] So why do you fail to complete the work? Tell me the reason. For it must lie either in me, or in you, or in the nature of the task. Now the thing itself is possible and is the only thing that is wholly within our power. It follows, then, that the fault must lie either in me or in you,

or more truly, in both at once. [34] Well then, is it your wish that we should at last make a start here on carrying out this design? Let's lay aside all that we have done up until now. Let's just make a start, and believe me, you'll see.

2.20 *Against the Epicureans and Academics*

[1] Propositions that are true and evident must necessarily be used even by those who contradict them; and just about the strongest proof that one could offer of a proposition being evident is the fact that even one who contradicts it finds himself having to make use of it. [2] If someone should contradict the proposition, for instance, that 'one universal statement is true', it is clear that he would be obliged to assert the contrary and say, 'There is no universal statement that is true.' Slave, that isn't true either. [3] For what else does the assertion come down to than this, 'If a statement is universal, it is false'? [4] Again, if someone should come forward and say, 'You should know that nothing can be known, but everything is uncertain,' or someone declared, 'Believe me, and it will be to your benefit, when I say: one shouldn't believe anyone whatever,' or a third, 'Learn from me, man, that it is impossible to learn anything; [5] I am the one who is telling you, and I will prove it to you if you so wish.' Now what difference is there between these people and (who shall I say?) those who call themselves Academics. 'Men, give your assent', they say, 'to the proposition that no one should give his assent; believe us when we say that no one can believe anyone.'

[6] And Epicurus likewise, when he wants to destroy the natural sense of fellowship that binds people together, makes use of the very thing that he is destroying. [7] What does he say, then? 'Don't be deceived, man, don't allow yourself to be led astray, or be mistaken; there is no natural sense of fellowship that binds rational beings together. Believe me. Those who say otherwise are deceiving you and misleading you with false arguments.' [8] Why is it that you care, then? Let us be deceived. Will you be any worse off if all the rest of us remain convinced that we do have a natural sense of fellowship with one another, and that we ought to preserve it by every possible means? No, your own position will be all the better, and more secure. [9] Why do you worry about us, man; why write such lengthy books? Is it for fear that one or other of us may be deceived into supposing

that the gods take care of human beings, or may suppose that the essence of the good lies in something other than pleasure? [10] Because if that is the case, you should lie down and go to sleep, and lead the worm's life that you've judged yourself to be worthy of; eat and drink, and copulate, and defecate, and snore! [11] What does it matter to you what the rest of us may think about these things, and whether or not our ideas are sound? For what do you have in common with us? What, do you worry about sheep because they offer themselves up to be shorn, to be milked, and finally to be slaughtered? [12] Wouldn't it be desirable that human beings could be charmed and bewitched by the Stoics into offering themselves up to you, and those like you, to be fleeced and milked? [13] Should you have talked in such a way, indeed, to your fellow Epicureans? Wouldn't it have been better to conceal these things from them and persuade them, above all others, that we're born as naturally sociable creatures, and that self-control is a good thing, so that everything should be reserved for you alone? [14] Or should this fellowship be maintained with some and not with others? And in that case, with whom? With those who maintain it in return, or with those who violate it? And who violates it more than you Epicureans do, who uphold doctrines such as these?

[15] What was it, then, that awakened Epicurus from his slumbers and impelled him to write what he did? What else than what is most powerful of all in human beings, nature, who constrains everyone to her will, groan and resist though he may. [16] 'For since you hold these antisocial views,' she says, 'write them down and hand them on to others, and stay awake at night because of them, and so become, through your own practice, the denunciator of your own doctrines.' [17] Though we speak of Orestes* as being pursued by the Furies and kept from his sleep, weren't the Furies and avenging spirits that pursued Epicurus even more ferocious? They woke him up when he was asleep and would allow him no rest, compelling him instead to proclaim his own ills, as do madness and wine in the case of the priests of Cybele.* [18] So mighty and so invincible is human nature! For how can a vine be moved to act, not like a vine, but like an olive tree? Or an olive tree in turn, not like an olive tree, but like a vine? That's impossible, inconceivable. [19] Neither is it possible, then, for a human being to lose his human affections altogether, and even men who are castrated can't have their desires as men entirely cut off.

[20] And so it was with Epicurus: he cut off everything that characterizes the man, the head of a household, the citizen, the friend, but the desires that are truly and properly human he couldn't cut off; for he couldn't do that, any more than the lazy-minded Academics can reject their own sense-impressions and blind themselves, in spite of all the efforts that they make to that effect.

[21] Oh what a misfortune it is that when man has received from nature measures and standards for discovering the truth, he doesn't go on to try to add to them and make up for what is missing, but does precisely the opposite, and if he possesses some capacity that would enable him to discover the truth, he tries to root it out and destroy it.

[22] What do you say, philosopher? What opinion do you hold about piety and sanctity?—'If you like, I'll prove that it's good.'—Yes, prove it so that our citizens may be converted and honour the divine, and finally cease to be indifferent about the most important matters.—'Do you have the proofs, then?'—Yes I do, thank goodness. [23] —'Well then, since you're so highly contented with that position, hear the opposite position: that the gods do not exist, and even if they do exist, they do not concern themselves with human beings, nor do we have anything in common with them; and this piety and sanctity that the common run of people talk about is nothing but a lie told by charlatans and sophists, or, by Zeus!, by lawmakers to scare and deter evildoers.' [24] —Excellent, philosopher! You've rendered a valuable service to our fellow citizens, and you've won back our young men, who were already tending towards contempt for the divine. [25] —'So that doesn't please you, then? Hear now how justice amounts to nothing, how a sense of shame is mere foolishness, how a father is nothing, how a son is nothing.'

[26] Well done, philosopher! Continue in this vein, persuade the young men, so that we may have many more people who think and talk like you. Was it through principles like these that our well-governed cities grew great; was it doctrines like these that made Sparta what it was? Are these the convictions that Lycurgus* instilled into its citizens through his laws and programme of education, namely, that slavery is no more shameful than noble, and freedom is no more noble than shameful? Those who died at Thermopylae,* did they die by virtue of such doctrines? And did the Athenians* abandon their city on the basis of any other principles than these?

[27] And then people who talk in this way go on to marry, and father children, and fulfil their duties as citizens, and get appointed to be priests and prophets! Priests of whom? Of gods who don't exist! And they themselves consult the Pythian priestess, to know her lies and interpret the oracles to others? Oh what colossal impudence, what imposture!

[28] What are you up to, man? You're refuting yourself every day, and are you unwilling all the same to abandon these frigid endeavours? When you eat, where do you carry your hand to, to your mouth or to your eye? When you take a bath, what do you step into? When do you call a pot a plate, or call a ladle a roasting spit? [29] If I were a slave of one of these gentlemen, even at the risk of being whipped to the bone every day, I would never stop tormenting him. 'Throw a bit of oil into the bath, boy.' I'd take some fish sauce and go and pour it over his head. 'What's this?'—'I had an impression that was indistinguishable from that of oil; it was just the same, I swear that by your fortune.'—'Here pass me the gruel.' [30] I'd bring him a dish full of vinegar. 'Didn't I ask you for the gruel?'—'Yes, master, this is gruel.'—'But surely it's vinegar?'—'Why that rather than gruel?'—'Take some and smell it, take some and taste it.'—'Well, how do you know, if it is true that our senses deceive us?' [31] If I had three or four fellow slaves who thought in the same way as I did, I'd soon make him explode with anger and hang himself, or else change his ideas. But as things are, men like this are making fun of us, they make use of all the gifts of nature while abolishing them in theory.

[32] Here we have people who are truly grateful and full of reverence! To look no further, they eat bread day after day and yet have the gall to say, 'We don't know if there's a Demeter, or Persephone, or Pluto'!* [33] Not to mention that, although they enjoy the night and day, the changing seasons, the stars, the sea, the earth, and the help that people provide for one another, they're not in the least impressed by any of these things, but merely seek to belch out their little problems, and after having exercised their stomachs, go off to take a bath. [34] As for what they're going to say, and about what, and to whom, and what their audience will gain from what they say, they've never given the slightest thought to any of that. I very much fear that some noble-minded young man may hear these doctrines and be influenced by them, and under that influence, perhaps, lose all the germs of nobility that he once possessed. [35] I fear that we may be

providing an adulterer with grounds for abandoning all shame in his actions; or that an embezzler of public funds may be able to put his hand on some specious argument derived from such teachings; or that someone who neglects his parents may gain additional effrontery from them.

What is good or bad, then, in your opinion, what is right or wrong? This or that? [36] But what is the use of arguing any further with these people, or giving them a hearing, or having one's own say, or attempting to convert them? [37] One would have much greater hope, by Zeus, of converting sexual perverts than people who have become so utterly deaf and blind.

2.21 *On inconsistency*

[1] There are some faults that people readily admit, whereas they admit others only with reluctance. No one will admit, for instance, to being stupid or unintelligent, whereas, on the contrary, you'll hear everyone saying, 'If only my luck matched up to my wits!' [2] They admit readily to timidity and say, 'I'm inclined to be a bit nervous, I admit, but you won't find me to be a fool.' [3] As for lack of self-control, no one willingly admits to that, and not at all to being unjust, or envious, or meddlesome, although most people will admit that they tend to give way to pity. [4] What reason can be found for this? The principal reason is that people are inconsistent and confused in their ideas about matters of good and evil, but the reasons vary otherwise according to the person, although it can generally be said that people are most unwilling to admit to anything that they consider to be shameful. [5] Timidity they imagine to be a mark of good sense, and pity a mark of good feeling, whereas stupidity is something that they see as being altogether slavish; and offences against society they will not admit in any circumstances. [6] Now, in the case of most faults, the main reason why people can be brought to confess to them is that they conceive them as being in some sense involuntary, as in the case of timidity and pity. [7] Injustice, on the other hand, isn't pictured as being in any way involuntary. In jealousy, though, there is again an involuntary element in most people's view, and that is accordingly something that they'll also admit.

[8] Living as we do among such people, who are so confused, and don't know what they're saying, or what evil they have within them,

or where they got it from, or how they can get rid of it, we should constantly be focusing our attention, I think, on the following thoughts: 'Could it be, perhaps, that I too am one of these people? [9] What kind of person do I picture myself as being? How do I conduct myself? Is it really as a wise person, as someone who has control of himself? Can I say for my part that I've been educated to face everything that may come? [10] Is it indeed the case, as is fitting for someone who knows nothing, that I'm aware that I know nothing? Do I go to my teacher as to an oracle, ready to obey? Or do I go to the schoolroom like a snivelling child, wanting only to gain second-hand information, and to understand books that I didn't previously understand, and, if the occasion should arise, expound them to others?' [11] At home, man, you've been boxing with your little slave, you've turned the house upside down, you've caused disturbance to your neighbours, and then you come to me with all the dignity of a sage, and sit down and pass judgement on how I've explained my text, and how—what shall I say?—I spoke any old nonsense that came into my head? [12] You've come here full of envy, humiliated because nothing's been sent to you from home, and you sit through the lesson reflecting about nothing other than how things stand between you and your father, or you and your brother. [13] 'What are people saying about me at home? At this moment they're thinking that I'm making progress in my studies, and they're saying, "He'll come back full of knowledge." [14] How I'd like to return home full of knowledge, but that demands a great deal of effort, and nobody sends me anything, and the baths are filthy here at Nicopolis, and things are bad for me at my lodgings, and bad here at the school.'

[15] And then people say, 'Nobody's any the better for attending a philosopher's school.' Well, who goes to the school, I ask you, with the intention of attaining a cure? Who goes there to submit his judgements to purification; who goes there to become fully aware of what he stands in need of? [16] Why are you surprised, then, if you go away again with the very same thoughts that you brought when you arrived here? The fact is that you didn't come here to lay them aside, or correct them, or exchange them for others. [17] Oh no, far from it. Consider this at least, whether you're getting exactly what you came for. You want to chatter about philosophical principles. Well then, haven't you become all the better at empty talk?

Don't these philosophical principles provide you with excellent material for making your displays? Aren't you adept at analysing syllogisms and equivocal arguments? Haven't you examined the premisses of the argument of 'the Liar', and of hypothetical syllogisms? So why should you still be vexed if you're getting exactly what you came for?

[18] 'Yes, but if my child or brother dies, or if I myself have to face death or torture, what good will such things do me?'

[19] But was it really for this that you came? Is it for this that you've sat down beside me? Has this ever been the reason why you've lit your lamp or stayed awake at night? Or when you went out for a walk, did you ever set some impression before your mind, rather than a syllogism, and subject it to examination together with your companions? When did you ever do anything like that? [20] And then you say, 'Philosophical principles are useless.' Useless to whom? To those who fail to make proper use of them. Eye salves aren't useless to those who rub them in when and as they ought; and jumping-weights aren't useless, but merely useless for certain people, while they're useful, on the other hand, to others. [21] If you want to ask me now, 'Are syllogisms of any use?', I'd reply that they are, and if you wish, I'll show you how.

'But what good have they been to me?'

Man, you didn't ask whether they're useful for you, but whether they're useful in general. [22] Let someone who's suffering from dysentery ask me whether vinegar is useful, and I'll tell him that it is.

'Is it useful for me, then?'

I'll reply, no. Seek first to stop your diarrhoea and heal your little ulcers. And you too, gentlemen, should first cure your ulcers, stop the discharge of your humours,* calm your mind, and bring it to school free from distraction; and then you'll know what power reason can have!

2.22 *On friendship*

[1] What one has set one's heart on, that one naturally loves. Do people set their hearts on things that are bad? Certainly not. Or on things that mean nothing to them? No again! [2] It remains for us to conclude, then, that they set their hearts on good things alone, [3] and if they have set their hearts on them, they love them too. Whoever has

knowledge of good things, then, would know how to love them too; but if someone is incapable of distinguishing good things from bad, and things that are neither good nor bad from the one and the other, how could he still be capable of loving? It is thus to the wise alone that the power to love belongs.

[4] 'How so?', someone says. 'I'm not wise, and yet I love my child all the same.'

[5] Goodness me, I'm amazed, to begin with, that you should admit to not being wise. For what is it that you lack? Don't you have the use of your senses; don't you distinguish between sense-impressions; don't you supply your body with the appropriate nourishment, clothing, and shelter? [6] Why do you admit, then, that you're lacking in wisdom? It is because, by Zeus, that you're often led astray by your impressions, and disturbed by them, and you often allow their persuasiveness to get the better of you. And so at one time you think them good, and at another time you think the same things to be bad, and then at another to be neither good nor bad; and in short, you find yourself exposed to distress, fear, envy, disturbance, and change. Thus, you admit to being lacking in wisdom. [7] And aren't you changeable, too, in what you love? Riches, pleasure, and, in a word, all external things you sometimes regard as being good and sometimes as bad; and in your relations with others, don't you regard the same people as being good at one time and bad at another, and aren't you sometimes well disposed towards them, and sometimes ill disposed, and don't you praise them at one time while criticizing them at another?

'Yes, that's just how I feel.'

[8] Well then, can someone who has been mistaken about somebody be his friend?

'Surely not.'

Or can someone who is liable to change his mind in the choice of a friend show him true good will?

'No again.'

[9] Well, haven't you often seen little dogs fawning on one another and playing together, which prompts one to exclaim, 'Nothing could be more friendly'? But to see what that friendship amounts to, throw a bit of meat between them, and you'll know. [10] And likewise, if you throw a small bit of land between yourself and your son, you'll know how impatient your son is to see you buried, and how greatly you in

turn long for the death of your son. And then you'll come to say, 'What a child I've raised! All this time he's been longing to see me buried!' [11] Throw a pretty girl between you, and both fall in love with her, the old man and the young; or again a scrap of glory. And if you have to risk your life, you'll end up repeating the words of the father of Admetus, '*You wish to behold the light, do you think that your father does not?*'*

[12] Do you suppose that this man didn't love his child when it was young, and that he wasn't in anguish when it had a fever, and didn't say many times over, 'If only I had the fever instead'? But then, when the test comes and is getting close, just see what words he comes up with! [13] Weren't Eteocles and Polynices offspring of the same mother and father? Weren't they brought up together, and didn't they frequently embrace one another? So that if anyone saw them together, I imagine, he would have laughed at the philosophers for expressing paradoxical ideas about friendship. [14] But when the throne was tossed between them, like a piece of meat, look at what they say:

> Eteo.—*Where before the walls will you stand?*
> Pol.—*Why do you ask that of me?*
> Eteo.—*I mean to confront and kill you.*
> Pol.—*And that is my desire too.* *

[15] For as a general rule—and one should have no illusions on the matter—there is nothing that a living creature is more strongly attached to than its own benefit. So whatever seems to him to be standing in the way of that benefit, be it a brother, or father, or child, or lover, or beloved, he will proceed to hate, reject, and curse. [16] For there is nothing that he loves so much by nature as his own benefit; for him this is father, and brother, and family, and country, and god. [17] Whenever we suppose, then, that the gods are standing in the way of our interest, we revile even them, and throw down their statues, and burn down their temples, as when Alexander ordered that the temple of Asclepius should be burned because of the death of his beloved.* [18] For that reason, if one identifies one's own benefit with piety, honour, one's country, one's parents, one's friends, all of them will be safeguarded; but if one places one's benefit in one scale and one's friends, country, and parents, and justice itself, in the other, the latter will all be lost, because they will be outweighed by one's

benefit. [19] For on whatever side 'I' and 'mine' are set, to that side the living creature must necessarily be inclined; if they're in the flesh, it is there that the ruling power will reside; if in choice, the ruling power will be there; if in external things, it will be there. [20] It follows that if I am where my moral choice is, in that case alone will I be the friend, the son, the father that I ought to be. For then it will benefit me to preserve my trustworthiness, my sense of shame, my patience, my temperance, my cooperativeness, and to maintain good relations with others. [21] But if I place myself in one scale, and what is right in the other, the saying of Epicurus then acquires full strength when he declares that 'the right is nothing at all, or at most, is what is valued in common opinion'.*

[22] It was through ignorance of this that the Athenians and Spartans came to quarrel with one another, and the Thebans with both of them, and the Great King came to quarrel with Greece, and the Macedonians with both of them, and in our own time, the Romans with the Getae, while in the remoter past, the events at Troy owed their origin to the same cause. [23] Paris was a guest of Menelaus, and anyone who saw the kindness that they displayed to one another would never have believed anyone who said they were not friends. But there was thrown between them a tempting morsel, a pretty woman, and the war broke out* because of her. [24] So when you now see friends or brothers who seem to be of one mind, don't be too quick to pronounce on their friendship, even if they swear to it, even if they declare that it is impossible that they should ever be parted. [25] For the ruling centre of a bad man can't be trusted; it is unstable, and unsure in its judgements, falling under the power of one impression after another. [26] Don't try to find out, like everyone else, whether these men had the same parents, or were brought up together, or had the same attendant during their childhood, but ask instead this one question alone, whether they locate their benefit in things outside themselves or in their choice. [27] If they locate it in external things, don't call them friends, any more than you call them trustworthy, or reliable, or courageous, or free; indeed, if you have good sense, don't even call them human beings. [28] For it isn't human judgement that makes them snap at one another, and abuse one another, and take to the desert or public places as wild beasts take to the mountains, and conduct themselves like bandits in the law-courts; it isn't human judgement that makes them become dissolute, and

turns them into adulterers and seducers, and leads them to carry out all the crimes that people commit against one another. All of this is brought about by one single judgement alone, that which incites them to place themselves, and all that is theirs, in the category of things that lie outside the sphere of choice. [29] If you hear, on the other hand, that these men truly believe that the good lies nowhere else than in choice, and in the right use of impressions, then you need not trouble to enquire any further whether they're father and son, or whether they're brothers, or whether they were at school together for a long time and are comrades, because even if that is the only thing that you know about them, you can confidently declare that they're friends, and likewise that they're faithful and just. [30] For where else can friendship be found than where fidelity lies, and where a sense of shame lies, and where there is respect for what is right and nothing other than that?

[31] 'But he's been taking care of me for so long, and yet didn't love me?'

How do you know, slave, that he didn't take care of you as he does when he cleans his shoes, or rubs down his beast of burden? And how do you know that, when you cease to be of any use as a utensil, he won't throw you away like a broken plate?

[32] 'But she's my wife, and we've been living together for so long.'

And how long did Eriphyle live with Amphiaraus, bearing him children too, and many of them? But a necklace came between them.* [33] What is a necklace? It is the judgement that one holds about things of that kind. That was the brutish factor; that was the force that broke the ties of love; that was what prevented the woman from remaining a wife, and the mother from remaining a mother.

[34] Whoever among you sincerely wants to be friend to another, or to win the friendship of another, should thus eradicate these judgements, and despise them, and banish them from his mind. [35] And when he has done so, he will, in the first place, be free from self-reproach, and inner conflict, and instability of mind, and self-torment; [36] and, furthermore, in his relations with others, he will always be frank and open with one who is like himself, and will be tolerant, gentle, forbearing, and kind with regard to one who is unlike him, as likewise to one who is ignorant and falls into error on the matters of the highest importance; and he will never be harsh with anyone because he fully understands the saying of Plato, that 'no mind is ever

willingly deprived of the truth'.* [37] But if you're not like this, you may act in every regard as friends do, drinking together, living together under the same roof, and sailing on journeys together, and may even have the same parents, yes, and so may snakes too, but they can never be friends and neither can you, as long as you hold these brutish and abominable judgements.

2.23 *On the faculty of expression*

[1] Everyone will read a book with greater pleasure and ease if it is written in clearer characters; isn't it also the case that everyone will listen with greater ease to discourses that are expressed in elegant and attractive language? [2] One shouldn't say, then, that there is no such thing as a faculty of expression, for that would be to speak as one who is both impious and cowardly. Impious because one would be slighting gifts bestowed by God, just as if one were to deny the usefulness of our power of vision, or of hearing, or indeed of speech itself. [3] Is it, then, for no purpose that God has given you eyes, and for nothing that he has infused them with a spirit that is so powerful and ingenious that it can reach far out and gather impressions of the forms of visible objects? What messenger is as swift and attentive as that? [4] Was it for nothing, furthermore, that God made the intervening air so active and elastic that vision can pass through it* as though through some taut medium? Was it for nothing that he made light, without which all the rest would be useless?

[5] Don't be ungrateful, man, nor yet forgetful of better gifts than these, but offer up thanks to God for sight and hearing, and, by Zeus, for life itself and all that supports it, for dried fruits, for wine, for olive oil, [6] remembering all the same that he has given you something better than all of these, the faculty that makes use of them, that tests them out, that passes judgement on the value of each. [7] For what is it that, with regard to each of these faculties, declares what value it holds? Is it each faculty itself? Have you ever seen our power of sight make any declaration about itself? Or our power of hearing? No, rather as servants and slaves, they've been appointed to perform work on behalf of the faculty that makes use of impressions. [8] And if you ask what is the value of each, of whom are you asking this? Who is to answer you? How, then, can any other faculty be superior

to that which makes use of all the others as servants, and tests each of them and passes judgement on it? [9] For which of them knows what it is, and what its work is? Which of them knows when one should make use of it and when one shouldn't? Which of them opens and closes our eyes, and turns them away from those things that one should turn them away from, and directs them towards others? Is it the faculty of sight? No, but that of choice. [10] Which is it that opens and shuts our ears? Which is it that makes us curious and questioning, or again, unmoved by what people are saying? [11] And when this faculty sees that all the other faculties are blind and deaf, and are unable to see anything apart from those acts that they have been appointed to perform in its service and at its bidding, unless it alone can see clearly, and can embrace all the rest within its view and determine the value of each, is it likely that it will declare anything other than itself to be supreme? [12] And what else does the eye do, when open, than see? But as to whether it ought to look at somebody's wife, and in what manner, what tells us that? The faculty of choice. [13] As to whether one should place any belief in what one is told, or not believe it, and if one does believe it, whether one should be upset by it or not, what tells us that? Isn't it the faculty of choice? [14] And the faculty of expression itself, and of the embellishment of language, if there is indeed a specific faculty of that kind, what else does it do, when the discourse touches on some topic, other than embellish the words and arrange them as a barber does with our hair? [15] But whether it is better to speak or keep silent, or better to speak in this way or that, and whether this is appropriate or inappropriate, or what is right moment for each discourse, and what use it will serve—is there any other faculty than that of choice that can tell us all of that? Would you have it step forward, then, and pass sentence against itself?

[16] 'But what if the matter stands like this instead,' someone says, 'and it is in fact possible for that which serves to be superior to what it is serving, the horse to the rider, the dog to the hunter, the instrument to the musician, the subject to the king?'

[17] What is it that makes use of everything else? Choice. What is it that takes charge of everything else? Choice. What is it that destroys the whole person, sometimes through hunger, sometimes through a noose, sometimes by hurling him over a cliff? Choice. [18] Can it be, then, that there is anything more powerful among human beings than

this? And how is it possible that what is subject to hindrance should be more powerful than something that is not subject to hindrance? [19] What things are capable by nature of hindering the faculty of vision? Choice and also things that lie outside the sphere of choice. The same is true of the faculty of hearing, and likewise that of speech. But what is capable by its nature of hindering the faculty of choice? Nothing that lies outside the sphere of choice, but only choice itself when it has become perverted. That is why it alone becomes vice and it alone becomes virtue.

[20] Well then, since it is so great a faculty and has been set above all the rest, let it step forward to tell us that the flesh is superior to everything else. No, even if the flesh proclaimed its own superiority, no one could endure its presumption. [21] Now what is it, Epicurus, that proclaims that judgement? What is it that wrote *On the End*, the *Physics*, *On the Canon*?* What is it that prompted you to grow a philosopher's beard?* What is it that wrote, when you were on the point of death, 'We're living our last day which is also a happy one'?* [22] Was it the flesh, or was it choice? And after that, can you admit to having anything superior to it, if you're in your right mind at least? Can you really be so deaf and blind?

[23] What, then, is one to despise one's other faculties? Heaven forbid! Does one say that there is no use or progress except in the faculty of choice? No, everything should be accorded its proper value. [24] For even a donkey has its use, though not as much as an ox has; even a dog has its use, though not as much as a slave has; and a slave too, though not as much as the other citizens have; and the citizens likewise, though not as much as the magistrates have. [25] Just because some things are superior to others, one shouldn't despise the use that the others can offer. The faculty of expression has its use too, though not as much as the faculty of choice has. [26] So when I speak in this way, no one should think that I'm asking you to neglect the art of speech, any more than I would have you neglect your eyes or ears or hands or feet, or your clothes and shoes. [27] But if you ask me, 'What is the most excellent of all things?', what am I to say? The faculty of expression? I cannot, but must rather say the faculty of choice, when it becomes right choice. [28] For it is choice that makes use of the faculty of expression, and of all the other faculties, both great and small. If it be rightly directed, a person becomes good; if it be badly directed, he becomes bad. [29] It is

through choice that we encounter good fortune or misfortune, and that we reproach one another or are pleased with one another. It is this, in a word, that brings about unhappiness when neglected, and happiness when properly tended.

[30] But to do away with the faculty of expression, and say that in reality it is nothing, is not only ungrateful to those who have given it to us, but cowardly too. [31] For someone who would want to do that seems to me to be afraid that, if there is any such faculty, we may not be able to despise it. [32] Such is the case, too, with those who claim that there is no difference between beauty and ugliness. What, could one be affected in the same way by the sight of Thersites and that of Achilles? Or by the sight of Helen* and that of some ordinary woman? [33] No, that is mere foolishness, indicating a lack of cultivation in people who are ignorant of the specific nature of each reality, and who fear that if one comes to appreciate its excellence, one will at once be carried away and placed within its power. [34] No, the important thing is this, to leave each thing in the possession of its own specific faculty, and then to consider the value of that faculty, and to learn what is the most excellent of all things, and to pursue that in everything, and make it the chief object of one's concern, regarding everything else as of secondary value by comparison, yet without neglecting even those other things, so far as possible. [35] For we must take care of our eyes too, though not as being the most excellent thing, but for the sake of what is most excellent, because it cannot attain its natural perfection unless it uses our eyes with prudence and chooses some things instead of others.

[36] What usually happens, then? People behave like a traveller who, when returning to his homeland, passes through a place where there is a very fine inn, and because he finds it pleasant, remains there. [37] Man, you've forgotten your purpose, you weren't travelling to this place, but passing through it. 'But it's a lovely inn.' And how many other inns are there that are just as nice, and how many meadows too! But only as places on the way. [38] The purpose that lies before you is to return to your homeland, to relieve your family from fear, to fulfil your duties as a citizen, to marry, to have children, to hold public office. [39] For you haven't come into the world to pick out the prettiest places, but to return and live in the place where you were born, and in which you've been enrolled as a citizen. [40] Something much the same happens in the present case too. It is through the

spoken word and instruction of this kind that one must advance towards perfection, and purify one's choice, and correct the faculty that makes use of impressions. Furthermore, the teaching of these principles demands a certain eloquence, requiring a certain variety and subtlety in the way in which they're expressed. [41] So people become captivated by all of this, and stop short at this point, one being captivated by matters of style, another by syllogisms, another by equivocal arguments, and another stopping off at another wayside inn of this kind, and they remain there and rot away, as though among the Sirens.*

[42] Your purpose, man, was to render yourself capable of using the impressions that present themselves to you in conformity with nature, and not to fail to attain what you desire, and not to fall into what you want to avoid, and never to suffer failure or misfortune, but to be free and immune to hindrance or constraint, as one who conforms to the governing order of Zeus, obeying it and finding satisfaction in it, and never finding fault with anyone, and never accusing anyone, being able to recite these verses with your whole heart, '*Guide me, Zeus, and thou, O Destiny.*'*

[43] And then, after having adopted this as your purpose, because some little turn of style strikes your fancy, or certain precepts appeal to you, will you stop off at that point, and choose to stay there, forgetting all that you have at home, and saying, 'What pretty things these are!' Why, who doubts that they're pretty? But only as a place of passage, a wayside inn. [44] For what is to prevent an orator who could vie with Demosthenes* from being unhappy? And what is to prevent someone who could analyse syllogisms like Chrysippus from being wretched, and suffering grief and envy, and, in a word, living in misery and distress? Nothing whatever. [45] You can see, then, that these were mere inns of no inherent value, while your aim was something quite different. [46] When I talk like this to some people, they think that I'm denigrating the study of rhetoric and of general principles. No, I'm not criticizing that, but only the notion that people should concentrate excessively on that, and place all their hopes in it. [47] If anyone causes offence to his audience by putting forward such ideas, you may mark me down as one of those offensive people; but when I see that one thing is most excellent and essential, I can't say that of something else merely to gratify you.

2.24 *To one of those whom he regarded as unworthy*

[1] Someone said to him, 'I've often come to you wanting to listen to you, and you've never given me any reply; [2] but now, if possible, do please say something to me.'—Do you think, said Epictetus, that when it comes to speaking, there is an art, as in everything else, that enables one who possesses it to speak with skill, while one who doesn't possess it will speak unskilfully?—'Yes, I think so.' [3] —That person, then, who by the use of speech brings benefit to himself, and is able to benefit others, would be speaking with skill, whereas someone who brings harm to himself and others would be unskilled in this art of speaking? You would find that some suffer harm while others gain benefit. [4] And of those who are listening, do all gain benefit from what they hear, or would you find that some gain benefit from it while others are harmed?—'That applies to them too,' the man said. [5] Just as there is a skill in speaking, there is also a skill in listening?—'It would seem so.' [6] —If you please, also consider the matter from this point of view. Whose art is it to play a musical instrument in accordance with the rules of the art?—'That of a musician.' [7] —Very well, and whose part is it, in your view, to make a statue in accordance with the rules of the art?—'That of a sculptor.'—And to look at the statue in a properly appreciative manner, does that also require some kind of skill?—'Yes, that requires one too.'

[8] If to speak as one ought requires a certain skill, then, don't you see that a skill is also required if one is to listen with benefit? [9] As for what is ultimately beneficial, let's leave that aside for the moment, if you please, since both of us are a long way off from anything like that. [10] But here is something that I think everyone could agree on, that it requires a good deal of practice in listening if one is to listen to philosophers. Isn't that so? [11] What should I talk to you about, then? Tell me now. What are you capable of hearing about? About what is good and bad? For whom? A horse?—'No.'—An ox, then?—'No.' [12] —What, a human being?—'Yes.'

Do we know what a human being is, then, and what his nature is, and what the concept of man is? Do we have our ears sufficiently open with regard to this question? Do you have any notion, indeed, of what nature is, and are you capable of following me to any adequate degree as I speak? [13] And could I make use of demonstrations with you? How can I? Do you have any understanding at all of what a proof is, and how one proves something, and by what means? Or what things resemble proofs without actually being so? [14] Do you know what truth is, or what falsehood is? And what follows from what, and what conflicts with what, or is in opposition to what, or in disaccord with what? But how am I to excite you to take an interest in philosophy? [15] How can I show you that a great many people have contradictory ideas, which makes them disagree about what is good and bad or beneficial and harmful, when you don't even know what a contradiction is? Show me, then, what I can achieve by entering into a discussion with you. Excite a desire in me. [16] Just as the sight of suitable grass excites a sheep's desire to eat, whereas if you offer it a stone or loaf of bread it remains wholly unmoved, so likewise some of us have a natural desire to speak when a suitable listener appears, and he himself excites that desire. But if he simply sits at our side like a stone or a clump of grass, how can he excite any such desire in a man? [17] Does the vine perhaps say to the farmer, 'Take care of me'? No, it shows by its very appearance that someone who takes care of it will derive profit from it, and so invites him to take care of it. [18] And at the sight of little children, with their charming and lively ways, who doesn't feel drawn to take part in their games, and to crawl with them and engage in baby talk? But who feels any desire to play or bray with a donkey? For even if it is small, it is nothing but a little donkey.

[19] 'Why is it, then, that you have nothing to say to me?'

I have this one thing alone to say to you, that whoever is ignorant of who he is, and what he was born for, and in what kind of world he finds himself, and with what people he is sharing his life, and what things are good or bad and what are honourable or shameful, and is someone who is incapable of following an argument or proof, and doesn't know what is true or false, and cannot distinguish between them: such a person will exercise neither his desires, nor his aversions, nor his motives, nor his designs, nor his assent, not his dissent, in accordance with nature, but being altogether deaf and blind, he'll go around thinking that he is somebody when in reality he is nobody at all. [20] And do you suppose that there is anything new in this? Isn't it the case that ever since the human race came into being, it is from this ignorance that all our errors and all our misfortunes have arisen? [21] Why was it that Agamemnon and Achilles fell out with one another? Wasn't it for want of knowing what is beneficial and what isn't? Doesn't one of them say that it is expedient to return Chryseis to her father, while the other says that it isn't? Doesn't one of them say that he ought to get someone else's prize, while the other says that he shouldn't? Wasn't it because of this that they came to forget who they were and what they had come for? [22] Why, what did you come for, man? To acquire mistresses or to fight?—'To fight.'—Against whom? Against the Trojans or the Greeks?—'Against the Trojans.'—You're turning away from Hector, then, to draw your sword against your own king? [23] And you, my good man, are turning away from your task as a king, '*To whom peoples are entrusted, and has such great cares*',* and are exchanging blows, instead, with the most warlike of your allies over a slip of a girl, when you ought to be treating him with every respect and seeking to protect him? Will you show yourself to be inferior to a clever high priest, who treats the noble warriors with every kind of attention? Do you see what kind of effects are brought about by ignorance of what is expedient?

[24] 'But I too am rich.'—What, richer than Agamemnon?—'But I'm handsome too.'—What, more handsome than Achilles?—'But I also have fine hair.'—Didn't Achilles have even finer hair, which was golden too? And didn't he comb it and dress it most elegantly? [25] —'But I'm strong too.'—Can you lift a stone of such size, then, as was lifted by Hector or Ajax?—'But I'm also of noble birth.' Have you a goddess for a mother, then, or a son of Zeus for a father? And what good did that do him when he sat down and wept for his girl? [26] —'But I'm an orator.'—And wasn't Achilles? Don't you see how he dealt with Odysseus and Phoenix, who were the cleverest of all the Greeks in the art of speaking, and reduced them to silence?*

[27] This is all that I have to say to you, and I couldn't summon up much enthusiasm even to say that much.

'Why not?'

[28] Because you haven't excited my enthusiasm. For what can I see in you to excite me, as horsemen are excited by thoroughbred horses? Your miserable body? It's shameful the way in which you tend it. Your clothing? That, too, is effeminate. Your bearing, your expression? Nothing there that's worth a second glance. [29] When you want to know what a philosopher has to say, don't ask, 'Have you nothing to say to me?', but simply show that you're capable of listening to him, and you'll see how you excite him to speak.

2.25 *On the necessity of logic*

[1] When someone who was attending his school said to him, 'Convince me of the usefulness of logic,' he replied: Would you like me to demonstrate it to you?—'Yes.' [2] —Then I must employ a demonstrative argument? And when the questioner agreed, he asked: [3] How will you know, then, whether I'm trying to mislead you with a sophism? The man offered no reply. So do you see, continued Epictetus, how you yourself are conceding that logic is necessary, since without it you can't even tell whether it is necessary or not?

2.26 *What is the distinctive characteristic of error?*

[1] Every error involves a contradiction; for since someone who commits an error doesn't want to do that, but to act rightly, it is clear that he isn't doing what he wants. [2] For what does a thief want to achieve? Something that is to his benefit. If theft, then, is contrary to his benefit, he isn't doing what he wants. [3] Now every rational mind is by nature averse to contradiction; but as long as someone fails to realize that he is involved in a contradiction, there is nothing to prevent him from carrying out contradictory actions; when he becomes aware of it, however, he must necessarily turn aside from the contradiction and avoid it, just as harsh necessity forces one to renounce what is false as soon as one realizes that it is false, although one assents to it as long as its falsity remains unapparent.

[4] Someone who is skilled in reasoning, and is able both to encourage and to refute, will thus be able to show each person the contradiction that is causing him to go astray, and make him clearly understand that he isn't doing what he wants, and is in fact doing what he doesn't want. [5] For if anyone can make that clear to him, he'll renounce his error of his own accord, but if you fail to show him, don't be surprised if he persists in it, being under the impression that he is acting rightly. [6] That is why Socrates, placing full confidence in this capacity, used to say, 'I'm not in the habit of calling another witness to speak in support of what I'm saying, but I always remain satisfied with the person who is engaging in discussion with me, and call on his vote and summon him as a witness, so that he alone suffices for me in place of all others.' [7] For

Socrates knew how a rational mind is moved: that being like a balance, it will incline whether one wishes it or not. Make the ruling centre aware of a contradiction, and it will renounce it; but if you fail to make it clear, blame yourself rather than the person whom you're unable to convince.

BOOK 3

3.1 *On personal adornment*

[1] He was visited one day by a young student of rhetoric whose hair was arranged in a rather too fussy manner, and whose clothing was in general very showy. Tell me now, said Epictetus, don't you think that there are some dogs that are beautiful, and some horses that are, and likewise in the case of every creature?—'I do', the young man said. [2] —Isn't it true of human beings too, that there are some who are beautiful and some who are ugly?—'Absolutely.'—In calling each of these things beautiful in its own kind, do we do so on the same grounds in all cases, or on special grounds in each case? [3] Look at the matter in this way. Since we can see that a dog is fitted by nature to do one thing, and a horse to do another, and a nightingale, if you like, to do yet another, it wouldn't be absurd for one to declare overall that each of them is beautiful precisely in so far as it best fulfils its own nature; and since each is different in nature, it would seem to me that each of them is beautiful in a different way. Isn't that so? The student agreed.

[4] So what makes a dog beautiful will make a horse ugly, and what makes a horse beautiful will make a dog ugly, if their natures are indeed different?—'It would appear so.' [5] —For what makes someone a fine pancratiast, I fancy, doesn't make someone a good wrestler, and would be absurdly out of place in a runner; and the same man who appears fine for the pentathlon would appear quite the opposite for the wrestling?—'Very true.' [6] —Then what makes a human being beautiful is just the same as what makes a dog or horse beautiful in its kind?—'Yes, it's the same.'—What makes a dog beautiful, then? The presence of a dog's distinctive excellence. And a horse? The presence of a horse's excellence. And of a human being, then? Surely it must be the presence of a human being's excellence? [7] So if you want to be beautiful for your own part, you should strive to achieve this, the excellence that characterizes a human being.

'But what is it?'

[8] Consider who it is that you praise when you praise people dispassionately: is it those who are just, or unjust?—'Those who are just.'—The temperate or the intemperate?—'The temperate.'—The

self-controlled or the dissolute?—'The self-controlled.' [9] —You should know, then, that if you make yourself a person of that kind, you'll be making yourself beautiful; but if you neglect these virtues, you're bound to be ugly, whatever techniques you adopt to make yourself appear beautiful.

[10] Beyond that, I'm not sure what else I can say to you; for if I say what I think, I'll offend you, and if I don't, think how I'll be acting, since you've come to me in the hope of gaining some benefit, and I will have brought you none at all; and you're coming to me as a philosopher, and I won't have spoken to you as a philosopher. [11] Besides, how could it be anything other than cruel for me to leave you unreformed? If you should come to your senses at some future time, you'd have reason to criticize me, saying, [12] 'What did Epictetus see in me, that when he saw me coming to him in such a state, he left me in the same shameful condition, without saying so much as a word to me? Did he despair of me so completely? [13] Wasn't I young; wasn't I capable of listening to reason? And how many other young men there are who commit innumerable errors of such a kind at that age! [14] I've heard mention of a certain Polemo* who, after having been a thoroughly dissolute youth, underwent a complete transformation. Granted that he didn't consider me to be another Polemo, but he might at least have corrected the way in which I wore my hair, he might have stripped me of my ornaments, he might have stopped me plucking out my body hair. But when he saw me looking like a—what shall I say?—he didn't say a word.' [15] For my part, too, I won't say what it is that you resemble; you'll say it for yourself when you return to your senses, and recognize what sort of people they are who behave in this way.

[16] If you should lay these charges against me at some future time, what defence would I be able to put forward? Yes, but what if I do speak and he won't pay any heed to me? After all, did Laius pay any heed to Apollo?* Didn't he go away and get drunk and dismiss the oracle from his mind? What, did that deter Apollo from telling him the truth? [17] While I for my part have no idea whether you'll listen to me or not, Apollo knew perfectly well that Laius would pay no heed to him, and he spoke all the same. [18] —'But why did he speak?'—And why is he Apollo? Why does he deliver oracles? Why has he appointed himself to that post, to be a prophet and fountain of truth, and have people from the entire civilized world coming to

consult him? And why are the words 'Know yourself' carved on the front of his temple, even if no one pays any attention to them?

[19] Did Socrates succeed in persuading all who approached him to take proper care of themselves? Not even one in a thousand. But all the same, since he had been appointed to this post by the deity, as he himself expressed the matter, he never abandoned it.* Why, what was it that he said even in front of his judges? [20] 'If you acquit me', he said, 'on condition that I should no longer act as I do at present, I won't accept your offer and won't cease to act as I do, but I'll go up to young and old, and in a word, to everyone I meet, and ask the same questions as I ask at present, and above all, I'll interrogate you, my fellow citizens, because you're most closely related to me.'* [21] Why are you so meddlesome, Socrates, why are you such a busy-body? What does it matter to you how we act? 'Why, what are you saying? You're my companion in life and share the same blood as me, and yet you neglect yourself, and supply your city with a bad citizen, your relations with a bad relation, and your neighbours with a bad neighbour.'

[22] 'Well, who are you, then?' Here it is no small thing to reply, 'I'm he whose duty it is to take care of human beings.' For when a lion comes along, it is no ordinary little ox that dares to confront him, but if the bull comes forward and confronts him, ask the bull, if you think fit, 'But who are you?' or 'Why do you care?' Man, in every species nature produces some exceptional individual, [23] among cattle, among dogs, among bees, among horses. Don't say to that exceptional individual, 'Who are you, then?' Or if you do, it will find a voice somehow or other to reply to you, 'For my part I'm like the purple in a robe: don't expect me to resemble the rest, and don't find fault with my nature for having made me different from the rest.'*

[24] What, then, am I a person of that kind? How could I be? And you, are you the kind of person who is capable of listening to the truth? If only you were! But all the same, since I've somehow been condemned to have a white beard and wear a rough cloak, and you're coming to me as a philosopher, I won't treat you cruelly or act as if I'd despaired of you, but will say to you, Young man, who is it that you want to make beautiful? [25] Learn first to know who you are, and then adorn yourself accordingly. You're a human being; that is to say, a mortal animal who has the capacity to make use of impressions in a rational manner. And what does it mean, to use them rationally?

To use them in accordance with nature and perfectly. [26] What is superior in you, then? The animal in you? No. The mortal? No. The capacity to make use of impressions? No. The rational element in you—that is what is superior in you. Adorn and beautify that; but as for your hair, leave it to him who made it in accordance with his will. [27] Well, what other names do you bear? Are you a man or a woman? A man. Then adorn yourself as a man, and not as a woman. A woman is by nature smooth-skinned and delicate, and if she is covered with hair, she is a prodigy, and is exhibited at Rome among the prodigies. [28] But the same applies to a man if he is not hairy, and if by nature he is devoid of hair, he is a prodigy; but if he himself cuts it off and pulls it out, what are we to make of him? Where shall we exhibit him, and what announcement shall we post up? 'I'll show you a man who would rather be a woman than a man.' [29] What a shocking spectacle! There won't be anyone who won't be shocked by such an announcement. By Zeus, I imagine that the men themselves who pluck out their hair do so without realizing what it is that they're doing.

[30] Man, what complaint do you have to bring against nature? That she brought you into the world as a man? What, ought she to bring everyone to birth as a woman, then? And in that case, what benefit would it have brought you to adorn yourself as you do? Why, if everyone was a woman, who would you have been adorning yourself for? [31] But this wretched thing displeases you, does it? Then why not make a thorough job of the matter and remove—how shall I put it?—the cause of all this hairiness? Turn yourself into a woman fully and completely, so that we may no longer be in doubt, rather than being half-man and half-woman. [32] Whom do you want to please? The women? Then please them as a man.

'Yes, but they like smooth-bodied men.'

Go hang yourself. But if they liked inverts, I suppose, you'd become one of those? [33] Is this your business in life, then; is this what you were brought into the world for, to make yourself appealing to licentious women? [34] Shall we make a man like you a citizen of Corinth, and quite possibly a city warden, or superintendent of the cadets, or general, or president of the games? [35] Come, even when you're married, will you continue to pluck out your hairs? For whom, and to what end? And when you've fathered boys, will you introduce them into the community with their hair plucked out in turn? Oh, what a fine citizen, what a fine senator, what a fine orator! Is it youths of that kind that we should have born and reared among us? [36] By the gods, young man, may that not be your fate! But once you've heard what I've had to say, go away and tell yourself, 'It wasn't Epictetus who told me all that—for how could he have come up with it?—but some kindly god speaking through his mouth. For it would never have entered the mind of Epictetus to say such things, because he isn't in the habit of speaking to anyone. [37] Well, let's obey the god, then, so as not to incur his anger.' No, if a raven gives a sign to you through its croaking, it isn't the raven that's giving the sign, but the god through him; and if he gives the sign through a human voice, will you pretend that it is the person himself who is saying these things, and so fail to recognize the power of the divinity, and to realize that he gives signs to some people in one way, and to other people in another way, but that when it comes to the highest and most important matters, he gives the sign through the noblest of his messengers? [38] What else does the poet mean when he says,

> *Since we ourselves warned him,*
> *By sending keen-sighted Hermes, the slayer of Argos,*
> *To tell him not to slay the man and court his wife.* *

[39] And just as Hermes came down to tell these things to Odysseus, so the gods are now telling you the same by sending Hermes 'the messenger, the slayer of Argos' to warn you not to overturn what is right and good, and not to meddle with it to no purpose, but to let a man be a man, a woman be a woman, and one who is beautiful be beautiful as a human being, and one who is ugly be ugly as a human being. [40] For you yourself are neither flesh nor hair, but choice, and if you render that beautiful, then you yourself will be beautiful. [41] So far I haven't summoned up the courage to tell you that you're ugly, since I have the impression that you'd prefer to hear anything rather than that. [42] Consider, though, what Socrates says to Alcibiades, that most beautiful of men in the bloom of his youth: 'Strive, then, to make yourself beautiful.' What does he mean by that? Curl your locks and pluck the hair from your legs? Heaven forbid! But rather, beautify your moral choice, and eradicate your bad judgements. [43] As for your poor body, how are you to deal with that? In accordance with nature. Another has taken care of that, leave it to him.

[44] 'What, should my body be left dirty, then?'

Heaven forbid! But the person who you are and were born to be, keep that clean, a man as a man, a woman as a woman, and a child as a child. [45] No, but let's pluck out the lion's mane too, so that he may not be left 'dirty', and the cock's comb, since he for his part too needs to be 'clean'! Indeed he should be, but as a cock, and a lion as a lion, and a hound as a hound.

3.2 *What a person must train himself in if he is to make progress, and that we neglect what is most important*

[1] There are three areas of study in which someone who wants to be virtuous and good must be trained: that which relates to desires and aversions, so that he may neither fail to get what he desires, nor fall into what he wants to avoid; [2] that which relates to our motives to act or not to act, and, in general, appropriate behaviour, so that he may act in an orderly manner and with good reason, rather than carelessly; and thirdly, that which relates to the avoidance of error and hasty judgement, and, in general, whatever relates to assent.

[3] Of these, the most important and most urgent is that which is concerned with the passions, for these arise in no other way than through our being frustrated in our desires and falling into what we want to avoid. This is what brings about disturbances, confusions, misfortunes, and calamities, and causes sorrow, lamentation, and envy, making people envious and jealous, with the result that we become incapable of listening to reason.

[4] The second is concerned with appropriate action; for I shouldn't be unfeeling like a statue, but should preserve my natural and acquired relationships, as one who honours the gods, as a son, as a brother, as a father, as a citizen.

[5] The third belongs to those who are already making progress, and is concerned with the achievement of constancy in the matters already covered, so that even when we're asleep, or drunk, or depressed, no untested impression that presents itself may catch us off guard.

'That's beyond our powers,' someone says.

[6] But philosophers nowadays neglect the first and second areas of study to concentrate on the third, dealing with equivocal arguments, and those that are developed through questioning, and those that are fallacious, like 'the Liar'.

[7] 'Yes, because when one is dealing with these matters, one needs to protect oneself against being deceived.'

Who must? One who is virtuous and good. [8] Is it in this regard that you fall short, then? Have you achieved perfection in the other areas of study? When a bit of money is involved, are you secure against deception? If you see a pretty girl, can you resist the impression? If your neighbour receives an inheritance, don't you feel a bite of envy? And are you lacking in nothing else at present than unshakeable judgement? [9] Even while you're studying these topics, you wretch, you're trembling with anxiety at the thought that someone may despise you, and are asking whether anyone is making remarks about you. [10] And if someone should come and tell you, 'A discussion developed about who was the best philosopher, and someone who was there said, "That fellow's the only true philosopher",' that little soul of yours, which measures hardly an inch, springs up to become a yard high; but if someone else who was there should say, 'You're talking rubbish, that fellow isn't worth listening to, what does he know? The first elements of the subject and nothing more,' you're distraught, you turn pale, and immediately exclaim, 'I'll show him what sort of a man I am, that I'm a true philosopher!' [11] From that very behaviour, it is clear what kind of man you are! Why do you want to show it in any other way than that? Don't you know that Diogenes* showed up one of the sophists in that way, by pointing at him with his middle finger,* and then, when the man flew into a rage, remarking, 'That's the man, I've pointed him out to you!' [12] For a human being is not something that can be shown in the same way as a stone or a piece of wood, by pointing with one's finger, but when one has shown what his judgements are, then one has shown what he is as a human being.

[13] Let's have a look at your judgements too. For isn't it clear that you set no value on your own choice, but look beyond to things that lie outside the sphere of choice, to think about what So-and-so will say about you, and what impression you make on people, whether they'll see you as a scholar, or as someone who has read Chrysippus and Antipater. And if you pass for someone who has read Archedemus too, you're over the moon. [14] Why are you still anxious that you may be failing to show us who you are? Would you like me to tell you what kind of a man you've shown yourself to be? One who presents himself as base, querulous, quick-tempered, and cowardly, and as

one who finds fault with everything, criticizes everybody, and is never at peace, and is a braggart. That is what you've shown us. [15] Go away now and read Archedemus; and then if a mouse falls over and makes a noise, you'll die of fright. For that is the sort of death that awaits you, the sort of death that—who was it now?—Crinus* met with. And he too thought very highly of himself because he could understand Archedemus.

[16] Wretch, aren't you willing to put aside these things that don't concern you? For they're suitable only for those who can learn them with an untroubled mind, for those who can rightly say, 'I don't give way to anger, distress, or envy; I'm free from hindrance and constraint. What is left for me to do? I have leisure, I have peace of mind. [17] Let's see how one should tackle equivocal arguments; let's see how, after having accepted a hypothesis, one may avoid being led on to any absurd conclusion.' It is to people of such a kind that these studies belong. When people are in a good way, it is fitting for them to light a fire, eat a meal, and, if they care to, even sing and dance; but when your ship is already sinking, you're coming to me and hoisting your topsails!

3.3 *What is the material that the good person works upon, and what should be the main object of our training?*

[1] The material that the good and virtuous person works upon is his own ruling centre, as that of a doctor or wrestling master is the human body, and that of a farmer is his land; and the task of the good and virtuous person is to deal with his impressions in accordance with nature. [2] Now, since it lies in the nature of every mind to give its assent to what is true, and to dissent from what is false, and to suspend judgement with regard to what is uncertain, it lies in its nature likewise to be moved by desire towards what is good, and by aversion from what is bad, and to remain indifferent towards what is neither good nor bad. [3] For just as Caesar's coinage may not be refused by a banker or a greengrocer, but he is obliged, if it is presented to him, to hand over what is sold for the price whether he wishes it or not, the same also holds true of the mind. [4] Immediately the good appears, it draws the mind towards itself, while the bad repels the mind from itself. Never will the mind refuse a clear impression of the good, any more than a man will

refuse Caesar's coinage. [5] On this hangs every action of both man and god.

That is why the good is preferred above every tie of blood. My father is nothing to me, but only the good.—'Can you be so hard-hearted?'—Yes, because that is my nature; that is the coinage that God has given me. [6] For that reason, if the good is different from what is right and just, they're all gone, father, brother, country, and the rest. [7] What, shall I neglect my own good so that you may have it, and shall I make way for you? What for? 'I'm your father.' But not a good. 'I'm your brother.' But not a good. [8] Yet if we place the good in right choice, the preservation of our relationships itself becomes a good. And besides, he who gives up certain external things achieves the good through that. [9] 'My father's depriving me of money.' But he isn't causing you any harm. 'My brother is going to get the greater share of the land.' Let him have as much as he wishes. He won't be getting any of your decency, will he, or of your loyalty, or of your brotherly love? [10] For who can disinherit you of possessions such as those? Not even Zeus; nor would he wish to, but rather he has placed all of that in my own power, even as he had it himself, free from hindrance, compulsion, and restraint.

[11] When different people use different coinage, a person offers his money and takes what can be bought in exchange for it. [12] A thief has come to the province as proconsul. What coinage does he use? Silver. Offer it to him and carry away what you wish. An adulterer has arrived. What coinage does he use? Pretty girls. 'Take the coin', the buyer says, 'and sell me that bit of stuff.' Give and buy. [13] Another has a taste for boys. Give him the coin and take what you wish. Another is fond of hunting. Give him a fine nag or hound, and though with sighs and groans, he'll sell in exchange whatever you wish; for another forces him from within to act in that way, the one who has established the currency.

[14] It is in accordance with this plan of action above all that one should train oneself. As soon as you leave the house at break of day, examine everyone whom you see, everyone whom you hear, and answer as if under questioning. What did you see? A handsome man or beautiful woman? Apply the rule. Does this lie within the sphere of choice, or outside it? Outside. Throw it away. [15] What did you see? Someone grieving over the death of his child? Apply the rule.

Death is something that lies outside the sphere of choice. Away with it. You met a consul? Apply the rule. What kind of thing is a consulship? One that lies outside the sphere of choice, or inside? Outside. Throw that away too, it doesn't stand the test. Away with it; it is nothing to you. [16] If we acted in such a way and practised this exercise from morning until night, we would then have achieved something, by the gods. [17] But as things are, we're caught gazing open-mouthed at every impression that comes along, and it is only in the schoolroom that we wake up a little, if indeed we ever do. Afterwards, when we go outside, if we see someone in distress, we say, 'He's done for,' or if we see a consul, exclaim, 'A most fortunate man'; if an exile, 'Poor wretch!'; if someone in poverty, 'How terrible for him; he hasn't money enough to buy a meal.'

[18] These vicious judgements must be rooted out, then; that is what we should concentrate our efforts on. For what is weeping and groaning? A judgement. What is misfortune? A judgement. What is civil strife, dissension, fault-finding, accusation, impiety, foolishness? [19] All of these are judgements and nothing more, and judgements that are passed, moreover, about things that lie outside the sphere of choice, under the supposition that such things are good or bad. Let someone transfer these judgements to things that lie within the sphere of choice, and I guarantee that he'll preserve his peace of mind, regardless of what his circumstances may be.

[20] The mind is rather like a bowl filled with water, and impressions are like a ray of light that falls on that water. [21] When the water is disturbed, the ray of light gives the appearance of being disturbed, but that isn't really the case. [22] So accordingly, whenever someone suffers an attack of vertigo, it isn't the arts and virtues that are thrown into confusion, but the spirit in which they're contained; and when the spirit comes to rest again, so will they too.

3.4 *To one who took sides in the theatre in an undignified manner*

[1] The governor of Epirus had shown his support for a comic actor in a somewhat undignified manner, and had been abused in public for doing so. When he then reported to Epictetus that he had been subjected to abuse, and expressed indignation at those who had insulted him, Epictetus said: Why, what was wrong in what they were doing?

They too were taking sides, just as you were, to which the man replied, [2] 'Is that the way, then, in which one expresses one's partiality?'

When they saw you, their ruler, the associate and procurator of Caesar, taking sides in that way, weren't they bound to take sides for their own part too in the same way? [3] Why, if one shouldn't take sides in such a way, you shouldn't do so either; but if one may, why be angry with them because they followed your example? Who else do the people have to imitate apart from you, their superior? Who are they going to look at when they go to the theatre, if not at you? [4] 'Look at how Caesar's governor is acting as he watches the show! He is shouting; well, I'll shout too. He is jumping from his seat; well, I'll jump up and down too. His slaves who are scattered around the theatre are crying out; well, since I don't have any slaves, I'll shout as loud as I can to make up for the lot of them!'

[5] You ought to know, then, that when you enter the theatre, you're entering as a pattern and example for everyone else, showing them how they should behave as spectators. [6] Why did they abuse you, then? Because everyone hates whatever stands in his way. They wanted one person to win the crown, and you wanted someone else to win. They were standing in your way, and you in theirs. It was you who proved the stronger, and they did what they could, by abusing what was standing in their way. [7] What do you want, then? That you should do what you please, and they shouldn't even say what they please? And what is surprising in that? Don't farmers revile Zeus when he stands in their way? Don't sailors revile him? And when do people ever stop reviling Caesar? What, then, is Zeus unaware of this? [8] Does Caesar receive no report about what people are saying about him? What does he do, then? He well knows that if he were to punish all who abuse him, he would have nobody left to rule. [9] What, then, as you enter the theatre, ought you to say, 'Come, let Sophron have the crown'? No, rather, 'Come, let me ensure that in this matter, I keep my faculty of choice in accord with nature. [10] No one is dearer to me than myself; it would thus be absurd that I should do harm to myself to enable another man to win a victory as a comic actor. [11] Then who do I want to see winning? Why, the victor: and in that way, the man whom I want to win will invariably win.'

'But I want Sophron to get the crown.'

Stage as many contests as you wish in your own house, and proclaim him a Nemean, Pythian, Isthmian, and Olympic* victor; but in public, don't claim more than your due and seize for yourself a right that belongs to everyone; [12] otherwise you must put up with being abused, because if you act as the crowd does, you're placing yourself on their level.

3.5 *To those who leave because of illness*

[1] 'I'm ill here,' someone says, 'and I want to go home.'

[2] What, were you never ill at home? Don't you want to examine whether you're doing anything that may contribute to the improvement of your choice? For if you're not accomplishing anything, it was pointless for you even to come here. [3] Go away, and attend to your domestic affairs. For if your ruling centre can't be kept in accord with nature, your little piece of land at least could be. You'll add to your small store of cash, look after your father in his old age, hang around in the marketplace, hold public office; and being of bad character, you'll do everything else badly. [4] But if you can recognize in your own mind that you're ridding yourself of some bad judgements, and taking on others in their place, and that you've transferred your centre of concern from things that lie outside the sphere of choice to those that lie within, and that if you sometimes cry, 'Alas!', it won't be because of your father or brother, but because of yourself—what reason is there for you to give any thought to your illness? [5] Don't you know that illness and death are bound to overtake us whatever we're doing? They seize the farmer at his plough, and the sailor out at sea. [6] And for your own part, what would you like to be doing when you're seized by them? For you surely will be seized by them whatever you're doing. If you could be doing something more worthwhile than what you're doing at present when that time comes, go and do it.

[7] For my part, I'd wish that death may overtake me when I'm attending to nothing other than my power of choice, to ensure that it may be unperturbed, unhindered, unconstrained, and free. [8] That is what I'd like to be engaged in when death finds me, so that I may be able to say to God, 'Have I violated your orders in any way? Have I used the resources that you gave me for anything other than the purpose for which they were given? Have I misused my senses or my preconceptions? Have I ever found fault with you in any regard? Have I ever made any complaint against your government? [9] I fell ill

when you wished it; so did others too, but I did so willingly. I suffered poverty because you wished it, but I rejoiced in it. I didn't hold public office since that wasn't your wish, and I never desired it. Have you ever seen me in any way dejected because of that? Haven't I always presented myself to you with a face shining with joy, ready to carry out whatever you might command, and to obey your least signal? [10] It is now your wish that I should leave the festival, and I take my leave, full of gratitude that you should have judged me worthy of taking part in this festival with you, and of viewing your works and understanding your governing order.' [11] May I be thinking such thoughts, writing such thoughts, reading such thoughts, when death overtakes me!

[12] 'But my mother won't be there to hold my head when I'm ill.'—Go home to your mother, then; for you deserve that someone should hold your head when you're ill. [13] —'But at home I have a nice little bed to lie down in.'—Go back to that little bed of yours, since you're the kind of person who deserves to lie in such a bed, even when you're in good health. So don't miss out on what you could be doing back there.

[14] But what does Socrates say? 'As one person rejoices in improving his land, and another his horse, so I rejoice day by day in observing that I myself am becoming better.'*—'Better in what? In weaving fine phrases together?'—Hush, man! [15] —'In putting forward fine theories?'—What do you mean? [16] —'Well, I can't see what else philosophers spend their time doing.'—Does it seem nothing at all to you that one should never find fault with anyone, whether god or human being, and never reproach anyone, and always have the same expression on one's face, whether going out or coming in? [17] These were the things that Socrates knew, while saying nonetheless that he knew and taught nothing whatever. But if someone was looking for fine phrases or fine principles, he would send them off to Protagoras or Hippias,* just as though, if someone had come in search of vegetables, he would have sent them off to a market gardener. Who of you sets this as his purpose, then? [18] Because if you did, you'd willingly undergo illness, hunger, and death. [19] If any of you has ever been in love with a pretty girl, he'll know that I'm telling the truth.

3.6 *Miscellaneous*

[1] When someone asked him how it is that, although more effort is devoted to the study of logic nowadays, greater progress was made in

the past, [2] Epictetus replied: In what area is the effort applied in our own time, and in what area was progress greater in earlier times? For in that to which effort is devoted nowadays, so also will progress be found in our day. [3] Now, in our own day people have been devoting their efforts to the solving of syllogisms, and in that, real progress has been made; whereas formerly they devoted their efforts to keeping their ruling centre in accord with nature, and progress was made in that regard. [4] Don't confuse one thing with another, then, and when you concentrate your efforts in one area, don't expect to make progress in another. But see if there is anyone among us who, if he strives to keep himself and his life in conformity with nature, fails to make progress. You won't find anyone who fails to do so.

[5] The good person is invincible because he never engages in any contest in which he is not superior. [6] 'If you want my land, take it; take my servants, take my public position, take my poor body. But you won't cause my desires to fail to attain their end, or my aversions to fall into what they want to avoid.' [7] This is the only contest that he enters into, the one that is concerned with things that lie within the sphere of choice; so how can he be anything other than invincible?

[8] When someone asked what is meant by common sense, he replied: Just as one might call the faculty that simply distinguishes between sounds common hearing, whereas that which distinguishes between musical sounds is artistic hearing, so there are likewise certain things that people whose minds are not altogether perverted can see by virtue of their general resources; such a condition of the mind is called common sense.

[9] It isn't easy to convert young men to philosophy, any more than one can catch soft cheese on a hook; but those who are naturally gifted, even if one tries to turn them away, attach themselves all the more strongly to reason. [10] And so Rufus* used to turn people away most of the time, using that as a test to distinguish the gifted from the ungifted. For he used to say, 'Just as a stone, even if you throw it into the air, will fall down to the earth by virtue of its own nature, so it is too with the gifted person: the more one tries to beat him off, the more he inclines towards the object to which his nature carries him.'

3.7 *To the inspector of the free cities, who was an Epicurean*

[1] When the inspector called in on him (the man was an Epicurean), Epictetus said: It is fitting for laymen like ourselves to enquire of you philosophers—just as those who arrive in a strange town do of the citizens who know the place—to ask you what is the best thing in the world, so that when we've learned what it is, we too may seek it out to have a look at it, just as visitors seek out the sights of a city.

[2] Now, hardly anyone denies that there are three things that make up human beings: mind, body, and external things. So all that remains for you to do is to answer the question, which is the best? What are we going to tell people? That it is the flesh? [3] Was it for this that Maximus sailed all the way to Cassiope* in winter with his son, conducting him on his way? Was it for the pleasure of the flesh? [4] When the visitor denied that, exclaiming, 'Heaven forbid!', Epictetus continued: Isn't it proper, then, to devote special attention to what is best in us?—'It is altogether proper.'—What do we have in us, then, that is better than our flesh?—'Our mind', the man said.—Are the goods of the best part of higher value, or those of the inferior part? [5] —'Those of the best.'—And the goods of the mind, do they lie within the sphere of choice, or outside it?—'Within it.'—Does the pleasure of the mind lie within the sphere of choice, then?—'It does.' [6] —And what gives rise to it? Does it arise of itself? No, that is inconceivable; for we must assume the prior existence of a certain essence of the good, by partaking of which we come to feel this pleasure in our mind.—He agreed to this point too. [7] —At what, then, does this pleasure of the mind arise? For if it is at the goods of the mind, the essence of the good has been discovered, because it is impossible that the good should be one thing while that in which we reasonably take delight should be another, or again, that if the antecedent is not good, what follows from it could be good; for if the consequent is to be justified, the antecedent must be good. [8] But this is something that you Epicureans should not admit, if you have any sense, because what you would then be saying would be inconsistent both with Epicurus and with the other doctrines of your school. [9] The only thing that is left for you to say, then, is that the pleasure of the mind is pleasure in bodily things, and these pleasures thus come to be what is of primary value, and the essence of the good.

[10] Maximus thus acted foolishly if he made his voyage for

anything other than the flesh, that is to say, for the sake of anything other than what is best. [11] And someone is acting foolishly too if he refrains from taking other people's property while he is sitting as a judge and is able to do so. But if you like, let's take care only that the theft be committed in secret, and in full safety without anyone knowing; [12] for Epicurus himself doesn't declare the act of theft to be bad, but only getting caught, and it is merely because one can't be sure of escaping detection that he says, 'Don't steal.'* [13] But I assume that if it is done cleverly and with proper care, we won't be found out. And besides, we have powerful friends in Rome, both men and women, and the Greeks are pusillanimous; none of them will dare to go to Rome about such a matter. [14] Why is it, then, that you refrain from pursuing your own good? That's foolish; it's silly. No, even if you were to tell me that you do refrain from it, I won't believe you. [15] For just as it is impossible to give your assent to what appears to be false, it is impossible likewise to abstain from something that seems to be good. Now wealth is good, and it is, one might say, what serves best for the securing of pleasures. [16] Why shouldn't you acquire it? And why shouldn't we try to seduce our neighbour's wife, if we can do so without getting caught? And if her husband spouts a lot of nonsense, why shouldn't we break his neck in addition? [17] That's what you should do if you want to be a philosopher of the right kind, a perfect philosopher, remaining true to your own doctrines! Otherwise you're no different from those of us who are called Stoics. [18] For we too speak in one way and act in another; we talk of what is fine and noble, but do what is shameful, while you're perverse in the opposite way, laying down shameful doctrines but acting nobly.

[19] In God's name, I ask you, can you imagine a city of Epicureans? 'I shan't marry.' 'Nor I, for one shouldn't marry.' 'Nor should one have children; nor should one perform any civic duties.'* So what will happen, then? Where are the citizens to come from? Who'll educate them? Who'll be superintendent of the cadets? Who'll be director of the gymnasium? And then, what will the young men be taught? What the Spartans were taught, or the Athenians? [20] Take a young man, I ask you, and bring him up in accordance with your doctrines. Your doctrines are bad; they're subversive of the state, ruinous to families, and not fitting even for women. [21] Give them up, man. You're living in a city of the empire; you must exercise your authority, judge in

accordance with what is right, keep your hands off other people's property, regard no woman as beautiful apart from your own wife, and regard no boy as beautiful, nor any piece of silverware or gold-ware. [22] You should seek out doctrines that are consistent with that pattern of behaviour, and with those as your guide, you'll abstain from the things that are so seductive to us, and are liable to lead us astray and overpower us. [23] But if, on the contrary, in addition to their seductiveness, we should have devised some such philosophy as yours, which will help to propel us towards them and give them added strength, what will come of that?

[24] In a piece of embossed silverware, what is best: the silver or the workmanship? The substance of the hand is mere flesh, but what is important is the works that the hand produces. [25] Now, appropriate actions are of three kinds:* first, those relating to mere existence, sec-ondly, those relating to existence of a particular kind, and thirdly, those that are themselves principal duties. And what are those? [26] Fulfilling one's role as a citizen, marrying, having children, honour-ing God, taking care of one's parents, and, in a word, having our desires and aversions, and our motives to act and or not to act, as each of them ought to be, in accordance with our nature. And what is our nature? [27] To be people who are free, noble-minded, and self-respecting. For what other animal blushes; what other animal has a sense of shame? [28] Pleasure should be subordinated to these duties as a servant, as an attendant,* so as to arouse our zeal, so as to ensure that we consistently act in accord with nature.

[29] 'But I'm rich and have need of nothing.'

Why do you still make a pretence, then, of being a philosopher? Your goldware and silverware are enough to satisfy you; what need do you have of philosophical doctrines?

[30] 'Yes, but I'm also serving as judge of the Greeks.'

Do you know how to judge? Who has given you such knowledge? 'Caesar has signed my credentials.'

May he give you credentials too certifying that you're a judge of music! And what good would that do you? [31] Besides, how did you come to be a judge? Whose hand did you kiss? That of Symphorus or Numenius?* Whose antechamber did you sleep in?* Who did you send gifts to? And then, don't you understand that your post as a judge is worth precisely the same as Numenius is worth?

'But I can throw anyone I want into prison.'

As you can throw a stone.

[32] 'But I can have anyone I want beaten with a cudgel.'

As you can a donkey. That isn't what it means to govern human beings. [33] Govern us as rational beings by showing us what is in our interest, and we'll follow you; show us what is against our interest, and we'll turn away from it. [34] Make us admire you, make us want to emulate you, as Socrates did with his followers. He was someone who truly knew how to govern his fellow men, because he led people to submit their desires to him, their aversions, their motives to act or not to act. [35] 'Do this, don't do that, otherwise I'll have you thrown into prison': it isn't in that way that one governs rational beings. [36] No, say instead, 'Do this as Zeus has ordained; otherwise you'll suffer punishment, you'll suffer injury.' What kind of injury? None other than not having done what you ought to do. You'll destroy the man of good faith in you, the man of honour, the man of moderation. You need look for no greater injuries than that.

3.8 *How should we train ourselves to deal with impressions*

[1] As we train ourselves to deal with sophistical questioning, so we should also train ourselves each day to deal with impressions, [2] because they too put questions to us.

'The son of So-and-so has died.'—Reply: That lies outside the sphere of choice, it is nothing bad.

'So-and-so has been disinherited by his father.'—That lies outside the sphere of choice, it is nothing bad.

'Caesar has condemned him.'—That lies outside the sphere of choice, it is nothing bad.

[3] 'He has been distressed by these things.'—That lies within the sphere of choice, it is something bad.

'He has endured it nobly.'—That lies within the sphere of choice, it is something good.

[4] If we adopt this habit, we'll make progress, because we'll never give our assent to anything unless we get a convincing impression.*

[5] 'His son has died.'—What has happened?—'His son has died.'—Nothing more than that?—'Nothing more.'

'His ship has gone down.'—What has happened? His ship has gone down.

'He has been taken off to prison.'—What has happened? He has been taken off to prison. But the observation 'Things have gone badly for him' is something that each person adds for himself.

[6] 'But Zeus is not acting rightly in all of this.'—Why? Because he has given you the ability to endure things, and has made you noble-minded, because he has prevented these things from being evils, because he has made it possible for you to suffer them and still be happy, because he has left the door open for you, for when things are no longer good for you? Go out, man, and don't complain.

[7] If you want to know how the Romans feel towards philosophers, listen to this. Italicus,* who had a very high reputation among them as a philosopher, once grew angry with his friends in my presence, claiming to have suffered something intolerable. 'I can't bear it,' he said; 'you'll be the death of me, you'll be making me just like him'—and he pointed at me!

3.9 *To an orator who was going to Rome in connection with a lawsuit*

[1] Someone called in on Epictetus while travelling to Rome in connection with a lawsuit about an honour that was due to him. After responding to Epictetus' enquiry about the reason for his journey, the man proceeded to ask him what he thought about the matter. [2] If you're asking me about what you're going to do in Rome, he replied, and whether you'll win or lose your case, I have no guidance to offer; but if you're asking me how you'll do, I can tell you that if your judgements are right, you'll do well, but if they're wrong, you'll do badly; for whatever a person does, he does on the basis of a judgement. [3] For what is it that makes you want to be elected as patron of the Cnossians?* Your judgement. And what prompts you to go off to Rome at the present time? Your judgement. And in winter too, at some risk and expense?

'Yes, because it is essential.'

[4] Who tells you that? Your judgement. If our judgements, then, are the cause of all that we undertake, when someone has bad judgements, just as the cause is, so will the result be too. [5] Well then, do we all have sound judgements, both you and your opponent alike? If so, how is it that you disagree? But is it that you have sound

judgement rather than he? Why? Because you think that is the case. But he thinks that too, and so do madmen. That is a bad criterion.

[6] Show me, then, that you have subjected your own judgements to some examination, and have paid attention to them. And since you're now sailing off to Rome in the hope of becoming the patron of the Cnossians, and aren't content to stay at home with the honours that you already had, but have set your heart on something greater and more splendid, have you set sail in such a way for the purpose of examining your own judgements, and rejecting any that you find to be unsound? [7] Whom have you ever visited for that purpose? What time have you devoted to yourself; what period of your life? Run through the years of your life; in your own mind if you're ashamed to do so in front of me. [8] When you were a child, did you examine your own judgements? Isn't it true that you used to do everything just as you do it now? And when you grew up to become an adolescent, when you listened to the orators and practised on your own account, did you imagine that you were deficient in anything? [9] And when, as a young man, you began to take part in public affairs, and to plead cases yourself and acquire a reputation, was there anyone who still appeared to you to be your equal? Would you have put up with it for a moment if someone had tried to cross-examine you to show that you had bad judgements? [10] Well then, what do you want me to say?

'Help me out in this matter.'

I have no rules of conduct to offer you in this, and if you have come to me for that purpose, you haven't come here as you should come to a philosopher, but as one would come to a greengrocer or a cobbler.

[11] 'With regard to what, then, do philosophers have rules to offer?'

With regard to this, to ensuring that whatever comes about, our ruling centre is and forever continues to be in accord with nature. Does that seem a small matter to you?

'No, but of the highest importance.'

Well then, does that require only a short time, as something that you can pick up in passing? Please do, if you can. [12] You'll go on to say, 'I had an encounter with Epictetus, but it was like being with a stone, with a statue.' The fact is that you've seen me and nothing more. But if one is to meet someone properly, as a person, one must become acquainted with his judgements, and show him one's own

judgements in one's turn. [13] Learn to know my judgements, show
me your own, and then you can say that you've met me. Let's cross-
examine one another; and if I'm harbouring any bad judgement, root
it out, or if you're harbouring any, bring it to light. That is what
meeting a philosopher is all about. [14] But no, instead you say, 'We're
passing through, and while we're waiting to hire our ship, we'll have
an opportunity to go and see Epictetus too. Let's see what he has to
say.' And then as you leave, 'Epictetus didn't amount to anything, he
murdered the language, used barbarous expressions.' For what else
would you be able to pass judgement on, coming here in the way that
you did?

[15] 'But if I turn to these matters,' someone says, 'I won't be a
landowner any more than you are, I won't own silver goblets any
more than you do, and I won't have fine cattle any more than you do.'
[16] To which it would perhaps suffice to respond, 'But I have no need
of such things, and even if you come to acquire many possessions,
you'll need more again, and whether you wish it or not, you're more
poverty-stricken than I am.'

[17] 'What do I have need of, then?'

What you don't have at present, stability, a mind in accord with
nature, and freedom from agitation. [18] To be a patron, or not to be a
patron, means nothing to me, but it matters to you. I'm not anxious
about what Caesar will think of me, and I flatter no one for that purpose. That is what I have in place of your vessels of silver and gold.
As for you, you may possess goldware, but your reason, your judgements, your assents, your motives, your desires, are earthenware one
and all. [19] But when I have all of these in accord with nature, why
shouldn't I devote some of my attention to the art of reasoning? I
have the leisure to do so, because my mind isn't distracted by all
kinds of different things. Could I find a task more worthy of a human
being than this? [20] For your part, you're at a loose end when you
have nothing to do; you go to the theatre to kill time. Why shouldn't
a philosopher cultivate his own reason? [21] You have crystal vases, I
the argument of 'the Liar'. You have Myrrhine glassware, I the denying argument.* To you, all the possessions that you have seem small,
while to me everything that I have seems great. Your desire is insatiable; mine is already fulfilled. [22] It is the same as when children
push their hand into a narrow-necked jar and try to extract nuts and
figs; if they fill their hand, they can't get it out again, and then burst

into tears. Drop a few of them and you'll get it out. And in your case, too, let your desire drop; don't hanker after so many things, and you'll get what you want.

3.10 *How ought we to bear our illnesses?*

[1] We should have each judgement ready at hand for when we have need of it; at table, such as relate to the table, at the baths, such as relate to baths, and in bed, such as relate to bed.

> [2] *Let not sleep descend on your weary eyes*
> *Before having reviewed every action of the day.*
> [3] *Where did I go wrong? What did I do? What duty leave undone?*
> *Starting here, review your actions, and afterwards,*
> *Blame yourself for what is badly done, and rejoice in the good.*

[4] We should keep these verses at hand to put them to practical use, and not merely use them by way of exclamation, as when we cry, 'Paean Apollo!'* [5] And again, when in a fever, we should have the judgements at hand that apply to that; let's make sure, if we're struck by a fever, that we don't cast all of that aside and forget it, saying, 'If I return to philosophy again, let things come about as they will,' and go away somewhere to take care of our poor body. Won't the fever go there too? [6] But to practise philosophy, what does that mean? Isn't it to prepare oneself to face every eventuality? Don't you under-stand, then, that what you're saying amounts to something like this: 'If I ever again prepare myself to face every eventuality with equa-nimity, let things come about as they will'? It is as if someone were to withdraw from the pancration because he has received some blows! [7] Though in the pancration, it is possible to withdraw from the con-test and so escape a beating, but in our case, if we were to abandon philosophy, what good would that do us? What should a philosopher say, then, in the face of each of the hardships of life? 'It is for this that I've been training myself; it is for this that I was practising.' [8] God says to you, 'Give me proof of whether you've competed in accord-ance with the rules, whether you've followed the proper diet, carried out the proper exercises, and have obeyed your trainer.' And then, when the time comes for you to act, will you quail? Now is the moment to suffer a fever; may it proceed as it should; to undergo thirst, may you undergo it in the right spirit; to undergo hunger, may

you undergo it in the right spirit. [9] Isn't that within your power? Who can prevent you? Yes, a doctor may prevent you from drinking, but he can't prevent you from bearing thirst in the right way; he may prevent you from eating, but he can't prevent you from facing hunger in the right way.

[10] 'But isn't it the case that I'm a scholar?'

And for what purpose do you pursue your studies? Isn't it so that you may be happy, slave? Isn't it so that you may achieve constancy of mind? Isn't it so that you may be in accord with nature and pass your life so? [11] What prevents you, then, when you have a fever, from keeping your ruling centre in accord with nature? Here is the proof of the matter; here is the testing point for a philosopher. For this too is a part of life, just as a walk is, or a sea-voyage, or a journey, so is a fever too. [12] You don't read when taking a walk, do you?—'No.'—Nor do you read when you're suffering from a fever. But if you walk in the right way, you're fulfilling your role as a walker, and if you undergo a fever in the right way, you're fulfilling your role as a fever patient. [13] What does it mean to undergo a fever in the right way? It is to find fault with neither God nor man; it is to refuse to allow yourself to be overwhelmed by what is happening, and to await death bravely and in the right way, and to do what you're told; when your doctor arrives, don't be afraid of what he might say, and don't rejoice too greatly if he says, 'Things are going nicely for you.' For what is good in what he is telling you? [14] After all, when you were in good health, what was good for you in that? And likewise, if he says, 'You're in a bad way,' don't be dejected. For what does it mean to be in a bad way? That the moment is close at hand in which your soul will be separated from your body. Now what is so terrible in that? If you're not drawing close to that now, isn't it the case that you will draw close at some future time? What, will the world be turned upside down if you should come to die? [15] Why do you flatter your doctor, then? Why do you say, 'If only you wish it, sir, I'll be well'? Why do you give him an opportunity to put on airs? Why not pay him just what is due to him? As I pay a shoemaker his due with regard to my foot, and a builder with regard to my house, why not the doctor with regard to my poor body, something that isn't my own, something that is by nature a corpse? These are the things that the moment demands from someone who is suffering from a fever; and if he accomplishes them, he is as he ought to be.

[16] For it isn't the business of a philosopher to safeguard these external things, his little store of wine or oil, or his poor body; but in that case, what? His own ruling centre. And how should he concern himself with external things? Only so far as to ensure that he doesn't behave towards them in any ill-considered manner. What occasion is left for fear, then? What occasion for anger? [17] What occasion is there left for fear when it comes to external things, to things of no value? [18] These, then, are two principles that we should always keep at hand: that outside the sphere of choice, there is nothing good or bad, and that we should guide events rather than follow them.

[19] 'My brother shouldn't have treated me in this way.' Indeed he shouldn't, but it's for him to see to that. For my part, however he treats me, I should conduct myself towards him as I ought. For that is my business, and the rest is not my concern. In this no one can hinder me, while everything else is subject to hindrance.

3.11 *Miscellaneous*

[1] There are certain punishments that are laid down as though by law against those who disobey the divine governing order: [2] 'Whoever shall regard anything as good other than those things that lie within the sphere of choice, let him be subject to envy and desire, let him flatter, let him be troubled in his mind; whoever shall regard anything other as evil, let him grieve, let him lament, let him be unhappy.' [3] Yet all the same, in spite of these harsh penalties, we cannot desist from thinking in such a way.

[4] Remember what the poet says with regard to strangers:

> *Stranger, it is not permitted, even if worse should come*
> *Than you, to dishonour a stranger; for all come from Zeus,*
> *Strangers and beggars.*

[5] You should also keep this thought at hand to apply in the case of a father: 'It is not permitted for me to dishonour you, father, even if worse should come than you, because all come from Zeus, the God of Paternity'; [6] and so too in the case of a brother, 'because all come from Zeus, the God of Kindred'. And likewise in all our other social relations, we shall find Zeus to be the overseer of them all.

3.12 *On training*

[1] In our training we shouldn't resort to unnatural and extraordinary practices, or otherwise we who profess to be philosophers will be no better than showmen. [2] For it is difficult also to walk along a tight-rope, and not only difficult, but dangerous too. For that reason, should we too practise walking along a tightrope, or setting up palms, or embracing statues?* In no way. [3] For not everything that is difficult or dangerous is suitable for training, but only what will contribute to our achieving the object of our strivings. [4] And what is the object of our strivings? To pass our lives without suffering any hindrance in our desires and aversions. And what does that mean? That we should neither fail to get what we desire, nor fall into what we want to avoid. It is, accordingly, towards that end that our training should be directed. [5] For without hard and unremitting training, it isn't possible for us to ensure that our desires won't fail to attain their object, or that our aversions won't fall into what they want to avoid, and you should know that if you allow your training to be directed outward, towards things that lie outside the sphere of choice, you won't have desire that is successful in attaining its object, nor will you have aversion that is secure from falling into what it wants to avoid. [6] And since habit is a powerful force that leads us where it will, when we've become accustomed to exercising our desires and aversions in relation to these external things alone, we must set a contrary habit in opposition to that habit, and when impressions are most inclined to make us slip, there we must apply our training as a counteracting force.

[7] I'm inclined to pleasure: I'll throw myself beyond measure in the opposite direction,* for the sake of training. I'm inclined to avoid hard work: I'll train and exercise my impressions to ensure that my aversion from everything of that kind will cease. [8] For who is a man in training? One who practises not exercising his desire, and practises exercising his aversion only in relation to things that lie within the sphere of choice, practising especially hard in matters that are difficult to master. So different people will practise hardest with regard to different things. [9] What purpose can it serve here, then, to set up a palm, or carry a leather tent around, and mortar and pestle?* [10] If you're irritable, man, train yourself to put up with abuse, and not get upset when you're insulted. Then you'll make such progress that,

even if someone hits you, you'll say to yourself, 'Imagine that you're embracing a statue.' [11] Train yourself next to use wine with discretion, not so as to be able to drink it in quantity—for there are some people who are so uncouth as to train themselves for that—but so as to be able to keep away, first of all, from wine, and then from a pretty girl, or a honey-cake. And then one day, by way of a test, if the occasion presents itself, you'll venture into the lists to see whether your impressions still get the better of you as they once did. [12] But to begin with, keep well away from what is stronger than you. If a pretty girl is set against a young man who is just making a start on philosophy, that is no fair contest. 'Pot and stone', so the saying goes, 'don't belong together.'

[13] After desire and aversion, the second area of study is concerned with your motives to act or not to act, so that they may be obedient to reason, and not be exercised at the wrong time, or in the wrong place, or improperly in any comparable respect.

[14] The third area of study is concerned with assent, and with what is plausible and attractive. [15] For just as Socrates used to say that we shouldn't live an unexamined life, we shouldn't accept any impression without subjecting it to examination, but should say to it, 'Wait, let me see who you are, and where you've come from'—just as night watchmen say: 'Show me your marks of identification'*—'Do you have that mark from nature that every impression must have if it is to be accepted?'

[16] And in conclusion, all the practices that are applied to the body by those who are giving it exercise may also be useful here if they're directed in some way towards desire and aversion; but if they're directed towards display, that is the sign of someone who has turned towards external things and is hunting for other prey, of one who is seeking for spectators to exclaim, 'Oh what a great man!' [17] Apollonius* was thus right when he used to say, 'If you want to train for your own sake, take a little cold water into your mouth when you're thirsty in hot weather and then spit it out again, without telling a soul.'

3.13 *What desolation means, and the nature of one who is desolate*

[1] Desolation is the condition of someone who is bereft of help. For a person is not desolate merely because he is alone, any more than he is

secure from desolation because he is in a crowd. [2] At all events, when we've lost a brother, or son, or a friend whom we've relied on, we say that we've been left desolate, even though we're often in Rome, where we run into such crowds and have so many people sharing the house with us, and sometimes, indeed, have a multitude of slaves. For the very notion of being desolate means that a person is helpless and exposed to those who wish to harm him. [3] That is why, when we're on a journey, we call ourselves desolate above all when we fall among robbers, for it isn't the mere sight of another person that delivers us from desolation, but the sight of one who is trustworthy, honest, and helpful. [4] If the bare fact of being alone was enough to make one desolate, one would have to say that even Zeus is desolate at the time of the conflagration of the universe, and laments to himself, 'How wretched I am, I have neither Hera, nor Athena, nor Apollo, and in a word have neither brother, nor son, nor grandson, nor any relation.'* [5] There are some indeed who say that he really does act like that when he finds himself alone at the conflagration of the universe; for they're unable to conceive how a person can live on his own, starting out as they do from this fact of nature, that human beings are naturally sociable, and have natural affection, and take joy in associating with one another. [6] But we ought to prepare ourselves nonetheless to be able to be self-sufficient, and to be able to live with ourselves, [7] and even as Zeus lives with himself, is at peace with himself, and reflects on the nature of his own rule, and occupies himself with thoughts that are worthy of him, so we too should be able to converse with ourselves, and know how to do without others, and not be at a loss about how to occupy ourselves; [8] we should reflect on the divine governing order, and the nature of our relationship with all other things, and consider how we have responded to events up until now, and how we are doing so at present, and what are the things that afflict us, and how these too can be remedied; and if any of these things need perfecting, we must perfect them in accordance with the principle of reason inherent in them.

[9] See how Caesar seems to provide us with profound peace:* there are no longer any wars and battles, no brigandage on any large scale, and no piracy, but it is possible for us to travel by land at any hour, or sail the seas from sunrise to sunset. [10] But can Caesar provide us with peace from fever too, from shipwreck, from fire, from earthquake, from lightning? Come now, can he provide us with peace

from love? He can't. From sorrow? He can't. From envy? No, he can't; from nothing of this kind. [11] But the teaching of the philosophers promises to provide us with peace from all such things. What does it say? 'If you'll pay heed to me, men, wherever you are, and whatever you're doing, you'll feel neither pain nor anger; you'll suffer neither constraint nor hindrance, but will pass your lives in peace and free from every trouble.' [12] When someone has this peace proclaimed to him, not by Caesar—for how would he be able to do so?—but by God through the voice of reason, [13] isn't he contented when alone, as he thinks and reflects, 'Now nothing bad can possibly happen to me; there can be no robber for me, no earthquake; everything is full of peace, full of tranquillity; and every road, every city, every fellow traveller, neighbour, companion, all are harmless. Another, to whom that care falls, provides me with food and clothing, another has given me senses and preconceptions. [14] When he no longer provides what is necessary, he sounds the recall; he has thrown the door open and says to you: "Go!" To where? To nothing that need cause you fear, but to that from which you came, to that which is friendly and akin to you, to the elements. [15] What there was of fire in you will return to fire, what there was of earth to earth, what there was of air to air, what there was of water to water. There is no Hades, no Acheron, no Cocytos, no Pyriphlegethon, but everything is filled with gods and divine spirits.'* [16] Whoever has this to reflect upon, and beholds the sea, moon, and stars, and enjoys the earth and sea, is no more desolate than he is bereft of help.

[17] 'Well, what if someone attacks me when I'm alone and murders me?' No, you poor fool, but that miserable body of yours!

[18] What kind of desolation is left, then, what helplessness? Why do we make ourselves worse than little children? When left on their own, what do they do? They gather up bits of pottery and scraps of earth, and build something out of them, and then pull it down again to build something new. And so they're never at a loss for something to pass their time. [19] For my own part, then, if the rest of you sail away, am I to sit down and weep because I've been left alone and left desolate? Won't I have my bits of pottery, won't I have my scraps of earth? Why, when children act in that way through simplicity of mind, are we to be rendered unhappy through our wisdom? [20] Any great power is perilous for a beginner.* One should thus bear such things according to one's capacity, but in accordance with nature . . .

[certain actions may be appropriate for a healthy person,] but not for a consumptive. [21] You should practise at one time to live like one who is ill, so as to be able, one day, to live like one who is healthy. Take no food, drink water alone; abstain from every desire at one time so as to be able, one day, to exercise your desires in a reasonable way. And if you do so in a reasonable manner, when you have some good in you, your desires too will be good.

[22] But no, we want to live as wise men all at once, and bring benefit to others. What kind of benefit? What are you up to? Have you been able even to help yourself? And yet you want to convert others to a good life. Have you even converted yourself? You want to be of benefit to them? [23] Show them through your own example what kind of men philosophy produces, and give up your empty talk! By the way in which you eat, bring benefit to those who eat with you, by the way in which you drink, bring benefit to those who drink, and by yielding to all of them, by giving way to all, by putting up with all, be of benefit to them in that way, and not by showering them with your spittle!*

3.14 *Miscellaneous*

[1] Just as bad choral singers in tragedy cannot sing properly on their own, but only along with many others, there are likewise some people who cannot walk around on their own. [2] If you're anyone at all, man, walk around on your own, and talk to yourself, and don't hide away in the chorus. [3] Put up with being laughed at on occasion; look around you, and give yourself a good shaking to find out who you really are.

[4] When someone drinks water alone, or adopts some other ascetic practice, he seizes every opportunity to tell everyone, 'I drink nothing but water.' [5] Why, do you drink water for the sole purpose of drinking water? Man, if it brings you any benefit to drink it, then drink it; otherwise you're acting in a ridiculous fashion. [6] But if it is of benefit to you and you drink water alone, don't talk about it to those who are irritated by people who drink nothing but water. What are you up to, then? Are you seeking to please those very people?

[7] There are some actions that are performed for their inherent value; others that are occasioned by circumstances; others that are performed

for purposes of practical management, or to accommodate others, or in pursuit of our own plans.

[8] There are two things that must be rooted out from human beings: presumption and lack of confidence. Presumption lies in supposing that there is nothing more that one needs, and lack of confidence in supposing that it is impossible that one can find serenity in the midst of so many adverse circumstances. [9] Now, as regards presumption, that can be removed by cross-examination, and Socrates was the first to do that* . . . but that the matter isn't impossible, that is something that you must examine and investigate; such an investigation will do you no harm, and one could just about say, [10] indeed, that the practice of philosophy consists in that, in investigating how it is possible to exercise one's desires and aversions without being subject to hindrance.

[11] 'I'm superior to you because my father is of consular rank.' [12] Another says, 'I've been a tribune and you haven't.' If we were horses, would you say, 'I have lots of barley and fodder' or 'I have lovely trappings'? What if you spoke in such a way and I replied, 'Be that as it may, let's run a race.' [13] Come, is there nothing in the human realm comparable to running a race in that of horses, by which it can be recognized who is better and who is worse? Is there no such thing as a sense of honour, or fidelity, or justice? [14] Show yourself to be better in these so that you may be better as a human being. But if you tell me, 'I have a powerful kick,'* I'll reply in my turn that 'You're priding yourself on what a donkey can do.'

3.15 *That we should approach everything with circumspection*

[1] In each action that you undertake, consider what comes before and what follows after, and only then proceed to the action itself. Otherwise you'll set about it with enthusiasm because you've never given any thought to the consequences that will follow, and then you'll give up in an ignominious fashion when one or another of them makes its appearance.

[2] 'I want to win an Olympic victory.' Well, consider what comes before and what follows after, and only then, if there is any advantage for you in it, actually set to work. [3] You must accept the discipline,

submit to a diet, abstain from eating cakes, train under orders, at a fixed time, in heat or cold, and you mustn't drink cold water or wine just as you wish; in short, you must give yourself up to your trainer as you would to a doctor, [4] and then, when the time comes for the contest, you must set about digging,* and sometimes dislocate your wrist, or sprain your ankle, and swallow quantities of sand, and get whipped—and then sometimes get defeated even after all of that! [5] When you've reflected about these things, go on then to become an athlete if you still want to; otherwise recognize that you're behaving as children do, who play at being athletes at one moment, and then at being gladiators, and then blow a trumpet, and then act out scenes that they have seen and admired. [6] For your own part likewise, you're sometimes an athlete, sometimes a gladiator, then a philosopher, then an orator, but nothing at all whole-heartedly; no, in the manner of an ape, you imitate everything that you see, and one thing after another is always catching your fancy, but it ceases to amuse you as soon as you grow accustomed to it. [7] For you've never embarked on anything after due consideration, nor after having subjected it to proper examination and tested it out, but always at random and in a half-hearted fashion.

[8] So it comes about that some people, after seeing a philosopher and hearing someone talking like Euphrates,*—and yet who is capable of talking like him?—want to become philosophers in their turn. [9] Consider first of all, man, what it is that you're taking on, and then your own nature too and what you're able to bear. If you wanted to be a wrestler, you'd have to look at your shoulders, your back, your thighs; [10] for different people are made for different things. Do you suppose that you can act as you do at present and yet be a philosopher? Do you suppose that you can eat as you do, drink as you do, lose your temper as you do, and be as irritable as you are? [11] You must stay up at night, toil away, overcome certain desires, become separated from those who are close to you, suffer scorn from a little slave, be laughed at by those whom you meet, and come off worse in everything, in power, in honour, in the courts. [12] When you've weighed up all of this, then approach philosophy if you think fit, if you're willing to give up all of this in exchange for serenity, freedom, peace of mind. Otherwise, don't come near, don't act as children do and be a philosopher at one time, and later a tax-collector, and then an orator, and then one of Caesar's procurators. [13] These things don't go together. You must be

just one man, either good or bad; you must devote your efforts either to your ruling centre or to external things; in other words, you must assume the part either of a philosopher or of a layman.

[14] After Galba* was murdered, someone said to Rufus, 'So is the universe under the rule of providence now?', to which he replied, 'Have I ever, even in passing, appealed to Galba as an example to show that the universe is under providential rule?'

3.16 *That we should enter into social intercourse with caution*

[1] Someone who associates regularly with certain people, for conversation, or for parties, or simply for the sake of sociability, is bound either to come to resemble them or else to convert them to his own way of life. [2] For if you place a dead coal beside a live coal, either the former will extinguish the latter, or the latter will set the former alight. [3] Since the risk is thus so great, we should be cautious in entering into such relations with laymen, remembering that it is impossible to rub up against someone covered with soot without getting sooty oneself. [4] For what will you do if he chats about gladiators, horses, or athletes, or still worse, about personalities: 'So-and-so is a bad person, So-and-so a good one; that was well done, that was badly done'; or again, if he mocks, if he ridicules, if he is ill-natured? [5] Do any of you have the skill that a good lyre-player possesses, of being able to tell, as soon as he touches the strings, which are out of tune, and so be able to tune his instrument? Or the power that Socrates had, always to be able to bring those who associated with him over to his own views? [6] How could you have? It is rather the laymen who are bound to bring you round to theirs.

[7] Why is it, then, that these people are stronger than you? Because all the rotten things that they say are drawn from their own judgements, while your smart talk comes only from your lips. As a consequence, it has no vigour, no vitality, and anyone would feel sick to hear your exhortations and miserable prattle about virtue, which you keep going on about. [8] And so laymen get the better of you; since judgement is all-powerful, judgement is invincible. [9] Until these fine thoughts, then, are firmly established in you, and you've acquired the power that is needed to guarantee your safety, I would advise you to be cautious about getting involved with laymen. Otherwise

everything that you write down in the schoolroom will melt away day by day like wax in the sun. [10] You should retire, then, to some place far away from the sun, as long as your opinions are like wax.* [11] That is the reason why philosophers recommend that we should even leave our homeland, because old habits distract us and hold us back from making a start on developing new ones, and we can't bear to have those who meet us say, 'Look, So-and-so has turned to philosophy, who used to be like this or that.' [12] Doctors likewise send patients with chronic disorders away to a different place and a different climate, and rightly so. [13] And you too should introduce new habits in place of your old ones; fix your ideas firmly within you, and exercise yourselves in them.

[14] But no, you go away from here to a theatre, to a gladiatorial show, to a gymnasium, to a circus; and then you return here from such places, and then you go back again, remaining always the same. [15] No fine habit is to be seen in you; you devote no care or attention to yourself, and fail to keep a watch on yourself, asking, 'How do I deal with these impressions that present themselves to me? In accordance with nature or contrary to it? How shall I respond to them? As I should or as I shouldn't? Do I declare to those things that lie outside the sphere of choice that they mean nothing to me?' [16] For if you have yet to achieve that frame of mind, flee from laymen, if you ever want to begin to be somebody.

3.17 *On Providence*

[1] Whenever you find fault with providence, just give the matter some thought and you'll recognize that what came about was in accordance with reason.

[2] 'Yes, but someone who is unjust comes off better.'

In what? In money. For in that regard he has the better of you because he flatters people, because he has no shame, because he stays awake at night. Is there anything surprising in that? [3] But look to see whether he is better than you in being trustworthy and honest. Because you'll find that not to be the case; but rather, in those things in which you're superior to him, you'll find that you're the one who is better off.

[4] I said one day to someone who was indignant at the prosperity of Philostorgus: Would you have been willing to go to bed with

Sura?*—'Heaven forbid', he replied, 'that such a day should ever arrive!' [5] —Why are you indignant, then, if he gets some reward for what he sells? Or how can you account a man happy if he acquires his prosperity through means that you abhor? What wrong is providence committing if it gives the better things to the better people? Or isn't it better to be honourable than to be rich? The man agreed. [6] So why are you indignant, man, if you have what is of greater worth? Always remember, then, and keep in mind that it is a law of nature that one who is superior has the advantage over one who is inferior in the respect in which he is superior, and you'll never again have cause for indignation.

[7] 'But my wife behaves badly to me.'

Very well. If someone asks you what the matter is, reply, 'My wife behaves badly to me.'—'And nothing more than that?'—Nothing more.

[What is the matter? [8] 'My father doesn't give me anything.'] Must you add further in your own mind that this is something bad, and so add a falsehood too? That's why it is not poverty that we should reject, but the judgement that we hold about it, and then our life will run happily.

3.18 *That we should not allow news to disturb us*

[1] Whenever any disturbing news is brought to you, you should have this thought ready at hand: that news never relates to anything that lies within the sphere of choice. [2] For can anyone ever bring word to you that you've harboured a mistaken assumption or wrong desire?—'In no way.'—He can report, however, that someone has died. Well, what is that to you? Or that someone is speaking badly of you. Well, what is that to you? [3] That your father is hatching some plan or other. Against what? Surely not against your choice? How could he? Why, against your poor body, against your wretched possessions; you're safe and sound, then: it isn't against you.

[4] But the judge has pronounced you guilty of impiety. In the case of Socrates,* didn't the judges pronounce that very judgement? Surely it's no business of yours if the judge has pronounced that judgement?—'No indeed.'—Then why worry about it any longer?

[5] Your father has a certain function that he must fulfil, or else, if he should fail to do so, he will have destroyed the father in him, the

man who loves his offspring and is gentle towards them. Don't seek to make him lose anything else because of that. For it never happens that when someone goes wrong in one thing, he suffers harm in another. [6] In your case, it is your function to defend yourself firmly, respectfully, and without anger. Otherwise you will have destroyed the son in you,* the man who is respectful and high-minded. [7] What, then, is the judge himself exempt from risk? No, he too runs an equal risk. Why are you still afraid, then, of the judgement that he'll pronounce? What does someone else's evil have to do with you? [8] Your own evil is to make a bad defence. That alone is what you need to guard against; but as to whether you're condemned or acquitted, that is someone else's business, and accordingly, someone else's evil. [9] —'So-and-so is making threats against you.'—Against *me*? No.—'He's criticizing you.'—It's for him to look to how he carries out his own business.—'He's going to condemn you unjustly.'—Poor wretch!

3.19 *What is the position of the layman, and what that of the philosopher?*

[1] The first difference between a layman and a philosopher is this, that the one says, 'Ah, how I suffer because of my child, because of my brother, ah, how I suffer because of my father,' whereas the other, if he can ever be compelled to say, 'Ah, how I suffer,' adds after a moment's thought, 'because of myself'. [2] For choice cannot be hindered or harmed by anything that lies outside the sphere of choice, but only by choice itself. [3] So if we too incline towards this latter course, and whenever we go astray, blame ourselves for it and remember that nothing except our own judgement is capable of causing us to become disturbed or confused, I swear to you by all the gods that we've made progress.

[4] But as things are, we've followed quite another course from the beginning. Already, when we were still little children, if we ever bumped into anything while we had our head in the clouds, our nurse didn't tell us off, but would hit the stone. Why, what had the stone done? Should it have shifted out of the way because of the foolishness of a child? [5] And again, if we couldn't find anything to eat after leaving our bath, our attendant would never try to damp down our appetite, but would beat the cook instead. Man, we didn't appoint you to

be attendant to the cook, did we? No, but to our son. Put him right; be of some use to him. [6] So even when we're grown up, we have the appearance of being children. For it is a child's part to be uncultivated in matters of culture, to be unlettered in matters of literature, and to be uneducated in life.

3.20 *That advantage may be gained from every external circumstance*

[1] With regard to intellectual impressions, almost everyone has conceded that the good and bad are in ourselves, and not in external things. [2] No one maintains that the proposition 'It's day' is good, or that the proposition 'It's night' is bad, or that the proposition 'Three equals four' is the greatest of evils. [3] But what do they say? That knowledge is good, and error is bad, so that even in regard to what is false, something good arises: the knowledge that it is indeed false. [4] The same should thus be true in life also. Is health a good and illness an evil? No, man. What, then? Health is good when put to right use, and bad when put to bad use.

'So it is possible to draw advantage even from illness?'

By God, isn't it possible to draw advantage even from death? And from lameness too; isn't that so? [5] Do you supposes that it was only some small benefit that Menoeceus* gained through his death?

'May anyone who talks like that gain the same sort of benefit as he did!'

Look here, man, didn't he preserve his character as a patriot, and as one who was high-minded, faithful, and noble-spirited? And if he'd survived, wouldn't he have lost all of that? Wouldn't he have acquired the opposite qualities? [6] Wouldn't he have assumed the character of a man who is cowardly, mean-natured, and hates his country, and attaches too much importance to his own life? Come, do you think he gained little advantage from his death? [7] Well, did the father of Admetus* gain any great advantage from living on as he did, in an ignoble and miserable fashion? And later on, wasn't he bound to die in any case? [8] You must cease—I abjure you by the gods!—cease to attach such value to what is purely material, and cease to make yourselves slaves, in the first place, of things, and then, on account of those things, of the men who are able to procure them for you or take them away from you.

[9] 'Is it possible, then, to derive advantage from these things?'
Yes, from all of them.

'Even from someone who insults you?'

And what advantage does a wrestler gain from his training partner? The greatest. And that man, too, who insults me becomes my
training partner; he trains me in patience, in abstaining from anger,
in remaining gentle. [10] You disagree; and yet the man who seizes me
by the neck, and gets my hips and shoulders into shape, renders
me some advantage, and the wrestling master does well to tell me,
'Raise up the pestle with both hands,' and the heavier the pestle is,
the more good it does me. And yet you say that if someone trains me
in abstaining from anger, he brings me no benefit? [11] It is simply
that you don't know how to draw advantage from other people. My
neighbour is a bad man? Bad to himself, but good to me. [12] This is
the magic wand of Hermes: 'Touch what you want', so the saying
goes, 'and it will turn to gold.' No, but bring me whatever you wish,
and I'll turn it into something good. Bring illness, bring death, bring
destitution, bring abuse or a trial for one's life, and under the touch
of the magic wand of Hermes, all of that will become a source of
benefit.

[13] 'And death, what will you make of that?'

Why, what else than make it something that can bring you honour,
and make it a means by which you can show in very deed what it
means to be someone who follows the will of nature?

[14] 'And illness, what will you make of that?'

I'll show its nature, I'll excel in it, I'll remain steadfast and serene,
I won't flatter my doctor, I won't pray for death. [15] What more do
you seek? Whatever you present to me I'll turn it into something
blessed and a source of happiness, into something venerable and
enviable.

[16] But no, instead you say, 'Take care not to get ill: it is something bad.' It is as if one were to say, 'Take care not to form the
impression that three is equal to four: that is something bad.' In
what way is it bad, man? If I come to think about it as I ought, can it
be of harm to me any longer? Won't it rather be a source of benefit
to me? [17] If I form the right idea about poverty, about illness, about
lack of office, isn't that enough for me? Won't all these things be of
benefit to me? How, then, am I to seek for good or bad any longer in
external things?

[18] But what does in fact happen? These ideas are accepted as far as the door, but no one carries them home with him; all at once everyone is at war with his slave-boy, with his neighbour, with those who mock us, with those who laugh at us. [19] Good for you, Lesbius,* for proving to me every day that I know nothing!

3.21 *To those who set out to become lecturers without due thought*

[1] Those who have taken in the principles raw and without any dressing immediately want to vomit them up again, just as people with weak stomachs bring up their food. [2] Digest them first, and then you won't vomit them up in this way. Otherwise they do indeed become nothing more than vomit, foul stuff that isn't fit to eat. [3] But after having digested them, show us some resulting change in your ruling centre, just as athletes show in their shoulders the results of their exercises and diet, and those who have become expert craftsmen can show the results of what they have learned. [4] A builder doesn't come forward and say, 'Listen to me as I deliver a discourse about the builder's art,' but he acquires a contract to build a house, and shows through actually building it that he has mastered the art. [5] And you for your part should follow a similar course of action: eat as a proper human being, drink as a proper human being, dress, marry, father children, perform your public duties; put up with being abused, put up with an inconsiderate brother, put up with a father, a son, a neighbour, a fellow traveller. [6] Show us these things to enable us to see that you really have learned something from the philosophers.

But no, instead you cry, 'Come and listen to me reading out my commentaries.' Away with you, look for someone to vomit over. [7] 'Yes, but I'll expound the teachings of Chrysippus to you like no one else can, and analyse his style with perfect clarity, and even mix in some of the brio of Antipater and Archedemus.' [8] So it is for this, then, the young men should leave their homelands and parents, to come and hear you expatiating on trifling points of language? [9] Shouldn't they return home as people who are patient and helpful towards others, and have minds that are free from passion and agitation, and are furnished with such provisions for their journey through life that they'll be able, by that means, to face up well to everything that comes about, and draw honour from it? [10] And how can you impart things to others that you yourself don't possess? For have

you done anything else from the beginning than spend your whole
time examining how solutions can be found for syllogisms, and for
equivocal arguments, and for arguments that are developed through
questioning?

'But So-and-so keeps a school; why shouldn't I do the same?'

[11] That is not something that one can set about at random, slave,
and without proper thought; one must be of an appropriate age, and
follow a certain way of life, and have God for a guide. [12] You disagree; and yet no one sails out from a harbour without first having
offered a sacrifice to the gods and having implored their help, nor do
people sow the fields in any casual manner, but only after having first
invoked the aid of Demeter;* so can anyone embark safely on such
important work as this without the aid of the gods? [13] And will those
who come to him then meet with good fortune in doing so? What else
are you doing, man, than profaning the Mysteries, and saying, 'Just
as there's a shrine at Eleusis, look, there's one here too. There's a
hierophant* there, I'll make one here too; there's a herald there, I'll
appoint one here too; there's a torch-bearer there, I'll have one here
too; there are torches there, there'll be torches here too. [14] The
words that are spoken are just the same; so what difference is there
between what happens there and what happens here?' Oh most impious of men, is there really no difference? Do these actions procure the
same benefit if they're conducted at the wrong place and at the wrong
time? Shouldn't they be approached with sacrifices and prayers, and
don't they require that a man should first have been purified, and
have his mind predisposed to the thought that he'll be coming to take
part in sacred rites, and rites, moreover, that are of great antiquity?
[15] Is it in this way that the Mysteries came to be of benefit; is it in
this way that we came to appreciate that all these things were established by men of old for our education and for the amendment of our
life? [16] But for your part you're divulging them to one and all, and
parodying them, and conducting them outside the proper time and
place, without sacrifices and without purification; you don't wear the
costume that the hierophant ought to wear, nor do you have the right
hair or headband, nor the right voice, nor are you of the right age, nor
have you kept yourself pure as he has, but you've been satisfied
merely to appropriate the words that he utters and recite them. Are
the words, then, sacred in themselves?

[17] It is in quite another way that we ought to approach these

matters. This is a great undertaking, a solemn mystery, not to be lightly granted to whoever comes along. [18] To be wise, indeed, is perhaps not even a sufficient qualification for taking care of the young; one should also have a special aptitude and predisposition, and yes, by Zeus, a particular physique also, and above all else, a vocation from God to fulfil this function, [19] as Socrates was called to fulfil that of cross-examining people, and Diogenes that of rebuking them in a regal manner, and Zeno that of instructing them and establishing philosophical doctrines.* [20] But you open up shop as a doctor with no other equipment than your medicines; as to when or how you should apply them, that you neither know nor have ever bothered to learn. [21] 'Look, that man has those eye salves, and I have just the same.' Do you have the ability, then, to make proper use of them? Do you have any idea when and how they'll do any good, and to whom?

[22] Why, then, are you gambling with matters of the highest importance? Why are you acting in such an ill-considered manner; why are you embarking on an enterprise for which you're entirely unsuited? Leave it to those who are capable of it, to those who can carry it out with distinction. Don't bring disgrace to philosophy for your part, too, through your own actions; don't range yourself among those who defame the profession. [23] But if philosophical principles hold a fascination for you, sit down and reflect on them within yourself, but don't ever call yourself a philosopher, and don't allow anyone else to apply that name to you. Say rather, 'He's mistaken, since my desires are no different from those that I formerly harboured, nor are my motives any different, nor is my assent, and in a word, I haven't changed in the least from my former state with regard to the way in which I deal with my impressions.' [24] That is what you should think and say about yourself, if you want to think aright. Otherwise, carry on gambling, and continue to act as you do now; for that suits you.

3.22 *On the Cynic calling*

[1] When one of his pupils, who was showing an inclination towards the Cynic calling, asked him, 'What sort of man should a Cynic be, and what idea should one form of that enterprise?', Epictetus replied: We'll consider the matter at our leisure, [2] but this much I can tell

you now, that anyone who embarks on such a great endeavour without the help of God will incur the wrath of God, and is wishing for nothing other than to disgrace himself in front of everybody. [3] For no one comes into a well-ordered household and says to himself, 'I ought to be the manager here,' or if he does, and the master of the house returns to see him ordering everyone around in a high-handed manner, he'll drag him outside and make him pay the price for it. [4] That is the way of things in this great city of the universe also. For here too there is a master of the house* who issues orders to one and all. [5] You for your part are the sun, and as you make your orbit round the heavens, you have the power to give rise to the year and the seasons, and to give growth and nourishment to the fruits of the earth, and to raise and calm the winds, and to warm the bodies of human beings in due measure; go now, and proceed on your circuit, and set all things in motion, from the greatest to the least. [6] As for you, you're a calf: when a lion appears, act as is proper for you, or else you'll rue the day. But you, you're a bull,* come forward and fight, because that is your part in life; it befits you and lies within your power. [7] And you, you're capable of leading the army against Troy: be Agamemnon. And you, you're capable of fighting against Hector in single combat: be Achilles. [8] But if Thersites* had come forward and claimed the command, either he wouldn't have got it, or if he had, he would have disgraced himself in front of a multitude of witnesses.

[9] So you too should consider this matter with proper care: it isn't what you think it is. [10] 'I wear a rough cloak even now, and I'll be wearing one then. I sleep on a hard bed now, and I'll sleep on one then. I'll take up a knapsack and staff, furthermore, and set off on my rounds, begging from those whom I meet, and abusing them. And if I see anyone pulling out his body hair, I'll give him a scolding, and likewise if his hair is dressed too fussily, or he struts around in purple robes.' [11] If you picture the Cynic calling as being something like that, keep well away from it, don't come near, because it is not for you. [12] But if you can form a proper idea of it in your mind and don't judge yourself unworthy, consider what a great enterprise it is that you're embarking on.

[13] First of all, with regard to what concerns you directly, you must no longer show yourself to be behaving in any respect as you do at present; you must bring no accusation against either god or man;

you must suppress your desires wholly and completely; you must direct your aversion only towards things that lie within the sphere of choice; you must harbour neither anger, nor malice, nor envy, nor pity; you mustn't find any wench beautiful, nor any scrap of reputation, nor any boy, nor a honey-cake. [14] For you must be clear in your mind about this point, that other people have walls and houses and darkness to protect them when they venture on anything of this kind, and have many means by which they can hide it away. A man shuts his door, he stations someone in front of his bedroom, saying, 'If anyone comes along, say: he's out, he's busy.' [15] But the Cynic, in place of all these defences, must make his own self-respect* his source of protection; or else he'll be disgracing himself while he's naked and in the open. His self-respect is his house, his door, the watchman in front of his bedroom, and his darkness. [16] No, he mustn't want to conceal anything that relates to him, or else he's lost, he has destroyed the Cynic in him, the man who lives in the open, the man who is free, and has begun to fear something outside himself, has begun to have need of concealment. Nor is he able to find concealment when he wants to. For where can he conceal himself, and how? [17] And if by any chance this educator of the general public, this pedagogue, should get caught, what he must suffer! [18] If he has these fears in his mind, then, how will he still have the confidence to watch over everyone else? It's out of the question, it's impossible.

[19] You must begin, then, by purifying your own ruling centre, and adopting this as your plan in life: [20] 'From this time forth, the material that I must work upon is my own mind, just as that of a carpenter is wood, and that of a cobbler is leather; for my work lies in making right use of my impressions. [21] This poor body of mine is nothing to me, and every part of it is nothing. Death? Let it come when it will, either to the whole of me, or to any part of me. [22] Banishment? And where can anyone banish me to? Hardly beyond the bounds of the universe. No, but wherever I go, the sun will be there, and the moon and the stars, and dreams, omens, and converse with the gods.'*

[23] And next, even when he is prepared in this way, the true Cynic can't remain satisfied with that, but must know that he has been sent to human beings by Zeus as a messenger,* to show them that they're wholly mistaken with regard to what is good and bad, and are seeking the nature of the good and the bad where it is not to be found, and

never think to look for it where it is; [24] he must know too that, as
Diogenes said when he was brought in front of Philip after the battle
of Chaeronea, that he has been sent as a spy. For the Cynic is in truth
a spy* who is seeking to find out what things are friendly to human
beings, and what are hostile; [25] and after having first spied out the
ground, he must come back to report the truth, without allowing
himself to be so overcome by fear that he designates as enemies those
who are not, or letting himself be disturbed or confused in any other
way by his impressions.

[26] He must be able, then, if the occasion presents itself, to raise
his voice and mount the tragic stage to speak like Socrates:* 'Alas,
men, where are you hurrying to? Like blind men, you're staggering
this way and that, you've strayed from the right path and are setting
off on quite another, you're looking for serenity and happiness where
they're not to be found, and when someone points you in the right
direction, you don't believe him. [27] Why are you seeking them
outside? In the body? That's not where they are. If you doubt that,
look at Myron, look at Ophellius.* Nor are they to be found in riches.
If you doubt that, look at Croesus,* look at the rich men of our own
day, and all the lamentations with which their life is filled! Nor are
they to be found in power. For if that were the case, those who've
been consul two or three times would surely be happy, and they
aren't. [28] Whom are we to believe about this matter? Those of you
who view the situation of such people from outside and are dazzled
by appearances, or the people themselves?* [29] What do the people
themselves say? Listen to them as they lament and groan, considering
their situation to be all the more miserable and perilous because of
those very consulships, and because of their eminence and glory. [30]
Nor are serenity and happiness to be found in royal power. Otherwise
Nero would have been happy, and so would Sardanapalus.* But even
Agamemnon himself wasn't happy, although he was a better man
than Sardanapalus and Nero; while all the rest are snoring, what is it
that he does? *'Many hairs does he pull from his head by their roots.'* And
what does he say? *'Thus do I wander,'* and *'In my anguish my heart
leaps from my breast.'**

[31] What is going badly for you, poor wretch? Your property? Not
that, but rather, you're *'rich in gold and rich in bronze'.** Your body?
Not that. So what is wrong with you? This, that you've neglected and
ruined that part of you, whatever it may be, by which we desire

things, or seek to avoid them, or exercise our motives to act or not to act. [32] In what way has this faculty been neglected? It remains ignorant of the true nature of the good for which it was born, and of the nature of what is bad, and of what properly concerns it, and of what is foreign to it. And whenever one of those things that are not its true concern finds itself in a bad way, it says, 'Oh alas, the Greeks are in danger!' [33] Ah, poor ruling centre, which alone remains neglected and uncared for! 'They're going to die at the hands of the Trojans!' And if the Trojans don't kill them, they'll never die at all I suppose? 'They'll die, but not all at one time.' What is the difference? For if it is a bad thing to die, it's bad whether they die at the same time or one after another. Will anything else come about than the separation of the soul from our poor body? 'Nothing else.' [34] And if the Greeks perish, does the door stand closed for you? Isn't it possible for you to depart from this life? 'Indeed it is.' Why these lamentations, then? 'Woe is me, a king and one who holds the sceptre of Zeus!' A king can't fall into misfortune any more than a god can. [35] Who are you, then? Truly a shepherd! For you're weeping as shepherds do when a wolf carries off one of their sheep, and the people you rule over are nothing more than sheep. [36] But why did you come to Troy anyhow? Your desire wasn't in peril, was it, or your aversion, or your motives to act or not to act? 'No,' he says, 'but my brother's poor wife has been abducted.' [37] Isn't it a considerable gain, then, to be rid of an adulterous wife? 'So are we to suffer the contempt of the Trojans?' What kind of people are they? Wise men or fools? If they're wise, why are you fighting against them? If they're fools, why do you care what they think?*

[38] Where is the good to be found, then, if it doesn't lie in these things? Tell us, sir messenger and spy. Where you don't expect, and where you don't want to look for it. Because if you had wanted to, you would have found it inside yourself, and wouldn't be wandering outside, seeking after things that are no concern of yours as though they were your own. [39] Turn your attention towards yourselves; learn to understand the preconceptions that you have. What sort of thing do you imagine the good to be? Serenity, happiness, freedom from constraint. Come then, don't you imagine it as something that is great by nature? As something that is precious? As something that lies beyond the reach of harm? [40] In what kind of material, then, should one seek for serenity and freedom from constraint? In that which is

slave or that which is free?—'That which is free.'—And your poor body, then, do you possess that as slave or free?—'We don't know.'—Don't you know that it is slave to fever, to gout, to eye diseases, to dysentery, to a tyrant, to fire, to iron, to anything that is stronger than itself?—'Yes, it is slave to those.' [41] —How is it possible, then, that anything that belongs to the body can be free from constraint? How can something be great or precious if it is by nature mere lifeless flesh, mere earth, mere clay? So then, do we possess nothing that is free? [42] —'Perhaps nothing at all.'—What, can anyone constrain you to give assent to what seems to you to be false?—'No one can.'—Or not to give assent to what seems to you to be true?—'No one can.'—Here, man, you can see that you have something in you that is free by nature.* [43] Now who among you can desire something, or feel an aversion from it, or feel a motive to act or not to act, or make preparations for something, or set something for yourself to do, without first forming an impression of what is to your advantage or what isn't fitting for you?—'No one can.'—Here, too, you can see that you have something in you that is beyond hindrance and free; [44] cultivate that, you wretches, pay attention to that, and seek your good there.

[45] And how is it possible for a man who owns nothing, and has neither clothes, nor home, nor hearth, and lives in squalor without a slave, without a country, to pass his life in serenity? [46] Look now, God has sent us someone to show us by his example that it is indeed possible. [47] 'Look at me, I am without a home, without a country, without possessions, without a slave. I sleep on the ground. I have neither wife nor children, nor a governor's palace, but only the ground and sky and a single rough cloak. [48] And yet, what do I lack? Isn't it the case that I'm free from sorrow, free from fear? Am I not free? When did any of you ever see me failing to attain what I desire, or falling into what I want to avoid? When have I ever cast any reproach at god or man? When have I ever accused anyone? Have any of you ever seen me with a sad expression on my face? [49] How do I treat those who inspire you with fear and awe? Don't I treat them as though they were slaves? Who, on seeing me, doesn't think that he's seeing his king and master?'*

[50] These are the words of a Cynic; this is his character, this his plan of life! No, you say, rather, that what makes a Cynic is a wretched knapsack, a staff, or strong jaws, or the way in which he swallows

down everything that one gives him, or stores it away, or outrageously insults those whom he meets, or shows off his fine shoulder.* [51] Do you see in what spirit you're planning to embark on such a great enterprise? Begin by picking up a mirror, and look at your shoulders, examine your loins and your thighs. You're going to enter your name for the Olympic Games,* man, not for some wretched second-rate contest. [52] At the Olympic Games it isn't possible simply to suffer defeat and then withdraw, but, in the first place, you must disgrace yourself in front of the entire civilized world rather than merely in front of the Athenians, the Spartans, or the people of Nicopolis, and secondly, one who leaves without good reason must undergo a flogging, and even before that will have suffered thirst and intense heat, and have swallowed any amount of dust.

[53] Consider the matter with great care; know yourself; consult the divinity; don't attempt this enterprise without God. For if God advises you to take this course, you may be sure that he wants you to become a great man or to suffer many a blow. [54] For this is a very pretty thread that is woven into the Cynic way of life, that he must be thrashed like a donkey, and that while being thrashed, he must love those who beat him as though he were the father or brother of them all. [55] Oh no, that's not how you'd react, but if someone beat you, you'd go and cry out in front of everyone, 'O Caesar, am I to suffer such things in breach of your peace? Let's go in front of the proconsul.' [56] But what is Caesar to a Cynic, what is a proconsul, or anyone other than Zeus who has sent him out on his mission, and whom he serves? Does he call upon anyone other than Zeus?* Isn't he convinced that in all these sufferings that he has to endure, it is Zeus who is placing these demands? [57] Now, Heracles, when he was meeting the demands of Eurystheus,* didn't regard himself as miserable, but unhesitatingly carried out everything that he was ordered to do. So shall one who is being trained by Zeus and is meeting his demands cry out and make complaint? Is such a man worthy of carrying the sceptre of Diogenes? [58] Listen to what he said to those who walked by while he was lying ill with a fever: 'You wretches,' he cried, 'aren't you going to stop? You'll travel all the way to Olympia to see wrestlers and athletes do battle with one another, and yet you have no wish to see a man fighting it out with a fever?'

[59] Oh yes, such a man would assuredly have reproached God, who sent him into this world, for having subjected him to undeserved

mistreatment! He who took such pride in confronting difficulties and offered himself as a spectacle to passers-by! Why, what could he have reproached God for? Because he is living in a good and proper manner? What can he accuse him of? That he is displaying his virtue more splendidly? [60] Come now, what does Diogenes say about poverty, about death, about hardship? How did he compare his happiness with that of the Great King?* Or rather, he thought there could be no comparison between them in that respect. [61] For where there are disturbances, and sorrows, and fears, and unsatisfied desires, and aversions that fall into what they want to avoid, and envies and jealousies, how can happiness find its way in among all of that? And wherever corrupt judgements prevail, all these failings must necessarily be present.

[62] When the young man asked him whether, if he fell ill and a friend invited him into his house to be nursed, he should accept the offer, Epictetus replied: But where will you find me a Cynic's friend? [63] For such a man would need to be another Cynic to be accounted worthy of being his friend. He would need to share the sceptre with him, and the kingdom,* and be a worthy minister, if he were to be judged worthy of becoming his friend, as Diogenes became the friend of Antisthenes, and Crates* of Diogenes. [64] Or do you suppose that if someone merely comes up to greet a Cynic, he'll become his friend, [65] and that the Cynic will think him worthy of being received by him? So if you see and consider the matter in such a way as that, you'd do better to look around for a nice little dung-hill to have your fever on, one that will shelter you from the north wind so that you won't die of cold. [66] But you'd prefer, I think, to go into someone's house for a while to fill your stomach. What reason do you have, then, even to attempt so great an enterprise?

[67] 'And marrying and having children,' the young man asked, 'is that something that a Cynic should undertake as a priority?'

If you give me a city of wise people,* replied Epictetus, it's quite likely that no one will readily embark on the Cynic life. [68] For whose benefit would it serve for him to adopt that way of life? If we suppose, nonetheless, that he did, there would be nothing to prevent him from marrying and having children. For his wife would be another person like himself, as would his father-in-law, and his children would be brought up in the same fashion. [69] But as things are set up at present, when we find ourselves as though in a battle-line, isn't it necessary that the Cynic should remain free from all distraction, to dedicate himself wholly to the service of God, and be able to walk about among people without being tied down by private duties, or being involved in social relationships that he cannot violate if he is to preserve his character as a virtuous and good person, and which he cannot maintain, on the other hand, without destroying his nature as a messenger, spy, and herald of the gods? [70] For consider, there would be some duties that he would have to fulfil towards his father-in-law, some that he would have to fulfil towards other relations of his wife, or towards his wife herself, so that he would finally be shut out from his calling to act as a sick-nurse and provider. [71] Not to mention all the rest: he would need a kettle to heat water for his baby, so that it could be washed in the bath-tub, and some wool for his wife when she has had a child, along with some oil, a cot, and a cup (see how the gear is mounting up), [72] leaving aside all the other things that would take up his time and distract him. What is left now, I ask you, of that king of ours, who has time to devote himself to the public interest, '*who has people to watch over and so many a care*'?* That king who must watch over everyone else, over those who are married, over those who have children, to see who is treating his wife well, who is treating her badly, and see who is quarrelling with others, and which house is at peace and which is not, just like a doctor who is making his rounds, and says, [73] 'You have a fever, and you have a headache, and you have gout; you must fast, you must eat, you mustn't take a bath; you need an operation, you need to be cauterized.' [74] What leisure will a man have for all of this if he is tied down by private duties? Wouldn't he have to provide clothing for his children? Come, wouldn't he have to send them to their schoolmaster with their writing tablets and their styluses, and, besides, get their little cot ready for them? For they could hardly be Cynics from the moment they leave their mother's womb! If he didn't attend to all of this, it would have been better to expose them at birth than to allow them to perish in such a way. [75] Do you see to what a level we're reducing our Cynic, and how we're depriving him of his kingdom?

[76] 'Yes, but Crates married.'

You're referring to a special case in which the marriage was prompted by love, and you're reckoning on a wife who was herself another Crates.* But our present enquiry is concerned with ordinary marriages in which special circumstances don't enter the picture, and in that context, we don't find that marriage, under present conditions, is a priority for a Cynic.

[77] 'In that case,' the young man asked, 'how will the Cynic help to keep human society in existence?'

In the name of God, who renders a greater service to the human race, those who bring two or three children with ugly snouts into the world to replace them, or those who keep watch over all human beings, so far as they can, observing what they do and how they pass their life, and what they devote their care to, and what they neglect in contravention of their duty? [78] And from whom did the Thebans draw greater benefit: from all the many men who left children behind for them, or from Epaminondas, who died childless? And did Homer contribute less to the common good than Priam, who fathered fifty worthless children, or than Danaus or Aeolus?* [79] And again, will a military command or the writing of a book be enough to absolve someone from marrying and fathering children, so that he shouldn't be thought to have exchanged his childlessness for nothing of value, and yet a Cynic's kingship not be thought to provide adequate exchange? [80] Could it be, perhaps, that we don't appreciate the greatness of the true Cynic, and fail to form an adequate notion of the character of Diogenes, but look instead towards those Cynics whom we now have in front of us, those dogs '*of the table that guard the doors*',* who follow the example of the masters in no way at all, except perhaps in farting in public, but in nothing apart from that. [81] Otherwise these Cynic ways wouldn't disconcert us, and we wouldn't be amazed that a Cynic doesn't marry or father children. He has the whole human race as his children, man, all the men as sons, all the women as daughters; and it is in that spirit that he approaches them all and tries to take care of them. [82] Or do you suppose that it is out of mere officiousness that he rebukes those whom he meets? No, it's as a father that he does so, as a brother, and as a servant of Zeus, who is father of us all.

[83] If you care to, ask me too whether he should get involved in public affairs.* [84] Blockhead, can you think of any higher form of public business than that in which he is already engaged? Or would you have him step forward at Athens to speak about revenues and resources when it is his business to speak to all humanity, Athenian, Corinthian, and Roman alike, not about resources and revenues, or peace and war, but about happiness and unhappiness, about good

fortune and bad, about freedom and servitude? [85] When someone is engaged in such important public business as that, you ask me whether he should play any part in public affairs? Ask me too whether he'll take any public post, and I'll reply again, Fool, what post could be more important than that which he already holds?

[86] It is also necessary, however, that the Cynic should have the right kind of body, because if he comes forward looking like a consumptive, all thin and pale, his witness would no longer carry the same weight. [87] For he must not only prove to laymen, by displaying the qualities of his mind, that it is possible to be virtuous and good without having the things that they set such store on, but he must also show through his bodily qualities that a plain and simple life lived in the open air has no deleterious effects even on the body. [88] 'Look, both I and my body bear witness to that truth.' That was the way of Diogenes, for he would walk around radiant with health, and would attract the attention of the crowd by the very condition of his body. [89] But a Cynic who arouses pity passes for being a beggar; everyone turns away from him; he arouses everyone's disgust. Nor should he look dirty, so as not to scare people away for that reason too, but even in his destitution, he should be clean and attractive.

[90] And furthermore, a Cynic needs to have great natural charm and a witty tongue (otherwise he becomes a pain and nothing more), so as to be able to respond readily to whatever comes along. [91] So when someone said to Diogenes, 'Are you the Diogenes who doesn't believe in the existence of the gods?', he retorted, 'And how could that be, if I regard you as being hateful to the gods?';* [92] or again, when Alexander stood over him while he was asleep and said, '*To sleep the whole night through ill befits a man of counsel.*' He replied while still half-asleep, '*Who has people to watch over and a multitude of cares.*'*

[93] But above all, the Cynic's ruling centre needs to be purer than the sun, otherwise he'll necessarily be nothing more than a gambler and a rogue, because he'll be reprimanding everyone else while being in thrall to some vice himself. [94] For consider how things stand: while the kings and despots of this world have their guards and arms that enable them to reprove people and to punish those who do wrong, however wicked they themselves might be, in the case of the Cynic, it is neither arms nor guards that give him that power, but his own conscience. [95] When he sees that he has watched over his fellow

human beings and has toiled on their behalf, and that he has slept
with a pure heart, and that his sleep has left it purer still, and when
he sees that his every thought is that of a friend and servant of the
gods, as one who shares in the government of Zeus, and is ready to
say on every occasion, 'Lead me, O Zeus, and thou, O Destiny,'* and 'If
this is what pleases the gods, so be it,' [96] why, then, shouldn't
he have the courage to speak with unsparing frankness to his own
brothers, to his children, and in a word, to all who are of the same
blood?

[97] That is why someone who thinks in such a way as this is no
mere meddler or busybody, because he isn't busying himself with
other people's affairs when he inspects the doings of human beings,
but is carrying out his own business; otherwise you should also call a
general a busybody when he inspects his troops, and reviews them,
and watches over them, and punishes those who misbehave. [98] But
if you reprove others while holding a little cake under your arm, I'll
say to you, Wouldn't you rather go off into a corner to devour what
you've stolen? [99] How are other people's affairs any concern of
yours? For who are you? Are you the bull of the herd; are you the
queen of the bees? Show me such tokens of authority as the queen has
by nature. But if you're a drone who is laying claim to sovereignty
over the bees, don't you think that your fellow citizens will drive you
away, just as bees drive away the drones?

[100] A Cynic must have such powers of endurance that he strikes
the crowd as being insensible and like a stone. No one can insult him,
no one can strike him, no one can assault him; as for his poor body, he
himself has handed that over for anyone to deal with as he thinks fit.
[101] For he keeps in mind that what is weaker must necessarily be
overcome by what is stronger, in that respect in which it is weaker,
and that his body is weaker than the crowd, as what is physically
weaker must be to what is stronger. [102] So he never enters into this
contest in which he can be defeated, but renounces once and for all
what is not truly his own, laying no claim to what is slavish. [103] But
when it comes to his capacity of choice and use of impressions, there
you'll see that he has so many eyes that you could say that Argus* was
blind by comparison. [104] Is over-hasty assent ever to be found in
him, or ill-considered impulse, or any frustrated desire, or any aversion
that falls into what it wants to avoid, or any unfulfilled purpose, or any
fault-finding, meanness of spirit, or envy? [105] It is to these matters

that he devotes all his attention and energy; but when anything else comes into play, he lies back and snores, and is wholly at peace. No one can rob him of his power of choice, or exert mastery over it. But over his poor body? Yes. [106] And over his miserable possessions? Yes, and over his offices and honours too. But what does he care about any of that? When anyone tries to scare him by means of such things, he says, 'Go and look for some children; they're afraid of empty masks, but I know that they're made of clay and have nothing inside them.'

[107] Such is the nature of the enterprise that you're considering. So I ask you, in the name of God, to defer your decision for a while, if you will, and check first whether you have the resources for it. [108] For see what Hector says to Andromache: '*Go rather into the house*', he tells her, '*and weave,*

> *But war shall be the business of men,*
> *Of all men, but of me most of all.*' *

[109] So aware was he of his own resources, and of her incapacity.

3.23 *To those who read and discuss for mere display*

[1] Tell yourself first of all what kind of person you want to be, and then act accordingly in all that you do. For in almost every other pursuit we see this to be the course that is followed. [2] Athletes first decide what kind of athlete they want to be, and then act accordingly. If someone wants to be a long-distance runner, he adopts a particular diet, a particular way of walking, a particular form of massage, and particular exercises; if someone wants to be a sprinter, these are all rather different; and if someone wants to be a pentathlete, they're more different again. [3] You'll find the same is true in the crafts, too. If you want to be a carpenter, you'll have to do such and such, if a blacksmith, certain other things. For in all that we do, unless we refer our actions to some end, we'll be acting at random; and if we don't refer them to an appropriate end, we'll go badly wrong.

[4] There is, besides, a particular end and a general end. First of all, I must act as a human being. What does that involve? That one shouldn't act like a sheep, even if one is gentle in one's behaviour, and one shouldn't act injuriously like a wild beast. [5] The particular end relates to each person's specific occupation and moral choice. The lyre-player must act as a lyre-player, the carpenter as a carpenter, the

philosopher as a philosopher, the orator as an orator. [6] So when you say, 'Come and listen to the lecture that I'm going to deliver to you,' check first of all that you're not embarking on it without due consideration; and then, if you find that you are in fact referring your actions to an end, consider whether it is the appropriate end. [7] Do you want to do good or merely be praised? At once you hear the answer, 'But what interest could the praise of the crowd have for me?', and that is rightly said. For it is of no concern to a musician, in so far as he is a musician, or to a geometer. [8] You want to be of benefit to others, don't you? In what? Tell us, so that we may rush off to your lecture-room. Now, is it possible to bring benefit to others where one has brought no benefit to oneself? No indeed, no more than someone who isn't a carpenter can be of use to others with regard to carpentry, or someone who isn't a shoemaker with regard to shoemaking.

[9] Do you want to know, then, whether you have gained any benefit? Bring forth your judgements, philosopher. What does desire promise? Not to fail in getting what one desires. What does aversion promise? Not to fall into what one wants to avoid. [10] Well now, do we fulfil what they promise? Tell me the truth. If you reply falsely, I'll say to you, 'The other day, when your audience gathered with no great enthusiasm and didn't applaud, you walked out feeling thoroughly dejected. [11] On another occasion, when you did receive some applause, you walked out asking everybody, 'What did you think of me?'—'Upon my life, sir, that was splendid.'—'How did I deliver that passage?'—'Which?'—'The one where I gave the description of Pan and the Nymphs.'—'Magnificently.' [12] —And then you come to me and claim that in your desires and aversions, you manage to remain in accordance with nature? Off with you, and try to persuade someone else! [13] And the other day, didn't you shower someone with praise contrary to your real opinion? Didn't you flatter that senator? Would you want your children to be as he is?—'Heaven forbid!' [14] —Then why did you praise him and dance attendance on him?—'He's a gifted young man who likes to listen to recitals.'—How do you know?—'He admires me.'—So you've come forth with your proof! What do you suppose, then? That these same people don't secretly despise you? [15] When a man who is conscious of never having done or thought anything of value finds a philosopher who tells him, 'You're wonderfully gifted, a man of unimpaired integrity,' what else do you suppose that he can say to himself except 'This fellow

is seeking to make use of me in some way'? [16] Or else, tell me, what work of genius has he produced? Look, man, he has been associating with you all this time; he has been listening to your discourses and has heard your lectures. Has he acquired self-restraint? Has he looked in on himself? Has he become aware of the bad state that he is in? Has he renounced his conceit? [17] Is he looking around for someone to instruct him?

'Yes, he's looking around.'

For someone who'll teach him about how he ought to live? No, you fool, about how he ought to speak! Because that is the reason why he admires even you! Listen to him. What does he say? 'This man writes in a most artistic style, even more elegantly than Dio.'* [18] This is something quite different. He isn't saying, is he, that 'This man is honourable, this man is trustworthy, this man has an untroubled mind'? And even if he did say that, I'd reply to him, 'Since this man is trustworthy, in what exactly does his trustworthiness consist?', and if he were unable to reply, I'd add, 'First learn what you're talking about, and then you can talk.'

[19] While you're in such a wretched state as this, then, and have such a hankering for praise, is it by counting the number of people in your audience that you wish to do good to others?—'Today I had a much bigger audience.'—'Yes, there were lots of people.'—'I think there must have been five hundred.'—'Nonsense, make it a thousand.'—'Dio never had as many people listening to him.'—'How could he?'—'And they have a fine feeling for points of style.'—'Beauty, Sir, can move even a stone.'

[20] Behold the language of a philosopher; behold the state of mind of one who wants to be of benefit to his fellow men! Here is a man who has listened to the voice of reason, who has read the Socratic literature as one should read Socratic works, and not as one reads those of Lysias and Isocrates!* 'Often have I wondered by what arguments . . .' No, but rather, 'by what argument', that runs more smoothly than the other.* [21] For have you read these writings in any other way than one reads cheap songs? Because if you'd read them as you ought, you wouldn't have lingered over such trifles, but would have turned your view to passages like these: 'Anytus and Meletus can kill me, but they cannot harm me,' and again, 'It has always been my nature not to pay any attention to my personal affairs, but only to the argument that seems to me on due consideration to be the best.'*

[22] And for that reason, who ever heard Socrates say, 'I know some-thing and teach it'? But rather, he used to send people elsewhere, one to one instructor, and one to another. People would thus come to him and ask him to introduce them to philosophers, and he would take them off and introduce them.* [23] But no, you fancy that as he was going along with them, he would say, 'Come and listen to me today as I deliver a discourse in the house of Quadratus.'* Why should I listen to you? Do you want to show me how elegantly you can string words together? You can do so very nicely, man; and what good does it do you?

'But give me some praise.' [24] —What do you mean by praise?—'Say "Bravo!" to me, or "That's marvellous!"'—Very well, I'll say that. But if praise is one of those things that philosophers class in the category of the good, what praise can I offer you? If it is a good thing to speak correctly, teach me that and I'll praise you.

[25] 'What, then, should one listen to fine talk without pleasure?' Heaven forbid! For my part, I don't even listen to a lyre-player without feeling pleasure. But surely that doesn't provide any reason why I should stand up and sing while strumming on a lyre? Listen to what Socrates says: [26] 'Nor would it be fitting for me, gentlemen of the jury, at my time of life, to appear before you and weave fine words together like a schoolboy.'* He says, 'Like a schoolboy'. For it is, in truth, an elegant accomplishment, to choose out pretty words and put them together, and come forward to read or recite them in a graceful manner, and then exclaim in the middle of the reading, 'On your life, I declare that there aren't many people who understand these things!'

[27] Does a philosopher invite people to come and listen to him? Isn't it the case, rather, that just as the sun draws its nourishment to itself without need for further action,* a philosopher likewise draws those whom he can benefit? What doctor ever invites anyone to come to him to be cured? Although I hear that doctors in Rome nowadays do invite custom; but in my day, it was they who were invited in. [28] 'I invite you to come and hear that you're in a bad way, and that you attend to everything except what you should be attending to, and that you don't know what is good or bad, and that you're miserable and unfortunate.' A fine invitation that would be! And yet if a philosopher's discourse doesn't produce that effect, it has no life in it, nor does the man who is delivering it. [29] Rufus was in the habit of saying, 'If you

find time to praise me, I'm saying nothing of value.' And indeed, he used to speak in such a way that each of us, as we sat in front of him, would imagine that someone must have been informing him of our faults, since he showed such a sure touch in assessing our condition, and setting each man's failings before his eyes.

[30] A philosopher's school, man, is a doctor's surgery. You shouldn't leave after having had an enjoyable time, but after having been subjected to pain. For you weren't in good health when you came in; no, one of you had a dislocated shoulder, another an abscess, another a headache. [31] Am I to sit, then, and regale you with pretty thoughts and fine sayings, so that you'll go out singing my praises, one having his shoulder just as it was when he brought it in, another having his head in the same state, another still having his fistula, and another his abscess? [32] Is it for this that young men are to travel away from home, and leave their parents, friends, relations, and what small property they have, so that they can shout, 'Bravo!' when you come up with your fine sayings? Is that what Socrates used to do, or Zeno, or Cleanthes?

[33] 'What, isn't there a special style that is used for exhortation?'

Who denies it? Just as there is a style that is employed for refutation or for didactic purposes. But who has ever mentioned a fourth style in addition, a style for display?* [34] So what is the nature of the style that is used for exhortation? It is the style that enables one to show an individual, or a number of people, the contradictions in which they're entangled, and that they're giving thought to everything other than what they truly want; for they want the things that are conducive to happiness, but are looking for them elsewhere than where they're to be found. [35] To achieve this end, is it necessary that any number of benches should be set out, and that an audience should be invited, so that you may lean on a cushion dressed in a fancy cloak or mantle and describe how Achilles met his death? I implore you, by the gods, to stop doing all that you can to bring noble names and deeds into disrepute. [36] Never is exhortation more effective than when the speaker makes his hearers clearly understand that he has need of them. [37] But tell me who, on hearing you recite or lecture or conduct a discussion, has come to feel greatly concerned about himself, and to look in upon himself, or has gone out saying, 'That philosopher has really shaken me, I should no longer act as I do'? [38] Isn't it true, on the contrary, that when you've met with any notable success,

one man says to another, 'What he said about Xerxes was most elegantly expressed,' to which the other replies, 'No, I preferred his
account of the battle of Thermopylae.' Is that what it means to listen
to a philosopher?

3.24 *That we should not become attached to things that are not within our power*

[1] Don't let that which is contrary to nature in another be an evil for
you, for you were born to share not in the humiliations or misfortunes
of others, but in their good fortune. [2] If anyone suffers misfortune,
remember that he suffers it through his own fault, since God created
all human beings to enjoy happiness, to enjoy peace of mind. [3] He
has provided them with the resources to achieve this, giving each
person some things as his own, and others not as his own. Those
that are open to hindrance, removal, or compulsion are not our own,
while all that is immune to hindrance is our own; and the nature of
the good and the bad he has granted to us among the things that are
our own, as was fitting for one who watches over us and protects us
like a true father.

[4] 'But I've parted from So-and-so and he's inconsolable.'

Man, why did he consider what is not his own to be his own? Why
didn't he reflect, when he enjoyed the pleasure of seeing you, that
you're mortal and that you're liable to move to another place? So he
is simply paying the penalty for his own foolishness. [5] But you,
why are you paying for anything? Why are you shedding tears for
yourself? Or is it that you too have failed to reflect on these things,
but have instead, like women of no value, taken delight in all that
you've enjoyed, the places, the people, and the way of life, as though
they would last for ever? And now you sit and weep because you can
no longer see the same people, or pass your time in the same places.
[6] You deserve, then, to be more wretched than crows and ravens,
which can fly wherever they please, and build their nests in different
places, and cross the seas without groaning or yearning for their
former home.

[7] 'Yes, but it's because they're irrational creatures that they feel
in that way.'

Has reason been granted to us by the gods, then, for our misfortune
and unhappiness, so that we may pass our lives in perpetual misery

and lamentation? [8] Or is everyone to be immortal and never leave home, but stay rooted in one spot like a plant? And if anyone from our circle leaves home, shall we sit down and weep, and then, if he comes back, dance about and clap our hands like children?

[9] Shall we not wean ourselves once and for all, and call to mind what we've learned from the philosophers [10] —unless we merely listened to them as one listens to weavers of spells—when they said that this universe constitutes only a single city, and that the substance from which it has been fashioned is single too, and that there must be a periodic revolution when one thing gives way to another, and when some things are dissolved while others come into being, and some things remain where they are while others are moved elsewhere; [11] that everything is full of friends, furthermore, first the gods and then human beings too, who by nature form one family with one another; and that some people must remain with one another, while others must leave, and that we should take delight in those with whom we live, without being upset to see others go away. [12] And that human beings, in addition to being noble-minded by nature and capable of feeling contempt for all that lies outside the sphere of choice, also possess this further quality, of not being rooted down or attached to the earth, but being able to move from one place to another, sometimes under the pressure of specific needs, sometimes merely so as to enjoy the spectacle.*

[13] It was something of this kind that happened to Odysseus, '*Cities of many men he saw, and learned their ways*', and earlier still, it fell to Heracles to travel around the entire inhabited earth, '*Viewing the wickedness of men and their lawful ways*',* banishing the former to clear the world of it, while introducing the latter in its place. [14] And yet how many friends do you suppose he had in Thebes, how many in Argos, how many in Athens, and how many new friends he gained as he was travelling around, considering that he would even take a wife when the moment seemed right to him, and father children; and these children he would abandon without lamentation or regret, and without feeling that he was leaving them behind to be orphans; [15] for he knew that no human being is an orphan, but that all have a father who takes care of them constantly and for ever. [16] Because to him it was not merely a matter of hearsay that Zeus is the father of human beings, but he truly regarded him as his own father, and called him so, and looked to him in all that he did. That is why he was able

to live happily wherever he was. [17] But it is impossible to be happy and yet yearn at the same time for things that are not at hand. For a being that is happy must be in possession of all that it wants; it must resemble a man who has eaten his fill; it must feel neither hunger nor thirst.

[18] 'Yes, but Odysseus yearned for his wife, and sat down on a rock and wept.'

And why do you put faith in everything that Homer says and believe his tales?* If it is indeed true that Odysseus wept, what could he have been but miserable? But what good and virtuous man can be miserable? [19] Truly this is an ill-governed universe if Zeus doesn't set out to ensure that his own fellow citizens should be happy like himself. No, that is unthinkable; it is sheer impiety to suppose any such thing, [20] and if Odysseus shed tears and wept, then he wasn't a good man. For how can someone be good if he doesn't know who he is? And who could know that if he'd forgotten that everything that comes into being is bound to perish, and that it isn't possible for one human being to live with another for ever and a day? [21] What follows, then? That to desire the impossible is the mark of a slave and a fool; it is the behaviour of one who is a stranger in the world, and is fighting against God through the only means that is available to him, through his own judgements.

[22] 'But my mother grieves at not seeing me.'

Then why hasn't she learned these principles? And I'm not saying that you shouldn't make an effort to stop her from grieving, but that we shouldn't wish at all costs for things that are not our own. [23] Now, someone else's grief is not my own concern, but my own grief is. It is thus my responsibility to put an end to it at all cost, because that is within my power; as to the grief of another, I'll strive to put an end to it so far as I am able, but won't strive to do so at all costs. [24] Otherwise I'll be pitting myself against the gods; I'll be setting myself in opposition to Zeus, and be ranging myself against him with regard to the ordering of the universe. And the penalty for this contest against God, and for this disobedience, won't be paid by my children's children, but by myself in person, both by day and by night, when I'm startled out of my dreams, when I'm troubled in my mind, when I tremble at every message, when my inner peace hangs on letters from other people. [25] Someone has arrived from Rome—'I only hope there's no bad news!' Why, what harm can come to you there when you're not even present? Someone has arrived from Greece—'I only hope there's no bad news!' Why, at this rate any place can be a source of misfortune to you! [26] Isn't it enough for you to be unhappy where you actually are, but must you be unhappy too beyond the seas and by correspondence? Is that the security in which your affairs stand?

[27] 'Yes, but what if my friends over there should die?'

Why, what else than that mortals have met their death? How can you wish to reach old age and yet, at the same time, not to see any of those whom you love come to die? [28] Don't you know that over a long stretch of time, many things of every kind are bound to occur? That a fever will get the better of one person, and a robber of another, and a tyrant of someone else again? [29] Such is the nature of the world around us, such is the nature of the people with whom we share it; heat or cold, an unsuitable diet, a journey by land or by sea, the winds of the air, dangers of every kind, will cause one person to perish, another to be driven into exile, another to be dispatched on an embassy, and another to be sent out on a campaign. [30] Sit down, then, and get upset by all of these things, and grieve, and be unfortunate and miserable, and be at the mercy of any external event, and not just of one or two, but of thousands and thousands.

[31] Is that what you've heard from the philosophers, is that what you've learned? Don't you know that this life is like a campaign? One man must keep guard, another go out on reconnaissance, and another go into battle. It isn't possible for all to remain in the same place, nor would it be better that they should. [32] But you neglect to perform the duties assigned to you by your general, and complain when you're given an order that's at all hard, and fail to realize to what state you're reducing the army, so far as you can; because if everyone follows your example, no one will dig a trench, or build a palisade, or keep watch at night, or expose himself to danger, but everyone will show himself useless as a soldier. [33] Again, if you embark on a ship as a sailor, settle down in a single spot and never leave it. If it should be necessary for you to climb the mast, refuse to do so; if you have to run along to the bow, refuse again. And what captain will put up with you? Won't he throw you overboard as a useless piece of tackle, a mere obstruction, and a bad example to the other sailors? [34] So likewise in the present case, the life of every one of us is a campaign, and a long one subject to varying circumstances. You must fulfil the role of a

soldier and carry out every deed as your general bids, [35] divining his
will so far as is possible. For there is no comparison between this general and an ordinary one, with regard either to his power or to the
superiority of his character. [36] You've been stationed in an imperial
city, not in some wretched little hole, and you're to be a senator for
life.* Don't you know that a man of that kind has little time to devote
to his domestic affairs, but must spend most of his time away from
home giving and receiving orders, or serving as an official, or going out
on campaign, or sitting as a judge? And then you tell me that you want
to be fixed in one spot like a plant and take root there. [37] —'Yes,
that's pleasant.'—But a sauce is pleasant too, and so is a pretty woman.
What else do those people say who make pleasure their end?

[38] Don't you realize what kind of men they are whose language
you've been using? That they're Epicureans and perverts? And then,
when you're behaving like them and sharing their opinions, you're
going to cite the words of Zeno and Socrates to us? [39] Why don't
you cast them away from you, as far as you can, those alien adorn-
ments that you've adopted, which are altogether unsuitable for you?
What else do these people desire than to sleep without hindrance or
compulsion, and when they've risen from their bed, to yawn at their
leisure, and wash their faces, and then read and write as the fancy
takes them, and then talk some nonsense or other, winning applause
from their friends whatever it might be, and then go out for a walk,
and having taken a short stroll, take their bath, eat, and go to bed, in
the kind of bed, moreover, in which such people are most likely to
sleep.* Need one say more? For it may easily be guessed.

[40] Come now, you for your part must also tell me about your own
way of life, the life that you aspire to follow as one who is eager for the
truth and seeks to emulate Socrates and Diogenes. What is it that you
want to do in Athens? [41] The very things that I've just mentioned?
Why do you call yourself a Stoic, then? When those who lay false
claim to Roman citizenship are severely punished, should those who
lay false claim to a title and calling as great and venerable as this be
allowed to escape without penalty? [42] Or is that quite impossible,
but that rather, a law that is divine, all-powerful, and inescapable
exacts the heavier penalties on those who commit the graver offences?
[43] For what does this law say? 'Let anyone who pretends to possess
qualities that have nothing to do with him be a braggart, be vainglori-
ous; let anyone who disobeys the divine order be base, be a slave, and

let him grieve, let him feel envy, let him feel pity, and, in a word, be miserable and lament.'

[44] 'What, then, would you have me pay court to So-and-so and approach his door?'*

If reason demands that for the sake of your country, of your family, of humanity, why shouldn't you go? You're not ashamed to visit the door of a shoemaker when you need shoes, or that of a market gardener when you need lettuces, and yet you're ashamed to visit the door of the rich when you have need of what they have to offer? [45] —'Yes, because I don't have any esteem for a shoemaker.'—Then don't have any for a rich man either.—'And I won't have to flatter the market gardener.'—Then don't flatter the rich man either. [46] —'In that case, how will I get what I need?'—Is that what I'm telling you, 'Go with the intention of getting what you ask,' rather than simply, 'Go so that you may do what is appropriate to you'?

[47] 'Then why should I go at all?'

To have gone there, and to have fulfilled your part as a citizen, a brother, a friend. [48] And besides, you should remember that you've come to see a shoemaker, a seller of vegetables, a man who has authority over nothing great or valuable, even if he sells his merchandise at a high price. You're going there like someone who's going in search of lettuces, and they cost an obol, not a talent. [49] Likewise in the present case too; the matter is worth the trouble of my going to his door. Very well, I'll go. It is also worth exchanging some words with him. Very well, I'll do so. Yes, but it is also necessary that I should kiss his hand and flatter him with various compliments. Be off with you! That would be like paying a talent. It is profitable neither to me, nor to the city, nor to my friends, thus to destroy the good citizen and friend in me.

[50] 'But if you don't succeed, people will think you haven't put any effort into it.'

Have you forgotten again why you went? Don't you know that someone who is virtuous and good never acts for the sake of appearances, but only for the sake of having acted rightly?

[51] 'So what benefit does he gain from having acted rightly?'

What benefit does someone gain from having written the name 'Dion' as it ought to be written? That of having written it.

'Is there no further reward, then?'

Do you seek any greater reward for a good person than that of accomplishing what is virtuous and right? [52] At Olympia you don't ask for anything further but think it quite enough to receive an Olympic crown. Does it appear to you to be such a small and worthless thing to be virtuous, good, and happy? [53] When the gods have introduced you into this city of the universe for that purpose, and it is now your duty to accomplish the work of a man, do you still hanker for nurses and the breast, and do you allow yourself to be moved and reduced to effeminacy by the weeping of poor foolish women? Will you never cease, then, to behave like a little child? Doesn't someone who acts like a child become the more ridiculous the older he grows?

[54] At Athens, did you never go to see anyone, visiting him in his house?—'Yes, the man I wanted to see.'—Here again, make up your mind to see this man, and see whom you want; only, do so in no submissive manner, and without desire or aversion, and then things will go well for you. [55] But that result doesn't depend on your going to the house or standing at the door, but on the judgements within you. [56] When you've come to despise external things and all that lies outside the sphere of choice, and have come to regard none of that as being your own, but to consider one thing alone to be yours, to judge and think rightly, and to exercise your motives, desires, and aversions rightly, what room is left for flattery or self-abasement? [57] Why do you still yearn for the peace that you enjoyed there, and for your familiar haunts? Wait a short while and these places will become familiar to you in their turn. And then, if you're so mean-spirited, weep and groan again when you have to leave these places too.

[58] 'How am I to show my affection, then?'

As fits a noble-minded person, as fits someone of good fortune; for reason never demands that we should be self-abasing or broken-spirited, or should become dependent on another, or should ever find fault with either god or human being. [59] That is how I would have you show affection, as one who observes these rules. But if as a result of this affection, or whatever it is that you call affection, you're going to be slavish and miserable, it does you no good to be affectionate. [60] And what is to prevent you from loving somebody as one who is subject to death, as one who may have to leave you? Did Socrates have no love for his children? He did, but he loved them as a free man, as one who remembered that his first duty was to be a friend to the gods. [61] That is why he didn't fail to fulfil any of the duties of a good man, either in making his defence, or in proposing a penalty for himself, or indeed at an earlier time when he was serving on the council or as a soldier.* [62] But we for our part find all manner of excuses to explain away our mean-spirited behaviour, some saying it is because of a child, others because of their mother, or others again because of their brothers. [63] Now it isn't fitting for us to be unhappy because of anyone else, but we should instead be happy because of everyone else, and first and foremost because of God, who has created us for this end. [64] Come, was there anyone at all whom Diogenes didn't love, a man who was so kind and benevolent that he cheerfully underwent any number of toils and physical hardships for the common good of humanity? Yes, he did love people, but in what way? [65] As was right and proper for a servant of Zeus, being at once full of care for others and obedient to God. [66] That is why he alone had the entire earth for his homeland, rather than any land in particular; and after he was taken captive, he didn't yearn for Athens and his friends and acquaintances there, but befriended the pirates themselves and tried to reform them. And later, when he was sold into slavery in Corinth, he lived there in just the same way as he had previously lived in Athens, and if he had gone off to the Perrhaebians,* he would have conducted himself in exactly the same manner.

[67] That is how one acquires freedom. He used to say accordingly, 'Ever since Antisthenes set me free,* I've ceased to be a slave.' [68] And how did Antisthenes set him free? Listen to what Diogenes says: 'He taught me what is my own and what isn't my own. Property isn't my own; relations, family, friends, reputation, familiar places, conversation with others, none of these are my own.' [69] What is your own, then? 'The proper use of impressions. He showed me that I possess that power free from all hindrance and constraint; no one can obstruct me; no one can force me to deal with impressions other than I wish. [70] Who still holds any power over me, then? Philip, Alexander, Perdiccas,* or the King of Persia? How could they? For someone who is destined to be overpowered by another human being must first have been overpowered well before by things.' [71] So accordingly, that person who doesn't allow himself to be overpowered by pleasure, or by suffering, or by glory, or by wealth, and who is capable, whenever he thinks fit, of spitting his entire miserable body into some tyrant's face and taking his leave—to what can such a man still be a slave; to whom can he still be subject? [72] But if he had continued to live a pleasant life in Athens, and had let himself fall under

the spell of the way of life there, his affairs would have been subject to everyone's control, and everyone who was stronger than him would have had the power to cause him distress. [73] How do you imagine he would have cajoled the pirates into selling him to some Athenian, so that he might be able to see the beautiful Piraeus again, and the Long Walls, and the Acropolis? [74] And as what sort of a man would you be seeing them, slave? As one who is slavish and submissive. [75] So what good would it do you?

'No, but as one who is free.'

Show me in what way you're free. Look, someone or other has seized hold of you, and takes you away from your accustomed way of life, saying, 'You're my slave, because it's in my power to prevent you from living as you want; it's in my power to set you free or abase you; whenever I please, you can be of good cheer again, and set off for Athens in the best of spirits.' [76] What do you say to this man who has enslaved you? Who are you going to offer to him as your emancipator? Isn't it the case that you daren't even look him in the face, but that, putting aside all further argument, you're going to beg him to set you free? [77] Man, you ought to set off joyfully for prison, hurrying on your way, and running ahead of those who are taking you there. And then, reluctant though you are to live in Rome, are you yearning for Greece? And when you have to die, you'll come weeping to us once more because you'll never see Athens again or be able to walk around in the Lyceum?*

[78] Was it for this that you left the land of your birth? What is for this that you've been seeking to attach yourself to somebody who could help you? Help you in what respect? To be able to analyse syllogisms with greater ease, or to deal methodically with hypothetical arguments? And was it for this reason that you left your brother, country, friends, and family, to be able to return home with knowledge of such a kind? [79] And so you didn't travel abroad to acquire firmness of mind; it wasn't to achieve impassibility; it wasn't to become secure from harm, and thus no longer blame anyone or find fault with anyone; and it wasn't to make it impossible for anyone else to wrong you, and so be able to maintain your social relationships without ever being subject to hindrance? [80] That is a fine piece of trading that you've accomplished, to be able to bring back syllogisms and equivocal and hypothetical arguments! Yes, if you care to, go and sit in the marketplace with a sign in front of you as the drug sellers

do. [81] Shouldn't you deny, rather, that you know even what you've learned, so as not to bring your philosophical doctrines into disrepute as being useless? What harm has philosophy ever done to you? What wrong has Chrysippus done you that you should set out to prove by your own example that his efforts were pointless? Didn't you have enough troubles at home to cause you sorrow and distress, without your having to travel abroad to add still more to their number? [82] And if you gain new friends and acquaintances, you'll have yet more reasons to lament, and so too if you get attached to another land. What reason do you have for living, then? To pile one sorrow on top of another to make yourself miserable? [83] And then you call this natural affection? What kind of affection, man? If it's good, it can't be the source of anything bad; if it's bad, I'll have nothing to do with it. I was born for the things that are good for me; I wasn't born for those that are bad.

[84] What, then, is the proper training for this? First of all, the highest and principal form of training, which stands, so to speak, right at the entrance, that whenever you become attached to anything, don't become attached as though it were something that cannot be taken away, but rather as though it were something like an earthenware pot or crystal goblet, so that if it should get broken, you'll remember what kind of thing it was and not get unduly upset. [85] So, too, in life, when you kiss your child, your brother, your friend, never let your imagination run free, or your transports carry you as far as they might wish, but hold them back, restrain them, like those who stand behind generals when they're riding in triumph and keep reminding them that they're mortal. [86] In the same way, you should remind yourself that what you love is mortal, that what you love is not your own; it has been granted to you just for the present, not irrevocably, and not for ever, but like a fig or bunch of grapes, for a particular season of the year; so that if you long for it in the winter, you're a fool. [87] And likewise, if you long for your son or friend at a time when he's no longer granted to you, you should know that you're longing for a fig in winter. For as winter is to a fig, so is every circumstance that arises from the general order of things in relation to the things that are destroyed in accordance with that circumstance. [88] From now on, whenever you take delight in anything, call to mind the opposite impression; what harm is there in your saying beneath your breath as you're kissing your child, 'Tomorrow you'll die'? Or similarly to your

friend, 'Tomorrow you'll go abroad, or I will, and we'll never see one another again.'

[89] 'But those are words of bad omen.'

Yes, and so are some incantations, but I don't mind, provided only that they do good. Do you call anything ill-omened except what signifies something bad for us? [90] Cowardice is ill-omened, meanness of spirit is ill-omened, as is sorrow, affliction, lack of shame. These are words of ill omen; and yet we oughtn't to shrink from uttering even these words, if it will enable us to guard against the things themselves. [91] But would you describe any word to me as ill-omened if it refers to something that follows from the course of nature? Say that it is also of bad omen for ears of corn to be harvested, because that signifies the destruction of the corn. Say that it is ill-omened, too, for leaves to fall, and for a fresh fig to turn into a dried one, and for grapes to turn into raisins. [92] For all these things involve change from a preceding state to a new and different one; it's not a matter of destruction, but of ordered management and administration. [93] Travelling abroad is like that: a change, and a small change; death is like that: a bigger change from what presently is, not into what is not, but rather into what presently is not.

[94] 'So I'll no longer exist, then?'

You won't exist, but something else will, of which the world then has need. For indeed, you came into being not when you wanted it, but when the world had need of you. [95] And so a virtuous and good person, keeping in mind who he is, and where he has come from, and by whom he was created, concentrates on one thing alone: how he may fill his post in a disciplined manner, remaining obedient to God: [96] 'Is it your will that I should continue to live? I'll live as a free person, someone of noble spirit, as was your desire, for you created me to be free from hindrance in all that is my own. [97] But now you no longer have need of me? Just as you will. Up until now, it was because of you that I've remained here, not for anyone else, and now I obey you and depart.' [98] —'How do you depart?'—'Again in accordance with your wish, as a free person, as your servant, as one who takes note of your commands and your prohibitions. [99] But as long as I remain in your service, what kind of person do you want me to be? A magistrate or a private citizen, a senator or a commoner, a soldier or a general, a teacher or the head of a household? Whatever post and rank you assign to me, as Socrates says, I'll die a thousand times rather than abandon it. [100] And where do you want me to be? At Rome, at Athens, at Thebes, or at Gyara?* I ask only one thing of you, that you remember me there. [101] If you send me to a place where it is impossible for anyone to live in accord with nature, I'll depart from this life, not out of disobedience to you, but because you will have sounded the signal for me to withdraw. I'm not abandoning you. Heaven forbid! But I realize that you no longer have need of me. [102] And yet if it is granted to me to live in accordance with nature, I seek no other place than that in which I am, nor any other company than that of the people with whom I'm living.'

[103] Both by night and by day, keep these reflections at hand; write them down, read them, make them the subject of your conversation, whether with yourself, or with another: 'Can you come to my aid in this matter?' And then approach someone else, and someone else again. [104] Then, if any of those things that are regarded as undesirable should happen, you'll gain some immediate relief, to begin with, from the thought that it wasn't unexpected. [105] For it is important to be able to say on every such occasion, 'I knew that I'd fathered a mortal';* for that is what you'll say, and furthermore, 'I knew that I was mortal,' 'I knew that I was likely to leave home,' 'I knew that I might be exiled,' 'I knew that I could be imprisoned.' [106] And then, if you reflect within yourself, and examine to what domain this event belongs, you'll remember at once that 'It belongs among those that lie outside the sphere of choice, that are not my own: so what does it matter to me?' [107] Then comes the principal question, 'Who was it who sent it?' Our ruler or our general, the state or the law of the state. 'Grant that it may come about, then, because I must obey the law in everything.' [108] Later on, if your imagination gnaws at you—for that is something outside your control—fight against it with your reason, wrestle it down, don't allow it to gain strength or pass on to the next stage, of picturing everything that it wants in the very way that it wants to. [109] If you're at Gyara, don't picture how one lives at Rome, and all the pleasures that you used to enjoy when you were there, and all that you might enjoy on your return; but since this is where you've been stationed, you should strive to live valiantly in Gyara, as befits someone who is living in Gyara. And if you're in Rome, don't picture the way of life in Athens, but rather make life in Rome your sole preoccupation.

[110] Then, in place of all other pleasures, introduce that of being

conscious that you're obeying God, and that you're accomplishing, not in mere word but in very deed, the work of a good and virtuous person. [111] For what a fine thing that is, to be able to say to oneself, 'What other people talk about in solemn tones in the schools, things that pass for being paradoxical, I'm now accomplishing in very fact, while they for their part are sitting there and making my virtues the subject of their discussions; it's about me that they're enquiring, it's me whom they're praising; [112] and Zeus wanted me to provide proof of all of this in my own person, while he for his part wanted to know whether he has a soldier in me who is such as he ought to be, a citizen who is such as he ought to be, and wants to present me to everyone else as one who can provide witness about those things that lie outside the sphere of choice. 'See that your fears have no foundation, he says, and that it is against reason that you desire what you desire. Don't seek for what is good for you outside yourselves; seek it within you, or else you'll never find it.' [113] That is why Zeus brings me here at one time and there at another, and exhibits me to humanity as one who is poor, who has no position of authority, who is ill, and sends me off to Gyara, and puts me in prison. It isn't because he hates me. Perish the thought! Who could hate the best of his servants? And it isn't because he neglects me, he who neglects not even the least of his servants, but rather because he is training me and making use of me as a witness in front of everyone else. [114] And when he has appointed me to perform such a service, shall I care any longer where I am, or in whose company, or what people are saying about me? Shouldn't I strain all my attention towards God, and to fulfilling his orders and commands?'

[115] If you keep these thoughts constantly at hand, and reflect on them constantly within your own mind to make them ready for use, you'll never have need of anyone else to encourage you or strengthen your resolve. [116] For dishonour, in truth, consists not in not having anything to eat, but in not having reason enough to preserve you from fear and distress. [117] But if, one fine day, you secure freedom from fear and distress, will any tyrant still exist for you, or guardsman, or member of Caesar's household? Or will the award of any high office still arouse your envy, or those who offer sacrifices on the Capitol* on entering into office, when you've been appointed to such a very important post by Zeus? [118] Only, don't make a parade of it, don't boast about it, but demonstrate it through your actions; and even if

no one notices, be content that you yourself are of sound mind and are living a happy life.

3.25 *To those who fail to achieve what they have proposed for themselves*

[1] Of the things that you initially proposed for yourself, consider which you have achieved and which you haven't, and how it gives you joy to recall some of them and pain to recall others, and, if possible, try to recover even those that have slipped from your grasp. [2] For those who are engaged in the greatest of contests shouldn't flinch, but must be prepared also to take blows. [3] For the contest that lies in front of us is not in wrestling or the pancration, in which, whether or not one meets with success, it is possible for one to be of the highest worth or of little, and by Zeus, to be most happy or most miserable; no, this is a contest for good fortune and happiness itself. [4] What follows, then? In this contest, even if we should falter for a while, no one can prevent us from resuming the fight, nor is it necessary to wait another four years for the next Olympic Games to come around, but as soon as one has recovered and regained one's strength, and can muster the same zeal as before, one can enter the fight; and if one should fail again, one can enter once again, and if one should carry off the victory one fine day, it will be as if one had never given in.

[5] Only, don't begin, through force of habit, to be glad to repeat the process all over again, so that you end up like a bad athlete, travelling round the athletic circuit to be beaten again and again, like quails that get into the habit of running from the ring.* [6] 'I'm overcome by the impression of a pretty girl. What of that, wasn't I overcome just the same the other day?' 'The desire comes over me to disparage somebody. For didn't I have a go at someone just the other day?' [7] You're talking as if you'd come off unscathed. It is just as if someone, when told by his doctor not to take a bath, were to say in return, 'But didn't I take a bath just the other day?' To which the doctor would respond, 'Well then, what did you feel like after the bath? Didn't you get a fever? Didn't you suffer a headache?' [8] And when you for your part disparaged someone the other day, weren't you acting like an ill-natured person; weren't you talking nonsense; didn't you feed that habit of yours by citing the example of your own previous actions? [9] Why do you talk, then, about the things that you did the other day?

You ought to have remembered them, I would have thought, in the same way as slaves remember the blows that they've received, to avoid repeating the same mistakes. [10] But the two cases aren't the same, because for the slaves it is the pain that brings back the memory, but in the case of your faults, what pain is there, what penalty? And when did you ever get into the habit of shunning bad actions?

3.26 *To those who are afraid of want*

[1] Aren't you ashamed to be more cowardly and base than a runaway slave? How do they manage when they run off and abandon their masters, and on what lands and servants can they rely? Isn't it true that after stealing just a little to tide them over for the first few days, they then make their way around by land and sea, devising one means after another to sustain themselves? [2] And what runaway slave ever died of hunger? But for your part, you tremble for fear that you may run out of the necessities of life, and you lie awake at night. [3] Poor wretch, are you so blind as not to be able to see where the lack of such necessities will lead? Where does it lead, then? To just the same place as a fever or a stone falling down on your head will lead you: to death. Haven't you yourself often said the very same thing to your companions; haven't you read many things that tend in the same direction, and written many such things? How often have you boasted that, as regards death at least, you're quite settled in your mind?

[4] 'Yes, but my family too will go hungry.'

What of that? Their hunger won't take them in any other direction than yours, will it? Isn't the journey below the same from everywhere? And the world below, isn't it the same? [5] Aren't you willing to look down below, then, with courage to confront every lack and want, to that place to which even the wealthiest, and holders of the highest offices, including kings and tyrants themselves, must finally descend, even if it could well be that you'll go down hungry while they're torn apart by indigestion and drunkenness? [6] Have you ever found it easy to catch sight of a beggar who wasn't old? One who hadn't reached an advanced age? But although they freeze by night and day, and make their bed on the ground, and have no food beyond the bare essentials, they've reached a state in which it is virtually impossible for them to die. [7] And yet you, who are of sound body, and have hands and feet, are you so very afraid of hunger? Can't you fetch water, or work as a scribe, or guide children to school, or guard somebody's door?

'But it's shameful to be reduced to such straits.'

You should learn first of all what is shameful, then, and only after that come to us and call yourself a philosopher. At present, though, you shouldn't even allow someone else to call you by that name. [8] Can something be shameful for you which is not of your own doing, for which you aren't responsible, which has come to you by accident, like a headache or a fever? If your parents were poor, or if they were rich and left their property to others, and never helped you out during their lifetime, is there anything shameful for you in that? [9] Is this what you've learned from the philosophers? Have you never learned that only what is shameful is blameworthy, and only what is blameworthy deserves blame? Now can one blame someone for something that is not of his own doing, for what he himself has not brought about? [10] Well then, was it you yourself who brought about this state of affairs, who made your father the kind of man he is? Or is it in your power to reform him? Is that granted to you? What, then, ought you to wish for what isn't granted to you, or be ashamed if you don't attain your wish? [11] And is this the habit that you've acquired from studying philosophy, to look to other people and hope for nothing from yourself? [12] Well then, groan and lament as you will, and eat in fear of not having any food tomorrow. And tremble with regard to your slaves, fearing that they'll steal from you, that they'll run away, that they'll die. [13] Live in such a way and never cease to do so; you've embarked on philosophy in name alone, you who have discredited its principles, so far as you are able, by showing them to be useless and unprofitable for those who adopt them! Never have you desired firmness of mind, serenity, impassibility; never have you attended any teacher with that purpose in mind, but many a teacher to learn about syllogisms. Never have you tested out any of these impressions for yourself, asking yourself, [14] 'Am I capable of bearing this or not? What remains for me to do?', but as if all were safe and sound for you, you've concentrated on the area of study which should come last, that which is concerned with immutability, so that you may be unchanging—in what? In your cowardice, your meanness of spirit, your admiration for the rich, your inability to achieve what you desire, your inability to avoid falling into what you want to avoid. These are the things that you've been so anxious to secure!

[15] Shouldn't you have begun by acquiring something from reason, and then tried to ensure that this was secure? Who did you ever see constructing a cornice around a building without first having a wall to build it around? And what kind of doorkeeper can one place on guard when there is no door for him to watch over? [16] But for your part, you're practising to acquire the ability to demonstrate—what? You're practising to avoid being shaken by sophistic arguments. Shaken from what? [17] Begin by showing me what you're preserving, what you're measuring, what you're weighing; and then show me, accordingly, your scales and your measure. [18] Or how long will you keep measuring worthless ashes?* Isn't this what you ought to be measuring: what it is that makes people happy, what makes their affairs prosper as they would wish, and what makes it possible for them never to blame anyone, never to find fault with anyone, and to submit to the governing order of the universe? Show me that.

[19] 'Look, I'll show you,' he says; 'I'm going to analyse some syllogisms for you.'

That's an instrument that we use to measure things, slave, it isn't what is measured. [20] That is why you're now paying the penalty for what you've neglected; you tremble, you lie awake at night, you consult with everybody, and if your plans don't seem likely to please everyone, you think that they've been badly thought out. [21] And then you're afraid of going hungry, so you suppose. But no, it's not hunger that you're afraid of, but of having no one to cook for you, and no servant to do the shopping, and no other servant to put your shoes on, and no other to dress you, and no others to give you a massage, [22] and no others to follow after you, so that when you've undressed at the baths and stretched yourself out like a man who has been crucified, you may be massaged on this side and that, and the masseur may then stand over you and say, 'Shift along, give me his side, take hold of his head, let me have his shoulder,' and after that, when you've returned home from your bath, you may cry out, 'Will no one bring me something to eat?', and then, 'Take the tables out, sponge them down.' [23] This is what you fear, that you may not be able to live the life of an invalid, since to know how healthy people live, you have, in truth, only to look at how slaves live, how labourers live, how genuine philosophers live, and how Socrates lived, even when he had a wife and children, and how Diogenes lived, and Cleanthes, while having to study at the same time and draw water.* [24] If this is what you want, you'll have it everywhere, and you'll live with full confidence. Confidence in what? In the only thing in which one can properly have confidence, in that which is reliable, that which is immune to hindrance, that which can never be taken away, that is to say, your own moral choice. [25] But why have you rendered yourself so useless and good for nothing in that respect that no one is willing to welcome you into his house, or bother himself with you? When an undamaged tool that is still usable has been thrown out, anyone who finds it will carry it off and count it a gain, but no one will think that of you, but everyone will count you a loss. [26] And so you're unable to render the service even of a dog or a cock. Why do you want to keep on living, then, being such a man as you are?

[27] Does any good man fear that he may run out of food? The blind don't run out of food, nor do the crippled; so will a good man run out of it? A good soldier doesn't fail to find someone to employ him and pay him his wages, nor does a good workman or a good cobbler; so will a good man fail to find anyone? [28] Does God so neglect his own creatures, his servants, his witnesses, the only people he can make use of as an example to the uneducated, to prove that he both exists and governs the universe wisely, and doesn't neglect human affairs, and that nothing bad ever happens to a good person, either during his lifetime or after his death?

[29] 'Yes, but what if he should fail to provide me with food?'

What else could that mean, then, except that, like a good general, he has given the signal to withdraw. I obey, I follow, speaking well of my commander, and singing hymns in praise of his works. [30] For I came into this world when it pleased him that I should do so, and I am now taking my leave in accordance with his wish; and while I lived, it was my part to sing hymns of praise to God, to myself, or to someone else, or in larger company. [31] It is not much that he has given me, and nothing in abundance; he doesn't wish me to live in luxury, for he didn't grant that to Heracles either, though he was his own son, but another reigned over Argos and Mycenae, while Heracles did as he was ordered, and toiled away and accomplished his labours. [32] As for Eurystheus, who bore the name of king, he didn't rule over Argos or Mycenae, since he didn't even rule over himself,

while Heracles was ruler and governor of the entire earth and sea, he
who purged the world of wickedness and iniquity, and introduced
justice and reverence, accomplishing that task unarmed and alone.*
[33] And again, when Odysseus was shipwrecked and cast ashore, did
he allow himself to be humiliated by his destitution; did he lose heart?
No, for how was it that he approached the young girls, to ask them for
the necessities of life, something that is thought to be most shameful
for one person to ask from another? '*Like a mountain-bred lion.*'*

[34] What did he place his trust in? Not in reputation, or riches, or
office, but in his own strength, that is to say, in his judgements about
what is in our power and what isn't. [35] For it is those judgements
alone that make us free, that render us immune to hindrance, that
raise up the head of those who have been subjected to ignominy, and
allow us to look into the faces of the rich with unaverted gaze, and
likewise into the faces of despots. [36] Such was the gift that philosophy could bestow, and yet instead of taking your leave with courage
in your heart, you'll go out trembling for your clothes and silverware?
Wretched man, is that how you've wasted your time up until now?

[37] 'But what if I should fall ill?' You'll face illness as you ought.
'Who'll take care of me?' God and your friends. 'I'll have a hard bed
to lie on.' But lie on it like a man. 'But I won't have a suitable house.'
Then you'll fall ill in an unsuitable place. 'Who'll prepare my food?'
Those who prepare it for the others also, you'll be ill like Manes.*
'And what will be the outcome of my illness?' What else but death?
[38] Why don't you reflect, then, that for man the source of all evils,
and of his meanness of spirit and cowardice, is not death itself, but
rather the fear of death? It is to confront this that you must train
yourself, [39] and it is towards that end that all your reasonings, all
your studies, and all your readings should be directed, and then you'll
recognize that it is in this way alone that human beings can attain
freedom.

BOOK 4

4.1 *On freedom*

[1] That person is free who lives as he wishes, who can neither be constrained, nor hindered, nor compelled, whose motives are unimpeded, and who achieves his desires and doesn't fall into what he wants to avoid. Who wishes, then, to live in error?

'No one does.'

[2] Who wishes to live as one who is subject to deception, and is impetuous, unjust, dissolute, petulant, and base?

'No one.'

[3] No one who is of bad character lives as he wants, and accordingly, he isn't free either. [4] And who wants to live in sorrow and fear, and feel envy and pity, desiring things without being able to attain them, and wanting to avoid things and yet falling into them?

'No one at all.'

[5] Do we find anyone who is of bad character, then, to be free from grief and fear, and secure from falling into what he wants to avoid, and from failing in his desires?

'Not a single one.'

So neither do we find any such person to be free. [6] If a man who has been twice consul should hear this, he'd forgive you provided that you added, 'But you for your part are a wise man, none of this applies to you.' But if you tell him the truth, namely, [7] 'You differ not a whit with regard to your being a slave from those who've been sold three times over,' what else are you to expect than a beating? [8] 'For how on earth can I be a slave?' he says. 'My father was free, my mother was free, and no one has a deed of sale for me; and besides, I'm a senator, and a friend of Caesar, and I've been a consul, and I own many slaves.' [9] In the first place, O most excellent senator, it could well be that your father was a slave in the same way as you are, and your mother too, and your grandfather, and all your ancestors in turn. [10] But even if they were wholly free, how does that affect you? Why, what if they were noble-minded and you're mean-spirited? If they were courageous and you're a coward? If they had self-control and you're licentious?

[11] 'And what', someone asks, 'does that have to do with being a slave?'

Does it seem to you that acting against one's will and under constraint, groaning all the while, has nothing to do with being a slave?

[12] 'Granted,' he replied, 'but who can compel me apart from Caesar, who is master of us all?'

[13] By your own admission, then, you have at least one master. And the fact that he is, as you say, the common master of us all should be no source of consolation for you, but you should recognize that you're merely a slave in a great household. [14] It is thus also that the people of Nicopolis are in the habit of exclaiming, 'Yes, by the fortune of Caesar, we're free men!' [15] All the same, let's put Caesar aside for the moment, if you please, and answer me this, have you never conceived a passion for anyone, girl or boy, slave or free?

[16] 'Why, what does that have to do with being a slave or free?'

[17] Were you never ordered by your beloved to do something that you didn't want to do? Have you never flattered your little slave? Have you never kissed his feet? And yet, if you were compelled to kiss Caesar's feet, you'd regard that as an outrage and the height of tyranny. Is slavery anything other than that, then? [18] Have you never gone out at night to somewhere where you didn't want to go? Or incurred expenses greater than you wished? Or given voice to groans and lamentations, and put up with being abused and having the door shut in your face? [19] If you're ashamed to confess to your own follies, see what Thrasonides says and does, he who had served on so many campaigns, perhaps even more than you have. First of all, he went out at night, at an hour when even Geta* didn't dare to venture abroad; now, if he'd been compelled to do so by his master, he would have gone out with many a cry, lamenting his bitter servitude, [20] but what does he in fact say? '*A little wench*', he says,

> *has enslaved me, a cheap one too,*
> *Me whom no enemy has ever enslaved.**

[21] Poor wretch, to be the slave of a young girl, and a cheap one at that! Why do you still call yourself a free man, then? And why do you boast of your campaigns? [22] Then he asks for a sword and gets angry with the man who, out of the goodness of his heart, refuses to hand it over to him, and he sends presents to the girl who despises him, and begs and weeps, and again, when he meets with some slight success,

is over the moon. [23] And yet even then, as one who hadn't yet learned to escape from desire and fear, how could he be a free man?

[24] Consider now, with regard to animals, how we apply the concept of freedom to them. [25] People rear tame lions in cages, and feed them, and some even take them around with them; and yet who would say that such a lion is free? Isn't it true that the softer the life that it leads, the more it is a slave? And what lion, if it acquired sense and reason, would want to be one of those lions? [26] Come, look at those birds over there, when they're caught and brought up in cages, what won't they suffer in their efforts to escape? Some would even prefer to starve to death rather than endure such an existence, [27] and those that survive do so barely and with difficulty, and pine away; and if they can ever find an opening, they'll make their escape. Such is the desire that they feel for their natural freedom, and for an independent and untrammelled life. [28] And what harm do you suffer from being shut in a cage? 'What a thing to ask! I was born to fly wherever I please, to live in the open air, to sing when I wish. You deprive me of all of that and then ask me, "What harm do you suffer?"'

[29] That is why we call free only those animals that won't put up with captivity, but escape through death as soon as they're captured. [30] Diogenes remarks accordingly somewhere that the only sure means to secure one's freedom is to be happy to die, and he writes to the king of the Persians, 'You cannot enslave the Athenian state,' so he says, 'any more than you can enslave the fishes.' [31] —'How so? Can't I capture them?'—'If you do,' he replies, 'they'll immediately leave you and be gone like fish. For as soon as you catch one of those, it dies; and if the Athenians come to die when they're caught, what good will you gain from your armed force?'* [32] This is the language of a free man who has examined the question in all seriousness and, as might be expected, has found the right answer. But if you look elsewhere than where it is to be found, why be surprised that you never find it?

[33] It is the slave's prayer that he may be set free without delay. Why so? Do you suppose that it is because he wants to hand over his money to the men who collect the five per cent tax?* No, it is because he imagines that up until now, as a result of not having obtained his freedom, he has lived a restricted and unhappy life. [34] 'If I'm set free,' he says, 'it will at once be happiness all the way; I'll no longer

have to defer to anyone, I'll no longer have to submit to anyone, and I'll talk to one and all as their like and equal; I'll travel where I choose; I'll come from where I please and go to where I please.' [35] The day then comes when he is set free, and all at once, having nowhere to eat, he looks around for someone to flatter, for someone to have a meal with. And then he either works through the sweat of his body, undergoing the most dreadful things, and if he does acquire a manger to feed at, has fallen into much harder slavery than that which he formerly had to endure; [36] or even if he makes his fortune, being a rough sort of fellow with poor taste, he falls in love with some worthless girl, and then grows miserable, sheds tears of regret, and yearns to be a slave again. [37] 'For what harm did it bring me? Someone else clothed me, and fed me, and shod me, and took care of me when I was ill, while I did little enough in his service. But these days, poor wretch that I am, what things I have to suffer, having to slave for several masters instead of just one. [38] Yet all the same,' he adds, 'if I get those rings,* then I'll live more prosperously and be as happy as can be.' First, in order to acquire them, he suffers what he deserves, and then, when he has got them, the story starts all over again. [39] He then says, 'If I go out on campaign, I'll be delivered from all my troubles.' So he goes on campaign, suffers all the hardships that a worthless slave has to suffer, but asks nonetheless to go out on a second campaign, and then a third.* [40] After that, when he adds the finishing touch and becomes a senator, he then becomes a slave indeed as he enters the Senate, to submit to the most splendid and luxurious slavery of all.

[41] Let him put aside his foolishness, then, and learn, as Socrates used to say, 'what each real entity* is', and not apply his preconceptions to particular cases merely at random. [42] For that is the cause of all human ills, that people aren't able to apply their general preconceptions* to the particular cases. [43] No, but one person thinks in one way, and another person in another. This person imagines that he is ill. Not at all, it is merely that he is applying his preconceptions wrongly. Another imagines that he is poor, another that he has a harsh father or mother, another that Caesar is ill-disposed towards him. But all of this means one thing and one alone, that people don't know how to apply their preconceptions. [44] Now, who doesn't have a preconception of what is bad, that it is harmful, that it should be avoided, that one should get rid of it by every possible means? One

preconception doesn't conflict with another, [45] but conflict can arise when one comes to apply it. What is this evil then, that is harmful and ought to be avoided? One person says that it is not to be Caesar's friend;* he has gone astray, he has failed to make a proper application, he is in distress, he is going in search of something that isn't relevant to the case in hand; because when he has actually become Caesar's friend, he has failed all the same to attain what he was seeking. [46] For what is it that every one of us is seeking? To live in peace, to be happy, to do all that one wants without being subject to hindrance or constraint. Now when he has become Caesar's friend, has he ceased to be subject to hindrance and constraint, and does he live in peace and happiness? Who shall we ask? Is there anyone who could be more worthy of our trust than this very man who has become Caesar's friend? [47] Come forward and tell us when you slept more peacefully, at the present time or before you became Caesar's friend? At once you'll hear the reply, 'Leave off, for heaven's sake, stop making fun of my predicament—you have no idea what miseries I have to suffer, poor wretch that I am. I'm unable to get any sleep, but first one person comes in and then another, saying that Caesar is already awake, that he is already coming out; and then come the troubles, then come the anxieties.' [48] Come, when did you dine with greater pleasure, now or before? Listen to what he has to say about this matter too. He says that if he isn't invited, he gets upset, but if he is, he dines like a slave in the presence of his master, being anxious all the while not to do or say anything stupid. And what do you suppose he is afraid of? Of being whipped like a slave? And how could he hope to escape as lightly as that? No, but as befits so great a man, a friend of Caesar, he is frightened that he may lose his head.

[49] And when did you bathe in greater tranquillity? When did you take your exercise at greater leisure? In short, which life would you prefer to lead, that of today or that of former days? [50] I could swear that no man is so stupid or so incurable as not to lament his misfortunes the more greatly the more he becomes Caesar's friend.

[51] So if neither those who are called kings, nor the friends of those kings, live as they wish, what free man can there still be?

Seek and you'll find; for nature has provided you with resources to enable you to discover the truth. But if you yourself are unable, through use of those resources alone, to go on to discover what follows, [52] listen to those who have made the enquiry. Does freedom seem to you to be something good?—'Yes, the greatest good.'—Is it possible, then, that one who obtains this greatest of goods should be unhappy or fare badly?—'No it isn't.'—So whenever you see people to be unhappy, miserable, and subject to grief, you should confidently declare them not to be free.—'I so declare.' [53] —Well then, we have now got away from buying and selling,* and such arrangements with regard to property; but if you're right in agreeing to the points that you have, whether it be the Great King* who is unhappy, or a little king, or a man of consular rank, or one what has been twice consul, he couldn't be free.—'Agreed.'

[54] Answer me, then, on this further point: do you regard freedom as being something great and noble, something of high value?— 'How could it not be?'—Is it possible, then, that someone who is in possession of something so great, so valuable, so noble, could be base-minded?—'Impossible.' [55] —So whenever you see someone grovelling in front of somebody else, or flattering him contrary to his real opinion, you may confidently declare that he isn't free, and not only if he is acting in this way for the sake of a wretched little meal, but even if it is for the sake of a governor's post or a consulship. No, but when people do this for the sake of trifles, you should call them petty slaves, and call the latter by the name that they deserve, slaves on a grand scale. [56] —'That too I concede.'

Does freedom seem to you to entail independence and self-determination?—'How could it be otherwise?'—So whenever anyone is subject to hindrance or compulsion from another, confidently declare that he isn't free. [57] And don't look, I ask you, to his grandfathers and great-grandfathers, or enquire about deeds of sale or purchase, but if you hear him say 'master' from his heart and with true feeling, even if the twelve fasces are being carried in front of him, then call him a slave; and if you hear him exclaiming, 'Wretch that I am, what things I have to suffer!', call him a slave too. In a word, if you see him wailing, complaining, and living unhappily, call him a slave in a purple-bordered robe.* [58] If he does nothing of that kind, however, don't yet declare that he is free, but get acquainted with his judgements, and see whether they're in any way subject to constraint, or hindrance, or unhappiness; and if you find that to be the case, call him a slave on holiday at the Saturnalia.* Say that his master is away from home; but he'll be back soon, and then you'll see what this man suffers! [59] —'Who'll be back?'—Whoever holds control over anything that the man desires, and can procure it or take it away.—'Do we have so many masters, then?'—Yes, so many. For even before these human masters, we have circumstances as our masters, and there are any number of those. [60] Because in truth, it is not Caesar himself whom people stand in fear of, but death, banishment, confiscation of their property, imprisonment, loss of civil rights. Nor does anyone love Caesar himself, unless Caesar happens to be a man of great worth, but it is riches that we love, or a post as tribune, praetor, or consul. As long as we love, hate, or fear these things, it necessarily follows that those who have power over them will be our masters. For that reason, we even worship such people as though they were gods, [61] because we suppose that anyone who has the power to confer the greatest advantages on us is divine. And then we wrongly lay down this minor premiss, 'This man has the power to confer the greatest advantages.' It is bound to follow that the conclusion drawn from these premisses must be false too.

[62] What is it, then, that sets a person free from hindrance and makes him his own master? For neither wealth, nor a consul's post, nor a governor's post, nor a kingdom make him so, [63] but something else needs to be found. Now what is it that ensures, when someone is writing, that he won't be subject to hindrance or obstruction?—'Knowledge of how to write.'—And when one is playing the lyre?—'Knowledge of how to play the lyre.'—It thus follows that in life, too, it must be knowledge of the art of living. [64] Now you've already learned this as a general principle, but consider it too in its specific applications. If someone desires any of the things that lie within the power of others, is it possible that he'll be free from hindrance?—'No.'—Is it possible that he'll be free from obstruction?—'No.' [65] —Then he can't be free either. Now consider this point: do we have nothing that is exclusively within our own power, or is that the case with everything, or are there some things that are within our own power while others are within the power of other people? [66] —'How do you mean?'—When you want your body to remain sound and whole, is that within your power or isn't it?—'No, that isn't within my power.'—And when you want it to be healthy?—'No, that isn't either.'—Or that it should be beautiful?—'That isn't either.'—And to live or die?—'No again.'—It thus follows that your body is not your own, but is subject to whatever is stronger than itself.—'Indeed.' [67] —And when it comes to your land, is it within your power to own what you want,

and for as long as you want, and just as you want?—'No.'—And your slaves?—'No.'—And your little house?—'No.'—And your horses?—'None of that.'—And if you should wish at all cost that your children should remain alive, or that your wife should, or your brother, or your friends, is that within your power?—'No, that isn't either.' [68]—Have you nothing at all, then, that is subject to your own authority, or exclusively within your power, or do you have something of that kind?—'I don't know.'

[69] Well, look at the question in this way, and think it over. Can anyone make you give your assent to what is false?—'No one can.'—In the matter of assent, then, you're free from hindrance and restraint.—'Agreed.' [70]—Come now, can anyone force you to direct your impulses towards anything that you don't want?—'Indeed he can. For when he threatens me with death or imprisonment, he can force me to it.' [71]—If you were to despise death, however, or chains, would you still pay any heed to him?—'No.'—Now, to despise death, is that your own act, or isn't it?—'It's my own act.'—And to exercise your impulses, is that your own act, or isn't it?—'Agreed, it's my own act.'—And to exercise your impulses not to act? That too is your own act. [72]—'Yes, but what if I have an impulse to go for a walk, and someone else prevents me?'—What can he prevent in you? Surely not your assent?—'No, but rather my poor body.'—Yes, as he could a stone.—'Granted, but I can no longer go for my walk.' [73]—And who told you that taking a walk is an act of your own that isn't open to hindrance? For my part, I said only that your impulse to do so isn't subject to hindrance. But when it comes to the use of our body, and its cooperation, you've learned long since that none of that is your own.—'I'll concede that too.' [74]—And can anyone force you to desire what you don't want?—'No one can.'—And to set an aim for yourself, or make a plan, or in general, to deal with the impressions that come to you?—'Not that either; [75] but when I form a desire, someone can hinder me from achieving that desire.'—If that desire is directed towards something that is your own, and isn't subject to hindrance, how can he hinder you?—'There is no way in which he can.'—Who is telling you, then, that someone whose desires are directed towards things that aren't his own isn't subject to hindrance? [76]—'But health, can't I desire that?'—In no way, nor anything else that isn't your own. [77] For that which is not in your power to procure or keep as you wish is not your own. Keep

not only your hands well away from it, but first and foremost your desire; otherwise you've delivered yourself into slavery, you've put your head under the yoke, if you attach value to anything that isn't your own, if you conceive a desire for anything that is subject to anyone else and is perishable.

[78] 'But isn't my hand my own?'—It is a part of you, but by nature it is nothing but clay; it is subject to hindrance and compulsion; it is a slave to everything that is stronger than itself. [79] And why just speak of your hand? It is your entire body that you ought to treat as a poor overburdened donkey, as long as it is possible, as long as it is permitted to you; and if it should be requisitioned, and a soldier seizes it, let it go; don't resist or grumble. Otherwise you'll get a beating, and you'll lose your poor donkey all the same. [80] But if that is the way that you should act with regard to your body, consider what is left for you to do with regard to everything else that is procured for the sake of the body. If your body is a little donkey, all those other things become bridles for the donkey, pack-saddles, shoes, barley, fodder. Let all of that go too; get rid of it more quickly and cheerfully than of the little donkey itself.

[81] And when you have undertaken this preparation, and have trained yourself in this way, to distinguish those things that are not your own from those that are, and those that are subject to hindrance from those that are not, and to regard the latter as being your concern, while the former are not, to keep your desire fixed on the latter and your aversion directed towards the former, will there then be anyone left whom you need fear?—'No one.'

[82] For what is there for you to be afraid about? About those things that are your own, in which your true good and evil lie? And who has any power over those? Who can take them away; who can impede them? No one, any more than he could impede God. [83] Or is it your body and your possessions that you fear for? For things that are not your own, for things that are nothing to you? And what else have you been studying for all this while, if not to distinguish what is your own from what isn't your own, and what is in your power from what isn't in your power, and what is subject to hindrance from what is immune to it? And for what purpose have you visited the philosophers? To be no less miserable and unfortunate than you were before? [84] You won't be free in that case from fear and agitation. And what does distress have to do with you? For it is expectation that gives rise to

fear, while distress arises from that which is present. And what will you still have any desire for? For things that lie within the sphere of choice, as being both your own and present, you have a measured and well-controlled desire; while for things that lie outside the sphere of choice, you have no desire, so as to allow no place to that irrational element which is violent and impetuous beyond measure.

[85] When this is the attitude that you hold towards things, what man could still be capable of inspiring you with fear? For what does one human being have in him that is of such a nature as to inspire fear in another human being, either in his appearance, his manner of talk, or his company in general, any more than a horse awakens fear in another horse, or a dog in a dog, or a bee in a bee?

[86] How is a citadel* destroyed, then? Neither by iron, nor by fire, but by judgements. For if we pull down the citadel in the city, have we also pulled down the citadel of fever, the citadel of pretty girls, or, in a word, the citadel within us, and shall we have driven out the tyrants whom we have inside us, whom we have exercising their sway over us day after day, sometimes the same ones, sometimes different? [87] But this is where we must begin; this is where we must set out from to destroy the citadel and drive out the tyrants: we must give up our poor body, and its various parts and faculties, and our property, reputation, public posts, honours, children, brothers, and friends, and regard all of that as being not our own. [88] And if the tyrants are driven out from there, what need do I have to raze the citadel, at least as far as I am concerned? For what harm does it do me if it is left standing? Why should I go on to expel the guards? For where am I conscious of them? It is against others that they direct their sticks, their spears, and their swords. [89] But for my part, I've never been hindered in the exercise of my will, or constrained to do anything against my will. And how could that be possible? I have submitted my impulses to God. It is his will that I should have a fever? That is my will too. It is his will that I should direct my impulses towards a certain thing? That is my will too. It is his will that I should desire something? That is what I want too. It is his will that I should get something? That is what I want too. He doesn't want that? Nor do I. [90] And so it is my will that I should die, my will that I should be tortured. Who can still hinder me, then, contrary to my own judgements; who can constrain me? No more than that would be possible with Zeus.

[91] This is also the way in which the more cautious travellers proceed. Someone has heard that the road is infested with robbers; he doesn't dare to set out alone, but waits to travel in the company of an ambassador, or quaestor,* or proconsul, and when he has attached himself to them, he can make the journey in safety. [92] Such is the way in which a prudent person acts in this world. 'There are many gangs of robbers, and there are tyrants, storms, difficulties, and losses of what we hold most dear. [93] Where can one find refuge? How can one pass on one's way without getting robbed? And what company should one wait for to make one's journey in safety? To whom should one attach oneself? [94] To that man, to this rich man, to that proconsul? And what good will it do me? The man himself is stripped bare, and groans and laments. And what if my fellow traveller himself should turn against me and become my robber? What am I to do? [95] I'll become a friend of Caesar; if I'm a companion of his, no one will do me any wrong. But first of all, to become his friend, what things I'll have to endure and suffer! How many times and by how many people am I bound to be robbed! [96] And then, even if I achieve my aim, Caesar too is mortal. And what if, for some reason or other, he should become my enemy? Would it be better for me to withdraw once and for all to a desert? Come, does no fever make its way there? [97] So what is to become of me? Is there no way of finding a fellow traveller who is reliable, trustworthy, strong, and incapable of treachery? [98] A prudent person thinks things over in this way, and comes to understand that if he attaches himself to God, he'll complete his journey in safety.

[99] 'What do you mean by "attaching himself to God?"'

This: that whatever God wants, this man wants too; and whatever God doesn't want, he doesn't want either.

[100] 'How can that be achieved, then?'

Why, how otherwise than by observing the wishes of God and his governing order? What has he given to me to be my own, and subject to my own authority, and what has he reserved for himself? He has given me whatever lies within the sphere of choice; he has made it to be subject to my control, and immune to hindrance and obstruction. This body formed from clay; how could he make that immune from hindrance? And so he has made it subject to the revolution of the universe, and likewise my property, my furniture, my house, my children, my wife. [101] Why shall I fight against God, then? Why should I want what I oughtn't to want, to keep at all cost what hasn't been given to me? So how am I to possess these things? On the terms on which they have been granted to me, and for as long as it remains possible. But he who has given them to me takes them away again. Why, then, shall I resist? Not to mention that I'd be a fool to try to force my way against one who is stronger than me; it would above all be wrong for me to do so. [102] For where did I get these things from when I entered the world? My father gave them to me. And who gave them to him? Who made the sun, the fruits of the earth, the seasons, and the society of human beings and the fellowship that binds them together?

[103] And then, when you've received everything from another, even your very self, will you complain and cast reproaches on the giver if he takes something away from you? [104] Who are you, and for what purpose have you come here? Wasn't it he who brought you here? Wasn't it he who showed you the light? Wasn't it he who gave you companions to work together with you? And senses too? And reason? And as what kind of being did he bring you here? Wasn't it as one who is mortal? Wasn't it as one who would live on the earth with a small portion of flesh, and would observe his governing order, and would accompany him in his procession and take part in his festival for a short period of time? [105] Aren't you willing, then, after having beheld his pageant and festival* for the time that is granted to you, to take your leave when he conducts you away, after having first paid obeisance to him and having thanked him for all that you've heard and seen? 'No, but I wanted to continue to take part in the festival.' [106] Yes, and the initiates at the Mysteries would like to continue the initiations, and the spectators at Olympia would doubtless like to watch more athletes; but the festival must have its end. Depart, then, as one who is grateful and reverent; make room for others; it is necessary that others, too, should come into the world as you yourself have come, and that once they've arrived, they should have room, and somewhere to live, and the necessities of life. But if those who came first don't make way, what will be left for them? Why are you so insatiable? Why are you never satisfied?

[107] 'Yes, but I want my young children and my wife to be with me.'

Why, are they yours? Don't they really belong to the one who gave them? To the one who also created you? So won't you give up what is not your own? Won't you surrender it to your superior?

[108] 'Why has he brought me here under these conditions?'

If they don't suit you, go away. He has no need of a spectator who is always complaining about his lot. He needs people to join in his festival and dances, so that they may, on the contrary, greet them with applause, and view them with reverence, and sing hymns in praise of the assembly. [109] As for grumblers and cowards, he won't be sorry to see them gone from the assembly; for even while they were present, they didn't behave as though they were at a festival, and didn't fill their proper place, but lamented instead and found fault with the deity, their lot, and their companions, unconscious of what had been granted to them, and the powers that they had received for the opposite use—greatness of soul, nobility of mind, courage, and the very freedom that we are now investigating.

[110] 'For what purpose have I received these gifts?'—To make use of them.—'For how long?'—For as long as the one who has lent them to you may please.—'But what if they're essential to me?'—Don't get attached to them, and they won't be; don't tell yourself that they're essential, and then they're not.

[111] This is what you should practise from morning to evening. Begin with the smallest and most fragile things, a pot, or a cup, and then pass on to a tunic, a dog, a horse, a scrap of land; and from there, pass on to yourself, to your body, and the parts of your body, and to your children, your wife, your brothers.* [112] Look around you in every direction, and cast these things far away from you. Purify your judgements so that nothing that is not your own may remain attached to you, or become part of yourself, or give you pain when it comes to be torn away from you. [113] And say while you're training yourself day after day, as you are here, not that you're acting as a philosopher (for you must concede that it would be pretentious to lay claim to that title), but that you're a slave on the way to emancipation. For that is true freedom.

[114] It was in this way that Diogenes was set free by Antisthenes, such that he said thereafter that he could never be enslaved by anyone. [115] So how did he react when he was captured; how did he behave towards the pirates?* He didn't call any of them master, did he? And here I'm not speaking of the name, because it isn't the word that I fear, but the state of mind expressed in the use of the name. [116] How he rebuked them for not giving enough food to their captives! And think how he conducted himself when he was offered up for sale! Did

he look for a master? No, but for a slave. And once he had been sold, how he behaved towards his master! He immediately began to argue with him, saying that he oughtn't to dress as he did, or have his hair cut in the way that it was, and he talked to him about his sons, telling him how they ought to live their lives. [117] And is there anything surprising in that? After all, if he had bought a trainer, would he have treated him as a servant or master when it came to gymnastic exercises? And likewise if he had bought a doctor, or an architect? Correspondingly, in whatever field, someone who possesses the relevant skill must necessarily exercise authority over one who lacks it. [118] So if someone possesses the knowledge of how we should live our lives in general, what else can follow than that he must be the master? For who is master of a ship?

'The helmsman.'

Why? Because anyone who disobeys him will be punished.

[119] 'But my master can flog me.'

But he can't do so with impunity, can he?

'No, that's what I thought too.'

But because he can't do so with impunity, it follows that he hasn't the power to do so; for no one can do wrong with impunity.

[120] 'And what punishment, in your view, does a man suffer if he throws his own slave into chains?'

The very fact of having thrown him into chains; for you yourself must concede that point if you want to preserve the principle that man is not a wild beast, but a civilized animal. [121] Consider now, when is a vine in a bad way? When it is acting contrary to its own nature. And a cock? Likewise. [122] And so too with a human being. Now, what is his nature? Is it to bite, to kick, to throw people into prison and cut their heads off? No, but to do good, to be helpful to others, to pray for them. So this master is in a bad way, whether you want to admit it or not, when he acts with brutality.

[123] 'You mean that Socrates didn't fare badly?'

No, but rather his judges and accusers.

'Nor Helvidius* at Rome?'

No, but the man who had him put to death.

[124] 'How do you mean?'

Just as you too wouldn't say that the winning cock, even if badly wounded, has fared badly, but rather the one that is defeated without suffering a scratch. Nor do you call a dog happy when it is neither on the hunt nor hard at work, but when you see it sweating, suffering, and broken by the chase. [125] What is paradoxical in asserting, then, that for every being, what is bad for it is that which is contrary to its nature? Is there any paradox in that? Didn't you say it yourself with regard to every other being? Why is it that you think otherwise in the case of man alone? [126] Why, when we say that man is by nature sociable, affectionate, and trustworthy, there surely isn't anything paradoxical in that?—'No, that isn't paradoxical either.' [127] —How is it, then, that he still suffers no harm when he is flogged, or thrown into prison, or decapitated? Isn't it that if he bears that in a noble spirit, he comes off with added profit and advantage, while the person who is truly harmed, and suffers the most pitiful and shameful fate, is the one who, instead of being human, turns into a wolf, a viper, or a wasp?

[128] Come, let us recapitulate the points that we've agreed. The person who isn't subject to hindrance is free, he who has everything at hand as he wants it; but one who is subject to hindrance, or constraint, or obstruction, or can be thrown into any difficulty against his will, is a slave. [129] And who is the person who is free from all hindrance? He who desires nothing that is not his own. And what are the things that are not our own? Those that are not within our power, either to have or not to have, or to have with certain qualities, or under certain conditions. [130] Our body is thus not our own, every part of it is not our own, and our property is not our own. So if you become attached to any of these as though it were your own, you'll suffer the punishment that a person deserves if he sets his aim on what is not his own. [131] This is the road that leads to freedom, this is the only deliverance from slavery, to be able to say one day with your whole heart,

> *Guide me, Zeus, and thou, O Destiny,*
> *To wheresoever you have assigned me.**

[132] But what do you say, philosopher? A tyrant calls upon you to say something that isn't worthy of you. Do you say it, or don't you? Tell me.—'Let me think about the matter.'—Think about it at this moment? What did you spend your time thinking about while you were at the school? Didn't you consider what things are good, and what are bad, and what are indifferent?—'Indeed I did.' [133] —And what conclusions did you arrive at?—'That what is just and honourable

is good, and what is unjust and shameful is bad.'—Living isn't a good, is it?—'No.'—And dying isn't an evil?—'No.'—And imprisonment isn't?—'No.'—But saying something that is ignoble and disloyal, and betraying a friend, and flattering a tyrant, what do you think of all of that?—'Those are bad things.' [134] —What then? No, you're not thinking about the matter, nor have you ever thought about it and come to a decision. For what sort of an enquiry is this, to ask whether it is fitting, when it is in my power, to secure the greatest goods for myself and avoid the greatest evils? A fine and necessary enquiry that is, one requiring long deliberation! Why are you making fun of us, man? One never makes an enquiry such as that. [135] No, if you truly imagined that shameful things were bad, and everything else indifferent, you would surely never have come to hesitate in this way, or anything like it, but would have been able to settle the question at once, as though by direct view in your mind's eye. [136] For when do you stop to consider whether black is white, or light is heavy? Don't you rely on the clear evidence of your senses? How is it, then, that you're now talking of examining whether one should avoid things that are indifferent more than those that are bad? [137] Actually this doesn't accord with the judgements that you hold; these things don't strike you as indifferent, but as the greatest of evils, and those other things don't seem bad to you, but rather things of no matter.

[138] For this is the habit that you have got into from the beginning. 'Where am I? In the school. And who are these people who are listening to me? I'm talking among philosophers. But now that I've left the schoolroom, away with all that talk which is fit only for pedants and fools!' That is how a philosopher comes to bear witness against a friend; that is how a philosopher turns parasite; [139] that is how he sells himself for money; that is how in the Senate a man doesn't say what he thinks, even though his judgement is crying aloud within him, [140] and not some wretched half-hearted judgement hanging on idle reasonings as though by a hair, but a robust and serviceable judgement that received its initiation by being tested in action. [141] Watch yourself to see how you react to the news—I won't say, that your child is dead, for how could you stand up to that?—but that your oil has been spilled, or all your wine has been drunk? You'd react in such a way [142] that a bystander, seeing you fall into such a passion, would simply exclaim, 'Philosopher, you talk quite differently

in the schoolroom. Why are you trying to deceive us? Why, when you're nothing but a worm, do you claim to be a man? [143] I'd like to stand over one of these philosophers when he is engaged in the act of love, to see how he deploys his efforts, and what words he utters, and whether he remembers his title and the arguments that he hears or recites or reads!'

[144] 'And what does all of this have to do with freedom?'

Nothing apart from this has anything to do with freedom, whether you rich folk wish it or not.

[145] 'And what proof can you bring of this?'

Why, what other than yourselves, who have this powerful master and live at his beck and call, you who faint if he merely looks at one of you with knotted brows, and pay court to old men and women, saying, 'I can't do that, I'm not allowed to.' [146] Why aren't you allowed to? And weren't you arguing with me just now and claiming that you're free? 'But Aprulla* has stopped me from doing it.' Tell the truth, slave, and don't run away from your masters, or try to disown them, and have the nerve to bring forward someone to attest that you're free when there are so many proofs to show that you're a slave. [147] In truth, when someone is compelled by the power of love to do something that is contrary to his opinion, even though he can see at the same time what is better, but can't summon up the resolve to follow it through, one might feel the more inclined to think him worthy of pardon because he has been seized by a passion that is violent and in some sense divine. [148] But who could bear with you, with your passion for old women and old men, you who wipe the noses old women and wash their faces, and try to win them over with gifts, and wait on them like a slave when they're ill, while you're praying at the same time for them to die, and are asking the doctors whether they're at last on the point of death? Or again, when for the sake of these great and venerable posts, you kiss the hands of other men's slaves, so making yourself the slave of people who aren't even free! [149] And then you strut around in front of me with grand airs as a praetor or consul! Don't I know how you came to be a praetor, and how you acquired your consulship, and who gave it to you? [150] For my part, I wouldn't even want to stay alive if I had to live by Felicio's favour, and put up with his pride and slavish arrogance; for I know what a slave is who is in the lap of fortune, as it seems, and is puffed up with pride.*

[151] 'And you, are you free?', the man asks.

By the gods, I want to be and pray to be, but I'm not yet able to look my masters in the face, I still attach value to my poor body, and I take great care to keep it whole and sound, despite the fact that it isn't so. [152] But I can show you a free man, to save you from having to search any longer for an example. Diogenes was free. How so? Not because he was born of free parents, for he wasn't, but because he himself was free, because he had cast off everything that could allow slavery to gain hold of him to enslave him. [153] Everything that he had he could easily let go; everything was only loosely attached to him. If you had seized all that he possessed, he would have abandoned it to you rather than follow after you for its sake; and if you had seized his leg, he would have let that go too; and if his whole body, he would have let his whole body go; and likewise his parents, friends, and country. For he knew from where it was that he had received these things, and from whom, and on what conditions. [154] As for his true ancestors, the gods, and his true country, these he would never have abandoned, nor would he have allowed any other person to surpass him in obedience and submission to them, and no one would have died for his country with a more cheerful heart than he. [155] For he never sought merely to give the impression of doing anything on behalf of the universe,* but he remembered that everything that comes about has that as its source, and is accomplished on behalf of that country, and is ordained by the one who governs it. See accordingly what Diogenes himself says and writes, [156] 'For this reason,' he says, 'it is permitted for you, Diogenes, to talk as you please with the king of the Persians, and Archidamas,* king of the Spartans.' [157] Was it because he was born of free parents? I suppose it was because Athenians, Spartans, and Corinthians were all children of slaves that they couldn't speak as they wished to those kings, but feared them and flattered them? [158] 'Why are you permitted to do so, then, Diogenes?' 'Because I regard this poor body as not my own, because I have need of nothing, because the law is everything to me, and all else is nothing.' These are the things that permitted him to be a free man.

[159] And so that you may not think that I'm offering you as an example a man who lived on his own, having neither wife, nor children, nor country, nor friends, nor relations, who might have turned him aside and caused him to deviate from his path, take Socrates and

consider a man who had a wife and young children, but didn't regard
them as being his own, and had a country, in so far as it was his duty,
and in the way in which that duty required, and had friends and relations, all of this subject to the law and to obedience to the law. [160]
That is why, when it was his duty to serve as a soldier, he was the first
to set out, and exposed himself to the dangers of war without sparing
himself in the least.* But he was sent by the Thirty Tyrants to arrest
Leon;* being sure in his mind that such a deed would be shameful, he
never even contemplated it, although he was well aware that he might
meet his death as a result, if things turned out that way. [161] But what
did that matter to him? For there was something else that he wanted
to preserve other than his body, namely, his character as a trustworthy man, as a man of honour. These are things that cannot be
violated, that cannot be reduced to subjection. [162] And later, when
he was on trial for his life* and had to defend himself, did he conduct
himself like a man who had children, who had a wife? No, but like a
man who lives on his own. And when he had to drink the poison,*
how did he behave then? [163] When he could have saved himself and
Crito said to him, 'Make your escape for the sake of your children,'
what did he reply? Did he regard that opportunity as a godsend? Not
at all, he thought only about what would be proper for him to do;
the rest he didn't even consider or take into account. For he didn't
want, so he said, to save his poor body, but to save that which finds
growth and is preserved through right action, and is diminished and
destroyed through wrong action.* [164] Socrates didn't save his life at
the cost of dishonour: he who had refused to put a motion to the vote
when the Athenians demanded it,* he who had held the Tyrants in
contempt, he who used to speak in such fine terms about virtue and
moral goodness. [165] This man could not be saved through dishonour, but it was by death that he was saved, not by flight. Just as a good
actor is saved when he stops at the point at which he should, rather
than by continuing to act beyond the proper time.

[166] 'But what will the children do, then?'

'If I had gone away to Thessaly, you would have looked after them;
so when I've gone down to Hades, will there be no one to look after
them?' See how he calls death by fair names, and mocks at it. [167] If
it had been you or I, we would at once have set out to show by philosophical reasoning that 'one needs to protect oneself against those
who act unjustly by repaying them in kind', and we would have

added, 'If I escape with my life, I'll be useful to many another, but if
I die, I'll be of use to no one.' For if it had been necessary, we would
have crawled out through a mousehole to get away. [168] And how
would we have been of any use to anyone? For how could we have
been if everyone else had still been in Athens? And even if we could
have been of some use alive, wouldn't we have been even more useful
to mankind if we had died when we ought, and as we ought? [169] And
now that Socrates is dead, the memory of him is no less useful to the
human race, or even much more useful than all that he did and said
while still alive.

[170] Reflect on these things, these judgements, these arguments,
and look at these examples, if you want to be free, if you desire freedom in accordance with its true value. [171] And why should you be
surprised if you have to purchase something of such value so dearly
and at such high cost? For the sake of what commonly passes for
freedom, some people hang themselves, others hurl themselves over
cliffs, and sometimes whole cities have perished. [172] So for the sake
of true freedom, which is secure against all treachery and is inviolable,
won't you return that which God has given you when he demands it
back? Won't you not only, as Plato says, practise to die,* but even to
suffer torture, to go into exile, to be flogged, and in a word, give up
everything that is not your own? [173] Otherwise you'll be a slave
among slaves, even if you become a consul ten thousand times; and
even if you ascend to the palace, you'll be no less a slave, and you'll
recognize that, as Cleanthes remarked, what the philosophers say
may conflict with common opinion but not with reason.* [174] For
you'll discover by experience that it is in fact true, and that the things
that are highly regarded and eagerly pursued are of no value to those
who acquire them, while those who have not yet acquired them fancy
that, once they do, they'll be in possession of all that is good; but
when they have them, there is the same scorching heat as before, the
same fierce agitation, the same sense of surfeit, the same desire for
what one doesn't have. [175] For freedom is not attained through the
satisfaction of desires, but through the suppression of desires. [176]
And so that you may come to know the truth of this, as you have
toiled hitherto for those other things, now transfer that same effort to
these instead; stay up at night so as to acquire a judgement that will
set you free, [177] and instead of paying court to a rich old man, pay it
to a philosopher, and be seen hanging around his doors. You'll incur

no disgrace by being seen there, and you won't come back empty-handed and without profit if you approach him as you ought. Have a try at least; there is no shame in trying.

4.2 *On association with others*

[1] This is a point to which you should attend before all others, that you should never become so intimately associated with any of your former friends or acquaintances that you sink down to the same level as them; for otherwise, you'll destroy yourself. [2] But if this thought worms its way into your mind, that 'I'll seem churlish to him, and he won't be as friendly to me as before,' remember that nothing is gained without cost, and that it is impossible for someone to remain the same as he was if he is no longer acting in the same way. [3] Choose, then, which you prefer: to be held in the same affection as before by your former friends by remaining as you used to be, or else become better than you were and no longer meet with the same affection. [4] For if the latter course is preferable, you should follow it immediately and not allow yourself to be distracted by other considerations, because no one can make progress if he is hesitating between two courses. No, if you've chosen this course above every other, if you want to devote yourself to this alone, you must put aside everything else. [5] Otherwise, if you're caught between two paths, you'll incur a double penalty, since you'll neither make progress as you ought nor acquire the things that you used to enjoy. [6] For before, when you aimed plainly and simply at things that are of no value, you made yourself agreeable to your companions. [7] You can't excel in two things at once, but in so far as you partake in one of them, you're bound to fall short in the other. If you no longer drink with the people whom you used to drink with, you won't seem as agreeable to them as you did before. Choose, then, whether you want to be a heavy drinker and pleasing to them, or a sober man and unpleasing to them. If you no longer sing with the people whom you used to sing with, you can't be held in the same affection by them. Here, too, you have to choose which you prefer. [8] For if it is better to have self-respect and be well behaved than have someone say of you, 'What a delightful fellow', you must give up all the rest, renounce it, turn your back on it, have nothing more to do with it. [9] But if that isn't to your taste, turn wholly and completely in the opposite direction, become one of those

perverts, one of those adulterers; act accordingly and you'll get what you want. Jump up and down too, and shout out your applause to the dancer. [10] But roles as different as these don't mix. You can't play Thersites* and Agamemnon at one and the same time. If you want to be Thersites, you must be humpbacked and bald; if Agamemnon, you must be tall and handsome and love your subjects.

4.3 *What things should be exchanged for what?*

[1] This is a thought that you should keep at hand to apply whenever you lose any external thing: what are you acquiring in exchange for it? And if it should be something more valuable, never say, 'I've lost out.' [2] You haven't lost out if you gain a horse in place of a donkey, an ox in place of a sheep, a fine deed in place of a bit of spare cash, a sense of shame in place of salacious talk. [3] If you keep this point in mind, you'll always preserve your character as it ought to be. Otherwise, you should consider that your time is being spent to no purpose, and that all the efforts that you're exerting on your own behalf will be squandered and run to waste. [4] It takes very little to spoil and upset everything: just some slight deviation from reason. [5] To capsize his ship, the helmsman doesn't need to make as much preparation as to keep it safe; he has only to steer a little too much into the wind and all is lost; and even if he does so inadvertently, because his attention has wandered, he is undone. [6] Such is the case here too: if you nod off just for a moment, all that you've amassed up until then is lost and gone. [7] Pay careful attention, then, to your impressions; watch over them unceasingly. For it is not something of little importance that you're trying to preserve, but self-respect, fidelity, impassibility, freedom from distress, fear, and anxiety, and, in a word, freedom. [8] At what price will you sell that? Consider how much it is worth.

'But I shan't get anything like that in exchange for what I'm giving up.'

If you do in fact get it, consider what it is that you're getting in exchange. [9] 'I have orderly conduct, he a tribune's post; he a praetor's post,* and I self-respect. But I don't shout out where it is unseemly, I won't jump up when I shouldn't, because I'm a free man and a friend of God, so I obey him of my own free will. [10] As for other things, there is none that I should lay claim to, neither body,

nor possessions, nor office, nor reputation—in a word, nothing whatever; nor is it God's wish that I should lay claim to them. For if it had
been, he would have made them good for me. But in point of fact he
hasn't done so, and in view of that, I cannot disobey any of his commands.' [11] Safeguard your own good in all that you do; and as for
the rest, simply take what is granted to you in so far as you can make
reasonable use of it, and be satisfied with that alone. [12] These are the
laws, these are the edicts, that have been transmitted to you from
above; it is these that you should set out to interpret; it is these that
you should submit to, not those of Masurius and Cassius.*

4.4 *To those who have set their hearts on living at peace*

[1] Remember that it is not only desire for office and wealth that
debases men and makes them subservient to others, but also desire for
quiet, and leisure, and travel, and learning. In a word, if you place
value on any external thing, whatever it may be, that will cause you to
become subject to others. [2] What difference does it make, then,
whether you set your desire on becoming a senator, or on not becoming one? What difference is there between saying on the one hand,
'Things are bad for me; I can't do a thing because I'm tied to my
books as though to a corpse,' and on the other hand, 'Things are bad
for me, I have no spare time for reading'? [3] For just as salutations
and public posts belong among external things that lie outside the
sphere of choice, so also does a book. [4] Or why is it that you want to
read? Tell me that. If you turn to reading for the sake of entertain-
ment or to acquire knowledge of some kind, you're frivolous and lazy.
But if you're directing your reading to the right end, what else could
that be than happiness? And if reading doesn't secure happiness for
you, what use does it serve?

[5] 'But it does secure that for me,' the man says, 'and that is why
I'm unhappy at being deprived of the opportunity.'

And what kind of happiness is that if virtually anything, I don't say
Caesar or a friend of Caesar, but a crow, a flautist, a fever, or a thousand
other things, can stand in the way of it? Now nothing characterizes
happiness better than the fact that it isn't subject to interruption or
obstruction. [6] I'm now called away to do something or another: I'll
go off at once, taking care to observe the standards that ought to be
maintained, so as to act with self-respect, with sure purpose, and

without desire or aversion with regard to external things; [7] and sec-
ondly, I pay attention to other people, to what they say, and to their
gestures, not doing so in any ill-natured manner or in the hope of
finding something to criticize or laugh at, but to enable me to look
back into myself to check whether I too am committing some fault.
'How can I stop doing so, then?' There was once a time when I too
used to commit these faults, but now no longer, thanks be to God.

[8] Come now, when you've acted in this way and attended to these
points, have you acted any worse than if you'd read a thousand lines
or written as many? For while you're acting, are you annoyed at not
being able to read? Aren't you satisfied to act in accordance with the
principles that you've learned through your reading? And so too
when you bathe, or when you take exercise? [9] Why don't you act
consistently, then, in all that you do, both when you're approaching
Caesar and when you're approaching some ordinary person? If you
keep yourself free from emotion, and remain imperturbable and
composed, [10] if you make yourself a spectator of events rather than
offering yourself as a spectacle, if you feel no envy for those who are
preferred above you, if you don't allow yourself to be flustered by
circumstances, what is there that you lack? [11] Books? How or for
what purpose?

'Doesn't reading help to prepare us for life?'

But life is full of many other things apart from books. It is as if an
athlete, on entering the stadium, should burst into tears because he
is no longer able to carry on training outside. [12] This is what you
were training for, this is what your jumping-weights were for, and
the sand too, and your young training partners. And are you now
looking for these when the time for action has arrived? [13] That is
just as if, in the sphere of assent, when we're presented with impressions, some of them convincing and others not, we should refuse to
distinguish between them and want to read a treatise *On Understanding**
instead.

[14] What, then, is the reason for this? It is because you have never
read and never written with this aim in view, to be able to deal in
accordance with nature with the impressions that present themselves
to us, but instead we stop at this, at learning what is said and being
able to explain it to someone else, and analysing syllogisms and examining hypothetical arguments. [15] So where our enthusiasm lies,
there also lies the obstacle. Do you want to have at any cost things

that are not within your power? Then be subject to hindrance, obstruction, and failure. [16] But if we read treatises *On Motivation* not merely to know what is said there about motivation, but so as to be able to direct our motives rightly; or a treatise *On Desire and Aversion* so that we may never fail in our desires or fall into what we want to avoid; or a treatise *On Appropriate Actions** so that we may keep in mind our social relationships and never act irrationally or in a way that conflicts with them [17] —if we approached our reading in that spirit, we wouldn't be vexed at being hindered with regard to our reading, but would be satisfied to accomplish the actions that are in accord with them, and we wouldn't be reckoning things up as we've been accustomed to do up until now, 'Today I've read this many lines, and I've written this many,' but would do so in this way instead, [18] 'Today I've formed my motives as the philosophers recommend, I haven't exercised any desire, I've confined my aversions solely to things that lie within the sphere of choice, I haven't allowed myself to be intimidated by So-and-so, or disconcerted by So-and-so, I've exercised my patience, my abstinence, my cooperativeness.' And thus we should be thanking God for what we ought to be thanking him for.

[19] But as it is, we don't realize that we ourselves, though in a different fashion, are coming to be just like everyone else. Someone else is afraid that he won't gain office, while you're afraid that you will. In no way should you be afraid, man! [20] But just as you laugh at someone who is afraid of not gaining office, so also laugh at yourself. For it makes no difference whether one thirsts for water because one has a fever, or one has a dread of water because one has rabies. [21] Or how could you still be able to say along with Socrates, 'If this is what God pleases, so be it!'* Do you suppose that if Socrates had wished for nothing other than to spend his time at the Lyceum or Academy,* and engage in conversation every day with the young men there, he would have been as happy to set out on the campaigns on which he so often served?* Wouldn't he have wept and groaned, saying, 'Poor unfortunate man that I am, I'm now in misery and misfortune when I might have been sunning myself in the Lyceum!' [22] Was this your task in life, to warm yourself in the sun? Wasn't it, rather, to be happy, and be free from hindrance and obstruction? And how would he still have been Socrates if he had lamented in that way? How would he still have been able to write hymns of praise* in prison?

[23] In a word, remember this, that if you attach value to anything at all that lies outside the sphere of choice, you've destroyed your choice. Not only is office outside that sphere, but also freedom from office; and not only want of leisure, but also leisure itself.

[24] 'Must I spend my life, then, in the midst of all this commotion?' What do you mean by commotion? Being among crowds of people? And what hardship is there in that? Imagine that you're at Olympia; think of it as a festival. There, too, one man shouts one thing and another shouts another, and one man does this and another does that, and one man knocks up against another, and there is a crowd of people at the baths. And yet who among us fails to take pleasure in the festival, and who isn't sorry to leave? [25] Don't be irritable, don't be oversensitive about what comes to pass. 'Vinegar is horrible because it's sour.' 'Honey is horrible because it upsets my digestion.' 'I don't like vegetables.' And likewise, 'I don't like having nothing to do: it's a desert.' 'I don't like a crowd: it's a commotion.' [26] Why, if things turn out in such a way that you find yourself living alone, or with few companions, call that peace and quiet, and make use of those circumstances as you ought; converse with yourself, work on your impressions, perfect your preconceptions. But if you get caught in a crowd, call it the games, call it a public gathering, call it a festival, [27] and join in the festival with everyone else. For what sight could be more pleasant to someone who loves his fellow human beings than a crowd of people? We look with pleasure at herds of horses and cattle, and are delighted to see a large fleet of ships; so is one to be distressed to see a crowd of people?

[28] 'But they deafen me with their shouting!'

Then it is your hearing that is impeded. What does that matter to you? Is your ability to deal with impressions hampered in the same way? And who can prevent you from exercising your desire and aversion in accordance with nature, and so too your motives to act or not to act? What commotion has power enough to do that?

[29] Just remember these general principles: 'What is mine, what isn't mine? What is granted to me? What does God want me to do now, and what doesn't he want?' [30] A short while ago, he wanted you to be at leisure, to talk with yourself, to write about these matters, and to read, listen, and prepare yourself. You've had time enough for that. Now he tells you, 'The time has come for you to proceed to the contest, show us what you've learned and how you've trained.

How long, then, are you going to carry out exercises on your own? It is now time for you to find out whether you belong among the athletes who are worthy of victory, or only those who travel around the world suffering one defeat after another.' [31] Why are you upset, then? There can be no contest without a commotion. There are bound to be many trainers, many people shouting out, many officials, and many spectators.

[32] 'But I wanted to live in peace and quiet.'

Well, lament, then, and groan, because you deserve nothing else. For what greater punishment can there be for one who is uneducated and disobeys the divine commander than to grieve and feel envy, and in a word, be miserable and unfortunate? Don't you want to deliver yourself from all of that?

[33] 'And how can I do so?'

Haven't you heard it repeatedly stated that you must completely eradicate desire,* and direct your aversion solely towards things that lie within the sphere of choice, and that you must give up everything, your body, possessions, reputation, and books or commotion, and office or freedom from office? For if you turn aside from this course, you've become a slave, you're subject to others, you're liable to hindrance and constraint, you're entirely in the power of others. [34] No, you should keep the saying of Cleanthes at hand, '*Guide me, O Zeus, and thou, O Destiny*'.* Is it your wish that I should go to Rome? To Rome I go. To Gyara? Then to Gyara. To Athens? Then to Athens. Into prison? Then into prison. [35] But if you once come to say, 'Oh when will one be able to get to Athens?', you're lost. For if this wish remains unfulfilled, it is bound to make you unhappy, or if it is fulfilled, you'll be puffed up with empty pride about things that oughtn't to be a source of pride; and on other hand, if you meet with obstacles, you'll suffer the misfortune of falling into what you want to avoid. [36] So be done with all of that.

'Athens is a fine city.'

But to be happy is finer still, and to be free from passion, and calm of mind, and be subject to no one else with regard to your own affairs.

[37] 'Rome is full of commotion and people who have to be greeted.'

But happiness compensates for all that is disagreeable. If the time comes for such things, then, why don't you suppress any aversion towards them? What need do you have to carry your burden like a donkey that is being rained with blows? [38] Or else, you should be clear that you're always bound to be the slave of the man who is able to secure your release, of the man who is able to hinder you in any regard, and that you'll have to serve him as an evil genius.*

[39] There is one path alone that leads to happiness—and keep this thought at hand morning, noon, and night—it is to renounce any claim to anything that lies outside the sphere of choice, to regard nothing as being your own, to surrender everything to the deity, to fortune, to consign the administration of everything to those whom Zeus himself has appointed to carry out that task, [40] and to devote yourself to one thing alone, that which is your own, that which is free from all hindrance, and when you read, to refer your reading to that end, and so too with your writing and your listening. [41] For that reason, I cannot call someone industrious merely because I hear that he reads and writes, and even if someone adds that he works away at it all night through, I couldn't yet call him industrious until I know what he is aiming at in doing so. For you wouldn't call a man industrious either because he stays awake for love of a young girl, and nor would I. [42] But if he acts in this way for the sake of his reputation, I call him ambitious, or if for money, avaricious, rather than industrious. [43] If, by contrast, he refers all his efforts to his own ruling centre, as he strives to bring it into accord with nature and to keep it so, in that case alone do I call him industrious. [44] For you should never praise or criticize a person for things that may be either good or bad, but for his judgements alone. It is these that are each person's special property; it is these that make his actions good or bad.

[45] Keeping these principles in mind, rejoice in what you have and be content with what the moment brings. [46] If you see that any of the things that you have learned about and enquired into are presenting themselves to you to be put into practice, then rejoice in them. If you have put aside malice and abuse, or indulge in them less, and so too over-hastiness, foul language, recklessness, or negligence, if you're not moved by the things that you were formerly moved by, or at least not to the same degree as before, you'll be able to view each and every day as a festival, today because you've conducted yourself well in this action, and tomorrow because you've acted well in another. [47] How much better reason does this provide for you to offer a sacrifice than because you've been appointed to be a consul or a governor! For these things come to you from yourself alone and from the gods. Remember

who it is that gives them, and to whom, and for what end. [48] If you're nourished by thoughts such as these, what need do you have to enquire any longer as to where you are to find happiness, and where you will please God? Aren't people just the same distance from God wherever they are? And wherever they are, don't they have just the same view of what is coming about?

4.5 *Against those who are quarrelsome and brutal*

[1] A virtuous and good person neither quarrels with anyone, nor, so far as he can, does he allow anyone else to quarrel. [2] In this matter, as in so much else, an example is set for us in the life of Socrates, who not only made a consistent practice of avoiding quarrels for his own part, but also tried to prevent others from quarrelling. [3] In Xenophon's *Symposium*, see how many quarrels he settled; and again, how patient he was in dealing with Thrasymachus, Polus, and Callicles,* and how patient he used to be with his wife, and with his son, too, when the latter tried to refute him with sophistical arguments.* [4] For he kept the thought firmly fixed in his mind that no one can exert control over another person's ruling centre; and he thus wanted nothing other than what was truly his own. [5] And what is that? It is not that we should try to make some other person act in accordance with his nature, because that is not within our power, but that while other people are attending to their own affairs as they think best, he himself should act nonetheless in accord with nature and continue to do so, attending to his own business alone in such a way that others too may be in accord with nature. [6] For that is the aim that a virtuous and good person should always set before him. Is it to become praetor? No, but if that is granted to him, to safeguard his ruling centre in those circumstances. To marry? No, but if it should be granted to him to marry, to keep himself in accord with nature in those circumstances. [7] But if he wishes that his son or wife should never commit a fault, he is wishing that things that are not his own should be his own; and becoming properly educated consists in this, in coming to know what is our own and what is not our own.

[8] What room is left for contention, then, if someone is in this state of mind? For is he surprised by anything that comes about? Does anything seem extraordinary to him? Doesn't he expect to receive worse and harsher treatment from the wicked than in fact comes to

him? Doesn't he count it a gain when anything that they do falls short
of the worst? 'That man abused you.' [9] I'm most grateful that he
didn't hit me. 'But he has gone on to hit you.' I'm most grateful that
he hasn't killed me. [10] For when did he ever learn, and from whom,
that man is a sociable creature who loves his neighbours, and that
injustice is of itself a cause of great harm to one who inflicts it?* Since
he has never learned that and never become convinced of it, why
shouldn't he follow the course that seems to him to be in his best
interest? [11] 'My neighbour has thrown stones at me.' Is it you who
has committed a fault, then? 'But things in my house have been
broken.' Are you some household utensil, then? [12] No, but choice.
So what means of defence have you been given to protect you against
such thing? Are you a wolf that you should bite back, and throw more
stones at them than they threw at you? But if you're seeking to act as
a human being, consider what resources you have; see what faculties
you brought into this world with you. Was it the savagery of a wild
beast? Was it the spirit of revenge? [13] When is a horse miserable,
then? When it is deprived of its natural faculties; not when it can't
sing like a cuckoo, but when it can't run. [14] And a dog? When it
can't fly? No, but when it can't follow the scent. So isn't it the case
likewise that a human being will be unhappy, not when he can't
strangle lions or embrace statues* (because he didn't come into the
world endowed with faculties for that), but when he has lost his kind-
heartedness, his trustworthiness?

[15] This is the kind of person whom people should '*gather
together to mourn because he has come into the world to meet with so
many evils*', and not, by Zeus, for '*the one who is born or the one who
has died*',* but the one whose lot it has been to lose while still alive
what is truly his own, not his inheritance, his wretched land and
house, his inn and his poor slaves—for none of these things truly
belong to a man, but all are foreign to him, and slavish, and subject
to others, given by their masters now to one person and now to
another—but rather the qualities that characterize him as a human
being, the imprints that he bore in his mind when he entered the
world, [16] resembling those that we look for on coins, so that if we
find them, we accept the coin, but reject it if we don't—'Whose
imprint does this coin carry? [17] That of Trajan? Accept it. That of
Nero?* Throw it away, it won't pass the test, it's rubbish.' So, too,
in the present case. What imprint do his judgements carry?

'Gentleness, sociability, patience, love of his neighbour.' Bring him to me, I'll accept him, I'll make him my fellow citizen, I'll accept him as a neighbour or a travelling companion. [18] See only that he doesn't carry the imprint of Nero. Is he quick to anger, is he prone to rage, is he discontented with his lot? [19] 'If the fancy takes him, he smashes the heads of those whom he meets.' Then why did you say that he is a man? Is it simply on the basis of its outward appearance that one judges the nature of a thing? Why, on that ground you could call a ball of wax an apple.* [20] No, it must also have the taste and smell of an apple; the external form doesn't suffice. So likewise, the presence of eyes and a nose doesn't suffice to show that someone is a human being, but he must also have such judgements as befit a human being. [21] Here is someone who doesn't listen to reason, and doesn't understand when he is refuted: he is a donkey. Here is one in whom all sense of shame is dead: he is a worthless creature, anything other than a human being. Here is someone who is looking for somebody to kick or bite: so he is neither a sheep nor a donkey, but some sort of wild beast.

[22] 'What, do you want me to make myself despised?'

By whom? By people of understanding? And how will such people be able to despise someone who is gentle and modest? By people who have no understanding? Why worry about them? Any more than a craftsman worries about people who have no knowledge of his craft.

[23] 'But they'll become all the more worked up against me.'

What do you mean by 'against me'? Can anyone injure your choice, or prevent you, when impressions present themselves to you, from dealing with them in accordance with nature?—'No one can.' [24] —Then why should you still be troubled, and why do you want to show yourself to be timid? Why don't you come forward instead to proclaim that you're especially amused by those who imagine that they're able to harm you? 'These slaves don't know who I am, or where my good and evil lie, and they have no access to those things that are truly my own.'

[25] It is in this way too that the inhabitants of a well-fortified city laugh at those who are besieging them: 'Why are those men going to all that trouble to no purpose? Our walls are secure; we have provisions that will last for a very long time, as will all the rest of our supplies.' [26] That is what renders a city secure and impregnable, and in the case of a human mind, it is nothing other than its judgements.*

For what manner of wall is so strong, or what manner of body so steely, or what property so safe against theft, or what reputation so unassailable? [27] All things everywhere are perishable and easily captured, and anyone who becomes attached to them in any way will necessarily be troubled in his mind, and worry about what the future will bring, and be subject to fear and sorrow, and is bound to be frustrated in his desires, and to fall into what he wants to avoid. [28] In view of this, aren't we willing to shore up the one and only means of safety that has been granted to us? And aren't we willing to renounce what is perishable and slavish, to devote our efforts instead to what is imperishable and free by nature? And don't we remember that no one can cause harm or bring benefit to any other person, but that it is a person's judgement alone about each thing that harms him, and upsets him, and this is what gives rise to dissension, and civil strife, and war? [29] What made Eteocles and Polynices* the enemies that they became was nothing other than the judgements that they held about the throne and about exile: that the latter is the greatest of evils, and the former the greatest of goods. [30] Now it lies in the nature of every being to pursue the good and avoid what is bad; and to regard anyone who deprives us of the former and involves us in the latter as an enemy, as a traitor, even if he is a brother, a son, or a father, because nothing is dearer to us than the good. [31] It thus follows that if these external things are good or bad, no father will be dear to his sons, and no brother dear to his brother, but the world will be filled on every side with enemies, traitors, and informers. [32] But if it is in applying choice as we ought, and in that alone, that the good lies, and in applying it wrongly, and in that alone, that evil lies, what place is left for dissension, what place is left for vilification? About what? About things that are nothing to us? Against whom? Against those who are ignorant, those who are wretched, those who have allowed themselves to be deceived about the most important issues.

[33] Socrates kept these principles in mind in his domestic life, putting up with his ill-tempered wife and unfeeling son. For in what way did she show her temper? In pouring as much water as she wanted over his head, and in treading his cake under her feet;* and what is that to me, if I regard these things as being of no concern to me? [34] To adopt such an attitude is my task, and no tyrant can hinder me in this, contrary to my own will, nor can any master, nor can the crowd hinder an individual, nor can the stronger hinder the weaker, because

this has been granted to us by God free from all hindrance. [35] These are the judgements that bring love into a household, and concord into a state, and peace among nations; and cause a person to be grateful to God, and confident at all times, in the conviction that the things that he is dealing with are not his own, and are of no value to him. [36] But for our part, we may be able to write about these matters, and give them our approval when we read about them, but we're very far from being convinced of them. [37] And so that proverb about the Spartans 'Lions at home, but foxes at Ephesus'* applies to us too: we're lions in the schoolroom but foxes outside.

4.6 *To those who are distressed at being pitied*

[1] 'It annoys me', someone says, 'to be pitied.'

Is this your doing, then, that you're pitied, or that of those who are doing the pitying? Well then, are you in a position to prevent this?

'It lies in my power, if I can show them that I don't deserve their pity.'

[2] But is this something that you have within your power, to deserve or not deserve pity?

'Yes, I think that it is in my power. But these people don't pity me for those things that, if anything, would be deserving of pity, that is to say, for my faults, but rather for poverty, lack of office, illnesses and deaths, and other things of that kind.'

[3] Are you ready, then, to convince the mass of people that none of these are in fact bad, but that one can be happy even when one is poor, and holds no office, and enjoys no honour; or are you ready to make a show to them of being a wealthy man and an official? [4] The second of these two approaches is that of a braggart, and a mediocre and worthless person. And consider what means you must adopt to uphold this pretence. You'll have to borrow some slaves, and own a few pieces of silverware, and show them off in public repeatedly, if possible, while trying to conceal the fact that they're always the same; and you'll need to have flashy clothing and all kinds of finery, and make a show of being honoured by the most eminent people, and try to dine with them, or at least make others believe that you're dining with them, and as regards your body, resort to mean tricks to appear better looking and of higher birth than you really are. [5] All this you

must set in train if you want to adopt the second course, to avoid being pitied.

As for the first course, it is both impracticable and long to attempt that very thing that Zeus has been unable to achieve, to convince everyone about what things are good and what are bad. [6] That power hasn't been granted to you, has it? The power that you've been granted is to convince yourself, and you have yet to do so. Then tell me, are you going to attempt to convince other people? [7] Why, who has lived with you as long as you've been living with yourself? And who could persuade you so convincingly as you could convince yourself? Who could be better disposed towards you and closer to you than you are to yourself? [8] How is it, then, that you haven't yet managed to persuade yourself to acquire this knowledge? Isn't it the case that everything is upside down at present? Is this what you've been anxious to learn: how to be delivered from grief, disturbance, and humiliation, and be free? [9] Haven't you heard, then, that there is only a single path that leads to that end: to give up things that lie outside the sphere of choice, and turn away from them, and acknowledge that they're not your own? [10] The opinion that someone else holds about you, then, what kind of a thing is that?—'Something that lies outside the sphere of choice.'—So isn't it nothing to you?—'Nothing at all.'—So while you continue to be disturbed and nettled by the opinions of others, do you suppose that you're properly convinced about what is good and bad?

[11] Won't you let other people be, then, and become your own teacher and your own pupil? 'Let others look to whether it is in their interest to be out of accord with nature and pass their lives in that condition, but as for me, no one is closer to me than I myself am. [12] How is it, then, that when I've listened to the arguments of the philosophers and have given my assent to them, my burden has in fact become none the lighter? Am I really so lacking in ability? And yet in everything else that I've wanted to engage in, I haven't been found to be so very incompetent, but I learned my letters quickly enough, and wrestling and geometry too, and how to analyse syllogisms. [13] Can it be, then, that reason has failed to convince me? In point of fact, there is nothing that I've so approved of from the beginning, or that I've liked better, and these are the matters that I now spend my time reading about, hearing about, and writing about. Up until now we haven't found a stronger argument than this.

[14] What is it that I lack, then? Can it be that the contrary opinions haven't been eradicated from my mind? Or can it be that the thoughts themselves haven't been properly exercised, that I haven't got into the habit of confronting them with the facts, but that instead, like old pieces of armour that have been stored away, they've grown rusty and no longer fit me? [15] Yet when it comes to wrestling, or writing, or reading, I'm not satisfied merely to learn, but I turn the arguments that are presented to me round and round in my mind, and I put together new ones, and equivocal arguments too. [16] Yet in the case of the essential principles, those that could serve as a starting point in enabling one to become delivered from grief, fear, passion, and hindrance, to become free, I neither train myself in them, nor do I devote such study to them as I ought. [17] And after that I worry about what other people will say about me, and whether I'll strike them as a man of note, a man who is happy.'

[18] Poor wretch, won't you see what you're saying about yourself? What kind of person do you view yourself as being? What kind of person in your thoughts, in your desires, in your aversions? And in your motives, preparations, and projects,* and in all other human activities? Instead of that, you're worrying about whether other people are pitying you?

[19] 'Yes, but I don't deserve to be pitied.'

So that is what is upsetting you? But if someone is upset, isn't he worthy of pity?

'Yes.'

How can it still be true, then, that you're being pitied without deserving to be? By these very feelings that pity awakens in you, you're making yourself worthy of pity. [20] What does Antisthenes say, then? Have you never heard it? 'It is a king's lot, Cyrus, to act well and be ill spoken of.'* [21] My head is perfectly well and everyone thinks that I have a headache. What does that matter to me? I don't have a fever and everyone is sympathizing with me as if I did. 'Poor man, you've had a fever all this while and it won't go away.' I assume a doleful expression and say, 'Yes, to be sure, it is quite some time that I've been unwell.'—'What will come of it, then?'—'As God wills.' And at the same time, I'm secretly laughing at those who are taking pity on me.

[22] So what is to prevent me from acting in the same way in the present case? I'm poor, but I have a correct judgement about poverty.

What does it matter to me, then, if others take pity on me because of my poverty? I hold no power, and others do. But I think as I ought to think about exercising power or not exercising it. [23] Let those who pity me look to that, but for my part, I'm neither hungry, nor thirsty, nor cold, and yet because in their own eyes they're hungry and thirsty, they imagine that the same must be true of me too. What shall I do for them, then? Am I to go around proclaiming, 'Don't be mistaken, men, all is well with me, I don't care a whit about poverty, or lack of office, or in a word, about anything other than having correct judgements; these I possess free from hindrance, and there is nothing else that I care about.' [24] Oh, what foolish talk is that? How can it still be true that I hold correct judgements if I'm not satisfied to be what I am, but get worked up about what other people will think of me?

[25] 'But other people will get more than I do, and be honoured above me.'

Why, what could be more reasonable than the fact that, if people devote their efforts to achieving a particular end, they'll have the advantage in those things to which they've devoted their efforts? They've devoted their efforts to obtaining public posts, you to your judgements. They to riches, you to the proper use of your impressions. [26] See whether they have the advantage over you in the things that you've devoted your efforts to and they've neglected; and whether their assent is more in accord with nature, whether they're more successful in achieving their desires, or in not falling into what they want to avoid, whether they're surer in achieving their goal in their designs, their purposes, their motives, whether they observe their duties as men, as sons, as parents, and then in all their other social relationships according to its name. [27] But if they hold public posts, aren't you willing to tell yourself the truth, that you do nothing for your part to achieve that, while they do everything, and that it would be altogether unreasonable for someone who takes pains over something to be less successful in achieving it than someone who doesn't.

[28] 'No, but because I take more care about forming correct judgements, it is more reasonable that I should exercise authority.'

Indeed, in that which you take trouble over, namely, judgements; but in those things that others have taken more trouble over than you, give way to them. It is just as if you were to claim, on the ground that you have correct judgements, you should be better at hitting the target in archery than archers are, or better at forging iron than blacksmiths are. [29] So stop being so earnest about your judgements, and turn your attention to the things that you wish to acquire; and then weep if you have no success in getting those, because then you deserve to weep. [30] But as it is, you claim to be occupied with other things, to be attending to other things, and as people rightly say, 'One form of business doesn't go together with another.'

[31] One man gets up at dawn and looks for someone from Caesar's household to salute, someone to whom he may address pleasing words, or to whom he may send a gift, and thinks how he may please the dancer, or how he may gratify someone by maligning somebody else. [32] When he prays, he prays for things like these; when he sacrifices, he sacrifices for things like these. The saying of Pythagoras '*Let not sleep descend on your weary eyes*' he applies for this purpose: [33] '*Where did I go wrong*' in dishing out flattery? '*What did I do?*'* Can it be that I acted as a free man, a man of noble character? And if he discovers any action of that kind, he rebukes and accuses himself, saying, 'Why did you have to say that? Wasn't it possible for you to lie? Even the philosophers say that there is nothing to prevent us from telling a lie.'*

[34] But if you've truly given attention to nothing else than how to make right use of your impressions, you should ask yourself as soon as you get up in the morning, 'What have I still to do to achieve freedom from passion? To achieve peace of mind? Who am I? Surely not a mere body? Or possessions, or reputation? None of these things. But what? I'm a rational living being.' [35] What is required, then, of such a being? Go over your actions in your mind. '*Where have I gone wrong*' with regard to achieving happiness? '*What did I do*' that was unfriendly, or unsociable, or inconsiderate? '*What have I not done that I ought to have done*' with regard to these matters?

[36] Since people differ so greatly, then, in their desires and actions, and in what they pray for, do you still want to have an equal share with others in those things to which you've devoted no effort but they've devoted every effort? [37] And after that, are you surprised that they take pity on you, and are you vexed by it? But they're not worried if you take pity on them. Why not? Because for their part, they're convinced that they're getting good things, while you on your side have no such conviction. [38] And so you're not contented

with what you have, but yearn for what they have, while they on their side are contented with what they have and don't yearn for what you have. For if you were truly convinced that, with respect to what is good, you're in possession of it while they've gone completely astray, you wouldn't even have given a thought to what they're saying about you.

4.7 *On freedom from fear*

[1] What makes a tyrant frightening?—'His guards', the man says, 'and their swords, and the chamberlains, and those who shut out people who try to enter.' [2] —Why is it, then, that when you bring a child in front of him when he is surrounded by his guards, the child isn't afraid? Is it because the child doesn't properly notice the guards? [3] Now, if someone is fully aware of them, and of the fact that they're carrying swords, and has come precisely because he wants to die, as the result of some misfortune, and is seeking an easy death at someone else's hand, he won't be frightened of the guards either, will he?—'No, because he wants the very thing that causes them to be frightening.' [4] —Well then, if someone who has no particular desire either to die or to live, but is happy to accept whatever is granted, comes into the presence of the tyrant, what is to prevent him from approaching him without fear?—'Nothing.' [5] —If someone feels the same, then, about his property, and his children, as that man feels about his body, and, in short, he has been brought into such a state by some madness or despair that he doesn't care whether he has them or not, but as children playing with bits of pottery* compete with one another in the game without caring about the bits of pottery, so he too has come to set no value on material things, but merely takes pleasure in the game and its moves, what tyrant could still inspire him with fear, or what guards, or what swords of theirs?

[6] Well then, if madness can cause people to adopt such an attitude towards these things, and habit too, as in the case of the Galileans,* can't reason and demonstration teach people that God has made all that is in the universe, and the universe itself as a whole, to be free from hindrance, and self-sufficient, and has made all the parts of it to serve the needs of the whole? [7] Now, all other animals have been excluded from being able to understand the divine governing order, but the rational animal possesses resources that enable him to reflect

on all these things, and know that he is a part of them, and what kind of part, and that it is well for the parts to yield to the whole. [8] And furthermore, because he is by nature noble-minded, great-hearted, and free, he sees that, of the things that pertain to him, he possesses some of them free from all hindrance and within his own power, while others are subject to hindrance and within the power of other people. Free from hindrance are those things that lie within the sphere of choice, while those that lie outside the sphere of choice are subject to hindrance. [9] And for that reason, if he regards his own good and advantage as lying in the former alone, the things that are free from hindrance and within his own power, he'll be free, contented, happy, invulnerable, magnanimous, reverent, and one who is grateful to God for everything, and never finds fault with anything that comes about, and never casts blame on anyone. [10] But if, on the other hand, he regards his good and advantage as lying in external things that lie outside the sphere of choice, he must inevitably be subject to constraint and hindrance, and be enslaved to those who have power over the things that he admires and fears; [11] and he must necessarily be impious because he thinks that God is causing him harm, and be unjust because he will always be trying to secure more than his proper share, and he is bound to be base and mean-spirited too.

[12] When someone has come to understand these things, what is to prevent him from living with a light heart and easy mind, calmly awaiting whatever may happen, and putting up with what has already happened. [13] Is it your wish that I should be poor? Bring it on, then, and you'll see what poverty is when it finds a good actor to play the part. Is it your wish that I should hold office? Bring it on. Is it your wish that I should be deprived of office? Bring it on. Is it your wish that I should suffer hardships? Bring those on too. [14] What, and exile? Wherever I go, all will be well with me, since that was also the case here, not because of the place but because of my judgements, and those that I'll carry away with me; for no one can take them away from me; they're the only things that are truly my own, and it is enough for me that I should possess them, wherever I am and whatever I'm doing.

[15] 'But the time has come for you to die.'

Why do you say 'to die'?* Don't make a tragedy of the matter, but tell it as it is: 'It is now time for the material of which you're composed to return to the elements from which it came.' And what is terrible in that? What element among all that make up the universe will be fated to perish? What new or extraordinary thing is going to come about? [16] Is it because of this that the tyrant awakens fear? Is it for this reason that the swords of the guards seem long and sharp? Let others be afraid of such things! For my part I've enquired into them, and no one holds any power over me. [17] I've been set free by God, I know his commands, no one has the power any longer to enslave me, I have the right emancipator, I have the right judges. [18] You hold mastery over my body? Why, what is that to me? Don't you have the power to send me into exile or throw me into chains? Again, I yield all of that to you, and my poor body in its entirety, at whatever time you wish. Test out your power on me, and you'll see how far it extends!

[19] Who can I still be afraid of? The chamberlains? Why, what could they do, shut the door on me? If they find me wanting to enter, let them shut the door on me!—'Why come to the door, then?'—Because I think it fitting for me to take part in the game as long as it lasts. [20] —'How does it come about, then, that you're not shut out?—Because if I'm not admitted, I have no wish to go in, but rather, I always want what actually comes about; for I judge whatever God wants as being better than what I want; I'll attach myself to him as a servant and follower, I'll share his impulses, I'll share his desires, and in a word, make his will my will. [21] Being shut out is something that can't happen to me, but only to those who try to force their way in. Why is it, then, that I don't try to force my way in? Because I know that nothing good is distributed inside to those who make their way in. No, when I hear anyone described as happy because he has been honoured by Caesar, I ask, 'What has he gained? Has he also gained the judgements that he ought to have if he is to govern a province? Has he gained the capacity to carry out the duties of a pro-curator?' Why, then, should I try to force my way in? They're scat-tering nuts and figs. [22] The children scramble to pick them up and fight among themselves; but men don't do so, because they regard this as being a trivial matter. And if one scatters bits of pottery, the children themselves don't scramble for them. [23] Provinces are being distributed. The children will look to that.* Or money. The children will look to that. A praetorship, a consulship. Let children scramble for those, let them have the doors closed in their face, let them suffer blows, let them kiss the hands of the giver, and of his slaves. [24] But

to me those are mere nuts and figs. But what if, by some chance, while he is throwing them out, a fig should land in my lap? I'll pick it up and eat it, since one can value even a fig to that degree. But as to stooping for it, or upsetting someone else or being upset by him, or flattering those who have access to the palace, no fig is worth as much as that, nor any of those other things that are not true goods, and which the philosophers have persuaded me not to regard as such.

[25] Show me the swords of the guards. See how big they are, and how sharp. So what do they do, these big sharp swords?—'They kill.' [26] —And a fever, what does that do?—'Nothing other than that.'—And a roof tile, what does that do?—'Nothing other than that.'—Do you wish, then, that I should stand in awe of these things, and bow down before them, and dance attendance on them as though I were a slave? Heaven forbid! [27] But once I've come to learn that all that comes into being must also perish so that the universe may not come to a standstill or be impeded, it no longer matters to me whether a fever brings that about, or a roof tile, or an armed guard, but if a choice has to be made, I know the guard would accomplish it in a swifter and less painful manner.

[28] Since I have no fear, then, of how a tyrant may treat me, and have no desire for any of the things that he can procure for me, why should I admire him any longer, why should I be in awe of him, why should I be afraid of his guards? Why should I rejoice if he speaks kindly to me and offers me a welcome, and why should I tell others how he spoke to me? [29] Is he Socrates, by any chance, or Diogenes, that his praise should provide proof of what I am? [30] Have I ever felt any urge to imitate his character? No, but to keep the game going, I come and serve him as long as he doesn't order me to do anything foolish or improper. If he should say to me, 'Go to Salamis and arrest Leon,'* I'll reply, 'Look for someone else, I won't take part in the game any longer.' [31] —'Take him off to prison,' the tyrant says of me; I follow, because that's part of the game.—'But you'll lose your head.'—And does he always keep his head, and those of you who obey him?—'But you'll be thrown out unburied.'*—Yes, if the corpse is myself, I'll be thrown out, but if I'm something other than the corpse, you should speak more intelligently, in accordance with the facts of the matter, and not try to scare me. [32] Things like that are frightening only to children and fools. But if anyone who has once entered a philosopher's school doesn't know what he

himself is, he deserves to fall prey to fear, and to continue to flatter those whom he previously flattered, if it is the case that he has yet to learn that he is neither flesh, nor bones, nor sinews, but that which makes use of these, that which governs impressions and understands them.

[33] 'Yes, but talk like this makes other people despise the laws.'

On the contrary, what principles are better suited to make those who follow them remain obedient to the laws? [34] Law isn't simply anything that lies within the power of a fool. And yet consider how, even with regard to men like that, these principles make us behave properly towards them, because they teach us not to claim in opposition to them anything in which they can gain the upper hand over us. [35] As regards our poor body, they teach us to give it up, and so, too, our property; and when it comes to our children, parents, brothers, to renounce them all, to let them go; our judgements mark the only exception, those judgements which, by the will of Zeus, are each person's own exclusive property. [36] What violation of the law is to be found in all of this, and what offence against reason? In the matters in which you're superior and stronger, there I give way to you; [37] where, by contrast, it is I who am superior, there you make way for me, because those matters are my concern, and not yours. Your concern is how to live in marble halls, and how your slaves and freedmen will serve you, and how you'll wear eye-catching clothes, and how you'll have many hunting dogs, and lyre-players, and tragic actors. [38] Do I lay claim to any of that? And have you, on the other hand, ever concerned yourself with judgements? Or with your own reason? Do you know what its constituent parts are, and how they're interconnected, and how it is ordered, and what capacities it has, and what their nature is? [39] Why do you take it amiss, then, if someone else who has studied these matters has the advantage over you in this area?

'But these are the most important matters of all.'

And what is to prevent you from turning your attention to them, and busying yourself with them? And who is better provided than you with books, and leisure, and people to help you? [40] Only turn your mind at last to these matters, and devote just a little time to your ruling centre. Consider what this is that you possess, and where it has come from, this faculty that makes use of everything else, and tests it out, and selects and rejects. [41] But as long as you devote your concern to external things, you'll own more of those than anyone else, but you'll have the ruling part of you just as you want it, filthy and neglected.

4.8 *To those who hastily adopt the outward appearance of philosophers*

[1] Never praise or criticize anyone for things that may be either good or bad, nor take that as evidence of aptitude or want of aptitude, and then you'll escape both hasty judgement and malice. [2] 'This man washes very quickly.' Is he doing anything wrong, then? Not at all. Well, what is he doing. Washing quickly. [3] 'So everything is done well, then?' By no means, but what is done as a result of correct judgements is well done, and what is done as a result of bad judgements is badly done. But until you know what judgement a person is acting upon in each of his actions, you should neither praise nor criticize his action. [4] Now one cannot easily determine the nature of a judgement from outward appearances. 'That man is a carpenter.' Why? 'Because he is using an adze.' What does that prove? 'That man is a musician because he is singing.' And what does that prove? 'That man is a philosopher.' Why? 'Because he is wearing a rough cloak and has long hair.' [5] And what is it that tramps wear? For that reason, if someone sees one of them behaving improperly, he immediately exclaims, 'Look at how the philosopher is behaving!' But he should rather have said, on the evidence of that misbehaviour, that the man wasn't a philosopher at all. [6] For if it formed part of the very nature and profession of a philosopher that he wore a rough cloak and had long hair, people would be justified in talking like that; but if those require rather that he should keep himself free from error, then why not refuse him that title as soon as he fails to fulfil that requirement? [7] For that is what we do when it comes to the other arts. When one sees someone making clumsy use of an axe, one doesn't say, 'What is the use of the carpenter's art? Look at how badly carpenters work,' but one says instead, 'That man is surely no carpenter, because he is so bad at handling an axe.' [8] Likewise, if one hears someone singing badly, one doesn't say, 'Look how musicians sing,' but rather, 'That man is no musician.' [9] It is only with regard to philosophy that people behave like this; on seeing someone behave in a way that conflicts with the requirements of the profession, they don't refuse him

the title of philosopher, but take it for granted that he is one, and conclude from the fact of his misbehaviour that philosophy serves no useful purpose.

[10] What is the reason for that, then? The reason is that we respect the conceptions that we form of a carpenter, and a musician, and likewise practitioners of the other arts, but not that of a philosopher; and because that conception is confused and ill-defined, we judge by external appearances alone. [11] And what other art can one acquire by adopting some particular costume and hairstyle, and which has no principles, subject matter, and end? [12] So what is the subject matter of a philosopher? It isn't a rough cloak, is it? No, but reason. What is his end? It isn't to wear a rough cloak, is it? No, but to reason correctly. What are his principles? Do they really have anything to do with how one can grow a long beard or have luxuriant hair? No, but rather as Zeno says, to know the elements of reason, and the nature of each of them, and how they're adapted to one another, and what consequences flow from all of this.* [13] Why aren't you willing, then, to begin by examining whether a man is truly fulfilling his profession as a philosopher if he behaves improperly, and only then cast aspersions against his way of life? But as things are, because he seems to you to be behaving badly while you're acting in a decent manner, you exclaim, 'Look at the philosopher!'—as though it were proper to call a man who is acting in that way a philosopher!—or again, 'So is that what a philosopher is?' Now you don't cry, 'Look at the carpenter!', when you know that one of them is an adulterer or you see him eating like a pig; nor do you exclaim in like circumstances, 'Look at the musician!' [14] And so you realize up to a certain point what the profession of a philosopher is, but you slip up and get confused through lack of attention.

[15] But even those who are called philosophers pursue their calling through means that are sometimes good and sometimes bad. No sooner have they put on a rough cloak and let their beard grow than they proclaim, 'I'm a philosopher!' [16] And yet no one says, 'I'm a musician,' simply because he has bought a plectrum and lyre, nor 'I'm a blacksmith,' because he has put on a felt cap and an apron. No, the costume is adapted to the art, and they take their name from their art and not from their gear. [17] For that reason Euphrates* said, 'For a long while I tried to conceal the fact that I was a philosopher, and this served me well. For in the first place, I knew that whatever I did

well, I did for my own sake and not for the sake of those who were looking on. It was for myself that I ate in a proper manner, that I maintained composure in my expression and way of moving; all of that was
for myself and God. [18] And furthermore, just as the contest was mine
alone, it was I alone who incurred the risks; if I did anything that was
shameful or improper, the cause of philosophy underwent no risk, and
I caused no harm to people at large by committing faults as a philosopher. [19] For that reason, those who were unaware of my intention
used to be surprised that, although all whom I frequented and lived
with were philosophers, I didn't become a philosopher myself.
[20] And what harm was there in making it recognized that I was a philosopher through what I did, rather than through the external signs?'

See how I eat, how I drink, how I sleep, how I endure things, how
I abstain from them, how I cooperate with others, how I exercise my
desires and aversions, how I maintain my social relationships, whether
natural or acquired, without becoming confused or obstructed; and
judge me by all of this, if you can. [21] But if you're so deaf and blind
as not to be able to regard even Hephaestus himself as a good smith
unless you see him with a felt cap* on his head, what harm is there in
not being recognized by a judge as foolish as that?

[22] It was thus that Socrates passed unrecognized by the great
majority of people, and they used to come to him and ask him to
introduce them* to philosophers. [23] Did he get annoyed by this, as
we would, and say, 'What, don't I look like a philosopher to you?' No,
he would take them off and introduce them, being satisfied merely to
be a philosopher in actual fact, and rejoicing to find that he wasn't
upset at not being taken for one. For he kept in mind what his true
business was. [24] And what is the business of a wise and virtuous
person? Is it to have many pupils? Not at all. Let those who take that
as their aim look to that. Is it to be able to expound difficult theories
with precision? Let others look to that too. [25] In what area, then, was
he someone of note, and wanted to be so? In the area where harm can
be suffered and help provided. 'If anyone can harm me,' he says, 'I'm
not achieving anything; if I'm waiting for someone else to help me, I
myself am nothing. If I want something and it is not accomplished,
then I'm miserable.' [26] It was in this great arena that he challenged
people to engage with him, and it seems that he never yielded to
anyone in—what do you suppose?—in proclaiming and asserting,
'I'm this sort of man'? Heaven forbid, but in actually being that kind

of man. [27] For again, it is the part of a fool and a braggart to say, 'I'm free from passion and imperturbable, and don't let it escape your notice, man, that while you're agitated and confused over things of no worth, I alone am immune to all disturbance.' [28] So it isn't enough for you to feel no pain, unless you proclaim in addition, 'Come along, then, all of you who are suffering from gout, fever, and headache, and who are lame and blind, and see how well I am and free from every disorder!' [29] What a display of vanity and vulgarity, unless you're able to show at once, like Asclepius,* how they too can be delivered from their ills, and are adducing your own good health as proof of that.

[30] Such is the course followed by the Cynic who is adjudged worthy to receive the sceptre and the crown* from Zeus, and says, 'So that you may come to see, men, that you're seeking for happiness and calm of mind, not where they're to be found, but where they're not to be found, [31] behold, I've been sent to you by God as an example; I have neither possessions, nor a house, nor a wife, nor children, nor even a bed, or a tunic, or a single piece of furniture, and yet see how healthy I am. Test me out, and you'll see that I have an undisturbed mind; hear what remedies and treatments have worked this cure on me.' [32] Now, that is true benevolence and noble-mindedness! But see whose work it is: it is the work of Zeus, or of one whom Zeus judges worthy to perform this service, such that he may never manifest anything to the crowd that would undermine the witness that he offers in favour of virtue and against external things.

> *Never did pallor descend on his fair features,*
> *Never did he wipe a tear from his cheeks.**

[33] Not only that, but he must neither yearn nor seek for anything, whether person, or place, or way of life, in the way that children do for the harvest time or the holidays, and he must surround and adorn himself on every side with self-respect, as others are protected by walls, and doors, and door-keepers.

[34] But as it is, no sooner do people feel drawn towards philosophy, as dyspeptics are towards food that they'll soon come to loathe, than they at once lay claim to the sceptre and the kingdom. Such a man lets his hair grow long, puts on a rough cloak, bares his shoulder, and quarrels with everyone he meets; and if he sees anyone with a thick warm cloak, he at once picks a quarrel with him. [35] First of all, man, you must undertake hard winter training;* examine your

impulses, and see whether they aren't those of a dyspeptic, of a woman seized with cravings during her pregnancy. Take care at first that you're not recognized for what you are; [36] practise philosophy for yourself alone for a short period. For this is the way in which fruit is produced; the seed must be buried for a time, and lie hidden, and grow little by little to come to maturity; but if it produces the ear before the stalk is properly jointed, it will never ripen, like those produced in gardens of Adonis.* [37] Now you too are a plant of this kind: you've bloomed before your time, and the winter will wither you. [38] See what the farmers say about seeds when the summer heat arrives before the proper season. They're worried that the seeds will shoot up too luxuriantly, and that a single frost will be enough to take them and expose their weakness. You should watch out too, man; [39] you've developed with impetuous haste, you've sprung forward to seize a scrap of glory before the proper season. You fancy that you're somebody, while being a fool among fools. You'll be taken by the frost, or rather, you already have been taken by the frost down at the root,* while up above you're still carrying a few flowers, and imagine for that reason that you're still alive and flourishing. [40] Allow us for our part at least to ripen as nature requires. Why do you expose us to the elements, why do you force us? We're not ready as yet to face up to the open air. Allow the root to grow, allow it next to bring forth its first joint, and then the second, and then the third; and in this way, the fruit will naturally force its way out, whether I wish it or not. [41] For who that has conceived and become pregnant with such great thoughts fails to become aware of his own resources, and to hurry on to act in accordance with them? [42] Why, a bull* doesn't fail to recognize the nature of his resources when a wild beast comes along, and he doesn't wait for someone to spur him on; nor does a dog that catches sight of a wild animal. [43] And if I for my part possess the resources of a good man, shall I wait for you to come and equip me for my own proper work? But as yet, I don't have these resources; take my word for it. Why, then, would you have me wither before my time, as you yourself have withered?

4.9 *To one who had become shameless*

[1] Whenever you see another person exercising authority in a public post, set against that the fact that you can do without a public post;

when you see another person living in wealth, look to what you have instead of that. [2] For if you have nothing in place of it, you're wretched indeed; but if you're capable of not having need of wealth, know that you have more than he does, and something of much greater value. [3] Another man has a beautiful wife; you have the power not to wish for a beautiful wife. Do you think these are small matters? And yet how much would those very men who are rich and powerful, and have beautiful wives, give to be able to despise riches and power, and those women whom they love and win? [4] Don't you know what kind of thirst one feels when one has a fever? It bears no resemblance to that of a healthy person. A healthy person takes a drink and his thirst is quenched, but the other, after some short relief, feels sick, turns the water into bile, vomits, suffers from colic, and feels much thirstier than before. [5] It is much the same to have wealth and yet feel a strong desire for that very thing, or have power and yet desire it, or pass one's nights with a beautiful woman and yet lust for her. To which may be added jealousy, and the fear of losing what one has, and shameful words, shameful thoughts, and improper deeds.

[6] 'And what do I lose?', someone asks.

Man, you used to be modest and now you're no longer so. Have you lost nothing? Instead of Chrysippus and Zeno, you now read Aristides and Evenus.* Instead of Socrates and Diogenes, you admire the man who is able to corrupt and seduce the largest number of women. [7] You want to be good-looking and make yourself so, although you're not, and want to display yourself in flashy clothing to attract women's attention, and if you come across some wretched perfume somewhere, you count yourself blessed. [8] But formerly you didn't even think about any of these things, but only about where you could find decent talk, a man of worth, a noble thought. As a consequence, you used to sleep like a man, bear yourself like a man, wear manly clothing, and speak in a manner appropriate to a good man. And then you say to me, 'I've lost nothing'? [9] What, is a bit of cash the only thing that a man can lose? Can't self-respect be lost; can't decency be lost? [10] For your part, perhaps, you no longer think that the loss of such things brings any penalty; but there was a time when you thought this to be the only loss and harm that really matters, and you were most anxious that no one should force you to abandon these principles and practices.

[11] Look, you have indeed been driven away from them, but by no

one other than yourself. Fight against yourself; restore yourself to decency, to self-respect, to freedom. [12] If someone had once told you this about me, that someone was forcing me to commit adultery, to wear clothes like yours, or perfume myself, wouldn't you have gone off and killed with your own hand the man who was subjecting me to such mistreatment? [13] And yet now, you don't want to come to your own assistance? And how much easier it is to offer assistance of that kind! There is no need for you to kill someone, or chain him up, or assault him, nor do you have to go to the marketplace; you have only to talk to yourself, the man most likely to be persuaded, and whom no one could more easily persuade than you can. [14] First of all, condemn your own actions, and then, after having condemned them, don't give up on yourself, and don't be like those mean-spirited people who, when they've given in on one occasion, surrender themselves completely, to be swept off, as it were, by the flood. [15] You should learn instead from what the wrestling masters do. The boy has taken a fall: 'Get up,' he says, 'and resume the fight until you grow strong.' [16] You too should think in some such way as that: you should know that there is nothing more tractable than the human mind. You only have to exert your will, and the thing comes about, and all is put right; whereas on the other hand, you only have to doze off, and all is lost. For ruin and deliverance alike come from within.

[17] 'And after all that, what good will I gain?'

And what greater good could you seek than this? Where once you were shameless, you'll have self-respect; where once you were faithless, you'll become faithful; where once you were dissolute, you'll have self-control. [18] If you're looking for anything other than things such as that, continue to act as you're now acting; for not even a god could still be able to help you.

4.10 *What should we despise and what should we especially value?*

[1] It is with regard to external things that all people fall into difficulty, fall into bewilderment. 'What shall I do? How will it be? How will it turn out? I only hope this, or that, doesn't happen to me.' [2] All of these are expressions of people who are preoccupied with things that lie outside the sphere of choice. For who says, 'How can I avoid giving my assent to what is false? Or how can I avoid refusing to accept what is true?' [3] If anyone is so gifted by nature as to be troubled by such

anxieties, I'll remind him of this: 'Why so anxious? This is within your power. Rest secure. Don't hasten to give your assent before applying the rule of conformity with nature.' [4] Again, if someone is worried about his desires, feeling that they may fail to achieve their end and miss their mark, or about his aversions, feeling that he may fall into what he wants to avoid, [5] I'll begin by giving him a kiss to congratulate him for having put aside the things that other people get exercised about, and their fears, to concentrate on his own business in the area where his true self lies. [6] And then I'll say to him, 'If you want your desires always to hit their mark, and want never to fall into what you want to avoid, never desire anything that is not your own, and never seek to avoid anything that is not within your power. Otherwise you're bound to fail in your desires, and bound to fall into what you want to avoid.' [7] What is difficult in that? What room is left for the questions 'How will it be?' and 'How will it turn out?' and 'I only hope that this or that doesn't happen to me.'

[8] Now doesn't the future lie outside the sphere of choice? —'Yes.'—And doesn't the nature of the good and the bad lie within the sphere of choice?—'Yes indeed.'—So whatever may happen, isn't it possible for you to make use of it in accordance with nature? Can anyone prevent you from doing so?—'No one can.' [9] —Then say no longer to me, 'How will it come about?', because whatever comes about, you'll be able to put it to good use, and the outcome will be fortunate for you. [10] What would Heracles* have been if he had said, 'How can I prevent a huge lion from coming my way, or a huge boar, or a savage man?' If a huge boar comes along, the contest that you engage in will be all the greater; if wicked men come along, you'll rid the world of wicked men.

[11] 'But what if I should die in doing so?'

You'll die as a good person, accomplishing a noble deed. Since you're bound to die in any case, you'll necessarily be caught doing something or other, whether working your farm, or digging, or suffering from indigestion or diarrhoea. [12] So what would you wish to be doing when death overtakes you? For my part I'd like to be carrying out some deed worthy of a human being, something beneficent, something that serves the common good, something noble. [13] But if I can't be caught doing anything as fine as that, I should like at least to be doing something that I can't be hindered from doing, something that is granted to me to accomplish, namely, putting myself right, striving to perfect the faculty that deals with impressions, and labouring to achieve peace of mind, while yet fulfilling my social duties, and if I should be so fortunate, pressing on the third area of study,* the one that is concerned with the attainment of security in one's judgements.

[14] If death overtakes me when I'm engaged in activities such as those, it is enough for me if I can raise up my hands towards God* and say, 'The faculties that I've received from you to enable me to understand your governing order and to follow it, I have in no way neglected; for my part, I haven't dishonoured you. [15] See how I've made use of my senses; see how I've made use of my preconceptions. Have I ever reproached you, have I ever shown discontent with anything that came about, or wished it otherwise? Have I ever violated any of my social relationships? [16] I'm grateful to you for having brought me into the world; I'm grateful, too, for the gifts that I've received from you; the length of time for which I've enjoyed the use of them is enough for me. Take them back again and assign me to whatever place you wish; they are yours one and all, and it is you who granted them to me.' [17] Isn't it enough to make one's departure from the world in such a state of mind? And what life could be better or more befitting than that of someone who thinks like this, and what end could be happier?

[18] But for this to be accomplished, one must accept difficulties of no small kind, and make sacrifices of no small kind. You cannot wish for a consulship and at the same time follow this path; you cannot set your heart on acquiring quantities of land and follow this path; you cannot worry about your poor slaves and yourself too. [19] No, but if you wish for anything that is not your own, what is really your own will be lost. This is the nature of the matter, that nothing can be gained without cost. [20] And what is surprising in that? If you want to be consul, you must stay up at night, rush this way and that, kiss men's hands, rot away at other men's doors, say and do much that isn't suitable for a free man, send presents to many people, and gifts of hospitality to some people every day. And what is the result of all of this? [21] Twelve bundles of rods, to sit three or four times on the tribunal, to give games in the Circus, and distribute lunches in little baskets.* If there is anything more in it than that, let someone show me! [22] Well then, to achieve freedom from passion, and freedom from disturbance, and to sleep soundly when you sleep, and to be fully awake when you're awake, to be afraid of nothing, and anxious about nothing, are you unwilling to make any sacrifice or any effort?

[23] But if you come to lose anything while you're engaged in this enterprise, or have to incur any expense to no purpose, or if someone else should get what you ought to have got, will you immediately become upset at what has happened? [24] Won't you balance what you have given against what you're receiving, and consider how much you've gained in return for how much? Do you really expect to get things of such value for nothing? How is that possible? 'One form of business and another.'* [25] You can't devote your attention both to acquiring external things and, at the same time, to your own ruling centre. [26] If you want the latter, you'll have to give up the former, or else you'll get neither the one nor the other, because you'll be pulled in two directions. So if you want the one, you'll have to give up the other. My oil will be spilled, my poor furniture lost, but I'll have peace of mind. While I'm away a fire will break out, and my books will be destroyed, but I'll deal with my impressions in accordance with nature.

'But I'll have nothing to eat.' [27] If I'm in such a bad plight, death is my harbour. And that is the harbour where everyone ends up; that is our refuge. As a consequence, nothing that happens to us in life is truly difficult. You can leave the house whenever you want and no longer be troubled by the smoke. [28] Why are you so anxious, then; why do you stay awake at night? Why don't you reckon up forthwith where your good and evil lie, and say, 'The one and the other lie within my power; no one can deprive me of the former, and no one can embroil me in the latter against my will. [29] So why don't I sit down and snore? All that is my own is safe. As for what is not my own, that will be the concern of whoever gets hold of it, as it is granted to him by the one who has mastery over it. [30] Who am I to wish that it should be this way or that? For that choice hasn't been granted to me, has it? I'm satisfied with those things that are under my own authority. I must make the best use of them that I can, and as for other things, let them be as their master pleases.'

[31] Does anyone who keeps these principles before his eyes lie awake at night, and '*toss from side to side*'? What does he wish for, what does he yearn for? For Patroclus, or Antilochus, or Protesilaus?* For when did he imagine that any of his friends would be immortal? And when wasn't he able to see quite clearly that tomorrow or the day after he or his friend would be bound to die?*

[32] 'Yes,' the man says, 'but I thought that he would survive me and bring up my son.'

Because you were a fool and you were reckoning on things that are uncertain. Why not blame yourself, then, rather than sit and cry like a little girl.

[33] 'Yes, but he used to set out my food for me.'

Because he was alive, you fool, but now he isn't. But Automedon* will see to your needs, and if he too should come to die, you'll find someone else. [34] If the pot in which your meal was cooked should happen to get broken, would you have to die of hunger because you no longer had your usual pot? Wouldn't you send someone out to buy a new one? 'No,' he says, [35] '*because no greater ill could could ever befall me.*'* Is that what you call an evil, then? And instead of getting rid of it, will you blame your master for not having warned you, so that from that time forth you might never stop grieving? [36] What do you think? Didn't Homer write these verses for the very purpose of showing you that when the noblest, the most perfect, the wealthiest, and the most handsome men don't hold correct judgements, there is nothing to prevent them from being miserable and utterly wretched?

4.11 *On cleanliness*

[1] There are some people who question whether social feeling forms part of human nature, and yet even these people wouldn't dispute, I think, that love of cleanliness undoubtedly forms part of it, and that it is by this, if anything, that man is distinguished from the other animals. [2] So when we see some other animal cleaning itself, we're accustomed to exclaim in surprise, 'Why, it's just like a human being!' And again, if someone finds fault with an animal for being dirty, we're inclined to say at once, by way of excuse, 'But after all, it isn't human.' [3] We thus regard cleanliness as a distinctive human quality, which we first received from the gods. Since the gods are by nature pure and undefiled, the closer human beings draw to them through reason, the more they feel attracted to purity and cleanliness. [4] But since it is impossible for human nature to be altogether pure, being compounded of such material as it is, the reason that it has received as part of its share strives to render it as clean as possible.

[5] The first and highest purity, then, and impurity likewise, is that which is manifested in the mind. But you wouldn't find the impurity

of the mind to be the same as that of the body, and when it comes to the mind, what other uncleanness could you find in it than that which soils it with regard to the execution of its own functions? [6] Now the functions of the mind are motivation to act or not to act, desire or aversion, preparation, design, and assent.* [7] What is it, then, that renders the mind dirty and impure with regard to the performance of these actions? Nothing other than its own bad judgements. [8] So the impurity of the mind consists accordingly of bad judgements, and its purification consists in the creation within it of the judgements that it ought to have. A pure mind is thus one that makes right judgements, for that kind of mind alone can escape confusion and pollution in its acts.

[9] We should endeavour as far as possible to achieve something similar with regard to the body too. It is impossible that there should not be some flow of mucus from a human being, since he is constituted in the way that he is. For that reason, nature has created hands, and has made our nostrils themselves like tubes to carry away the fluids. So if anyone sniffs them up again, I say that he isn't acting as is appropriate for a human being. [10] It was impossible that our feet should not get muddy, or dirty at all, when we pass through filth of that kind; nature has thus provided us with water and with hands. [11] It was impossible that some dirt should not get left behind on our teeth when we've eaten; and so nature says to us, 'Clean your teeth.' Why? So that you may be a human being, and not a wild beast or a pig. [12] It was impossible that through our sweat and the rubbing of our clothes, some uncleanness should not be left behind on our body and need to be cleaned off; for this reason, we have water, oil, hands, a towel, a scraper, and everything else that is used for cleaning the body. [13] Not in your case? But a smith will remove the rust from his iron, and has tools made for that purpose, and you yourself will wash your plate before you eat, unless you're irredeemably dirty and unclean; and yet when it comes to your poor body, you don't want to wash it and make it clean?

'Why should I?', the man says.

[14] I'll tell you again: in the first place, to act as is appropriate for a human being, and secondly, so as not to disgust those whom you meet. [15] You're doing something of that kind even here, without realizing it. You think that you have the right to give out a bad smell. Very well, you may have it. But do you think that those who sit by

you, or recline by you at table, should have it too, and those who kiss you? [16] Oh, go off into the desert somewhere, as you deserve, and live there alone, taking pleasure in your own odours. But living in a city as you do, what sort of a person do you think you're showing yourself to be, to behave in such a thoughtless and inconsiderate manner? [17] If nature had entrusted a horse to your care, would you have neglected it and failed to look after it? Well then, think of your own body as a horse that has been entrusted to you; wash it, wipe it, make it such that no one will turn away from you, no one will seek to avoid you. [18] And who doesn't want to avoid a man who is dirty, who smells, and whose skin looks even worse in colour than someone who has been spattered with dung? In the latter case, the smell rises merely from the outside and is accidental, but in the other, it arises from neglect, and thus comes from within, as though from some form of putrefaction.

[19] 'But Socrates rarely took a bath.'*

And yet his body looked radiant. Why, it was so attractive and pleasing that the most handsome and high-born men were greatly taken with him, and preferred to sit beside him rather than by those who had the finest features.* He might never have bathed or washed, if he had so pleased, but the rare baths that he did take had their effect.

[20] 'But Aristophanes says, "*I speak of pallid men who go barefoot.*"'

Yes, and he also says that Socrates 'trod the air' and stole people's clothes at the wrestling school.* [21] And yet all who have written about Socrates say precisely the opposite, attesting that he was pleasant not only to listen to, but also to look at. The same is written about Diogenes, too. [22] For even by our outward appearance, we shouldn't do anything to frighten people away from philosophy, but should show ourselves to be appealing and untroubled with regard to our body, too, as in everything else. [23] 'See, people, that I have nothing and have need of nothing. See how, although I have no house, and no city, and am an exile, if it so happen, and have no hearth, I live a happier and more untroubled life than all the high-born and wealthy; and you can see that even my poor body comes to no harm as a result of my hard way of life.' [24] But if someone were to say that to me when he had the appearance and expression of a condemned man, what god could ever persuade me to have anything to do with philosophy, if it is indeed that kind of person that it produces? Perish the thought! I wouldn't want to, even if I should become a wise man as a consequence.

[25] I'd prefer for my part, by the gods, that a young man who is just beginning to feel drawn towards philosophy should come to me with well-dressed hair, rather than having it dishevelled and dirty. For one could then detect some notion of beauty in him, and a desire for elegance;* and where he supposes it to lie, there he cultivates it. [26] And then all that one needs to do is to show him where it does lie, saying, 'Young man, you're seeking the beautiful, and rightly so. Know, then, that it grows up in that part of you where you have your reason. It is there that you should seek it, where you have your motives to act and not to act, where you have your desires and aversions. [27] For that is what you have in you that is of an exceptional nature, while your poor body is by nature nothing more than clay. Why trouble yourself about it to no purpose? If you learn nothing else, time will at least teach you that it is nothing.' [28] But if this young man should come to me befouled and dirty, with moustaches down to his knees, what can I say to him, what point of resemblance can I start from to draw him on? For what has he ever concerned himself with that has anything to do with beauty, [29] so that I might be able to change his point of view by saying, 'Beauty doesn't lie there, but here'? Would you have me say to him, 'Beauty doesn't lie in being befouled, but in reason'? For does he in fact feel any desire for reason? Has he any notion of it? Go and persuade a pig that it oughtn't to roll around in the mud. [30] That was why the discourses of Xenocrates could grip the mind even of a Polemo, because he was a young man who had a love for beauty; he had come to Xenocrates with the first glimmerings of an aspiration toward the beautiful, but he was looking for it in the wrong place.*

[31] Besides, nature hasn't made dirty even the animals that live with human beings. Does a horse roll around in the mud, or even a well-bred dog? No, but pigs do, and filthy geese, and worms, and spiders, the creatures that are banished the furthest from human company. [32] So don't you, who are a man, want even to be like one of those animals that live in the company of man, preferring to be a worm or spider instead? Will you never take a bath, in whatever way you like; won't you wash yourself in cold water if you don't care to use hot water? Won't you be clean when you come here, so that those who associate with you may enjoy your company? What, would you accompany us even into the temples in such a state, where it is forbidden to spit or blow your nose, you who are nothing but spittle and rheum.

[33] What then, is anyone asking you to beautify yourself? Heaven forbid, except in that which constitutes our true nature, in our reason and in its judgements and activities; but as regards our body, only so far as to keep it clean, only so far as not to cause offence to other people. [34] But if you hear that one shouldn't wear purple robes, you have to go off and smear your cloak with dung or rip it apart.

'But how can one have a fine cloak?'

Man, you have water: wash it. [35] Look, here is a lovable young man, here is an old man worthy to love and be loved in return, to whom a man will entrust the education of his son, to whom daughters and young men will come perhaps, so that he may deliver his lessons from a dung-hill! [36] Every eccentricity springs from something in human nature, but this comes close to being not human at all.

4.12 *On attention*

[1] When you relax your attention for a short while, don't imagine that you'll be able to recover it whenever you please, but bear this in mind, that because of the error that you've committed today, your affairs will necessarily proceed far worse in every respect. [2] For to begin with, and most seriously of all, a habit of inattention will grow up in you, and then a habit of deferring any effort to pay attention. So you should be aware that you'll be constantly putting off to an even later time a happy and appropriate way of life, a life that is in accord with nature and will remain so. [3] Now, if it brings any advantage to put things off, it will bring even greater advantage to give them up entirely; but if it brings no advantage, why don't you maintain your attention consistently? 'Today I'd like to play.' [4] Well, what is to prevent you from doing so attentively? For is there any area of life to which our attention should not be extended? Will you do anything worse, then, by paying attention, or better by not attending? And is there anything whatever in life [5] that is done better by those who remain inattentive? Does an inattentive carpenter carry out his work with greater precision? Does an inattentive helmsman steer his vessel more safely? And is any function of lesser importance accomplished better through inattention? [6] Don't you realize that when you've let your mind roam free, it is no longer in your power to call it back, either to decorum, or to self-respect, or to good order? But instead you do everything that comes into your head; you follow your impulses.

[7] 'To what things should I pay attention, then?'

In the first place to those general principles that you should always have at hand, so as not to go to sleep, or get up, or drink or eat, or converse with others, without them, namely, that no one is master over another person's choice, and that it is in choice alone that our good and evil lie. [8] No one has the power, then, either to procure any good for me or to involve me in any evil, but I alone have authority over myself in these matters. [9] So accordingly, when I'm secure with regard to those, what reason do I have to be troubled by external things? What tyrant can strike fear into me, what kind of disease, what poverty, what obstacle?—'But I haven't pleased So-and-so.' [10] —Is he an action of mine, then; is he a judgement of mine?—'No.'—Then why should I trouble myself any longer? —'But he passes for being a man of some importance.'—Let him look to that, and those who think him so, [11] but I for my part have someone whom I must please, whom I must submit to, whom I must obey, namely, God, and after him, myself. [12] He has commended me to myself, and has brought it about that my choice should be subject to myself alone, giving me rules for the right use of it; and when I follow those rules with due care, I pay no heed to anyone who says anything different, I give no thought to anyone who makes use of equivocal arguments. [13] Why do I get annoyed, then, with those who criticize me in the most important matters? Why should I be troubled in that way? For no other reason than the fact that I lack training in that area. [14] For, in truth, knowledge always despises ignorance and the ignorant, and this applies not only to the sciences but also to the arts and crafts. Take any shoemaker you please, and he holds the mass of people in contempt with regard to his own work; and take any carpenter, too.

[15] It is necessary first of all, then, to keep these principles at hand, and to do nothing without them, but keep our mind directed to this end, that we should pursue nothing external, and nothing that is not our own, but rather, as he who is all-powerful has ordained, pursue without reservation such things as lie within the sphere of choice, and all the rest only in so far as it is granted to us. [16] And next, we must remember who we are, and what name we bear, and strive to direct our appropriate actions according to the demands of our social relationships, [17] remembering what is the proper time to sing, the proper time to play, and in whose company, and what will be out of

place, and how we may make sure that our companions don't despise us, and that we don't despise ourselves; when we should joke, and whom we should laugh at, and to what end we should associate with others, and with whom, and finally, how we should preserve our proper character when doing so. Whenever you deviate from any of these rules, you suffer the penalty at once, [18] not from anything that comes from outside, but from the very action itself.

[19] What, is it possible thenceforth to be entirely free from fault? No, that is beyond us; but this at least is possible: to strive without cease to avoid committing any fault. For we must be contented if, by never relaxing our attention, we manage to escape a small number of faults. [20] But now, when you say, 'From tomorrow I'll pay attention,' be clear that what you're really saying is, 'Today I'll be shameless, importunate, and mean-spirited; it will lie within the power of others to cause me distress; I'll lose my temper today; I'll fall prey to envy.' [21] See how many evils you're bringing down on yourself. But if it would be good for you to pay attention tomorrow, how much better it would be to do so today, so that you may be able to achieve the same tomorrow also, and not put it off once again until the following day.

4.13 *To those who talk too readily about their personal affairs*

[1] When someone seems to have talked frankly to us about his personal affairs, we are somehow impelled to reveal our own secrets to him in turn, and we regard that as being frankness. [2] This comes about partly because, after hearing our neighbour's confidences, it seems unfair not to reply in kind by giving him a share of our own; and also because we think that we won't give such people the impression of being frank if we keep quiet about our personal affairs. [3] People are indeed often accustomed to say, 'Now that I've told you all about my affairs, will you tell me nothing about your own? How is that?' [4] A further point is that we think that we can safely place trust in somebody who has already told us his own secrets, because the thought comes to us that he would never divulge our secrets for fear that we would respond by divulging his. [5] It is in this way that soldiers at Rome catch out incautious people. A soldier sits down beside you in civilian dress and begins to speak ill of Caesar; and then you in turn, as if you'd received a pledge of his good faith because he

was the one who had initiated the abuse, begin to give voice, too, to what you think, and then you're arrested and put in chains. [6] We experience something similar in everyday life. For even though this man has safely entrusted his secrets to me, I for my part don't entrust mine to anyone who comes along; [7] no, I listen and keep silent, if I'm that kind of person, but he goes out and tells everyone what he has heard. And then, when I come to learn what has happened, I too, if I'm actually like him, tell everyone his secrets out of a desire for revenge, and so I besmirch and am besmirched. [8] If I bear in mind, however, that one person cannot harm another, but it is each person's own actions that bring harm or benefit to him, I achieve this much at least, that I don't act in the same way as he has done, but I nevertheless suffer what I must as a result of my own foolish talk.*

[9] 'Yes, but after hearing your neighbour's secrets, it is unfair not to give him a share of your own in return.'

[10] Did I invite your confidences, man? Did you tell me about your affairs on condition that you should hear about mine in return? [11] If you're a chatterbox and take anyone whom you meet to be a friend, do you wish that I too should come to be like you? Why then, if you did well to entrust your confidences to me but it wouldn't be good for me to trust you, do you want me to be so rash as to do so? [12] It is just as if I had a water-tight barrel and you had one with a hole in it, and you came and entrusted your wine to me, for me to store it in my barrel, and you then complained that I for my part didn't entrust my wine to you! No indeed, because your barrel has a hole in it. [13] So how could things still be on an equal basis? You've entrusted your confidences to one who is trustworthy, one who has self-respect, one who regards his own actions as being either harmful or beneficial, and nothing that is external as being so. [14] And would you have me entrust my confidences to you, to someone who has dishonoured his own faculty of choice, and wants to gain a bit of cash, or some post or other, or advancement at court, even if that means murdering his own children, as Medea* did? [15] Where is the equality in that? But show me that you're trustworthy, honourable, reliable; show me that your judgements are full of benevolence, show me that your barrel isn't leaky, and then you'll see how, instead of waiting for you to make confidences to me, I myself will invite you to listen to mine. [16] For who wouldn't want to make use of a sound barrel; who wouldn't respect a benevolent and trustworthy adviser; who wouldn't gladly

welcome someone who is ready to share his difficulties, as if sharing a load, and by doing so lighten them for him?

[17] 'Yes, but I trust you, and you don't trust me.'

In the first place, you don't trust me either, but you're simply a chatterbox, and for that reason, you can't keep anything back. For if it is true that you trust me, entrust your confidences to me alone. [18] But the fact is that as soon as you see anyone who is at leisure, you sit down beside him and say, 'Brother, there is no one who is better disposed to me and dearer to me than you; do please listen to my confidences,' and you do that with people who are complete strangers to you. [19] But even if you do trust me, it is plainly because you think me to be someone who is trustworthy and honourable, and not because I've spoken to you about my own affairs. [20] Permit me, then, to reach the same judgement about you. Show that if someone tells someone else about his own affairs, it follows that he is trustworthy and honourable. For if that were so, I would go around telling everybody about my affairs, if that would make me trustworthy and honourable! But that isn't the case; to be so one needs to have judgements that are of no commonplace character. [21] If you see someone, then, who devotes every concern to things that lie outside the sphere of choice, and subordinates his own choice to them, you may be sure that this person has thousands of people who constrain and obstruct him. [22] There is no need to resort to pitch or the wheel* to make him declare what he knows, but the slightest nod from a pretty girl, if it should so happen, will be enough to shake him, as will a friendly gesture from someone at Caesar's court, or desire for a public post, or an inheritance, or countless other things of that kind. [23] So you must remember that, as a general rule, confidences require trustworthiness and corresponding judgements; [24] and where can these be easily found nowadays? Or let someone show me somebody who is of such a mind that he can say, 'I concern myself only with what is my own, with what is immune to hindrance, with what is by nature free. Such is the nature of the good that I possess; as for all the rest, may it come about as God may grant: it makes no difference to me.'

FRAGMENTS

1. What does it matter to me, says Epictetus, whether everything is made up of atoms, or of indivisible parts, or of fire and earth? Isn't it enough to know the true nature of good and bad, and the proper bounds of our desires and aversions, and also of our motives to act or not to act, and to make use of these as rules to order the conduct of our life, and renounce those things that are beyond us? It may well be that the latter are incomprehensible to the human mind, but even if one should assume that they're fully comprehensible, what advantage would it bring to understand them? Shouldn't we say that those who assign that as being necessary to the philosopher's enquiry are giving themselves pointless trouble? Is the Delphic admonition also super-fluous, then, 'Know yourself'?—'No, it isn't,' he replies.—So what does it mean? If one told a chorus singer to know himself, wouldn't he respond to that instruction by paying attention to the other singers in the chorus so as to sing in harmony with them?—'Yes.'—And like-wise with a sailor? Or a soldier? Do you suppose, then, that man is a creature who has been made to live all alone, or for society?—'For society.'—By whom?—'By nature.'—As to what nature is, and how it administers the universe, and whether or not it really exists, these are matters that we need not bother about any further now.

2. He who is discontented with what he has, and with what has been granted to him by fortune, is one who is ignorant of the art of living, but he who bears that in a noble spirit, and makes reasonable use of all that comes from it, deserves to be regarded as a good man.

3. All things obey and serve the universe, both earth, and sea, and sun, and all the other stars, and the plants and animals of the earth; and our body, too, obeys it, both in sickness and in health, as the uni-verse wills, and both in our younger years and in old age, and as it passes through every other change. It is thus reasonable, too, that what lies within our own power, namely, the decision of our will, shouldn't be the only thing that sets itself in opposition to it; for the universe is mighty and superior to us, and has taken better counsel on our behalf than we can, by embracing us, too, in its governing order

in conjunction with the whole. And besides, to act against it is to align
ourselves with unreason, and while bringing nothing but a futile
struggle, it involves us in pains and miseries.

4. Of existing things, God has placed some within our power, and
others not within our power. Within our power he has placed the most
important thing, that through which he himself is happy, the power to
deal with impressions. For when that capacity is rightly exercised,
there is freedom, serenity, cheerfulness, constancy, and there is justice,
too, and law, and self-control, and virtue in its entirety. But as to
everything else, God hasn't placed that within our power. It is thus
necessary that we, too, should be of one mind with God, and by drawing this distinction, we should seek to obtain by every means those
things that lie within our power, but entrust those that don't lie within
our power to the universe, and if it should have need of our children,
our country, our body, or anything whatever, be glad to yield it up.

5. Who among us doesn't admire the saying of Lycurgus* the
Spartan? For when he had been blinded in one eye by one of his fellow
citizens, and the young man was handed over to him by the people for
him to exact whatever vengeance he might wish, he refrained from
doing so, but gave him a proper education instead, made a good man
of him, and presented him in the theatre; and when the Spartans
showed surprise, he said, 'When I received him from you, this man
was offensive and violent, and I'm returning him to you as someone
who is well behaved and public-spirited.'

6. But this above all is the work of nature, to bind together and harmo-
nize our motives with what we conceive to be fitting and beneficial.

7. To suppose that we'll be viewed with disdain by others if we don't resort
to every means to injure the first enemies we encounter is the mark of
thoroughly ignoble and foolish people; for we generally say that someone
can be recognized as contemptible by, among other things, his incapacity
to do harm, whereas it is much more by his incapacity to do good.

8. Such was, and is, and will be the nature of the universe, and it isn't
possible that things should come into being in any other way than
they do at present; and not only have human beings participated in

the process of change and transformation along with all the other creatures that live on the earth, but also those beings that are divine, and, by Zeus, even the four elements, which are changed and transformed upwards and downwards, as earth becomes water, and water air, and air is transformed in turn into ether. If someone endeavours to turn his mind towards these things, and to persuade himself to accept of his own free will what must necessarily come about, he will live a very balanced and harmonious life.

9. An eminent philosopher of the Stoic school . . . drew out of his little bag the fifth book of the *Discourses* of the philosopher Epictetus, which have been edited by Arrian, and are doubtless in agreement with the writings of Zeno and Chrysippus. In that book, which is of course written in Greek, we find this sentence: 'The visions of the mind (which the philosophers call *phantasiai*), by which the human mind at the very first sight of anything is impelled to the perception of that thing, are subject neither to his will nor to his control, but through a certain power of their own, force themselves on people's awareness; but acts of assent (which they call *sunkatatheseis*), by which these visions are recognized, are subject to the human will and under its control. So when some terrifying sound comes from the sky or from a falling building, or news of some danger is suddenly announced, or something else of that kind occurs, even the mind of a wise person is bound to be disturbed, and to shrink back and grow pale for a moment, not from any idea that something bad is going to happen, but because of certain swift and unconsidered movements which forestall the proper functioning of the mind and reason. Before long, however, this wise person of ours refuses to give his assent to *tas toiautas phantasias* (that is to say, these terrifying visions of the mind), but rejects and spurns them, and sees nothing in them that ought to inspire him with fear. And that is the difference, they say, between the mind of a wise person and that of a fool, that the fool thinks that the things that initially strike the mind as harsh and terrible really are such, and then, as if they are truly to be feared, goes on to approve them by his own assent, *kai prosepidoxazei* (the expression that the Stoics use when discussing this topic); whereas one who is wise, after being briefly and superficially affected in his colour and expression, *ou sunkatatithetai* [does not give his assent], but retains the consistency and firmness of the opinion that he has always had about mental

visions of this kind, namely, that such things are in no way to be feared, but arouse terror only through false appearances and empty alarms. This is what the philosopher Epictetus thinks and says, in accordance with the doctrines of the Stoics, as I read in the book mentioned above.

10. I have heard Favorinus say that the philosopher Epictetus declared that most of those who gave the appearance of practising philosophy were philosophers of this kind, *aneu tou prattein, mechri tou legein* (that is to say, 'without deeds, only so far as words'). There was an even stronger expression that he was in the habit of using, as Arrian has recorded in the books that he wrote about his discourses. For when, so Arrian says, Epictetus noticed a man who had lost all sense of shame, and had misdirected his energies, and was corrupt in his morals, bold and impudent in his speech, and devoted attention to everything other than his own soul—when he saw a man of that kind, says Arrian, also embarking on the study and pursuit of philosophy, and engaging with physics, and studying dialectic, and examining and investigating many theoretical matters of that kind, he would invoke the help of gods and men, and often, while doing so, would reproach the man in these terms: 'Man, where are you putting these things? Check to see whether the vessel is clean. If you put them into your conceited mind, they're ruined; and if they rot, they turn into urine or vinegar or perhaps something worse than that.' Surely there could be nothing weightier, nothing truer than these words in which the greatest of philosophers declared that the writings and teachings of philosophy, when poured into a false and degenerate person, as though into a dirty and polluted vessel, are spoiled and (as he himself says *kunikōteron* [in a somewhat Cynic tone]) turn into urine or perhaps something even fouler than that.

The same Epictetus, moreover, as we have also heard from Favorinus, used to say that there are two vices that are much graver and more hateful than all others, namely, want of endurance and want of self-control, when we are unable to bear and endure the wrongs that we ought to bear, and cannot hold back from those pleasures and other things that we ought to hold back from. And so, he said, if someone could take these two words to heart, and use them to govern and control himself, he will be free from fault for the most part and live a most peaceful life. These two words, he used to say, are *anechou* and *apechou* [bear and forbear].

10a. When the safety of our souls and respect for our true selves are at stake, one may have to do something even without prior thought, according to a saying of Epictetus, which Arrian quotes with approval.

11. Now when Archelaus* sent for Socrates, saying that he would make him rich, Socrates told the messenger to take back the following reply: 'At Athens one can buy four quarts of barley-meal for an obol,* and there are springs that run with water.' For if what I have isn't enough for me, it is enough to satisfy me, and it is thus enough for me. Or don't you see that Polus* didn't act the part of Oedipus the King with finer voice, or with greater pleasure, than he acted that of Oedipus at Colonus,* the vagabond and beggar? Then shall a man of noble character show himself inferior to Polus, by failing to perform well in any role that the Deity assigns to him? Won't he rather follow the example of Odysseus,* who was no less distinguished in rags than in a fine purple cloak?

12. There are some people who can be ill-tempered in a gentle way, and who, quite calmly and as though without anger, do everything that those who are carried away by their anger would do. We must be on our guard, then, against the error of such people, as something far worse than becoming furiously angry. For those who fly into a passion soon have their fill of vengeance, while others prolong it for a considerable time like people who are suffering from a light fever.

13. 'But I see the good and virtuous', someone says, 'dying from hunger and cold.'—But don't you also see those who aren't good and virtuous dying from luxury, pretension, and vulgarity?—'Yes, but it's shameful to rely on someone else for one's support.'—And who relies on himself alone for his support, you wretch? Only the universe does so. Whoever finds fault with providence, then, because the wicked aren't punished, and because they're rich and powerful, is acting just as though, if the wicked had lost their eyes, he said they weren't being punished because their fingernails were in good order. Now, I would say that there is much more difference between virtue and property than there is between eyes and fingernails.

14. .... bringing forward those grumpy philosophers who think pleasure is not something natural, but something that follows upon things

that are natural, such as justice, self-control, freedom. Why, then, does the soul take delight in lesser goods, those of the body, and find peace in them, as Epicurus says, and yet not find pleasure in its own goods, which are the greatest? Yet nature has also given me a sense of shame, and I often blush when I think that I'm saying something shameful. It is that emotion that won't permit me to regard pleasure as a good thing and the end of life.

15. In Rome the women have Plato's *Republic* in their hands because he says that women should be held in common. For they pay heed only to the words, and not to what the man actually means, since he doesn't recommend that people should marry and live together, one man with one woman, and then go on to say that wives should be shared, but he does away with that kind of marriage and introduces another in place of it. But in general people are pleased to find ways to excuse their own faults; since philosophy says, indeed, that we shouldn't even stretch out our finger without due reason!

16. One should know that it isn't easy for a person to arrive at a firm judgement unless, day after day, he states and hears the same principles, and at the same time applies them to his life.

17. When we're invited to a banquet, we take whatever is served, and if anyone should ask his host to serve him with fish or cakes, he would be thought eccentric; and yet in the wider world, we ask the gods for things that they don't give us, irrespective of the many things that they actually have given us.

18. Smart fellows they are, he said, who pride themselves on those things that are not within our power. 'I'm better than you,' one says, 'because I own plenty of land while you're half-dead with hunger.' Another says, 'I'm of consular rank,' and another, 'I'm a procurator,' and another, 'I have good thick hair.' And yet one horse doesn't say to another, 'I'm better than you because I have plenty of fodder, and plenty of barley, and bridles of gold, and richly worked saddles,' but rather it says, 'I can run faster than you.' And every creature is better or worse in so far as it is made so by its own specific virtue or vice. Can it be, then, that man is the only creature to have no specific virtue, so that he has to look instead to his hair, and his clothes, and his forebears?

19. When their doctor fails to offer them any advice, people who are ill get angry and think that he has given up on them. Why shouldn't one take the same attitude towards a philosopher, and so conclude that he has despaired of one ever achieving a sound state of mind if he no longer gives one any useful advice?

20. Those whose bodies are in good condition can endure both heat and cold; and so, likewise, those whose souls are in fine condition can endure anger, and grief, and every other emotion.

21. Agrippinus can be rightly praised for this reason, that although he was a man of the very highest worth, he never praised himself, but would blush even if someone else praised him. He was a man of such a kind, said Epictetus, that when he was struck by any difficulty, he would write in praise of it; if fever was his lot, in praise of fever, if disrepute, in praise of disrepute, if exile, in praise of exile. And one day, he said, when Agrippinus was about to take his morning meal, a man arrived to tell him that Nero was ordering him to go into exile; 'Very well,' he said, 'we'll eat our meal in Aricia.'

22. When Agrippinus was serving as governor, he used to try to persuade the people whom he sentenced that it was proper for them to be sentenced. 'For it is not as an enemy', he said, 'that I pass sentence against them, but as an overseer and guardian, just as a doctor encourages the man whom he is operating on, and persuades him to offer himself up.'

23. Nature is wonderful, and, as Xenophon* says, 'full of love for her creatures'. At any rate, we love our body and take care of it, the most unpleasant and foulest of all things; why, if we had to take care of our neighbour's body for just five days, that would be more than we could bear. For think what it would be like to get up in the morning and clean someone else's teeth, and then, after he had attended to a certain necessary function, to wash the relevant parts. In truth, it is amazing that we should love something for which we have to perform so many services day after day. I stuff this sack* here, and then I empty it; what could be more tedious? But I have to serve God; and for that reason, I stay here and put up with having to wash this poor wretched body of mine, and feed it, and shelter it. When I was younger, there was also another duty* that was assigned to me, and yet

I put up with that too. So why can't you bear it, then, when nature, which gave us our body, takes it away again?—'I love it,' someone says.—Well, but isn't it nature, as I was saying just now, that has given you the very love that you feel for it? But this same nature also says, 'Let it go now, and trouble yourself no longer.'

24. If someone dies young, he finds fault with the gods [because he is having to leave the world before his time, but if he remains alive when old, he finds fault with them too] because he is continuing to live when it was high time that he was at rest; but all the same, when death approaches, he wants to stay alive, and sends for the doctor, telling him to spare no trouble or effort. How extraordinary people are, he said, to be unwilling either to live or to die.

25. Before you attack anyone in an aggressive and threatening manner, remember to tell yourself that you're not a wild animal; and then you'll never commit any violent act, and will thus pass through life without having to repent or be called to account.

26. You're a little soul carrying a corpse around, as Epictetus used to say.

27. He said, too, that we must find an art of assent, and in the sphere of our motives, take good care that they're exercised subject to reservation, and that they take account of the common interest, and that they're proportionate to the worth of their object; and we should abstain wholly from desire, and exercise aversion towards nothing that is not within our power.

28. So the struggle, he said, is over no slight matter, but whether we are to be mad or sane.

HANDBOOK

1.1. Some things are within our power, while others are not. Within our power are opinion, motivation, desire, aversion, and, in a word, whatever is of our own doing; not within our power are our body, our property, reputation, office, and, in a word, whatever is not of our own doing. 2. The things that are within our power are by nature free, and immune to hindrance and obstruction, while those that are not within our power are weak, slavish, subject to hindrance, and not our own. 3. Remember, then, that if you regard that which is by nature slavish as being free, and that which is not your own as being your own, you'll have cause to lament, you'll have a troubled mind, and you'll find fault with both gods and human beings; but if you regard only that which is your own as being your own, and that which isn't your own as not being your own (as is indeed the case), no one will ever be able to coerce you, no one will hinder you, you'll find fault with no one, you'll accuse no one, you'll do nothing whatever against your will, you'll have no enemy, and no one will ever harm you because no harm can affect you.

4. Since you're aiming, then, at such great things, remember that you'll have to exert no small effort to attain them, and that you'll have to renounce some things altogether, while postponing others for the present. But if you want to have both these things and public office and riches too, you'll quite possibly not even gain the latter because you're aiming at the former too, and you'll certainly fail to get the former, through which alone happiness and freedom can be secured.

5. Practise, then, from the very beginning to say to every disagreeable impression, 'You're an impression and not at all what you appear to be.' Then examine it and test it by these rules that you possess, and first and foremost by this one, whether the impression relates to those things that are within our power, or those that aren't within our power; and if it relates to anything that isn't within our power, be ready to reply, 'That's nothing to me.'

2.1. Remember that desire promises the attaining of what you desire, and aversion the avoiding of what you want to avoid, and that he who falls into desire is unfortunate, while he who falls into what he wants to avoid suffers misfortune. If you seek to avoid, then, only what is contrary to nature among those things that are within your own power, you'll never fall into anything that you want to avoid; but if you attempt to avoid illness, or death, or poverty, you'll suffer misfortune.   2. Remove your aversion, then, from everything that is not within our power, and transfer it to what is contrary to nature among those things that are within our power. For the present, however, suppress your desires entirely; for if you desire any of the things that are not within our power, you're bound to be unfortunate, while those that are within our power, which it would be right for you to desire, aren't yet within your reach. But use only your motives to act or not to act, and even those lightly, with reservations and without straining.

3. With regard to everything that is a source of delight to you, or is useful to you, or of which you are fond, remember to keep telling yourself what kind of thing it is, starting with the most insignificant. If you're fond of a jug, say, 'This is a jug that I'm fond of,' and then, if it gets broken, you won't be upset. If you kiss your child or your wife, say to yourself that it is a human being that you're kissing; and then, if one of them should die, you won't be upset.

4. When you're about to embark on any action, remind yourself what kind of action it is. If you're going out to take a bath, set before your mind the things that happen at the baths, that people splash you, that people knock up against you, that people steal from you. And you'll thus undertake the action in a surer manner if you say to yourself at the outset, 'I want to take a bath and ensure at the same time that my choice remains in harmony with nature.' And follow the same course in every action that you embark on. So if anything gets in your way while you're taking your bath, you'll be ready to tell yourself, 'Well, this wasn't the only thing that I wanted to do, but I also wanted to keep my choice in harmony with nature; and I won't keep it so if I get annoyed at what is happening.'

5. It isn't the things themselves that disturb people, but the judgements that they form about them. Death, for instance, is nothing terrible, or else it would have seemed so to Socrates too; no, it is in the judgement that death is terrible that the terror lies. So accordingly, whenever we're impeded, disturbed, or distressed, we should never

blame anyone else, but only ourselves, that is to say, our judgements. It is the act of an ill-educated person to cast blame on others when things are going badly for him; one who has taken the first step towards becoming properly educated casts blame on himself; while one who is fully educated casts blame neither on another nor on himself.

6. Don't pride yourself on any excellence that is not your own. If a horse were to say in its pride, 'I'm beautiful,' that would be bearable; but when you exclaim in your pride, 'I have a beautiful horse,' you should be clear in your mind that you're priding yourself on a good quality that belongs to a horse. What is your own, then? The use of impressions.* So when you're in harmony with nature through the right use of impressions, you should then be proud of yourself; for then you'll be taking pride in some good of your own.

7. When you're on a voyage and your ship has set anchor, if you should go ashore to fetch water, you may pick up a little shellfish or bulb on the way, but you have to keep your attention directed towards the ship, and turn round constantly in case the captain calls you back; and if he does, you must cast these things aside, if you don't want to be thrown on board trussed up like a sheep. So in life too, if in place of some little bulb or shellfish, a little wife and child should be granted to you, there is nothing wrong with that; but if the captain calls, you must give up all of these things and run to the ship, without even turning around to look back. And if you're an old man, you shouldn't even wander any distance from the ship, so as not to be missing when the call comes.

8. Don't seek that all that comes about should come about as you wish, but wish that everything that comes about should come about just as it does, and then you'll have a calm and happy life.

9. Disease is an impediment to the body, but not to choice, unless choice wills it to be so. Lameness is an impediment to the leg, but not to choice.* And tell yourself the same with regard to everything that happens to you; for you'll find that it acts as an impediment to something else, but not to yourself.

10. With regard to everything that happens to you, remember to look inside yourself and see what capacity you have to enable you to deal

with it. If you catch sight of a beautiful boy or woman, you'll find that you have self-control to enable you to deal with that; if hard work lies in store for you, you'll find endurance; if vilification, you'll find forbearance. And if you get into the habit of following this course, you won't get swept away by your impressions.

11. Never say about anything, 'I've lost it,' but rather, 'I've given it back.' Your child has died? It has been given back. Your wife has died? She has been given back. 'My farm has been taken from me.' Well, that too has been given back. 'Yes, but the man who took it is a rogue.' What does it matter to you through what person the one who gave it to you demanded it back? So long as he entrusts it to you, take care of it as something that isn't your own, as travellers treat an inn.

12.1. If you want to make progress, reject such thoughts as these: 'If I neglect my affairs, I'll have nothing to live on,' or, 'If I don't punish my slave-boy, he'll turn out badly.' For it is better to die of hunger, but free from distress and fear, than to live in plenty with a troubled mind; and it is better that your slave should be bad than that you should be unhappy. Make a start, then, with small things. 2. A drop of oil is spilled, a little wine is stolen; say to yourself, 'Such is the price at which equanimity is bought; such is the price that one pays for peace of mind.' For nothing can be acquired at no cost at all. When you summon your slave-boy, keep in mind that he may not obey, and even if he does, he may not do what you want; but he is hardly so well placed that it depends on him whether you're to enjoy peace of mind.

13. If you want to make progress, put up with being thought foolish and silly with regard to external things, and don't even wish to give the impression of knowing anything about them; and if some people come to think that you're somebody of note, regard yourself with distrust. For you should recognize that it isn't easy to keep your choice in accord with nature and, at the same time, hold onto externals, but if you apply your attention to one of those things, you're bound to neglect the other.

14.1. If you want your children and wife and friends to live for ever, you're a fool, because you're wanting things that aren't within your power to be within your power, and things that aren't your own to be your own. And likewise, if you want your slave-boy never to commit a fault, you're an idiot, because you're wanting badness not to be badness, but something else. If you make it your wish, however, not to fail in your desires, that lies within your power. So exercise yourself in that which you can achieve. 2. Everyone is subject to anyone who has power over what he wants or doesn't want, as one who is in a position to confer it or take it away. If anyone wants to be free, then, let him neither want anything nor seek to avoid anything that is under the control of others; or else he is bound to be a slave.

15. Remember that you should behave in life as you do at a banquet. Something is being passed around and arrives in front of you: reach out your hand and take your share politely. It passes: don't try to hold it back. It has yet to reach you: don't project your desire towards it, but wait until it arrives in front of you. So act likewise with regard to your children, to your wife, to public office, to riches, and the time will come when you're worthy to have a seat at the banquets of the gods. And if you don't even take these things when they're in front of you, but view them with contempt, then you'll not only share in the banquets of the gods, but also in their rule. For it was by acting in such a way that Diogenes, and Heraclitus,* and others like them, deservedly became divine and were called so.

16. When you see someone weeping in sorrow because his child has gone away, or because he has lost his possessions, take care that you're not carried away by the impression that he is indeed in misfortune because of these external things, but be ready at once with this thought, 'It isn't what has happened that so distresses this person— for someone else could suffer the same without feeling that distress— but rather the judgement that he has formed about it.' As far as words go, however, don't hesitate to sympathize with him, or even, if the occasion arises, to join in his lamentations; but take care that you don't also lament deep inside.

17. Remember that you're an actor in a play, which will be as the author chooses, short if he wants it to be short, and long if he wants it to be long. If he wants you to play the part of a beggar, act even that part with all your skill; and likewise if you're playing a cripple, an official, or a

private citizen. For that is your business, to act the role that is assigned to you as well as you can; but it is another's* part to select that role.

18. When a raven croaks* inauspiciously, don't allow yourself to be carried away by the impression, but immediately draw a distinction within your mind, and say, 'None of these omens apply to me, but only to my poor body, to my paltry possessions, or my reputation, or my children, or my wife. But for me every omen is favourable for I want it to be so; for whatever may come about, it is within my power to derive benefit from it.'

19.1. You can be invincible if you never enter a contest in which the victory doesn't depend on you. 2. So whenever you see someone being preferred above you in the awarding of honours, or holding great power, or enjoying high repute in any other way, take care that you don't get carried away by the outward impression and count him as happy; for if the nature of the good is one of the things that lie within our power, there can be no place for either envy or jealousy, and you yourself won't want to be a praetor or senator or consul, but a free man. Now there is one path alone that leads to that: to despise everything that doesn't lie within our own power.

20. Remember that what insults you isn't the person who abuses you or hits you, but your judgement that such people are insulting you. So whenever anyone irritates you, recognize that it is your opinion that has irritated you. Try above all, then, not to allow yourself to be carried away by the impression; for if you delay things and gain time to think, you'll find it easier to gain control of yourself.

21. Day by day you must keep before your eyes death and exile and everything else that seems frightening, but most especially death; and then you'll never harbour any mean thought, nor will you desire anything beyond due measure.

22. If you set your desire on pursuing philosophy, prepare from that moment to be subject to ridicule, and to have many people mocking you, and saying, 'Look, he's come back to us having become a philosopher all of a sudden!' and 'Where do you suppose he picked up that supercilious air?' You shouldn't assume an air of self-importance, but should

hold fast to the things that seem best to you, as one who has been appointed by God to this post; and remember that if you hold true to the same principles, those who laughed at you will later come to admire you; but if you allow these people to get the better of you, you'll merely be laughed at twice over.

23. If it should ever come about that you turn to external things because you want to gratify another person, be clear that you've lost your plan in life. Be content, then, to be a philosopher in all that you do, and if you also want to be viewed as one, show yourself that you are, and you'll be able to achieve that.

24.1. Don't allow these thoughts to upset you: 'I'll live unhonoured, and be nobody anywhere.' For if it is a bad thing to be unhonoured, you cannot be in a bad state as a result of someone else's actions, any more than you can be brought into shame in that way. It is no business of yours, surely, to gain a public post or be invited to a dinner party? Certainly not. So how can this still be a source of dishonour? And how will you be 'nobody anywhere' if you only need to be somebody in those things that are within your own power, and in which it is possible for you to be a man of the highest worth? 2. But your friends will be left unhelped? What do you mean by 'left unhelped'? They won't receive any little payouts from you, nor will you be able to grant them Roman citizenship. Well, who told you that these are things that are within our power, rather than being other people's business? And who is able to give to another person something that he himself doesn't have? 'Then get hold of some money', a friend says, 'so that we too may have some.' 3. If I can get some while preserving my self-respect, trustworthiness, and generosity of mind, show me the way and I'll get it; but if you require me to lose the good things that I have to enable you to acquire things that aren't good, consider how unfair you're being, or how foolish. After all, what would you rather have? Money, or a faithful and self-respecting friend? So help me instead to become such a person, and don't require me to do things that would cause me to lose those qualities.

4. 'But my country', he says, 'will receive no help from me, so far as I can offer it.' Here again, what kind of help do you mean? It won't acquire any arcades or baths through your good offices. And what of that? For it doesn't acquire shoes either through the good offices of a blacksmith, or arms through those of a cobbler; it is enough that each

person fulfils his own function. And if you provide your country with another citizen who is trustworthy and self-respecting, would you bring it no benefit? 'Indeed I would.' Well then, in that case you wouldn't be of no use to it. 'What place shall I hold in the state, then?', he asks. Whatever place you can hold while maintaining your trustworthiness and self-respect. 5. But if, out of a wish to help the state, you sacrifice those qualities, what use could you be to it, when you've turned out to be shameless and untrustworthy?

25.1. Has someone been honoured above you at a banquet, or in being saluted, or in being summoned to give advice? If these things are good, you ought to rejoice if someone else has secured them; but if they're bad, don't be aggrieved that you haven't secured them. And remember, too, that if you don't resort to the same means as other people to acquire things that aren't within our power, you can't lay claim to an equal share of them. 2. For how can someone who doesn't hang around somebody's door claim an equal share with someone who does? Or if he doesn't join the man's retinue when he goes out along with the other person? Or he doesn't sing his praises along with the other person? You'll be unjust, then, and thoroughly greedy, if you refuse to pay the price for which these things are marketed, and want to get hold of them for nothing. 3. Well, at what price are lettuces sold? An obol perhaps. If someone pays the obol, then, and gets the lettuces, while you pay nothing and get nothing, don't suppose that you're worse off than the man who gets the lettuces; for while he has his lettuces, you have your obol, which you haven't given away. 4. Things follow the same course in the present case too. You haven't been invited to somebody's dinner party? Of course not, because you haven't paid the host the price at which he sells the dinner; he sells it for praise, he sells it for attention. Very well, then, pay him the price for which it is sold, if it is in your interest. But if you want to make no payment and still receive the goods, you're greedy and foolish. Do you have nothing, then, in place of the dinner? Why, of course you have: you haven't been obliged to praise a man whom you didn't want to praise, you didn't have to suffer the insolence of the people at the door.

26. The will of nature may be learned from those events in life in which we don't differ from one another. For instance, when someone else's

slave-boy breaks a cup, we're ready at once to say, 'That's just one of those things.' So you should be clear, then, that if your own cup gets broken, you ought to react in exactly the same way as when someone else's does. Transfer the principle to greater matters too. Someone else's child or wife has died; there isn't anyone who wouldn't say, 'Such is our human lot.' And yet when one's own child or wife dies, one cries out at once, 'Oh poor wretch that I am.' But we ought to remember how we feel when we hear that the same thing has happened to others.

27. Just as a target isn't set up to be missed, so nothing that is bad by nature comes into being in the universe.

28. If someone handed over your body to somebody whom you encountered, you'd be furious; but that you hand over your mind to anyone who comes along, so that, if he abuses you, it becomes disturbed and confused, do you feel no shame at that?

29. [See Discourse 3.15.1–13.]

30. Appropriate actions are measured on the whole by our social relationships. He is your father: you're obliged to take care of him, to give way to him in everything, to put up with it if he scolds you or strikes you. 'But he's a bad father.' Do the ties of nature bind you, then, only to a good father? No, but to a father. 'My brother is wronging me.' Very well, maintain the relation that you have towards him; don't look to what he is doing, but to what you must do if you are to keep your choice in harmony with nature. For no one will cause you harm if you don't wish it; you'll have been harmed only when you suppose that you've been harmed. In this way, then, you'll discover the appropriate actions to expect from a neighbour, from a fellow citizen, from a general, if you get into the habit of examining your social relationships.

31.1. As regards piety towards the gods, you should know that the most important point is to hold correct opinions about them, regarding them as beings who exist and govern the universe well and justly, and to have made up your mind to obey them and submit to everything that comes about, and to fall in with it of your own free will, as something that has been brought to pass by the highest intelligence. For if you follow that course, you'll never find fault with the gods or accuse them of having neglected you.

2. But it isn't possible for you to achieve this in any other way than by withdrawing your conception of good and bad from the things that are not within our power, and placing it in those things alone that are within our power. For if you regard any of the former as being good or bad, it will necessarily follow that, whenever you fail to get what you want or fall into things that you want to avoid, you'll blame and hate those who are responsible. 3. For it lies in the nature of every living creature that it should flee from and seek to avoid those things that seem harmful to it, and pursue and admire those that are helpful and all that gives rise to them. Accordingly, it is impossible for someone who thinks that he is suffering harm to take pleasure in what he thinks to be responsible for that harm, just as it is impossible for him to take pleasure in the harm itself. 4. And so it comes about that even a father is abused by his son if he fails to give him a share of the things that pass for good; and it was this that caused Eteocles and Polynices* to become enemies: the idea that the throne was a good thing. That is why a farmer reviles the gods, and so too a sailor or merchant, and those who have lost their wives and children. For where a person's interest lies, there too lies his piety. It follows that whoever takes care to exercise his desires and aversions as he ought is taking care at the same time that he'll act with piety. 5. But it is also appropriate on each occasion to offer libations and sacrifices, and first fruits, in accordance with the customs of our forebears, and do so with purity, and in no casual or perfunctory manner, and neither stingily nor beyond what we can afford.

32.1. When you take recourse to divination, remember that you don't know how that matter in question will turn out, but that you've come to discover that from the diviner; but if you are indeed a philosopher, you already know when you arrive what kind of thing it is. For if it is one of those things that are not within our power, it follows with absolute certainty that it must be neither good nor bad. 2. So you should bring neither desire nor aversion to the diviner, and you shouldn't approach him with trepidation, but as one who fully recognizes that every outcome is indifferent and of no concern to you, and that whatever it may be, it will be possible for you to make good use of it, and that no one can prevent you from doing so. So approach the gods with confidence, as your advisers, and afterwards, when some advice has been granted to you, remember who it is that you have taken as your advisers, and whom you will be disregarding if you disobey them. 3. Resort to divination as Socrates* thought right, in matters in which the enquiry relates exclusively to the outcome, and where neither reason nor any technical knowledge provides the means that are required to discover the point in question. So accordingly, when it is your duty to share a friend's danger or that of your country, you shouldn't resort to divination to ask whether you should share that danger. For even if the diviner should warn you that the omens from the sacrifice are unfavourable, and it is clear that death is portended, or mutilation of some part of your body, or exile, reason requires all the same that, even in the face of these risks, you should support your friend and share the danger of your country. Pay heed, then, to that greater diviner the Pythian Apollo,* who cast out of his temple the man who failed to come to the help of his friend when he was being murdered.

33.1. Lay down from this moment a certain character and pattern of behaviour for yourself, which you are to preserve both when you're alone and when you're with others.

2. Remain silent for the most part, or say only what is essential, and in few words. Very infrequently, however, when the occasion demands, do speak, but not about any of the usual topics, not about gladiators, not about horse-races, not about athletes, not about food and drink, the subjects of everyday talk; but above all, don't talk about people, either to praise or criticize them, or to compare them. 3. If you're able to so, then, through the manner of your own conversation bring that of your companions round to what is fit and proper. But if you happen to find yourself alone among strangers, keep silent.

4. Don't laugh much, or at many things, or without restraint.

5. Refuse to swear any oath at all, if that is possible, but if it isn't, refuse as far as you're able.

6. Avoid parties that are hosted by outsiders and people who have no knowledge of philosophy, but if you do have occasion to attend them, take great care that you don't fall back into a layman's state of mind. For you should be clear that if your companion is polluted, anyone who rubs up against him is bound to become polluted too, even if he himself happens to be clean.

7. In things relating to the body, take only as much as your bare need requires, with regard to food, for instance, or drink, clothes, housing, or household slaves; but exclude everything that is for show or luxury.

8. As regards sexual relations, keep yourself pure, so far as you can, until you marry; but if you do indulge, confine yourself to what is lawful. Don't make yourself tiresome, however, to those who indulge, or be over-critical, and don't constantly call attention to the fact that you don't behave like them.

9. If someone reports to you that a certain person is speaking ill of you, don't defend yourself against what has been said, but reply instead, 'Ah yes, he was plainly unaware of all my other faults, or else those wouldn't have been the only ones that he mentioned.'

10. There is no need on the whole to go to public shows, but if you ever have occasion to do so, show yourself as not taking sides for anyone other than yourself, that is to say, wish only that what actually does happen should happen, and that only the man who actually does win should win; for if you do that, you'll meet with no hindrance. But refrain entirely from shouting out, or laughing at anyone, or getting over-excited. And after you've left, don't talk much about what has taken place, except in so far as that contributes to your own improvement; for such talk would suggest that you were impressed by the spectacle.

11. Don't go casually or readily to people's public readings;* but if you do go, preserve your dignity and composure, taking care at the same time not to make yourself disagreeable.

12. When you're due to meet somebody, and in particular one who is regarded with high respect, put this question to yourself: 'What would Socrates or Zeno have done in this situation?' And then you'll have no difficulty in making proper use of the occasion. 13. When you're going to meet some very powerful man, put the thought to yourself that you won't find him at home, that you'll be shut out, that the door will be closed in your face, that he'll pay no heed to you. And if, in spite of all that, it is your duty to go, then go, and put up with whatever comes about, and never tell yourself, 'It wasn't worth the trouble.' For that is the mark of a layman, of someone who can be upset by externals.

14. In your conversation, avoid talking at length or overmuch about your own exploits or the dangers that you've faced; for pleasant though it may be for you to recall your perils, it is not as pleasant for others to listen to everything that has happened to you.

15. Abstain too from trying to arouse laughter, for that is behaviour that can easily slip into vulgarity, and tends at the same time to cause your neighbours to view you with less respect. 16. It is dangerous likewise to engage in smutty talk. So when anything like that comes up, you should, if the occasion presents itself, even reproach the person who has resorted to such talk; or if that isn't possible, show by your silence at least, and your blushes and frowns, that you're displeased at what is being said.

34. When you receive an impression of some pleasure, take care not to get carried away by it, as with impressions in general; but rather, make it wait for you, and allow yourself some slight delay. And next, think about these two moments in time, that in which you'll enjoy the pleasure, and that in which you'll come to repent after having enjoyed it and will reproach yourself; and set against all of that how you'll rejoice if you've abstained from the pleasure, and will congratulate yourself for having done so. If you think, however, that a suitable occasion has come for you to engage in this task, take care that you're not overcome by its allure, and by the pleasantness and attraction of it; but set against this the thought of how much better it is to be conscious of having gained a victory over it.

35. When you've decided that you ought to do something and are doing it, never try to avoid being seen to do it, even if most people will probably view it with disapproval; for if it isn't right to do it, avoid doing it in the first place, but if it is, why be afraid of those who'll reproach you without justification?

36. Just as the propositions 'it is day' and 'it is night' are entirely meaningful when taken separately, but become meaningless when joined into one, so likewise it may make sense with regard to your body to take the larger share at a dinner, but it makes no sense at all with regard to the maintenance of proper social feeling. So when you're eating with another person, remember to look not only at the value that the dishes set before you will have for your body, but also at the value of maintaining proper respect for your host.

37. If you take on a role that is beyond your power, you'll not only disgrace yourself in that role, but you'll also neglect to take on that which you might have been capable of filling.

38. Just as, when walking around, you take care not to tread on a nail or sprain your ankle, so take care likewise to avoid harming your ruling centre; and if we observe this rule in every action, we'll undertake the task in a more secure fashion.

39. Each person's body is the measure for his property,* as the foot is for a shoe. If you abide by this principle, then, you'll maintain due measure, but if you pass beyond it, you'll find yourself falling, so to speak, over a cliff. It is the same in the case of a shoe: if you pass beyond what the foot requires, you'll first get a gilded shoe, and then a purple one, and then an embroidered one; for as soon as you've passed beyond the measure, there is no limit.

40. As soon as they reach the age of fourteen, women are called mistresses by men. And so when they see that they have no other function than to become bedfellows of men, they set to work to beautify themselves, and place all their hopes in that. It is worth our while, then, to make them aware that they're valued for nothing other than being modest and self-respecting.

41. It is a sign of a lack of natural aptitude to spend much time on things relating to the body, by taking a large amount of exercise, for instance, and eating too much, drinking too much, and spending too much time emptying one's bowels and copulating. No, these things should be done in passing, and you should devote undivided attention to your mind.

42. When someone acts badly towards you, or speaks badly of you, remember that he is acting or speaking in that way because he regards that as being the proper thing for him to do. Now, it isn't possible for him to act in accordance with what seems right to you, but only with what seems right to him. So if he judges wrongly, he is the one who suffers the harm, since he is the one who has been deceived. For if anyone should think a true composite judgement* to be false, the judgement itself isn't harmed, but the person who has been deceived. If you start out, then, from this way of thinking, you'll be gentle with someone who abuses you, for in each case you'll say, 'That is how it seemed to him.'

43. Everything has two handles, and it may be carried by one of these handles, but not by the other. If your brother acts wrongly towards

you, don't try to grasp the matter by this handle, that he is wronging you (because that is the handle by which it can't be carried), but rather by the other, that he is your brother, he was brought up with you, and then you'll be grasping the matter by the handle by which it can be carried.

44. The following assertions don't form a coherent argument: 'I'm richer than you, therefore I'm better than you' or 'I'm more eloquent than you, therefore I'm better than you'; no, it is these that do: 'I'm richer than you, therefore my possessions are superior to yours' or 'I'm more eloquent than you, therefore my way of speaking is superior to yours.' But you yourself are neither your possessions nor your way of speaking.

45. Someone takes his bath in a hurry; don't say that he bathes badly, but that he does so in a hurry. Someone drinks a large amount of wine. Don't say that he drinks badly, but that he drinks a large amount. For until you've determined from what judgement he is proceeding, how do you know whether he is acting badly? And so in that way it won't come about that you receive convincing impressions of some things but give your assent to others.

46.1. Never call yourself a philosopher, and don't talk among laymen for the most part about philosophical principles, but act in accordance with those principles. At a banquet, for example, don't talk about how one ought to eat, but eat as one ought. Remember how Socrates so completely renounced all outward show that when people came to him and asked to be introduced to philosophers, he would take them along and introduce them, so readily did he submit to being overlooked.* 2. And accordingly, if any talk should arise among laymen about some philosophical principle, keep silent for the most part, for there is a great danger that you'll simply vomit* up what you haven't properly digested. So when the day arrives when someone tells you that you know nothing, and you, like Socrates, aren't upset by that, you may be sure that you're making a start on your work as a philosopher. For sheep, too, don't vomit up their fodder to show the shepherds how much they've eaten, but digest their food inside them, and produce wool and milk on the outside. And so you likewise shouldn't show off your principles to laymen, but rather show them the actions that result from those principles when they've been properly digested.

47. When you've become adapted to a simple way of life in bodily matters, don't pride yourself on that, and likewise, if you drink nothing but water, don't proclaim at every opportunity that you drink nothing but water. And if at any time you want to train yourself to endure hardship, do it for your own sake and not for others; don't embrace statues,* but if you ever find yourself extremely thirsty, take some cold water into your mouth and then spit it out again, without telling a soul.*

48.1. The condition and character of a layman is this: that he never expects that benefit or harm will come to him from himself, but only from externals. The condition and character of a philosopher is this: that he expects all benefit and harm to come to him from himself.

2. The signs of one who is making progress are that he criticizes no one, praises no one, blames or accuses no one, and never speaks of himself as being anyone of importance, or as one who has any knowledge. And if he is praised, he laughs within at the person who is praising him, and if anyone finds fault with him, he makes no defence. He goes about like an invalid, taking care not to disturb any part of him that is getting better until he has achieved lasting recovery. 3. He has rid himself of every desire,* and has transferred his aversion to those things alone that are contrary to nature among the things that are within our own power. He is moderate in his motives whatever they may be directed towards. If he gives the impression of being foolish or ignorant, he doesn't mind. In a word, he keeps guard against himself, as though he were an enemy lying in ambush for himself.

49. When someone is filled with pride because he is able to understand and interpret the works of Chrysippus, say to yourself, 'If Chrysippus hadn't written in such an obscure style, this person wouldn't have anything to pride himself on.' But what is it that I want? To understand nature and to follow it. So I look around for someone who can interpret it, and having heard that Chrysippus can, I go to him. But I don't understand his writings, so I look for someone who can interpret them. Up to this point, there is nothing to be proud of. But when I find the interpreter, what remains for me to do is to apply his precepts;

that is the only thing that gives any ground for pride. But if what I value is the mere act of interpretation, what else have I achieved than to have become a literary scholar instead of a philosopher? The only difference is that I'm interpreting Chrysippus rather than Homer. So when someone says to me, 'Read me some Chrysippus,' I blush rather than feeling any pride, when I'm unable to show that my actions match up to his words and are consistent with them.

50. Whatever rules of conduct are set for you, hold to them as if they were laws, as if it would be an act of impiety for you to transgress them; as to what anyone says about you, pay no heed to it, since in the end that is not your concern.

51.1. How much longer will you delay before you think yourself worthy of what is best, and transgress in nothing the distinctions that reason imposes? You've acquired knowledge of the philosophical principles that you ought to accept, and have accepted them. What kind of teacher, then, are you still waiting for, that you should delay any effort to reform yourself until he appears? You're no longer a youth; you're a full-grown man. If you're now negligent and idle, and are constantly making one delay after another, and setting one day and then another as the date after which you'll devote proper attention to yourself, then you'll fail to appreciate that you're making no progress, but will continue to be a layman your whole life through until you die. 2. So you should think fit from this moment to live as an adult and as one who is making progress; and let everything that seems best to you be an inviolable law for you. And if you come up against anything that requires an effort, or is pleasant, or is glorious or inglorious, remember that this is the time of the contest, that the Olympic Games have now arrived, and that there is no possibility of further delay, and that it depends on a single day and single action whether progress is to be lost or secured. 3. It was in this way that Socrates became the man he was, by attending to nothing other than reason in everything that he had to deal with. And even if you're not yet a Socrates, you ought to live like someone who does in fact wish to be a Socrates.*

52.1. The first and most necessary area of study in philosophy is the one that deals with the application of principles, such as, 'Don't lie.' The second deals with demonstrations, for instance, 'How is it that we oughtn't to lie?' The third confirms and analyses the other two, for instance, 'How is this a demonstration?' For what is a demonstration, what is logical consequence, what is contradiction, what is truth, what is falsehood? 2. The third area of study is necessary, then, because of the second, and the second because of the first, but the most necessary, and that on which we should dwell, is the first. But we do the opposite; for we spend our time on the third area of study, and employ all our efforts on that, while wholly neglecting the first. And so it comes about that we lie, while having at hand all the arguments that show why we oughtn't to lie.

53.1. On every occasion we should have these arguments at hand:

> Guide me, O Zeus, and thou, O Destiny,
> To wheresoever you have assigned me;
> I'll follow unwaveringly, or if my will fails,
> Base though I be, I'll follow nonetheless.*

2. 　　　　Whoever rightly yields to necessity
　　　　　We accord wise and learned in things divine.*

3. 'Well, Crito, if that is what is pleasing to the gods, so be it.'*

4. 'Anytus and Meletus can kill me, but they cannot harm me.'*

EXPLANATORY NOTES

The notes to the text are keyed to the books, chapters (i.e. individual Discourses), and paragraphs of the *Discourses*, the chapters of the *Handbook*, or the numbers of the fragments. All references, if not otherwise identified, are to the *Discourses*. References only by paragraph are to the Discourse being discussed. All dates are AD unless otherwise indicated.

DISCOURSES

PREFATORY LETTER

This letter, written separately by the historian Arrian (*c*.86–160) to an otherwise unknown Lucius Gellius, was attached to the manuscripts of the *Discourses* in antiquity. Arrian presents the *Discourses* virtually as a literal record of Epictetus' conversations; we do not know if this is the case or if Arrian has exercised more creativity in writing them than he claims. See Introd., pp. viii–ix and n. 3; Dobbin, pp. xx–xxiii; Long, 39–41.

BOOK 1

1.1 For an illustrative reading of this Discourse, see Introd., pp. xxii–xxiii and nn. 43–4. Most of the figures cited are politicians who faced with equanimity punishment and ill-treatment by Roman emperors. Two of them (Thrasea Paetus and Helvidius Priscus) were adherents of Stoicism; but Epictetus extracts a Stoic message from all these cases. Stoics did not oppose imperial rule as such but resisted abuse of imperial power, especially when that made it impossible for other politicians to play their role honourably: see M. T. Griffin, *Seneca: A Philosopher in Politics* (Oxford, 1976; repr. 1992), 363–6; P. A. Brunt, 'Stoicism and the Principate', *Papers of the British School at Rome*, 43 (1975), 7–35.

1.1.10 *Zeus*: the father of the gods in the traditional Greek pantheon. Like other Stoics, Epictetus uses Zeus, God, or 'the gods' interchangeably. (There is no equivalent in Greek for the capitalized 'God'; 'God' or 'god' is simply the singular form of 'gods'. The capitalized 'God' is used in this translation in line with the normal English convention.) However, Epictetus has a preference for phrases suggesting monotheism, and is sometimes seen as having an unusually personal view of divinity, although this view has also been challenged. Epictetus often presents human rational agency or autonomy as a god-given faculty. See Introd., pp. xii–xiii, xvii–xix, and text to nn. 13, 28, 33, 35; also LS 46 and 54 on Stoic ideas on divinity.

1.1.19 *Lateranus*: Plautus Lateranus, consul designate in 65, was executed for his role in the Pisonian conspiracy against the emperor Nero.

1.1.20 *Epaphroditus*: a freedman (ex-slave) who became influential in the reigns of Nero (54–69) and Domitian (81–96); he owned, but subsequently freed, Epictetus (see Introd., p. vii and n. 1); we know nothing more about this incident.

1.1.26 *Thrasea*: Thrasea Paetus, consul in 56, a prominent opponent of Nero's tyranny, was condemned by Nero in 66 and then committed suicide.

1.1.27 *Rufus*: Musonius Rufus (*c*.30–*c*.101), the most famous Roman Stoic teacher in his day and Epictetus' teacher, challenges the ethical grounds on which Thrasea prefers death by suicide to exile. Stoic thinkers regarded suicide as an ethically valid response to situations in which one could no longer lead a good human life; but the precise conditions of a justified suicide were debated by them (LS 66 G–H). The late Roman Republic and early Empire saw a series of famous suicides, often linked with Stoic principles: see M. T. Griffin, 'Philosophy, Cato, and Roman Suicide', *Greece and Rome*, 33 (1986), 64–77, 192–202.

1.1.28 *Agrippinus*: a Roman senator who joined the Pisonian conspiracy against Nero in 66, was tried along with Thrasea, and was exiled: his estate in Aricia lay on his route to exile.

1.2 For an illustrative reading of this Discourse, see Introd., pp. xxiii–xxiv and nn. 45–7.

1.2.12 *Agrippinus*: see note on 1.1.28: Florus is unknown. Taking part in musical or dramatic festivals as a performer (as Nero did) was seen as demeaning by Roman senators and as inconsistent with the proper conduct of their role in life.

1.2.18 *purple*: the senatorial toga (Roman outer garment) was edged by a single purple stripe, thus distinguishing it from the normal adult toga. Agrippinus presents the exceptionally courageous response that is required by his assessment of his ethical character as analogous to this distinctive purple stripe (see also Helvidius Priscus in 22).

1.2.19 *Helvidius Priscus*: son-in-law of Thrasea Paetus (see note on 1.1.26), and praetor in 70; he challenged the authority of Vespasian (emperor 69–79) on Stoic grounds, and was executed around 75.

1.2.25 *genitals*: Greek athletes (all male) exercised and performed naked. The testicles, the mark of his status as a 'man' (26), were seen as integrally linked with from the proper performance of his role as athlete.

1.2.29 *beard*: the beard, relatively common among Greeks but not Romans, had been associated with philosophers at Rome since the mid-second century BC, and Epictetus presents it as inseparable from his philosophical role.

1.2.33 *Socrates*: famous Greek philosopher (469–399 BC), executed by the Athenian people because of his philosophical challenges to received religious and ethical beliefs. He was seen as an important influence on the evolution of Stoicism, and as one of the very few people who may have achieved the Stoic ideal state of wisdom. Epictetus gives Socrates a very prominent role as philosophical exemplar (see Long, ch. 3).

1.2.36 *not too bad*: translation suggested by Long, 240 n. 7; the alternative translation 'not better' makes less good sense, given Socrates' exceptional quality. See also *Handbook* 51.3.

1.2.37 *Milo*: a famous Greek athlete (sixth century BC).

1.3.1 *children of God*: Stoicism regularly presents human beings, by contrast with non-human animals, as sharing rational agency with God (or the gods); see note on 1.1.10.

1.3.3 *two elements*: the contrast between body and mind or reason does not reflect Stoic psychological theory, according to which the mind is a physical entity (LS 45 C–D, 53). Epictetus uses the contrast to mark an ethical distinction between using our rational agency in a way that reflects the aspiration towards virtue or in the opposite way (3–6); see Long, 158–62; Gill, 98–100.

1.4 The concept of ethical development is of fundamental importance in Stoicism, given their belief that all humans are capable of developing towards complete virtue, or 'wisdom'. Here, Epictetus focuses on the individual (rather than social) strand in development, seen as leading to the recognition that virtue alone is the only thing that is worth pursuing, by contrast with which other things are 'matters of indifference' (or 'externals', as Epictetus often puts it). He stresses to his students that studying Stoic ethical treatises is not just an academic exercise, but is intended to have a practical effect, namely, helping us to take forward our ethical development. See Introd., pp. ix–x, xiv–xv, and nn. 5–7, 19–22.

1.4.1 *rid himself of desire*: this advice reflects the Stoic belief that only virtue (and not the 'indifferents' that are the usual objects of desire) is a proper object of desire. Since most people, including Epictetus' students, do not yet understand fully what virtue is, they should avoid desire for the present—while still aiming at forming a better understanding of what is truly desirable. See 4.4.33; *Handbook* 2.2, 48.3; also Inwood, 119.

1.4.6 *Chrysippus*: (*c*.280–*c*.206 BC), third head of the Stoic school and the main systematizer of Stoic theory; author of many handbooks (all now lost), including *On Motivation* (14), which is relevant to the topic of this Discourse. Expounding the treatises of Stoic thinkers such as Chrysippus seems to have formed the main pedagogic activity in Epictetus' school.

1.4.13 *jumping-weights*: these were used by athletes to increase the length of a jump (thrown by the jumper in mid-air), and to develop muscles in training, which is referred to here.

1.4.16 *five denarii*: the price of an inexpensive book.

1.4.24 *My dear Crito*: Plato, *Crito* 43d; also cited in 1.29.18, 4.4.21; *Handbook* 53.3. Socrates' equanimity in the face of imprisonment and execution (by hemlock poisoning: 14.23) is compared favourably with the passionate grief of figures in Greek epic and tragedy such as Priam and Oedipus (25); on tragedy, see, further, 1.28.

1.4.29 *benefactor*: i.e. Chrysippus.

1.4.30 *Triptolemus*: the Greek mythical inventor of the plough and the first to sow grain.

1.5 There were two main branches of Scepticism (which denied the possibility of achieving knowledge) in antiquity, the Academic Sceptics and the Pyrrhonists (see LS 68–72). A typical Sceptic argument was denial of the difference between what is seen in dreams and in real life (6–7). In fact, the main target of this Discourse is not so much Scepticism as such but various mental attitudes, including Sceptical ones, that prevent someone from listening to reason. Epictetus seems most interested in the kind of ingrained defectiveness of character that holds one back from listening to good ethical advice and trying to improve (3, 5, 8–9).

1.6.1 *providence*: the belief that the natural universe was purposive and providentially shaped, rather than randomly formed, was maintained by Stoics as well as a number of other ancient philosophers, including Plato and Aristotle, though it was denied by the Epicureans (see LS 54; contrast LS 13). See D. Sedley, *Creationism and its Critics in Antiquity* (Berkeley, 2007).

1.6.10 *constitution*: rationality, exemplified here by the capacity for rational inference, was seen by Stoics as a distinctive capacity of (adult) human beings, by contrast with non-human animals. Subsequently, Epictetus stresses, rather, the distinctively human capacity for reflective understanding (12–22). This idea is linked with the initial claim about providence by suggesting that humans are uniquely capable of understanding the providential order in the universe (19–22). See Inwood, ch. 2.

1.6.23 *Phidias*: the huge gold-and-ivory statue of Zeus by the fifth-century BC sculptor Phidias was included in the Seven Wonders of the World in antiquity.

1.6.32 *Heracles*: a famous, semi-divine hero in Greek myth; the Labours of Heracles consisted largely of ridding the world of monsters and wicked men. Along with Odysseus (and philosophers such as Socrates and Diogenes the Cynic), he was sometimes seen as embodying the Stoic ideal of wisdom, as indicated in 34.

1.6.37 *'Bring on me . . . may happen'*: the human capacity to endure misfortune is presented as one of the distinctively human capacities provided by a divinely shaped universe (37–43).

1.7 Logic (or dialectic) formed one of the three main branches of philosophy in the Stoic curriculum; it continued to be important in Stoicism in the early Imperial period, and Epictetus is a prime source for logic in this period: see J. Barnes, *Logic in the Imperial Stoa* (Leiden, 1997), ch. 3, also appendix (on 1.7); P. Crivelli, 'Epictetus and Logic', in Scaltsas and Mason. Epictetus' attitude to logic is quite complex. Sometimes, as here, he stresses the inherent importance of logic as an exercise of human rationality and as a component in making progress towards complete wisdom (for this as a standard Stoic idea, see LS 33 B–D; Long, *Stoic Studies* (Cambridge, 1996), ch. 4); see also 1.17, 2.25. Elsewhere, he emphasizes that logic is only of value if it is integrated with ethics as part of the search for a good human life (1.18, 2.23.41; *Handbook* 52).

1.7.17 *If the premises remain*: here, the reference is to premises that are time-dependent and no longer valid as the argument proceeds (over time).

1.7.32 *Rufus*: Musonius Rufus, Epictetus' Stoic teacher; the Capitol was one of the main political buildings in Rome (it burnt down twice in 69 and 80, during the period in which he may have been studying with Musonius).

1.8 See note on 1.7. The focus here is on the idea that training in dialectic (which, in Stoicism, included both formal logic and rhetoric), while valuable, has its dangers. It can distract us from trying to take forward our ethical development and can encourage students to take undue pride in acquiring these skills (5–10). The fact that Plato was a master of verbal expression, both logical and rhetorical, does not mean that such skill is an essential part of being a philosopher (11–16).

1.8.1–3 *enthymemes*: these are incomplete forms of syllogistic reasoning, commonly used in rhetorical contexts.

1.8.11 *Plato*: c.429–347 BC, famous Greek philosopher, whose many dialogues show a mastery of dialectical and rhetorical skill.

Hippocrates: fifth-century BC founder of Greek medicine, traditionally regarded as the author of many treatises, of which some show skill in argumentation or style.

1.8.14 *if I could be counted*: Epictetus refers to his own lameness, while modestly disowning the status of being a philosopher.

1.9 Epictetus explores a series of ideas centred on the capacity for rational agency and autonomy that human beings have in common with gods (or the divine principle in nature). One is the idea of the universe as a community or city shared by gods and humans (1–7; cf. LS 57 F(3), 67 L). Another is that our possession of rationality enables us to escape from subjection to bodily needs (1.9.8–15, 26), and to cope with adverse circumstances (18–21, 27–34), by understanding that all we really need for happiness depends on us, and not on acquiring 'indifferents'. Socrates' attitude is taken as exemplary in this respect (16–17, 22–24).

1.9.16 *You must wait for God*: this refers to Plato, *Phaedo* 61b–62e, where Socrates presents suicide as a crime against God, unless we are given a signal that death is necessary. In general, Stoics thought that suicide was sometimes a justified response to a situation in which one could no longer lead a good human life (LS 66G–H); but the suicide should not be 'without proper reason', as Epictetus puts it (17).

1.9.24 *abandon it*: this paraphrases Plato, *Apology* 29c, 28d–e, where Socrates insists he will persist in his 'divine mission' of philosophizing even at the risk of death.

1.9.28 *happened to me*: this incident, and the exchange between Musonius Rufus and the young Epictetus in 29–32, illustrate that human beings can (and should) respond to adversity by recognizing that the pathway to happiness lies in their own hands, not those of others.

1.10 This Discourse takes its starting point from a long-standing debate in Graeco-Roman intellectual life about the respective merits of the practical (or active) and the theoretical life. Epictetus begins by recalling the case of an older man who, when back in the hurly-burly of Rome, could not maintain his resolution to devote himself to the contemplative, rather than practical, life (2–6). Then, in line with earlier Stoic thinking on this topic, he insists that philosophy is just as much a form of action as business or politics, and deserves just as much energy and application, among the young as well as the old (7–13).

1.10.8 *due to read over in my lessons*: this passage, along with other evidence, indicates the normal practice in Stoic, and other, philosophical schools in this period; the teacher and his students would discuss and explain a given text, e.g. a treatise by Chrysippus (see 1.4).

1.11 This Discourse is relatively unusual in presenting a full-scale dialogue between Epictetus and a fully characterized interlocutor, an anxious father who could not bear to stay at his daughter's bedside during her illness. The dialogue is closely based on the Socratic method of *elenchus* (systematic refutation by cross-examination), which is presented in many early Platonic dialogues (5–26; see also Long, 77–8). The later part of the dialogue (27–38) focuses on an idea often seen as central for Socratic, as well as Stoic, psychology, namely, that people always act in line with their beliefs about what is for the best, even when they see themselves as overwhelmed by their passions. See Plato, *Protagoras* 355a–357e; 1.18.1; *Handbook* 42; also T. Brennan, 'Stoic Moral Psychology', in B. Inwood (ed.), *The Cambridge Companion to the Stoics* (Cambridge, 2003), ch. 10, esp. 265–9.

The refutation of the father centres on the idea that a course of action cannot be natural unless it is also rational (8, 17–18), and on leading him to see that his response in abandoning his daughter was not rational, and is therefore not natural (24–6). The dialogue presupposes central Stoic ideas, that parental love is a prime expression of the natural human desire to benefit others, and that this desire is appropriately expressed in engagement in family and communal roles and relationships (LS 57 E–F; also Introd., p. xv and n. 20).

1.11.28 *precise explanation*: Epictetus might have various points of Stoic theory in mind here, including their belief that most human emotions are based on false judgements about value and lead to confused and contradictory states of mind. See LS 65; Brennan, 'Stoic Moral Psychology' (cited in note to 1.11), 269–74; Gill, 251–60.

1.11.31 *Achilles . . . Patroclus*: Achilles' intense grief for his dead friend Patroclus in Homer, *Iliad* 18, had been criticized in Plato, *Republic* 388a–b.

1.12 This Discourse centres on the idea that 'following God' (often taken in Greek philosophy as a formula for the goal of human life) consists in accepting things that happen to us as the inevitable result of divine providential power. This is not an abandonment of freedom; true freedom lies not in wishing for whatever we want to happen, but in rational acceptance of what does happen and exercising our god-given ability for rational agency in things that fall within our power (9–12, 15, 32–5). See Introd., p. xvii and nn. 28–30.

1.12.1–3 *With regard to the gods*: the survey in 1–3 outlines possible ancient positions rather than specifying the ideas of different schools. However, the ideas are usually seen as those of (1) atheists (a rare view in antiquity), (2) Epicureans, (3) Aristotle; (4) and (5) may be Stoic, though (5) was also sometimes ascribed to Socrates.

1.12.3 *'Not a movement . . . escapes you'*: quotation from Homer, *Iliad* 10.279–80, Odysseus speaking to his patron god, Athena.

1.12.13 *Dion*: (and Theon) are often used as stock names in Greek philosophy.

1.12.23 *Socrates*: in Plato's *Crito*, Socrates is presented as refusing to be helped to escape from prison and, in *Phaedo* 98d–99a, he accepts his imprisonment, even while regarding his sentence as unjustified.

1.13 The title and opening of this Discourse stresses the Stoic idea that all aspects of human life, including eating one's meals, give scope for acting virtuously or badly. However, most of the passage focuses on proper treatment of slaves. It reflects the Stoic view that the institution of slavery is a matter of convention or law, and that in reality all human beings are equal in their possession of reason. As elsewhere in Stoic writings, this leads to the advice to treat slaves humanely rather than advocacy of the abolition of slavery.

1.13.5 *laws of the dead*: formal laws are treated as relating only to the body, or the 'corpse', as Epictetus sometimes puts it (1.19.9), not the mind or reason shared by all human beings.

1.14 Epictetus supports the idea of divine omniscience by referring to the Stoic doctrine that all natural processes are permeated by God (identified with the 'active cause' in nature; LS 46 A–C, 47 O–R) (1–6). He also argues that if human minds can grasp many 'impressions' (perceptions and thoughts) at once, God will be able to do the same on a cosmic scale (7–9). Human beings share with God the possession of rationality, the basis of moral agency; this is presented as a divinity, or 'guardian spirit' (*daimōn*) (for this idea, see LS 63 C(3–4), based on Chrysippus).

1.14.10 *shadow of the earth*: i.e. the part of the earth covered by night at any one time.

1.15 Epictetus advises those having difficulties in interpersonal relationships to focus on what lies within their own agency, rather than responding with anger, which is a misguided emotion, according to Stoicism (LS 65 E). Philosophy can help each person aim to bring the 'ruling centre' (or mind) into accordance with nature, that is, to achieve virtue (LS 63 A–C; 1.14.3–4), although the progress towards virtue naturally takes time; indeed, perhaps a lifetime (7–8).

1.16 Another discussion of divine providence (see 1.6), with some new elements. The fact that other animals do not need clothing and shoes shows divine providential care for humans, since we do not need to provide this for them (1–6). Also, the decorative features of human bodies, such as the presence or absence of a beard, serve a providential function by differentiating the genders (10–14). An appropriate response to divine providence is to celebrate it in philosophical discourse, which is a kind of hymn (15–21), like the Stoic 'Hymn to Zeus' of the second Stoic head, Cleanthes (LS 54 I). On the Stoic anthropocentric view of divine providence implied here, see LS 54 N, P, 57 F(7); also R. Sorabji, *Human Minds and Animal Morals* (London, 1993), ch. 10; D. Sedley, *Creationism and its Critics in Antiquity* (Berkeley, 2007), 231–8.

1.17 In this Discourse, couched as a dialogue between Epictetus and an unspecified interlocutor, the main focus is on the idea of the self-sufficiency of human reason. Epictetus begins with a formally conducted argument that the only thing that can analyse reason is reason itself (1–3), and then presents logic as the proper vehicle for this process of analysis (6–12). He also criticizes the tendency to rely on interpreters (even philosophical interpreters such as Chrysippus), rather than on our own judgement (13–18). All that interpretation (for instance, by means of divination) can show is a truth we could find out for ourselves, namely, that we have an inalienable, god-given capacity for rational agency (20–9). On the latter theme, see Introd., pp. xii–xiv.

1.17.6 *logic*: in fact, we find various orders of subjects in the Stoic curriculum, suggesting that there was no fixed order (LS 26 B–E), and Epictetus sometimes presents logic as the last subject to be tackled (e.g. 3.2.5–6).

1.17.11 *Cleanthes*: the first three heads of the Stoic school were Zeno (334–262), Cleanthes (331–232), and Chrysippus (*c*.280–206) (all BC).

1.17.12 *Antisthenes* (*c*.450–360 BC), a follower of Socrates; for his stress on definition in education, see D.L. 6.17.

Socrates: as presented in Plato's early dialogues, his enquiries focused on the definition of terms, especially the nature of the virtues; see also Xenophon, *Memorabilia* 1.1.16.

1.17.14 *all . . . do wrong . . . against their will*: one of the famous paradoxical ideas associated with Socrates (e.g. Plato, *Protagoras* 395d; Xenophon, *Memorabilia* 3.9.5), adopted by Stoicism; see also 1.18, 1.28.

1.7.16 *in Latin*: the most widely spoken language in the Roman Empire, so Epictetus could ask almost anyone for help in interpretation.

1.17.20 *entrails*: examining the entrails of sacrificial victims was a standard means of establishing the will of the gods (e.g. whether they were favourable to the sacrifice or not) in Greek and Roman religious practice.

1.18 This Discourse explores the implications of the Stoic theory of value for interpersonal relations. All people aim at what they think is beneficial for them (1–2), and wrongdoing is a matter of error, like being blind or deaf in one's mind; so we should pity such people rather than being angry at them (10). If we are angry, this shows that we are attaching value to external things, such as clothes or household items, rather than our own state of mind and character (11–17). We should train ourselves, like an athlete, with a view to becoming invincible to challenges of all kinds to our good character (18–23). Epictetus assumes Stoic thinking on human psychology and emotions (see T. Brennan, 'Stoic Moral Psychology', in B. Inwood (ed.), *The Cambridge Companion to the Stoics* (Cambridge, 2003), 265–74). Epictetus develops the implications of this theory for our attitudes to other people (see also 1.28), followed by Marcus Aurelius, *Meditations* 2.1, 5.28 (see Long, 250–2).

1.18.9 *pity . . . rather than hate*: pity is generally seen by Stoics as a (misguided) emotion or passion; but here pity is presented as a generalized and rational response to human error and thus justified.

1.18.15 *iron lamp*: see also 1.29.31. This anecdote made Epictetus' lamp quite famous, and it was later sold as a souvenir of the philosopher for 3,000 drachmas (a large sum: see Dobbin, 171)—which showed a quite different attitude to material possessions from the one Epictetus was recommending!

1.19 Here, Epictetus argues that we can be impervious to the power of tyrants and other powerful people once we realize that their power does not extend to what is really important, our state of mind and ethical character (see 1.1.21–5; 1.29.5–8). It is natural to pursue what we see as beneficial for us; this is basic to the Stoic idea of natural development (conceived as 'appropriation', or 'attachment', *oikeiōsis*, 15), although this is also compatible with the (equally natural) desire to benefit other people (12–13). However, it is when we make mistakes about the real nature of what benefits us that we attach value to powerful people and trivial things such as political status (16–29). On Epictetus' special interest in the doctrine of development as 'appropriation', including the interplay between the personal and social strands of this process, see Introd., pp. xv–xvi and nn. 22–3.

1.19.6 *Fever*: there were three temples to Fever in Rome; prayer to Fever was designed to make one immune from it.

1.19.11 *sun . . . for its own sake*: the sun and other heavenly bodies were conceived as living divinities in Stoicism; the sun nourished itself by drawing in air and fire in its movement across the sky (Dobbin, 180).

1.19.12 *Rain-giver and Fruit-bringer*: Stoics appeal to such stock epithets of Zeus as proof that gods benefit other inhabitants of the universe (on Stoic theology, see LS 54).

1.19.17 *Felicio*: a common name for a slave or (here) freedman.

1.19.24 *tribune*: an important Roman political magistrate.

1.19.26 *priesthood of Augustus*: in Roman culture, priesthoods were public or political appointments. Augustus (63 BC–AD 14), first emperor of Rome, was deified after his death and had a continuing cult, which was especially important in Nicopolis, a city he founded, after his victory at nearby Actium in 31 BC.

1.20 This Discourse begins with some of Epictetus' favourite themes, that reason examines itself and that the capacity to examine our impressions is a crucial function of reason (1–6; see also 1.1.1–13); this is compared with the assayer's skill in testing the validity of coins (7–10). Epictetus stresses that this process of examination is necessarily a long and demanding one, in part because of the many different views put forward about the proper goal (*telos*) of a human life, which are presented here as arguments about our essence or most important part (13–17). He focuses on Epicurus, whose ethical position was often contrasted to that of Stoicism, since he saw pleasure, including the pleasure of the body, as constituting human happiness (LS 21). Epicurus' real position is much more subtle and credible than presented here by Epictetus (see Gill, 100–26).

1.21 Here, Epictetus briefly states the common idea (see also 3.23) that adopting Stoic ethics makes you independent from concern with what other people think about you, since you realize that achieving what matters depends on you yourself.

1.21.4 *mad*: Stoics describe as 'mad' or 'fools' all those who fall short of being wise, although, strictly, this includes virtually all of us.

1.22 It was standard Stoic doctrine that all human beings naturally form certain beliefs, or 'preconceptions'; this claim forms part of the Stoic defence of the possibility of knowledge against Sceptics. Epictetus, more unusually, insists that disagreement results from the application of these shared preconceptions to particular cases (1–8). He then defines education as learning how to apply preconceptions properly, for instance, recognizing that we should only call 'good' things that are within our power, and not 'externals' (9–16). Although he acknowledges that this restricted account of 'good' will arouse criticism from many people, he ridicules the type of person who makes this objection (17–21). On preconceptions and Epictetus' treatment of the idea, see LS 40 (esp. S) and LS i. 253; also Dobbin, 188–90; on Stoic ideas of 'good' and the contrast with 'indifferents', see LS 58, 60.

1.22.5 *quarrel . . . arose*: the quarrel between Greek leaders that starts the action of the whole poem in Homer, *Iliad* 1, is used as an illustration of Epictetus' general point.

1.23 Epictetus criticizes Epicurus for failing to acknowledge the natural human instinct to benefit others, including family and community. The root cause of Epicurus' mistake is, he suggests, his core claim that pleasure, including bodily pleasure, is the human good (1; see also 1.20.17). Although Epictetus' critique has some basis in comments made by Epicurus expressing caution about familial and political involvement, Epictetus caricatures the Epicurean view, presenting it as systematically antisocial. Epictetus judges Epicurus by reference to the Stoic thesis that the desire to benefit others and to engage in familial and communal life forms a natural part of human development (see Introd., p. xv). For a fuller and more nuanced account of Epicurean thinking on society, see LS 22; E. Brown, 'Politics and Society', in J. Warren (ed.), *The Cambridge Companion to Epicureanism* (Cambridge, 2009); also Dobbin, 194–200.

1.23.10 *exposed*: the infanticide of unwanted (or defective) newborn children was not normally seen as criminal in antiquity.

1.24 Cynicism, a philosophical movement advocating a simple life (following nature, not convention) founded by Diogenes (mid-fourth century BC), influenced Stoicism from its origins. Epictetus often presents Diogenes as an exemplar of the ideal wise person. Here, he stresses that the austere lifestyle and indifference to loss of possessions and status recommended by Cynicism represent a model for Stoics to follow too. See 3.22; also W. Desmond, *Cynics* (Stocksfield, 2008); M. Schofield, 'Epictetus on Cynicism', in Scaltsas and Mason, esp. 75–80 on the 'scouting' metaphor in 3, 6.

1.24.11 *oil-flask . . . knapsack*: typical simple possessions of the itinerant Cynic, but also typical normal 'hand-luggage' of any ancient traveller.

1.24.12 *toga*: the Roman outer garment, with broad purple hem for senators, narrow hem for equestrians (wealthy citizens, the next class down from senators), and plain for other citizens.

1.24.16 *'Hang the palace . . . receive me?'*: the first line is from an unknown tragedy; the second is line 1390 from Sophocles' *Oedipus the King* (see 'Oedipus' in 18).

1.24.20 *door stands open*: for suicide (see note on 1.1.27).

1.25   Epictetus explores the implications of the key Stoic claim, that good
          and bad fall within what is up to us, whereas everything else is a matter
          of indifference (1). He maintains that recognizing the force of this claim
          renders more detailed instructions unnecessary (3–6). Life is compared
          to a game; what matters is playing the game well, even if the rules are
          dictated by forces outside our control (7–11). Similarly in logic, even if
          the hypotheses or premisses are set by others, it is up to us to decide
          what inferences we accept (11–13). It is also up to us how long we
          remain within the game of life, since suicide is always an option (18–
          25). Typically, the difficulties we experience in life derive from the false
          value we place on externals (26–31).

1.25.8   *Saturnalia*: a Roman festival involving play-acting and the election of
          a 'king' to preside over the festival.

1.25.10 *Briseis*: another reference to the quarrel at the start of Homer's *Iliad*
          (see also 1.22.5–8).

1.25.13 *another*: i.e. Zeus (see 3), who has given us choice that cannot be com-
          pelled.

1.25.20 *Gyara*: an island in the Aegean used as a place of exile in the early
          Roman Empire.

1.25.27 *senators*: in Roman theatres, senators had special seats at the front of
          the audience.

1.26   This is another Discourse on the importance of training in logic as
          a basis for living a good life (see 1.7, 1.8, 1.17). Logic offers us a neutral
          context for learning to reason correctly, which can then be applied to
          the more difficult area of ethical life (3–4, 10, 14, 17).

1.26.5   *parents*: the arguments in 5–7 are designed to show that training in logic
          is needed to address the question what constitutes a useful education.

1.26.13 *student*: evidently, in Epictetus' school a student might be set a task by
          another, more senior, student; Epictetus suggests that both of them
          have shown different weaknesses in reasoning.

1.26.18 *unexamined life*: see Plato, *Apology* 38a.

1.27   It is difficult to determine which of our impressions (perceptions and
          thoughts) are true, and this leads some thinkers to adopt a Sceptical
          position (1–2). However, Epictetus urges us to tackle this problem by
          counteracting plausible (but false) ethical ideas with ones that are better
          grounded, thus avoiding the passions that stem from misguided beliefs
          (3–14). Tackling the arguments of the Sceptics against common sense
          is a challenge that Epictetus declines; their claims are contrary to plain
          facts, and there are more pressing (ethical) problems to address (15–21).

1.27.2   *Pyrrhonists and Academics*: the main Sceptic schools in ancient thought
          (see 1.27.15 and 1.5; also LS 68–72).

1.27.8   *Sarpedon*: this passage paraphrases Homer, *Iliad* 12.322–8.

1.28   The main focus here is on the idea that we should examine our 'impressions' as carefully in ethical questions as in factual ones (1–6), and try to establish sound criteria and apply them appropriately (28–33). When people go wrong in their impressions (Epictetus cites notable cases from Greek tragedy and epic), we should not be angry with them but pity and correct them (7–13; see note on 1.18). We also need to recognize that the true 'tragedy' in such cases is the original ethical mistake and not the material destruction and loss of life that results (14–27, 31–2). See also A. A. Long, *Stoic Studies* (Cambridge, 1996), 277–81; Long, 76–7.

1.28.7   *master of my plans*: Euripides, *Medea* 1078–9, lines often read as showing *akrasia* (giving way to emotions against one's better judgement), but interpreted by the Stoics as showing bad judgement in the face of competing ethical claims. See C. Gill, 'Did Chrysippus Understand Medea?', *Phronesis*, 28 (1983), 136–49; Gill, 258–9.

1.28.13   *Odyssey too*: the seduction of Helen, wife of Menelaus (king of Sparta in Greece), by Paris, prince of Troy, caused the Trojan War, which forms the background of Homer's *Iliad* and *Odyssey*.

1.28.24   *to make war*: Epictetus summarizes key incidents in the plot of Homer's *Iliad*, especially Achilles' anger with Agamemnon at the seizure of his prize-bride Briseis (books 1 and 9), and his grief at the resulting death of his close friend Patroclus (book 17).

1.28.32   *Hippolytus*: Epictetus refers to fifth-century Athenian tragedies, of which we still have two plays by Sophocles called *Oedipus* (probably *Oedipus the King* is meant), and Euripides' *Hippolytus*, though the other two named are lost.

1.29   This is the longest Discourse in Book 1 and the fourth longest in all four books. The main theme is that what really matters in human life is within our power and that what other people have power over, such as our body and life, are matters of relative indifference. Socrates is taken as an exemplar whose actions and attitudes express this idea (1–29, including 16–21 on Socrates). This does not mean we should necessarily identify ourselves fully with our situation; we should see our specific context or role as providing the vehicle of progress towards virtue (33–49). Epictetus concedes that not everyone will accept these principles, although this does not invalidate them (30–2, 64–6).

1.29.18   *so be it*: paraphrase of Plato, *Apology* 30c and *Crito* 43d (on the significance of Socrates for Epictetus, see Long, ch. 3).

1.29.21   *my lamp*: see 1.18.15.

1.29.31   *Saturnalia*: see note on 1.25.8.

1.29.41   *masks, and high boots, and robes*: Epictetus uses the standard costume of Greek tragedy to make the point that we should not identify ourselves unreflectively with our role and context.

1.29.66   *a child*: Epictetus refers to Plato's depiction of Socrates' calm response to his impending death by hemlock poisoning (see *Phaedo* 116d, 117d).

1.30   Epictetus restates his usual emphasis on the idea that human agency
        is invulnerable to external circumstances by presenting a dialogue
        with God (the 'another' in 1, as in 1.25.13). The dialogue stresses that
        learning this lesson in school will be invaluable for Epictetus' students
        in the rigours of future life.

BOOK 2

2.1   Epictetus argues that if we recognize the importance of focusing on
        what is 'up to us', this will make us cautious about things that fall within
        our choice and confident about things that do not, such as death—
        which is the reverse of the conventional way of thinking about such
        things (1–20). The second half maintains (partly through dialogue
        form) that true freedom is freedom from misguided passions such
        as fear (21–9; see also 4.1), and that the aim of philosophical study
        should be to gain the kind of caution and confidence that the Discourse
        recommends.

2.1.8   *the nets*: beaters used to drive deer into nets by stretching a rope with
        brightly coloured feathers across openings in the woods.

2.1.13 *'To die . . . dishonour'*: a verse from tragedy of unknown authorship
        (Nauck, frag. adesp. 88).

2.1.15 *bogeys*: a reference to Plato, *Phaedo* 77e.

2.1.19 *stands open*: suicide, which was seen by Stoics as a reasonable course of
        action under extreme circumstances (see LS 66 G–H).

2.1.26 *turned his slave around*: this ritual, as well as paying 5 per cent (or
        'a twentieth') of the slave's value in tax, formed part of the legal process
        of freeing a slave.

2.1.32 *Socrates write*: an initially puzzling comment since Socrates (like
        Epictetus himself) wrote nothing, though other writers presented
        his philosophical dialogues. But Epictetus goes on to explain that by
        'writing' he means that Socrates used his characteristic method of
        systematic, logical cross-examination (*elenchus*) on others, or on himself
        if there was no one else there. See Long, 73–86, esp. 73, on Epictetus'
        use of Socratic method in the *Discourses*.

2.2   Epictetus argues that if you keep firmly in mind that what matters fun-
        damentally is 'up to us', you will not be anxious if summoned to court
        as a defendant. He takes Socrates as an exemplar, tried in 399 BC for
        corrupting the young and for impiety, but presented by Plato and
        Xenophon as emotionally undisturbed.

2.2.8   *reminded Socrates*: this passage is loosely based on Xenophon, *Apology* 2–3.

2.2.15 *Anytus and Meletus*: two of the prosecutors at Socrates' trial (the refer-
        ence is to Plato, *Apology* 30c). This passage is also referred to in
        1.29.18, 3.3.21.

2.3   Epictetus maintains that testing whether a person is good or bad is much more difficult than testing the validity of coins (such as the Greek silver coin, the drachma, 2–3), or of logical arguments (syllogisms, 4–5).

2.3.1 *Diogenes*: the Cynic, often used by Epictetus as a good exemplar, like Socrates (see also 3.22).

2.4 In Stoic political and social theory we find a combination of radical (or Cynic) and more conventional strands, and both of these appear also in the *Discourses* (see LS 67; Long, 57–64, 233–44). However, here, the interlocutor, already known as an adulterer (1), cites the more radical Stoic ideas opportunistically (8–9) to excuse his actions, and his excuses are briskly rejected by Epictetus.

2.4.8 *women common property*: an idea found in our evidence for the *Republic* of Zeno, founder of Stoicism (LS 67 B(4)) and also in Plato, *Republic* 457d–464b.

worthy of Socrates: Socrates is presented as taking part in symposia (similar to modern dinner-parties) by Plato and Xenophon; as Socrates is a moral exemplar for Epictetus, the comment here is sarcastic.

2.4.9 *the citizens*: for the idea of the state as a theatre shared by everyone (but still compatible with the validity of private property), see LS 57 F(7).

2.4.10 *Archedemus*: either a Stoic philosopher from Tarsus or a commentator on Aristotle's *Rhetoric*, but in either case not a well-known writer.

2.5 This Discourse discusses a central theme in Stoic ethics: that what matters, ultimately, in human life is not obtaining so-called good things such as health and property (in Stoic terms, 'indifferents') but doing so in a way that is compatible with acting virtuously. The project of trying to live a virtuous life is compared with playing a game well, even if we cannot determine the outcome of the game. Although it is natural for us to prefer health to disease, a broader understanding of the place of humanity in nature should lead us to accept that illness and death are also integral parts of living a complete human life. See LS 58, 64; also Introd., pp. xiv–xv and nn. 19, 22.

2.5.18 *Socrates*: the following passage paraphrases Plato, *Apology* 27a–e, in which Socrates challenges one of his prosecutors (Anytus) about the accusation of impiety made against him. Socrates' bravery in court is taken to show that he knows how to play the game of life well even in extreme circumstances.

2.5.24 *the foot*: for this image, which goes back to Chrysippus, a leading third-century BC theorist of Stoicism, see also 2.6.10, 2.10.4.

2.6 The theme here is similar to 2.5, though with greater stress on the (apparently) negative circumstances we may have to accept as the consequence of trying to lead a virtuous human life.

2.6.9 *Chrysippus*: see note on 2.5.24.

2.6.15 *Chrysantas*: see Xenophon, *Cyropaedeia* 4.1.3. By stopping his hand in response to the order to retreat, he consciously left himself open to a counter-attack by his intended victim.

2.6.26 *emulating Socrates*: according to Plato, *Phaedo* 60d–61b, Socrates wrote hymns in prison in response to a dream while awaiting his execution.

2.7   Some Stoics argued for the validity of divination (prophesying the future by examining the livers of sacrificial victims or by the behaviour of birds), on the ground that it was compatible with the Stoic theory of divine providence and determinism (LS 42 C–E). However, Epictetus takes a robustly ethical, and equally Stoic, attitude to divination, maintaining that divination cannot establish what is really good or bad, which depends on the exercise of rational choice (see 1.17.18–24).

2.7.8   *Gratilla*: the wife of a Roman senator, exiled by Domitian, emperor 81–96, generally regarded as tyrannical in his behaviour.

2.8   This Discourse treats the idea that human beings are (potentially) good in a way that non-human animals are not, because they alone have the capacity for reason, which is shared with gods. This is a standard Stoic theme (cf. LS 54 N–P, 63 D–E); but Epictetus gives special emphasis to the idea that our reason is an internal god (11–14; see also Long, 142–7).

2.8.18 *Phidias*: a famous fifth-century BC sculptor who designed images of Athena for the Parthenon in Athens, and Zeus for Olympia, the latter holding a symbol of victory (20).

2.8.26 *never deceives*: spoken by Zeus in Homer, *Iliad* 1.526.

2.9   The first part of this Discourse (1–12) develops the theme of 2.8, that to try to act virtuously is to express our distinctively human nature. The second part (13–22) stresses that being a Stoic is not just an academic exercise, but a matter of embedding Stoic ethical principles in your life and character.

2.9.8   *complex proposition*: logical propositions only fulfil their function when they are taken as a whole; and the same applies to the ethical life of human beings (9–10).

2.9.20 *baptized*: this might suggest that Epictetus has Christians in mind (with whom Jews were often confused at this time), but both Jews and Christians used baptism as an initiation ritual.

2.9.22 *rock of Ajax*: in Homer, *Iliad* 7.264, Ajax used a large rock to beat down Aeneas.

2.10   The first theme here (1–13) is that we should conceive our ethical life as combining the role of a human being (a rational and potentially virtuous agent) with our specific social or family role; for this Stoic idea, see 1.2 and Cicero, *On Obligations* 1.107–25; also Long, 232–44. The second theme is that loss of good ethical character or virtue is the only real loss, and is a harm that we impose on ourselves.

2.11   The Stoics believed that all human beings naturally form 'preconceptions' (*prolēpseis*) about fundamental ideas such as good, which provide the basis for forming a true understanding of these ideas. Disagreements between different people about these notions (13) are taken by Sceptics as showing that knowledge of the truth cannot be found. Epictetus, however, explains disagreement as stemming from the failure to apply our preconceptions appropriately in specific cases (7–12). The role of philosophy is to help us to examine these ideas systematically and form a true understanding of them (which, for Epictetus, means rejecting the Epicurean conception of what is good) (13–24). See also 1.22; LS 40 N–T; Long, 79–80, 102–3.

2.12 Epictetus takes Socrates as his model of how to engage people in argument in a way that enables them to reflect usefully on how they should live. As well as referring explicitly to Xenophon's *Symposium* (15), the Discourse alludes to Plato's *Gorgias* 474a, 472c (5). It also refers to Socrates' method of systematic cross-examination (6–11) and to the theme that we should only rely on the judgement of someone who has moral expertise (17–24; see Plato, *Crito* 47–8; *Protagoras* 312–13). See also Long, 86–9.

2.12.16 *'With sure skill . . . a great quarrel'*: quotes Hesiod, *Theogony* 87.

2.13 Epictetus claims that if anyone exhibits anxiety, this shows that he has not realized that what matters fundamentally is 'up to us', and does not depend on other people (10–11). Recognizing this fact enables us to confront anyone, however powerful, without anxiety, a point illustrated by the way in which certain philosophers behaved in their encounters with important rulers.

2.13.2 *lyre-player*: the lyre (*kithara*) was played by singers to accompany their songs, like a modern guitar.

2.13.13 *'Shift . . . other'*: Homer, *Iliad* 13.281.

2.13.14 *Zeno . . . Antigonus*: Zeno was the founder of Stoicism, and Antigonus a third-century BC king of Macedon, which dominated Greece at that time. For this incident, see D.L. 7.6.

2.13.24 *as a slave*: this passage refers to Socrates' bravery in defying the Thirty Tyrants, who governed Athens in 404–3 BC (see Plato, *Apology* 32c–e) and in his trial and in prison (shown in Plato's *Apology*, *Crito*, and *Phaedo*). It also refers to the indomitable attitude shown by Diogenes the Cynic in confronting Philip and Alexander (rulers of Macedon in the late fourth century BC), and the pirates who captured him (see D.L. 6.38, 43, 74).

2.13.26 *'In you . . . state'*: a verse quotation of unknown origin.

2.14 This Discourse is presented as being spoken to Naso (perhaps the Julius Naso mentioned in Pliny's *Letters* 4.6, 5.21, 6.6, 6.9), a man who is experienced in warfare and politics but not philosophy (17–18). The first part offers an overview of key Stoic themes in ethics and the interface between ethics and the study of nature (7–13), while the latter part refers to Stoic ideas about divine providence (25–7) (see Introd., p. xvi–xvii and nn. 28–30).

2.14.23 *festival*: versions of this comparison, which was traced back to the fifth-century thinker Pythagoras, are common in Hellenistic and Roman thought; Epictetus uses it to underline the idea of divine providence (see also 1.6.19–21).

2.15 This rather straightforward Discourse maintains that tenacity of purpose is only admirable if the original decision is well judged. Epictetus alludes to some recurrent Stoic themes: that suicide can be reasonable under certain circumstances (6; see LS 66 G–H); that virtue expresses itself in consistency of judgement and character (1–2; see LS 61 A); and that virtue or wisdom is like health, or 'good tone or sinew', whereas folly is like sickness, or 'bad tone or sinew' (2–3, 15–17, 20; see also LS 65 R–T).

2.16 Epictetus here offers extended treatment of his recurrent theme that what matters fundamentally is 'up to us', rather than 'externals' (see Introd., p. xii–xiii and n. 14).

2.16.17 *slept in a temple*: 'incubation' with the hope of having a prophetic vision or dream was a common Greek and Roman religious practice, especially in the cult of Asclepius, god of healing; for Epictetus' criticism of divination, see note on 2.7.

2.16.30 *Dirce . . . Marcian aqueduct*: the fountain of Dirce was in Thebes (in Greece), and the Marcian aqueduct brought water to Rome.

2.16.31 *'The baths . . . Marcian water'*: this is a parody of Euripides, *Phoenician Women* 368.

2.16.33 *pieces of stone and a pretty rock*: refers to the Acropolis at Athens, and the Parthenon temple (see 32).

2.16.44 *Heracles*: the Greek hero performed his famous twelve labours at the command of King Eurystheus, who remained safely in his palace. Stoics used mythical heroes such as Heracles as prototypes of the wise person's wish to benefit humanity by virtuous action (e.g. Cicero, *On Ends* 3.66).

2.16.45 *Procrustes or Sciron*: robbers punished by the Athenian hero Theseus.

2.17 The main theme of this Discourse is that logic (or dialectic) can be helpful in taking forward our ethical progress, but only if approached in the right way and not as an end in itself. In this connection, Epictetus also refers to the importance of applying our preconceptions correctly (1–14; see also 1.22, 2.11), the three topics of practical ethics (15–16, 31–3), and Medea as an exemplar of moral error on a grand scale (19–22).

2.17.16 *first field*: a distinctive feature of Epictetus' thought is a three-topic programme of practical ethics. This consists in (1) studying the proper objects of desire; (2) guiding our motives to action towards appropriate actions, and (3) examining with care the impressions to which we should give assent. Logic is seen as especially helpful for the third topic or field. See also 31–3, 3.2.1–5; Introd., p. xvi and n. 26; Gill, 380–9.

2.17.20 *what do I care?*: Epictetus presents the decision of Euripides' Medea (*Medea* 791–6, paraphrased here) to kill her own children in revenge against the husband who had abandoned her as an example of a (massive) mistake in the first ethical topic, namely, determining the proper object of desire. Medea was a favourite exemplar of error in Stoic moral theory, from Chrysippus onwards; see 1.28.7–11; Gill, 258–9; Long, 76–7.

2.17.34 *"the Liar"*: a famous logical puzzle or paradox (see also 2.18.18, 2.21.17), discussed at length by Chrysippus; see Cicero, *Academica* 2.95–6; LS 37 I.

2.17.35–6 *Xenophon . . . Plato . . . Antisthenes*: well-known thinkers and writers of the fifth and fourth centuries BC. All three wrote Socratic dialogues, and Epictetus may have in mind comparisons between the different styles of these dialogues.

2.17.40 *Antipater and Archedemus*: the former was head of the Stoic school from *c*.152 to *c*.129 BC, and the latter was also a second-century BC Stoic thinker.

2.18 Epictetus stresses the importance of habit in training yourself to make your responses to experiences ('impressions') match your most profound convictions. An emphasis on habituation is characteristic of Platonic–Aristotelian, rather than Stoic, ethical thought in this period. But Epictetus has in view a purely cognitive or rational process, rather than the non-rational habituation stressed in Platonic–Aristotelian thought: see Gill, 130–8, 144–5.

2.18.17 *'the Master'*: a logical puzzle; see also 2.19.

2.18.18 *"the Liar" or "the Silent One"*: on 'the Liar', see note on 2.17.34; on the Silent One, see Cicero, *Academica* 2.93; Sextus Empiricus, *Against the Professors* 7.416.

2.18.20–1 *'Then whenever . . . wise and virtuous men'*: quotation based on Plato, *Laws* 854b.

2.18.22 *he won*: see Plato, *Symposium* 218a–219c (Socrates rejects the invitation to make love to the youthful and handsome Alcibiades).

Heracles: traditional founder and first victor at the Olympic Games.

pancratiasts: athletes taking part in an 'all-in' boxing and wrestling competition.

2.18.29 *sailors call upon the Dioscuri*: i.e. Castor and Pollux, patron gods of sailors and travellers in general.

2.18.32 *'One who delays . . . wrestling with ruin'*: quotation from Hesiod, *Works and Days* 413.

2.19 Here, Epictetus presents himself as able only to report the complex debate among earlier Stoic thinkers raised by the 'Master' argument (1–4, 8–9; see LS 38); in this respect he is like a *grammatikos* (teacher of language and literature) or literary historian (7–13). But in ethics it is not enough just to report the views of others; you have to embed the principles in your actions and attitudes if you are to be a true Stoic and not just a reporter of Stoic teachings (20–4, 29–34).

2.19.1 *Diodorus*: Diodorus Cronus, leader of the 'dialectical' school of philosophy (d. 284 BC), who taught Zeno, founder of Stoicism.

2.19.2 *Cleanthes . . . Antipater*: heads of the Stoic school in 262–232 BC and *c*.152–*c*.129, respectively.

2.19.5 *Panthoides*: early third-century BC member of the 'dialectical' school (criticized by Chrysippus).

2.19.7 *Hector . . . Priam . . . Paris . . . Deiphobus . . . Hecuba*: those named here are famous members of the Trojan royal family in Homer's *Iliad*.

Hellanicus: a Greek writer on history, myth, and ethnography, *c*.480–395 BC.

2.19.9 *Archedemus*: second-century BC Stoic (for the point made, see 2.19.1–6).

2.19.10 *island of Calypso*: mythical island; see Homer, *Odyssey* 5.1–268, 7.244–66.

2.19.13 *pleasure, pain*: the claim that only virtue is really good is a key principle of Stoic ethics (LS 58, 60–1).

2.19.14 *Diogenes*: head of the Stoic school, early to mid-second century BC. The point is the analogy between merely reporting literary facts and philosophical ideas (see note on 2.19). The suggestion that these ideas would really come from Hellanicus is just a joke.

2.19.20 *Epicureans . . . Peripatetics*: Epicureans claimed that pleasure, not virtue, formed the human good, and the Peripatetics, followers of Aristotle, maintained that things such as health and wealth were goods (not 'indifferents' as the Stoics thought) and that they made some contribution to happiness (LS 21, 24 K–L).

2.19.23 *Phidias*: see 2.19.26 and note on 2.8.18.

2.20 Epictetus supports the Stoic approach by arguing that both the Academic Sceptic and Epicurean philosophies are in various ways self-refuting. The Academic position attacked is that certain knowledge of truth is not achievable (1–5, 28–35); the Epicurean view attacked is that human beings do not have an in-built motive to benefit each other (as the Stoics maintained; LS 57 F) (6–21), and that gods do not provide moral norms and sanctions for human life (22–7). Epictetus presents a crude caricature of the other positions: see also 1.5, 1.23; and for better accounts of the other theories, see LS 22–3, 68–70.

2.20.17 *Orestes*: he is presented as pursued by the Furies in revenge for his murder of his mother Clytemnestra (e.g. in Aeschylus, *Oresteia*).

priests of Cybele: they were supposed to work themselves up into a frenzy and castrate themselves (see also 19).

2.20.26 *Lycurgus*: the traditional founder of Sparta's famously stable and ordered political system.

Thermopylae: site of a battle in which all three hundred Spartans defending a mountain pass against the Persians died bravely in 480 BC.

Athenians: the people of Athens twice abandoned their city rather than surrender to the Persians (480, 479 BC).

2.20.32 *Demeter . . . Persephone . . . Pluto*: these gods are selected here because Demeter and her daughter Persephone (and also Pluto, god of the underworld, who keeps Persephone underground in winter) are linked with the growth of food and seasonal renewal.

2.21   Starting from people's general reluctance to admit failings that are their own fault (1–7), Epictetus presents studying philosophy as, fundamentally, a practical activity, designed to enable someone to become an ethically better person, though this also depends on studying logic with the proper attitude (8–22).

2.21.22 *your humours*: Epictetus' use of medical language reflects the widespread idea in this period (adopted especially by the Stoics) that philosophy was a form of 'therapy' for misguided beliefs and emotions, which are presented as 'illnesses' (LS 65 L, O, R–S).

2.22   Epictetus maintains that the only secure basis for stable affection (*philia*, in Greek, covers both 'friendship' and affectionate feelings for one's family) is well-grounded moral understanding. Otherwise, conflict can arise with one's family and friends as people pursue what they see as beneficial for themselves and fail to recognize that what is really beneficial is good for both parties (18–21, 34–7). See LS 67 P; Introd., pp. xiv–xvi and nn. 19–23; Long, 198–9.

2.22.11 *'You wish . . . does not'*: quotation from Euripides, *Alcestis* 691.

2.22.14 *Where before . . . my desire too*: quotation from Euripides, *Phoenician Women* 621–2. The brothers Eteocles and Polynices fight for rule in Thebes after their father, Oedipus, blinds himself and goes into exile.

2.22.17 *beloved*: Hephaestion, Alexander's close friend, who died on campaign with him in 324 BC.

2.22.21 *'the right . . . common opinion'*: not an exact quotation (the closest parallel we have is Athenaeus 12.547a); see also LS 21 O–P.

2.22.22–3 *It was through ignorance . . . war broke out*: Epictetus refers to a series of historical wars in Greece and the Roman Empire, and then to the legendary Trojan War, started by the seduction of Menelaus' wife, Helen, by Paris (also called Alexander).

2.22.32 *came between them*: Eriphyle, won over by the bribe of a necklace, persuaded her husband to join Polynices in his attempt to gain the throne in Thebes (see note on 2.22.14).

2.22.36 *'no mind . . . deprived of the truth'*: quotation from Plato, *Sophist* 228c; also referred to in 1.28.4.

2.23   Rhetoric (or 'the faculty of expression'), along with logic, forms part of the branch of philosophy that the Stoics call dialectic. This Discourse expresses the standard Stoic view that rhetoric has value, but that it should, ultimately, be combined with ethics (and physics) to make up complete virtue (LS 31 B–D; also 26 A–E). Ethical virtue is presented here as the proper use of the capacity for choice (7–22), as often in the *Discourses*.

2.23.4 *vision can pass through it*: the Stoics saw vision and other senses as active, rather than passive, functions in which *pneuma* ('breath') originates from the ruling centre, or mind (LS 53 G–H).

2.23.21 *On the End . . . On the Canon*: these three works must have been on ethics, physics, and logic; they do not survive, though we have fragments of *On Nature* (which is probably what Epictetus means by *Physics*).

a philosopher's beard: see note on 1.2.29.

'*We're living . . . a happy one*': quotation from Epicurus' famous death-bed letter (LS 24 D). Stoic and Platonic critics of Epicurus claim that the courage and benevolence expressed in that letter are inconsistent with Epicurus' own ethical principles (e.g. Cicero, *On Ends* 2.98–9; Plutarch, *Moralia* 1089F–1090A, 1099D–E).

2.23.32 *Thersites . . . Achilles . . . Helen*: Thersites is described by Homer as unusually ugly (*Iliad* 2.216–19), whereas Achilles is presented as an exemplar of youthful good looks. Helen of Troy was famous for her exceptional beauty.

2.23.41 *Sirens*: enchanted women who lured people to their death by the beauty of their songs (Homer, *Odyssey* 12.39–54, 158–200).

2.23.42 '*Guide me . . . O Destiny*': quotation from Cleanthes' *Hymn to Zeus*; see also 3.22.95, 4.131, and *Handbook* 53, which cites three more lines. On the meaning of these lines for Cleanthes and Epictetus' use of them, see S. Bobzien, *Determinism and Freedom in Stoic Philosophy* (Oxford, 1998), 346–51.

2.23.44 *Demosthenes*: famous fourth-century BC orator, whose style was presented as exemplary.

2.24 Epictetus talks in a very critical way to someone whom he regards as lacking in understanding of what it means to be a good human being (11–12) and who has no serious interest in listening and responding to sound teaching on this subject, as is indicated by his words and appearance (4–5, 15–18, 28–9).

2.24.21–3 *Why was it . . . such great cares*: quotation from Homer, *Iliad* 2.25; paragraphs 21–2 refer to the quarrel between Agamemnon and Achilles in *Iliad* 1.

2.24.26 *to silence*: this refers to Achilles' powerful speeches in Homer, *Iliad* 9.

2.26 For the content, see 2.12, where Socrates' ability to show people their self-contradiction is presented as exemplary of philosophical method. 2.26.6 is close to 2.12.5.

BOOK 3

3.1 Like 2.24, this is a very critical Discourse, directed at a young man whose elegant style and smooth skin indicate to Epictetus that he does not understand what it means to be male, let alone a human being. His point is not just that the young man does not have, like Epictetus, the beard that is the mark of a philosopher (24), but that he plucks out his body hair and makes himself look like a woman or an invert (14, 26–32, 35, 42).

3.1.14 *Polemo*: head of the Platonic Academy *c*.314–*c*.276 BC and teacher of Zeno, founder of Stoicism. He was converted to philosophy by Xenocrates, the previous head of the Academy (D.L. 4.16); see also 4.11.30.

3.1.16 *did Laius . . . Apollo?*: Apollo told Laius that if he had a son the child would kill his father and marry his mother, but Laius went on to have a child; the story forms the basis of Sophocles, *Oedipus the King*.

3.1.19 *Did Socrates . . . never abandoned it*: this passage is based on Plato, *Apology* 28e.

3.1.20 *'If you acquit me . . . related to me'*: a paraphrase of Plato, *Apology* 29c, e, 30a.

3.1.23 *'For my part . . . different from the rest'*: for the images, see 1.2.18, 30–2; for the idea, see Cicero, *On Ends* 3.66.

3.1.38 *Since we ourselves . . . court his wife*: quotation from Homer, *Odyssey* 1.37–8.

3.2 This Discourse offers a full statement of Epictetus' three-topic programme of practical ethics, and restates his standard view that study of philosophy, including logic, while potentially valuable, is only worthwhile if it leads towards real-life ethical improvement. See also notes on 2.17, 2.17.16.

3.2.11 *Diogenes . . . middle finger*: Diogenes the Cynic; pointing with the middle finger was a rude gesture.

3.2.15 *Crinus*: a little-known Stoic philosopher who was reported to have died in this way.

3.3 Epictetus' discussion of ethical training assumes the normal Stoic view that all human beings have the natural capacity to recognize and respond to what is good, presented here as a kind of 'coin', and to see the lesser value of other types of 'coin' (1–4, 11–13); the key criterion is distinguishing what is and is not 'up to us' (14–15). He also assumes that acting according to our social or family role is only worthwhile as long as this is compatible with our understanding of what is good (5–9); see 1.2, 2.10; also Introd., pp. xiv–xvi and nn. 19–23; Long, 237–8.

3.4 Epictetus here offers practical advice to a governor about maintaining impartiality in theatrical competitions (and so avoiding abuse from the audience), while also suggesting the key Stoic theme that we should focus on keeping what is up to us in harmony with nature rather than trying to ensure the success of other people in competitions (9–11).

3.4.11 *Nemean, Pythian, Isthmian . . . Olympic*: these were the four regular Panhellenic festivals, which included competitions.

3.5 Epictetus responds to someone (presumably a student) who wants to go home because he is ill by saying that the important thing, whether well or ill, is to press on with trying to become a better person, as Socrates did and urged others to do.

3.5.14 *'As one person . . . becoming better'*: the closest parallels to this passage are Xenophon, *Memorabilia* 1.6.8, and Plato, *Protagoras* 318a.

3.5.17 *Protagoras or Hippias*: famous fifth-century sophists who (unlike Socrates) claimed to be able to teach rhetoric and to make people better. Plato's Socrates sends young men to such sophists to learn these things (e.g. Plato, *Protagoras* 311a, 314e–316a), though his claims that he admires them seem ironic.

3.6 This is a collection of short passages on familiar themes, rather like those in the *Handbook*.

3.6.10 *Rufus*: Musonius Rufus, Epictetus' teacher.

3.7 As elsewhere, Epictetus offers a crude and simplistic view of Epicurean ethics, assuming that their claim that pleasure is the highest good rules out virtuous actions and attitudes and other-benefiting motives (see note on 1.23). The generalized contrast between goods of the body and goods of the mind (2–10) ignores the fact that, for both Stoics and Epicureans, the mind was a bodily entity; see LS 16, 53; also Gill, 29–66.

3.7.3 *Cassiope*: we are not sure which Maximus is meant here: the Cassiope mentioned is probably in Corcyra (modern Corfu).

3.7.12 *'Don't steal'*: there is some basis for this statement (see LS 22 A(4–5)); but it oversimplifies Epicurus' thinking on justice (see LS 22 as a whole, esp. M(4)).

3.7.19 *one shouldn't marry . . . civic duties*: see D.L. 10.119 for this Epicurean view; however, this needs to be set against the positive valuation of friendship (LS 22 F–I, O), and Epicurus' own concern for his friend's children in his death-bed letter (LS 24 D). For more sympathetic discussion of Epicurean thinking on this topic, see E. Brown, 'Politics and Society', in J. Warren (ed.), *The Cambridge Companion to Epicureanism* (Cambridge, 2009); J. Warren, *Facing Death: Epicurus and his Critics* (Cambridge, 2004), ch. 5.

3.7.25 *of three kinds*: this threefold division of appropriate actions (an important category in Stoicism) is not paralleled elsewhere; on 'appropriate actions', see LS 59.

3.7.28 *as an attendant*: Epictetus here reverses the Epicurean claim that the virtues should be 'attendants' to pleasure (i.e. instrumental to it) (LS 21 O).

3.7.31 *Symphorus or Numenius . . . did you sleep in?*: those named seem to be freedman influential at court; sleeping in the antechamber enables one to be first to take part in the morning greeting (*salutatio*) of important people.

3.8 Epictetus offers concrete illustrations of how we can train ourselves to examine impressions and to avoid describing things as 'good' or 'bad' unless they fall in the category of what is 'up to us' (see Introd., pp. xiii–xiv and nn. 14–16).

3.8.4   *convincing impression*: in Stoic theory, this is an impression that self-evidently confers knowledge of the object in question (LS 40), though here Epictetus is only focusing on the question of what is or is not 'up to us'.

3.8.7   *Italicus*: the identity of this person, the exact point of the anecdote, and the connection (if any) with the preceding part of the Discourse are unclear. Romans were, traditionally, sceptical about the value of philosophy; presumably Italicus had an amateurish or limited understanding of what it meant to be a philosopher.

3.9   Epictetus tries to explain what his philosophical teaching can offer to someone who is only superficially interested in philosophy (see esp. 1, 12, 14).

3.9.3   *patron of the Cnossians*: for a Roman to be a representative of the people of Cnossos (the main city in Crete) in their dealings at Rome would be a prestigious role.

3.9.21   *Myrrhine . . . the denying argument*: Myrrhine glassware was highly coloured and very expensive; the denying argument was studied extensively by Chrysippus (D.L. 7.197).

3.10   Epictetus explains that philosophy can train us to bear illness properly by underlining that the only things that matter, fundamentally, are 'up to us' (10, 18) and that things that happen to us, including illness and even death (14), are relatively unimportant.

3.10.4   *verses . . . 'Paean Apollo'!*: these are lines 40–4 of the *Golden Verses*, ascribed to the sixth-century BC thinker Pythagoras, but almost certainly written much later. The practice of nightly reflection and self-examination was a widely adopted practice in Hellenistic and Roman philosophy: see e.g. Seneca, *On Anger* 3.36. Epictetus stresses that we should embed this practice in our life and not merely chant the verse like a ritual cry (such as 'Paean Apollo!').

3.11   These two points are linked by the Stoic idea of the divine order as providing a moral framework for human life (LS 63 C(3–4)). In 1–2 Epictetus recasts as a divine law the standard Stoic view that passions derive from treating as good and bad things that lie outside the scope of choice (LS 65 B, D). In 4–6, quoting Homer, *Odyssey* 14.56–8, he suggests that Zeus, father of the gods, provides the moral basis for showing proper respect for one's father.

3.12   In giving advice on ethical training, Epictetus refers again to his three-topic programme of practical ethics, focused on management of desire (4–12), motivation (13), and assent (14–15); see 3.2.1–5 and note on 2.17.16. He also discourages extravagant or ostentatious modes of ethical training and seems to have certain Cynic practices in mind.

3.12.2   *tightrope, or setting up palms, or embracing statues*: the first two seem to be purely acrobatic or athletic practices ('setting up a palm' appears to mean climbing up a pole with only hands and feet, like those who climb palms). The third (done naked in cold weather) is ascribed to Diogenes the Cynic as a way of hardening himself (D.L. 6.23). Epictetus combines these practices, perhaps to make them look ridiculous.

3.12.7 *opposite direction*: a similar method of ethical training is recommended by Aristotle, *Nicomachean Ethics* 2.9, 1109^{b}1–7, as a way of learning how to 'hit the mean' in actions and feelings.

3.12.9 *palm . . . leather tent . . . mortar and pestle*: for 'palm', see note on 3.12.2. Cynics were, typically, itinerant, and carried a few items needed for their simple way of life. But the items mentioned here are excessive for this purpose; again, Epictetus seems to be parodying the Cynic lifestyle. In 3.20.10 a pestle is used for athletic training, but it is not clear that is meant here.

3.12.15 *marks of identification*: tokens used for identification in this period.

3.12.17 *Apollonius*: we do not know who Epictetus has in mind; it may have been Apollonius of Tyana, a celebrated Neo-Pythagorean thinker and ascetic in the first century AD.

3.13   Epictetus maintains that Stoic principles offer the only secure basis for avoiding a sense of desolation and helplessness, since they teach us to be self-sufficient (6–7) while also accepting whatever may happen to us, including our death (14–17). He assumes the standard Stoic view that we are composed of material elements, which dissolve at death (15).

3.13.4 *even Zeus . . . relation*: Zeus was identified in Stoic theory with the active principle (*pneuma*, or fiery air) in the universe; the universe experiences periodic conflagrations, when all other elements are converted into fiery air (LS 46–7). In Greek mythology, Hera is the wife of Zeus, and Athena and Apollo are his children. In 3.13.7 Zeus, as god and embodiment of divine order (LS 54), is taken as a model for human rationality and self-sufficiency.

3.13.9 *profound peace*: Augustus, the first Roman emperor, claimed to have brought peace throughout the Roman Empire, and this was an aspiration (sometimes achieved) of later emperors, to which Epictetus refers here.

3.13.15 *There is no Hades . . . divine spirits*: the Stoics (like the Epicureans) did not accept the truth of the traditional beliefs about the afterlife (or underworld), linked with the names cited here. Stoics thought that the universe as a whole was pervaded by divine agency and providence (LS 46, 54).

3.13.20 *for a beginner*: the remainder of this Discourse seems to be a separate discussion, which has become attached to 3.13.

3.13.23 *spittle*: Epictetus imagines an immature and over-enthusiastic philosophy lecturer spitting out his presentation at his audience.

3.14   Here we have a collection of sayings on themes typical of the *Discourses*.

3.14.9 *Now as regards . . . to do that*: for Socratic cross-examination as designed to counteract presumption, see e.g. Plato, *Lysis* 210e; *Sophist* 230a–d. There seems to be a gap in the Greek text at this point.

3.14.14 *powerful kick*: kicking was one of the techniques used by pancratiasts, who combined boxing and wrestling.

3.15 Epictetus compares the training required to become a Stoic with the single-minded and rigorous preparation needed to aim at victory in the Olympic games; for this theme, see 3.25.1–5; also Long, 107–12.

3.15.4 *digging*: this seems to refer to covering yourself with dust or mud before a wrestling match (D.L. 6.27).

3.15.8 *Euphrates*: a Stoic lecturer of the first century AD, possibly also taught by Musonius Rufus; see also 4.8.17–20.

3.15.14 *Galba*: an emperor assassinated after a short period of rule in AD 69 (the 'year of the four emperors'). This comment seems unconnected with the rest of the Discourse.

3.16.10 *like wax*: lecture notes would normally be written with a stylus on wax tablets.

3.17.4 *Sura*: Philostorgus, an unknown person, seems to have been prepared to gain wealth by sleeping with Sura, presumably Palfurius Sura, a senator under the Flavian emperors.

3.18 Epictetus stresses that the only harm you can experience is that of becoming an ethically bad person, which depends on your own choice, and not on external circumstances; for this idea, see also the argument put forward by Socrates in Plato, *Gorgias* 472–9; also Long, 70–4.

3.18.4 *Socrates*: he was condemned for impiety (more precisely, not worshipping the gods the city worshipped) in 399 BC. Epictetus suggests the condemnation was unjust; at any rate, Socrates did not regard it as significant.

3.18.6 *the son in you*: Epictetus assumes that playing your social or family role properly is a matter of doing so in accordance with virtue. See note on 3.3.

3.20 Epictetus discusses again the core Stoic claim that what is good or bad depends on our agency (or on the way we use things) and that everything else is 'a matter of indifference' (or an 'external thing', as Epictetus puts it). See LS 58; Introd., pp. xiii–xiv and nn. 14, 17–19.

3.20.4–5 *lameness . . . Menoeceus*: Epictetus may be alluding to his own lameness. Menoeceus, in Greek myth, gave up his life to save his own city of Thebes.

3.20.7 *the father of Admetus*: Pheres, who is presented in Euripides' *Alcestis* as refusing to die to save the life of his son in spite of being very old himself (see also 2.22.11).

3.20.19 *Lesbius*: evidently a critic of Epictetus (of whom we know nothing beyond this passage).

3.21 Here again, Epictetus stresses that becoming a Stoic teacher requires special natural capacities (18), quasi-religious commitment (12–16), and sustained training of a kind that leads to a real change in one's character and way of life (3–6, 8–9, 22–3). It is not a matter of superficial mastery of certain intellectual techniques and ideas which you can 'vomit' up again in the form of presentations and commentaries (1–2, 10, 16, 24).

3.21.12 *Demeter*: see next note.

3.21.13 *hierophant*: a priest who initiates worshippers in religious mysteries; this and the other roles mentioned here are linked with mystery cults, such as that of Demeter, goddess of corn, agriculture, and renewal of life, at Eleusis (near Athens). For the idea of the truths of philosophy as 'mysteries' that require intense training and preparation to understand properly, see also Plato, *Symposium* 210–11; *Phaedo* 69c, 81a.

3.21.19 *philosophical doctrines*: Epictetus here identifies three functions of philosophy that are especially associated with Socrates and the founders of Cynicism and Stoicism (Diogenes and Zeno). Long, 56–8, suggests that Epictetus aimed to combine all three functions in the ethical teachings presented in the *Discourses*. For the related idea of philosophy as a mode of 'therapy' for the mind (3.2.20), see note on 2.21.22.

3.22 In this, one of the longest of the Discourses, Epictetus underlines the demanding nature of the Cynic mission, if properly carried out. Cynicism, founded by Diogenes (*c*.412/403–*c*.324/321 BC) was a radical philosophical movement marked by extreme simplicity of lifestyle and the ideal of following nature while rejecting all that is merely conventional in human life. Cynicism was an important influence on early Stoicism and, though lapsing in importance in the later Hellenistic period, was taken seriously as a rigorous and ascetic mode of life by first-century AD Stoics, including Seneca, Musonius, and Epictetus. In this Discourse, Cynicism comes close to being an idealized version of the Stoic philosophical mission (whose demands Epictetus often stresses); but there are still a number of distinctively Cynic features.

3.22.4 *master of the house*: Stoic idea of God, linked with providential care for all that happens in the universe (see LS 46, 54).

3.22.6 *bull*: person of exceptional gifts, capable of conferring special benefits on humanity (see Cicero, *On Ends* 3.66); compared with heroic leaders in Homer's *Iliad*, Agamemnon and Achilles (rather than Thersites); on these figures see note on 3.22.7–8.

3.22.7–8 *Agamemnon . . . Thersites*: well-known figures in Homer's *Iliad*, often used as examples by Epictetus. Agamemnon was the leader of the Greeks at Troy, Achilles was the greatest Greek warrior who killed Hector, leader of the Trojans, and Thersites was an inferior fighter who challenged the authority of Agamemnon and was suppressed by Odysseus, another Greek leader (*Iliad* 2.211–77).

3.22.15 *self-respect*: the Cynic lifestyle, itinerant, homeless, with minimal clothing and goods, satisfying all his physical needs in public, was sometimes seen as expressing 'shamelessness' (*anaideia*); but here, Epictetus presents a Cynic's inner shame, or self-respect (*aidōs*), as his protection.

3.22.19–22 *You must begin . . . with the gods*: these paragraphs reflect a Stoic (rather than distinctively Cynic) ideal; 22 suggests the Stoic idea of the universe, especially the heavenly bodies, as pervaded by divine rationality (LS 54).

3.22.23 *by Zeus as a messenger*: on this image for the philosopher's mission, see K. Ierodiakonou, 'The Philosopher as God's Messenger', in Scaltsas and Mason.

3.22.24 *Philip . . . spy*: the Cynic is like a spy because he undergoes difficulty and danger to find out the truth (about what matters in human life) and reports this to people. D.L. 6.43 tells us that Diogenes, captured after the battle of Chaeronea (338 BC), described himself to Philip of Macedon as a spy on Philip's 'insatiable greed'; see also 1.24.3–10; M. Schofield, 'Epictetus on Cynicism', in Scaltsas and Mason, 75–80.

3.22.26 *like Socrates*: the description of Socrates and the start of the speech echoes Plato, *Clitophon* 407a–b.

3.22.27 *Myron . . . Ophellius*: probably well-known athletes or gladiators of the time.

Croesus: last king of Lydia (sixth century BC) and famous for his wealth.

3.22.28 *the people themselves*: Epictetus here uses language (especially 'dazzled by appearances') that evokes the idea of judging the real worth of the tyrannical character-type in Plato, *Republic* 577a.

3.22.30 *Nero . . . Sardanapalus*: Nero was Roman emperor in 54–68; his behaviour became extreme and tyrannical in the later years of his rule. Sardanapalus was the last king of Babylon and famed for luxury.

Many hairs . . . from my breast: these three quotations are from Homer, *Iliad* 10.15, 5.91, 94–5 (referring to Agamemnon).

3.22.31 *'rich in gold and rich in bronze'*: quotation from Homer, *Iliad* 18.289.

3.22.33–7 *Ah, poor ruling centre . . . what they think*: Epictetus comments on the worries of a king such as Agamemnon (leading the Greek army against the Trojans) in the light of the Stoic thesis that death and other 'indifferents' are not really bad things.

3.22.42 *free by nature*: on Epictetus' claim that our capacity for choice is fundamentally unconstrained or 'free', see Introd., p. xiv and nn. 17–18; on 'freedom' in Stoic theory, see also 4.1.

3.22.49 *king and master*: the Cynic is 'king' because he is master of himself (i.e. in control of anything that can affect his happiness), whereas conventional kings are subject to external circumstances. See also 93–6, 3.21.19; Schofield (cited in note to 3.22.24), 80–4.

3.22.50 *fine shoulder*: Epictetus here lists features of dress, attitude, and physique that form part of the popular stereotype of the Cynic, while indicating that what makes a real Cynic is a matter of ethical character and understanding.

3.22.51 *Olympic Games*: for this image for the philosophical life, see 1.18.18–23, 3.15.

3.22.56 *other than Zeus*: there are many anecdotes showing Diogenes treating kings (such as Philip and Alexander) with indifference or contempt; see e.g. 3.22.90–2 and note on 3.22.24.

3.22.57 *Heracles . . . Eurystheus*: see also notes on 1.6.32, 2.16.45.

3.22.60 *the Great King*: i.e. the king of Persia.

3.22.63 *sceptre . . . kingdom*: see note on 3.22.49 (also 'king' in 3.22.72).

Antisthenes . . . Crates: Antisthenes (mid-fifth to mid-fourth century BC), pupil of Socrates, was regarded as a major influence on Diogenes the Cynic, and Crates (late fourth to early third century BC) was a follower of Diogenes.

3.22.67 *city of wise people*: this is a Stoic political ideal, put forward in Zeno's *Republic* (LS 67 A–B), but here linked with the question whether a Cynic should marry or not.

3.22.72 *'who has . . . care'*: Homer, *Iliad* 2.25.

3.22.76 *another Crates*: Hipparchia, an exceptional case of a woman who became a Cynic and lived as a Cynic with her husband, Crates (D.L. 6.96).

3.22.78 *Epaminondas . . . Priam . . . Danaus . . . Aeolus*: Epaminondas (d. 362) was a famous Theban general; in Greek myth, Priam had fifty children, Danaus fifty daughters, Aeolus six sons and six daughters.

3.22.80 *dogs 'of the table . . . doors'*: quotation from Homer, *Iliad* 22.69. The name Cynic means 'dog-like', referring to their very simple, virtually animal, mode of life. While holding up Diogenes as an ideal, Epictetus is dismissive of contemporary Cynics, who merely adopt the 'dog-like' style without the ethical substance.

3.22.83 *he should get involved in public affairs*: this was a standard expectation of the Stoic wise person (LS 57 F(8), 67 W(3)), but not the Cynic, as Epictetus explains.

3.22.91 *when someone . . . hateful to the gods?*: for this incident, see D.L. 6.42.

3.22.92 *To sleep . . . multitude of cares*: quotation from Homer, *Iliad* 2.24, 25.

3.22.95 *'Lead me . . . Destiny'*: quotation from Cleanthes, *Hymn to Zeus*; see note on 2.23.42.

3.22.103 *Argus*: a mythical creature with many eyes.

3.22.108 *'Go rather . . . most of all'*: Homer, *Iliad* 6.490–2.

3.23 Epictetus contrasts the role of a philosophical teacher with that of the 'sophist', or display lecturer, a role that was becoming well known in Epictetus' time (*c*.55–135). Epictetus lived in the early part of the period we associate with the Second Sophistic in Graeco-Roman culture, i.e. 60–230. The sophist, who deploys display or 'epideictic' oratory, presents *ekphraseis* (verbal pictures), e.g. of Pan and the

Muses (11), and retells mythological or epic stories, e.g. the death of Achilles (35), or dramatic episodes from history, e.g. the Persian Wars (38). The philosophical teacher, by contrast, such as Socrates (21–2, 25) or Musonius Rufus (29) offers a less superficially attractive—but much more valuable—kind of discourse, namely, therapy for the mind (27–31).

3.23.17 *Dio*: Dio Chrysostom, a celebrated sophist of the period (*c*.40–*c*.110); see also 19.

3.23.20 *Lysias and Isocrates*: famous Athenian orators of the late fifth and fourth centuries BC.

Often have I wondered . . . than the other: Epictetus here imagines a conversation about the style of the opening of Xenophon's *Memorabilia* (which reports the dialogues of Socrates).

3.23.21 *'Anytus and Meletus . . . the best'*: this passage quotes Socrates in Plato, *Apology* 30c (also 1.29.18, 2.2.15), and modifies *Crito* 46b.

3.23.22 *People would thus . . . introduce them*: see note on 3.5.17.

3.23.23 *discourse . . . house of Quadratus*: recitations in the houses of rich men were common in the Roman Empire; Quadratus is used as a stock name for the hosts of these recitations.

3.23.26 *'Nor would it be fitting . . . like a schoolboy'*: see Plato, *Apology* 17c.

3.23.27 *just as the sun . . . further action*: the Stoics believed that the rays of the sun consisted of vapours drawn up to feed its fires. See also note on 1.19.11.

3.23.33 *for display*: display (or 'epideictic') oratory was a recognized style in rhetoric, along with the forensic and deliberative styles. But Epictetus stresses that this is *not* a fourth style in philosophical teaching, which can rank alongside the styles of exhortation, refutation, and didactic teaching. For the suggestion that these three styles are combined in Epictetus' modes of ethical teaching, as shown in the *Discourses*, see Long, 54–7; and on the link between these styles and philosophers such as Socrates and Zeno, see note on 3.21.19.

3.24 This rather long Discourse focuses on the challenges of managing interpersonal relationships for someone trying to lead a Stoic life. If we have good reasons to travel (for instance, to attend a philosophical school, 78), we should not be deterred by missing our relatives or worrying about how they are (4, 18, 22, 27). We should be affectionate towards other people in a way that recognizes that, ultimately, our happiness does not depend on their continued life (58–68, 82–8). We should also, during our lives, engage fully in social and political activities, but without compromising our ethical principles (44–56). See also, on these themes, 1.2, 2.10; also Introd., pp. xv–xxi and nn. 20–3; Long, 232–50, esp. 248–9.

3.24.9–12 *Shall we not wean . . . the spectacle*: here, Epictetus sets the theme of the challenges of travel in the broader context of the Stoic world-view.

He refers to the idea of the universe as a single substance animated by divine agency or rationality (or as a city of gods and humans), which experiences decomposition and change as well as periodic interruption (see LS 46–7; also 57 F(3)).

3.24.13 *Odysseus, 'Cities . . . lawful ways'*: as elsewhere, Odysseus and Heracles are presented as exemplary figures, and possible embodiments of Stoic 'wisdom'; see also (on Heracles), Cicero, *On Ends* 3.66; quotations are from Homer, *Odyssey* 1.3 and 17.487 (slightly modified). Heracles' treatment of women is presented much less favourably in Greek comedy and tragedy (e.g. Sophocles, *Women of Trachis*) than it is in 14–15.

3.24.18 *Yes, but Odysseus . . . believe his tales?*: quotation from Homer, *Odyssey* 5.82. For criticism of Homer and other poets for misrepresenting heroes (that is, not bringing out their qualities as moral exemplars), see also Plato, *Republic* 387d–392a.

3.24.31–6 *life is like a campaign . . . senator for life*: here Epictetus is using military and political language to symbolize the Stoic ideal of life as a campaign or mission. However, Stoicism also presents political engagement as a natural part of the best human life (LS 57 F(8)).

3.24.38–9 *Epicureans . . . likely to sleep*: here, as elsewhere, Epictetus gives a caricature of what the pursuit of pleasure meant for Epicureans (contrast LS 21, esp. B(5)).

3.24.44 *'What . . . his door?'*: the theme shifts in 44–56 to a different kind of social challenge, that of calling on a socially or politically important person for some purpose, but doing so without compromising one's ethical principles.

3.24.61 *in making his defence . . . as a soldier*: Socrates did not display his wife and children in court, as was often done in Athenian courts, to arouse the jury's sympathy: Plato, *Apology* 34c. For his (bold) counter-penalty on being convicted (i.e. free meals at public expense for life), see Plato, *Apology* 36b–e; and on his earlier service in war and on the council, see 28d–e, 32b.

3.24.66 *Perrhaebians*: a tribe living in a mountainous area on the borders of Thessaly and Macedon, exemplifying a remote or inaccessible region. The incidents about Diogenes' capture by pirates and slavery are designed to show his indomitable spirit (on such incidents, see W. Desmond, *Cynics* (Stocksfield, 2008), 20–1).

3.24.67 *Antisthenes set me free*: Antisthenes (famous for his austere ethic) set Diogenes free (symbolically) by his teaching; on 'freedom' in this sense, see 4.1.

3.24.70 *Philip, Alexander, Perdiccas*: kings of Macedon during Diogenes' lifetime.

3.24.77 *Lyceum*: a public gymnasium in Athens, also the site of Aristotle's philosophical school.

3.24.100 *Gyara*: a Greek island famous as a place of exile (see also 109, 1.24.19).

3.24.105 *I'd fathered a mortal*: this saying (attributed either to Solon or Anaxagoras) became famous in Hellenistic and Roman philosophy as an expression of fortitude in the face of misfortune.

3.24.117 *sacrifices . . . Capitol*: a normal part of the ritual undertaken by those holding magistracies in Rome; the Capitol was a hill in the centre of Rome and site of many temples.

3.25   For the comparison of preparation for the philosophical life to training for the Olympics (3–4), see also note on 3.15. For the stress on the importance of building up appropriate attitudes by consciously adopting good habits, see note on 2.18.

3.25.5 *like quails . . . the ring*: the implication seems to be that fighting quails, once defeated, are more inclined to run away.

3.26   Epictetus speaks sternly to someone whose fear of what the future may hold shows that his grasp of the real meaning of Stoic philosophy is as yet only skin-deep (13, 15–20, 39).

3.26.18 *measuring worthless ashes*: because of his failure in (ethical) measurement (18–20), the person addressed is attaching value to mere 'externals', such as danger or death, which are not fundamentally important.

3.26.23 *draw water*: according to D.L. 7.168, Cleanthes, the second head of the Stoic school, was so committed to studying with Zeno, despite his poverty, that he worked at night as a gardener to support his studies.

3.26.32 *unarmed and alone*: Epictetus takes as exemplary the attitude of Heracles (son of Zeus), who showed that he had a genuinely 'kingly' attitude by benefiting humanity by his seven labours, while Eurystheus, who made him carry out these labours, showed that he was not a real king because he did not rule himself. On Stoic rethinking of the notions of freedom and kingship, see also 4.1.

3.26.33 *'Like a mountain-bred lion'*: the quoted phrase is Homer, *Odyssey* 6.130. Odysseus shows his indomitable spirit by covering his naked body with a branch and asking for shelter and food from the attendants of Nausicaa, princess of Phaeacia.

3.26.37 *like Manes*: this puzzling phrase apparently alludes to a comment attributed to Zeno, who, when ill, asked to be treated 'like Manes', i.e. like a slave (Manes is a common slave name); Musonius fragment 18 A (Hense's edition). For Epictetus, a possible further layer of meaning is that *manes* means 'corpse' or 'shade' in Latin; so the person should be treated in a way that prepares him for death (the inevitable final outcome of human life, 38).

BOOK 4

4.1   Though very long, this Discourse is centred on a single idea, that real freedom consists in recognizing that everything that really matters is 'up to us' and that what is not 'up to us' is relatively unimportant. This message is stated in 1–5, recapitulated in 128–31, and summed up again in 174–6. Real slavery derives from surrendering our choice to things outside our power, such as objects of erotic desire, status, or wealth (15–23, 45–50, 144–9). A related theme is that real freedom derives from accepting all that happens as part of the providential work of fate or God (99–106, 131). Epictetus distinguishes this concept of freedom from conventional legal and political freedom (6–14, 33–40, 54–62). The point is sometimes brought out in a quasi-Socratic dialectical style (45–56, 132–7). The Discourse closes with pictures of Diogenes and Socrates as exemplars of freedom in the real sense, one rejecting conventional society, the other living a principled life within it (151–8, 159–69). See Long, 27–9, 208–10; also S. Bobzien, *Determinism and Freedom in Stoic Philosophy* (Oxford, 1998), ch. 7; M. Frede, *A Free Will: Origins of the Notion in Ancient Thought* (Berkeley, 2011), ch. 5.

4.1.19 *Thrasonides . . . Geta*: Thrasonides seems to be a mercenary soldier and Geta his slave.

4.1.20 *'A little wench . . . ever enslaved'*: quoted lines from Menander, *The Hated One*.

4.1.30–1 *You cannot enslave . . . armed force*: the quotations appear to be from letters ascribed to Diogenes the Cynic (these letters do not survive).

4.1.33 *five per cent tax*: levied on owners giving freedom to their slaves; see also 2.1.26.

4.1.38 *rings*: members of the equestrian order (the order below the highest, senatorial, class at Rome) were entitled to wear gold rings.

4.1.39 *and then a third*: by a law of Julius Caesar, three military campaigns were a prerequisite for becoming a municipal senator.

4.1.41 *entity*: the reference seems to be to Xenophon, *Memorabilia* 4.6.1; but this is also a very common theme in Platonic depictions of Socratic dialectical enquiry.

4.1.42 *apply . . . preconceptions*: see note on 1.22.

4.1.45 *Caesar's friend*: this was a semi-official role in the Roman Empire, like being a modern government adviser or minister.

4.1.53 *buying and selling*: i.e. buying and selling slaves, the normal mode of acquiring them at this period.

Great King: the king of Persia, a standard example of great power.

4.1.57 *twelve fasces . . . purple-bordered robe*: the consul (highest Roman magistrate) was preceded by twelve attendants (lictors), carrying 'fasces' (rods), symbolizing the power to punish people. Roman senators wore a purple-bordered toga.

4.1.58 *Saturnalia*: a festival when slaves were treated as if they were free (see also 1.25.8).

4.1.86 *citadel*: i.e. mind, or 'ruling centre', in Stoic terms. The metaphor goes back to Plato (*Republic* 560b; *Timaeus* 70a), and is adopted by Marcus Aurelius, *Meditations* 8.48.3.

4.1.91 *quaestor*: Roman magistrate in charge of provincial finances.

4.1.105 *pageant and festival*: see note on 2.14.23.

4.1.111 *This is what . . . your brothers*: on the approach to interpersonal relationships assumed here and in 107, see note on 3.24.

4.1.114–15 *Diogenes . . . pirates*: see notes on 3.24.66–7.

4.1.123 *Helvidius*: see note on 1.1.

4.1.131 *Guide me . . . assigned me*: see note on 2.23.42.

4.1.146 *Aprulla*: evidently, a rich old woman; the imagined speaker aims to inherit her wealth after her death.

4.1.150 *Felicio . . . with pride*: Felicio was a freedman of Nero; Epictetus seems here to refer to his own experience as the slave of Epaphroditus, an ex-slave of Nero's.

4.1.155 *the universe*: the ideal of cosmopolitanism (being a citizen of the universe) was adopted by both Cynicism and Stoicism; see W. Desmond, *Cynics* (Stocksfield, 2008), 199–2008; LS 67 A, K, L.

4.1.156 *Archidamas*: i.e. Archidamas III, fourth-century BC king of Sparta.

4.1.160 *exposed . . . in the least*: on Socrates' bravery in battle, see Plato, *Apology* 28e; *Symposium* 219e–221b.

sent . . . to arrest Leon: on this incident, see Plato, *Apology* 32c. Leon was a leading figure in the opposition to the Thirty Tyrants.

4.1.162 *on trial for his life*: see Plato, *Apology* 34d–e.

drink the poison: see Plato, *Phaedo* 117a–e.

4.1.163 *he thought only about . . . wrong action*: a paraphrase of Socrates' response in Plato, *Crito* 47d, to Crito's suggestion (45d–46a) that Socrates should try to escape from prison for the sake of his children.

4.1.164 *he who had refused . . . demanded it*: Socrates (who happened to be president of the Athenian council on that day) refused to put an illegal motion to the vote in the Assembly, in spite of popular pressure to do this; see Plato, *Apology* 32b; Xenophon, *Memorabilia* 1.1.18.

4.1.172 *practise to die*: see Plato, *Phaedo* 64a.

4.1.173 *what the philosophers say . . . with reason*: there is no other record of this comment by Cleanthes. However, the Stoics, like Plato's Socrates, were famous for their 'paradoxes', i.e. ideas that run counter to what most people believe but which have a strong underlying rationale, such as that only the wise person is 'free' in a full sense (LS 67 A(4)).

4.2 Epictetus points out that, if you want to make ethical progress, you may have to break with former friends who are not living by the same standards as those to which you aspire. On Stoic thinking on the interplay between the personal and social aspects of ethical development and Epictetus' attention to this interplay, see Introd., pp. xiv–xv and nn. 19–23.

4.2.10 *Thersites*: an ugly common soldier who challenged Agamemnon, leader of the Greeks, on his management of the Trojan War; see Homer, *Iliad* 2.212–77; see also 2.23.32, 3.22.7–8.

4.3 Epictetus urges his listeners not to aim at exchanges that are profitable in terms of 'externals' (such as wealth or social status), but at those that enable us to develop ethically, and to accept readily the loss of other things.

4.3.9 *tribune's post . . . praetor's post*: important Roman magistracies.

4.3.12 *Masurius and Cassius*: distinguished legal experts in the early second century.

4.4 Epictetus stresses again the need to focus our concern on what is 'up to us', pointing out that philosophical study is directed, ultimately, to a practical objective and is not an end in itself.

4.4.13 *On Understanding*: i.e. a Stoic treatise on gaining knowledge by correct use of impressions. This is a standard topic (and treatise title) in Stoic logic or dialectic, which included theory of knowledge.

4.4.16 *On Motivation . . . On Desire . . . On Appropriate Actions*: the titles listed are familiar topics in Stoic ethics.

4.4.21 *'If this is what God pleases . . . so be it!'*: Plato, *Crito* 43d, slightly modified; see also 1.4.24.

Lyceum or Academy: public gymnasia where Socrates held many of his philosophical dialogues.

he would have been as happy . . . often served: see first note on 4.1.160.

4.4.22 *hymns of praise*: see Plato, *Phaedo* 60d; D.L. 2.42.

4.4.33 *eradicate desire*: see note on 1.4.1.

4.4.34 *'Guide me . . . O Destiny'*: see note on 2.23.42.

4.4.38 *evil genius*: an exceptional case in the *Discourses* of a phrase evoking popular magic or folklore (though used ironically).

4.5 Epictetus shows that adopting Stoic ethical principles will prevent us from quarrelling with other people because we will realize that our happiness is, fundamentally, 'up to us' and does not depend on what others do to us.

4.5.3 *Thrasymachus, Polus, and Callicles*: these are conspicuously aggressive interlocutors of Socrates in Plato, *Republic* book 1, and *Gorgias*.

sophistical arguments: this does not match any incident in the Socratic dialogues we have; the closest parallel is Xenophon, *Memorabilia* 2.2.

4.5.10 *injustice . . . who inflicts it*: a recurrent idea in Plato (e.g. *Crito* 49b; *Gorgias* 468–75; *Republic* 588e–589c, also adopted by Stoicism); see also Long, 70–2.

4.5.14 *strangle lions or embrace statues*: the first act is superhuman or heroic (we may be reminded of Heracles), the second evokes Diogenes (see 3.12.2).

4.5.15 *'gather together . . . who has died'*: quotations are from a fragment of

Euripides, *Cresphontes*, urging us, paradoxically, to grieve at someone's birth, rather than his death.

4.5.17 *Trajan . . . Nero*: emperors in 98–117 and 54–68, respectively. The coins are accepted or rejected on the basis of the good (Trajan) or bad (Nero) character of these emperors.

4.5.19 *call . . . an apple*: this refers to a lump of beeswax used in leather sewing, which was described as 'the cobbler's apple'.

4.5.26 *judgements*: for the city–mind analogy, see note on 4.1.86.

4.5.29 *Eteocles and Polynices*: see note on 2.22.14.

4.5.33 *In pouring . . . under her feet*: there are various ancient sources for these incidents (though they do not appear in Plato's works); the cake was a present from Alcibiades, of whom Socrates' wife, Xanthippe, was jealous.

4.5.37 *'Lions . . . Ephesus'*: the Spartans were successful militarily in mainland Greece but not in Asia Minor (modern Turkey), where Ephesus is situated.

4.6 Epictetus maintains that the only secure way to avoid being pitied by other people is to recognize that what matters, ultimately, is things within our power, and that there is no reason to pity someone who fails to gain 'externals' such as power and wealth.

4.6.18 *motives, preparations, projects*: on the precise sense Epictetus gives to these terms and on how his usage relates to Stoic terminology more generally, see Inwood, 224–34.

4.6.20 *What does Antisthenes . . . spoken of*: for this incident, about the philosopher Antisthenes (student of Socrates and teacher of Diogenes) and Cyrus, king of Persia in the fifth to fourth centuries BC, see D.L. 6.3.

4.6.32–3 *Let not sleep . . . What did I do?*: from the *Golden Verses* ascribed to Pythagoras (lines 40 and 42) (3.10.2 gives lines 40–4, including the quotations cited here), ascribed ironically to the type of person being criticized here.

4.6.33 *a lie*: the Stoics thought that the wise person (though not necessarily other people) could legitimately lie on certain occasions. See also the 'noble lie' used by the rulers in Plato's ideal state (*Republic* 414b–e).

4.7 Epictetus maintains that a proper understanding of what is and is not 'up to us' confers freedom from fear of powerful people and of what they can provide or impose on us, including death.

4.7.5 *bits of pottery*: presumably used for dice or some similar game.

4.7.6 *Galileans*: Epictetus seems to mean the Christians, who were widely regarded as perversely defiant in their refusal to worship the emperor. This becomes clear in a famous exchange of letters between the emperor Trajan and the younger Pliny, a provincial governor, in 112.

4.7.15 *to die*: for death as decomposition into the elements of which all things are made up, see also 3.13.15.

4.7.23 *children will look to that*: in this slightly puzzling passage Epictetus presents political positions as no more valuable than nuts and figs (things that only children should run to pick up). However (24), if one happens to find oneself with a fig (i.e. political position) in one's lap, one should accept it, and play the role appropriately. For Epictetus' attitude to political roles, see also 1.1.19–29, 1.2.12–24.

4.7.30 *'Go . . . Leon'*: see second note on 4.1.160.

4.7.31 *thrown out unburied*: an insult to the dead. Diogenes asked to be thrown out unburied, but with his trusty staff at his side to keep off the dogs and birds (D.L. 6.79).

4.8   Epictetus argues that one should judge who is and who is not a philosopher not by the fact that they have the typical philosophical look (with beard, long hair, and rough cloak), but by the extent to which their behaviour shows they are living according to the principles to which they are committed.

4.8.12 *elements of reason . . . all of this*: the closest parallel to this passage is provided by Stoic definitions of the nature of logic or dialectic (one of the three branches of philosophy); see LS 31 A; also Long, 119–20.

4.8.17 *Euphrates*: see also 3.15.8. Unusually he combined the roles of sophist or public lecturer and Stoic philosopher; correspondingly, he dressed in a conventional way.

4.8.21 *Hephaestus . . . felt cap*: divine patron of blacksmiths and other crafts; the felt cap was typically worn by blacksmiths.

4.8.22 *introduce them*: see note on 3.23.22.

4.8.29 *Asclepius*: god of healing. Worshippers slept in his temples overnight with the aim of being cured by dreams that the god sent or by his interventions.

4.8.30 *sceptre and the crown*: on Cynics and 'kingship', see note on 3.22.49.

4.8.32 *Never did pallor . . . cheeks*: Homer, *Odyssey* 11.529–1.

4.8.35 *winter training*: for this theme, see also 3.15, 3.25.1–5.

4.8.36 *gardens of Adonis*: early spring domestic gardens (dedicated to Adonis), which played a role like modern greenhouses.

4.8.39 *at the root*: a botanical mistake, since it is the exposed parts of plants that are frosted, but not a deliberate one, it would seem.

4.8.42 *bull*: for this comparison, see 3.22.6.

4.9.6   *Aristides and Evenus*: authors of erotic stories.

4.9.10 *Heracles*: another reference to Heracles' labours; see also 1.6.32, 2.16.45, 3.26.32.

4.10.13 *third area of study*: see note on 2.17.16.

4.10.14 *If death . . . towards God*: for a similar speech in Stoic writings on practical ethics, see Seneca, *On Peace of Mind* 11.3–4 (addressed there to Fortune).

4.10.21 *If you want . . . little baskets*: these are the marks of being a Roman consul, namely, having attendants with twelve rods (see note on 4.1.57), judging trials, officiating at the games; the 'lunches in little baskets' were the dole (*sportula*) distributed by wealthy Roman patrons to their clients.

4.10.24 *'One form . . . another'*: the full form of this proverb is cited in 4.6.30: 'One form of business doesn't go together with another.'

4.10.31 *'toss . . . side' . . . Protesilaus*: the quoted lines are from Homer, *Iliad* 24.5, referring to Achilles' distress after the death of his much-loved friend Patroclus; the three men named were close friends of his, now dead.

bound to die: in *Iliad* 18.95–100, Achilles accepts that his own death will come soon after his vengeance on Patroclus' killer. For Epictetus' attitude towards these epic and tragic situations, see note on 1.28. For similar criticism of Achilles' extravagant grief at the death of Patroclus, see Plato, *Republic* 387d–388d.

4.10.33 *Automedon*: charioteer of Achilles and Patroclus, he became Achilles' companion after the death of Patroclus.

4.10.35 *'because . . . befall me'*: Homer, *Iliad* 19.321.

4.11 Epictetus' whole-hearted commendation of cleanliness is perhaps surprising in the light of his own adoption of a very simple lifestyle and idealization of Diogenes the Cynic. But it fits in with his advice that people should play their social roles appropriately (provided this is compatible with trying to act virtuously, 1.2, 2.10), and with his criticism of those who think that just adopting a scruffy appearance makes one a philosopher (4.8); note also his negative view of those who adopt the Cynic style but not the ethical content. See notes on 3.12.2, 3.22.80.

4.11.6 *Now the functions . . . assent*: on Epictetus' terminology for types of psychological agency, see note on 4.6.18.

4.11.19 *Socrates rarely took a bath*: see Plato, *Symposium* 174a.

finest features: Plato, *Symposium* 175c–e, 217–18, 223a–b.

4.11.20 *But Aristophanes . . . wrestling school*: Aristophanes, *Clouds* 103 (modified), 179, 225. Epictetus' point is that Aristophanes' evidence is of no value; *Clouds* (423 BC) does offer a ridiculous caricature of Socrates.

4.11.25 *notion of beauty . . . and a desire for elegance*: the idea that elegance, or decorum, constitutes the outward mark of virtue evokes Cicero, *On Obligations* 1.93–6 (based on the theory of the second-century BC Stoic Panaetius).

4.11.30 *That is why . . . in the wrong place*: see note on 3.1.14.

4.13 Epictetus criticizes those who speak indiscreetly about their own affairs, on the grounds that this shows that such people lack judgement both about how to treat others and how to conduct their own lives autonomously.

4.13.7–8 *no, I listen . . . foolish talk*: the line of thought seems initially puzzling, because Epictetus appears to associate himself with some quite unprincipled attitudes and behaviour. However, we need to note the qualifying phrases 'if I'm that kind of person' and 'if I'm actually like him'. Epictetus is imagining the response of someone who has the same malicious motives as the other (like the military spy in 5–6) but who can keep his mouth shut until the right moment. Epictetus' own view (that we are responsible for our own harm or benefit) reappears in 8. The last clause in 8 ('as a result of my own foolish talk') seems to be meant hypothetically. If Epictetus suffers from what he says, that is his responsibility, and not that of anyone else.

4.13.14 *Medea*: see note on 2.17.20.

4.13.22 *pitch . . . wheel*: ancient methods of torture.

FRAGMENTS

These are passages taken from other ancient writings that are said to be by Epictetus, and that seem to be based on lost versions of Epictetus' teachings by Arrian. The most common source is John Stobaeus' anthology of moralizing passages (fourth century AD). Only passages now thought by scholars likely to be by Epictetus have been included. The numbering is that of the edition of Epictetus' works by Heinrich Schenkl (Leipzig, 1916). References to *Disc.* refer to the *Discourses*. References by number alone are to other fragments.

1   The claim that the ultimate aim of studying all three branches of Stoic philosophy (logic, ethics, and physics) is to enable one to improve one's ethical character is a common theme in Epictetus, especially in connection with logic (e.g. *Disc.* 2.23, 3.2). Here, unusually, the first part of the passage concerns physics. The idea that, whether or not the universe is made of atoms (the Epicurean view) or elements (the Stoic view), we can still commit ourselves to Stoic ethical principles is restated sometimes in Marcus Aurelius' *Meditations* (e.g. 4.3, 10.6, 12.14).

3   The idea that ethical progress can be understood, in part, as bringing our wishes and decisions into line with the universe, by producing in ourselves the kind of order and rationality that is built into the universe, is a central Stoic theme (see LS 63 C(3–4)). Marcus Aurelius restates this theme often (e.g. *Meditations* 2.16, 3.5, 4.4). Epictetus normally refers to God, rather than the universe, in this connection (see e.g. *Disc.* 1.14, 1.16). See also the latter part of 4 and 6.

5   *Lycurgus*: he was the legendary founder of the distinctive Spartan constitution, which was widely admired by ancient philosophers for its stability and focus on character training.

6   For this theme, see also 3.

8   For the Stoic idea that the universe (including human beings) is composed of the four elements and that everything is transformed into these and the elements into each other, see LS 47; see also *Disc.* 3.13.15; this

theme is restated often by Marcus Aurelius (e.g. *Meditations* 2.3, 10.7, 11.20).

9   This passage is presented by the second-century author Aulus Gellius (19.1.14–21) as summarizing part of Book 5 of Arrian's *Discourses* of Epictetus; the phrases cited here in transliterated Greek (also translated by Gellius) are actual quotations. The passage is also cited in Augustine, *City of God* 9.4. The passage is an important piece of evidence for 'pre-emotions' in Stoicism and part of it forms LS 65 Y. On 'impressions' and 'assent', see Introd., pp. xiii–xiv and nn. 15–16; on 'pre-emotions' (involuntary reactions that fall short of being 'emotions' in the full sense), see LS 65 X. The wise person does not 'assent' to these impressions because he knows that such external events are not 'bad' in a real sense; on the wise person's 'good emotions', see LS 65 F, W. See also M. R. Graver, *Stoicism and Emotion* (Chicago, 2007), esp. chs. 2, 4.

10   This passage is also taken from Aulus Gellius (17.19); the phrases in inverted commas seem to be quotations from Epictetus. For the main point, see note on 1.

11   *Archelaus*: king of Macedon in the fifth century BC.

    four quarts of barley-meal for an obol: a substantial amount of a subsistence food for a small price.

    Polus: a famous actor in the fourth century BC (after Socrates' death, in fact).

    Oedipus the King . . . Oedipus at Colonus: the two plays are surviving fifth-century BC plays by Sophocles.

    Odysseus: he is disguised in rags throughout books 14–21 of Homer's *Odyssey*.

12   This response of controlled anger should not be confused with the wise person's absence of misguided emotion or 'good emotion' (see note on 9).

14   This passage supports the Stoic idea of pleasure, rather than the Epicurean claim that pleasure is the overall goal of life (LS 21). The description of the (Stoic) philosophers as 'grumpy' is ironic. The Stoic idea of 'pleasure' presented here is normally characterized as 'joy' (LS 65 F).

15   The Roman women mentioned presumably think that Plato is advocating promiscuous erotic relations between married people for pleasurable purposes. In fact, as the passage points out, Plato's proposals in *Republic* book 5 are to do away with marriage (and private property) altogether, at least in the ruling, 'guardian' class, in order to create single-minded commitment to the political role of this class and thus create a state that is 'just' in Plato's sense (457d–464b).

21   See note on *Disc*. 1.1.28.

22   Agrippinus was governor of Crete and Cyrenaica under Claudius (emperor 41–54). The idea of punishment as a form of quasi-medical treatment, beneficial to the person punished, is prominent in Plato,

Gorgias 476a–481b, and the last sentence of this passage evokes 476d especially. On Plato's *Gorgias* as an influential work for Epictetus, see Long, 70–4.

23   *Xenophon*: the quoted words are based on *Memorabilia* 1.4.7.

 sack: the stomach.

 another duty: the sexual urge.

26–8   The remaining three fragments are all taken from Marcus Aurelius, *Meditations*. 26 from *Meditations* 4.41; 27 from *Meditations* 11.37; 28 from *Meditations* 11.38.

HANDBOOK

The *Handbook* (Greek, *Encheiridion*) is a selection by Arrian of themes taken from the *Discourses*, of which there were originally eight books. The passages (or 'chapters') are of different types. Some (e.g. 1, 2, 5, 30–1) seem to be designed to provide concise and striking formulations of ideas that recur throughout the *Discourses* (presumably, including those we have lost). Many passages offer specific advice about what practices to adopt in order to set about living the kind of philosophical life recommended by Epictetus (e.g. 3, 4, 6, 10, 11, 12). One passage (33) exceptionally consists of a series of short pieces of moral advice that are not obviously related to Epictetus' normal Stoic framework. The *Handbook* has been much used, from Marcus Aurelius onwards, as a source of Stoic ethical advice for 'self-help' or 'guide to life purposes' (see Introd., pp. xxx–xxxii and nn. 49–54). However, the *Discourses* present the philosophical framework and the modes of discourse that enable us to make more complete sense of the nature of Epictetus' ethical teaching.

The notes highlight certain Discourses that explain more fully ideas or advice offered in brief form in the *Handbook*. References by numbers alone (e.g. 'see 2') are to other chapters in the *Handbook*.

1   A concise statement of Epictetus' most recurrent theme: see Introd., pp. xiii–xiv and nn. 14–16.

2   A restatement of the theme of 1, focusing on desire and aversion. For the idea of suppressing desire for the present, see also 48.3, and note on *Disc.* 1.4.1.

3   On this topic, see also *Disc.* 3.24.84–8.

5   See also *Disc.* 1.28, 3.3.14–15, 3.8.

6   *The use of impressions*: on the use of impressions, see 1.5 and note on 1.

7   See 3 and note on 3.

9   *leg . . . choice*: for the contrast between 'leg' and 'choice', see *Disc.* 1.1.23–4, 1.18.17, 1.19.8.

12   See also 13 and *Disc.* 1.4.

15   *Diogenes . . . Heraclitus*: Diogenes the Cynic, and Heraclitus, a Presocratic thinker of the sixth–fifth century BC who was influential in shaping Stoic ideas.

17   *another's*: i.e. God, conceived as source of providential fate. On playing
      your role in life properly, see *Disc.* 1.2, 2.10.

18   *raven croaks*: this is used as an example of prophesying the future by
      observing birds, a widespread Greek and Roman practice. On Epictetus'
      attitude to prophecy, see *Disc.* 2.7.

19   On this theme, see also note on *Disc.* 1.19.

27   The idea that a target is set up to be missed is absurd or inconceivable;
      the presence of badness in the universal is presented as equally absurd.
      See LS 54 on the Stoic providential world-view.

29   This chapter, exceptionally, reproduces one of the Discourses (3.15.1–13)
      excluding the final para (14) which seems to be an intrusion.

30   See *Disc.* 3.3.5–10; also *Disc.* 1.2 and 2.10.

31   On correct attitudes towards the gods, see also *Disc.* 1.12, 1.13, 1.14.

31.4 *Eteocles and Polynices*: see also *Disc.* 2.22.14–21.

32   On Epictetus and prophecy, see *Disc.* 2.7.

32.3 *Socrates*: there is no obvious source for this comment in our surviving
      evidence for Socrates.

      Pythian Apollo: this story underlines the point being made, that you do
      not need to consult a prophet in cases where there is a strong moral
      obligation to act in a certain way; Apollo himself shows this by throw-
      ing out of his temple someone who has failed to act properly.

33   This chapter consists of a series of moral instructions with little obvious
      linkage with Stoic philosophy (except in 33.12) and is unlike the rest of
      the *Handbook* in this respect.

33.11 *public readings*: recitations of new writings were a normal way of intro-
      ducing them to the educated public.

36   This chapter depends on an analogy between logical contradiction (e.g.
      between 'it is day' and 'it is night' if asserted at the same time) and
      ethical contradiction, in cases where one ethical claim is in competition
      with another.

39   *Each person's . . . for his property*: i.e. bodily needs should set the stand-
      ard for the property required; otherwise, we have no objective limit by
      which to restrict luxurious possessions.

42   For this theme, see also *Disc.* 1.28.

      composite judgement: i.e. two judgements linked with 'and'; see also
      Disc. 2.9.8.

46.1 *being overlooked*: see note on 3.23.22.

46.2 *vomit*: for this image, used for speaking with superficial understanding,
      see also *Disc.* 3.21.5.

47   *embrace statues*: see note on *Disc.* 3.12.2.

      take some cold water . . . soul: see *Disc.* 3.12.16.

48.3   *of every desire*: see note on 2.

49   For this kind of criticism, see also *Disc.* 2.17.34–40, 2.19.6–15.

51   On the kind of commitment required by the philosophical life, see (also using the comparison with preparing for the Olympic games) *Disc.* 3.15, 3.25.1–5.

51.3   *to be a Socrates*: see also *Disc.* 1.16.36.

52   The criticism of focusing on more sophisticated types of study when we have not grasped the more basic or fundamental is close to *Disc.* 3.2.6–7, where he is also concerned with the ethical consequences of making this mistake. But the philosophical topics he discusses here are different from those of 3.2.1–5, and seem to fall wholly within logic (though they have ethical implications).

53   The Platonic passages quoted in this chapter are cited frequently in the *Discourses*, but not the Euripides fragment. Elsewhere, Epictetus cites only the first line of the Cleanthes passage (see note on *Disc.* 2.23.42).

53.1   *Guide me . . . nonetheless*: quotation from Cleanthes, *Hymn to Zeus*.

53.2   *Whoever . . . divine*: quotation from Euripides fragment 965 in Nauck's edition.

53.3   *'Well, Crito . . . so be it'*: quotation from Plato, *Crito* 43d (modified).

53.4   *'Anytus . . . harm me'*: quotation from Plato, *Apology* 30c–d.

INDEX OF NAMES

Entries refer to the *Discourses*, cited by book, chapter, and paragraph (e.g. 1.27.2), with references at the end to the Fragments (e.g. fr. 5) or *Handbook* (e.g. 3 or 15.2). This index does not include references to Epictetus as speaker in the *Discourses* or to names used in a generic way, e.g. 'Caesar' (meaning the Roman emperor), or phrases such as 'by Zeus'.

INDEX OF MAIN THEMES

Entries refer to the *Discourses*, cited by book and chapter (e.g. 2.4) or book, chapter and paragraph(s) (e.g. 1.28.6–10), with references at the end to the Fragments (e.g. fr. 9) or *Handbook* (e.g. 32).

The Oxford World's Classics Website

www.worldsclassics.co.uk

- Browse the full range of Oxford World's Classics online

- Sign up for our monthly e-alert to receive information on new titles

- Read extracts from the Introductions

- Listen to our editors and translators talk about the world's greatest literature with our Oxford World's Classics audio guides

- Join the conversation, follow us on Twitter at OWC_Oxford

- Teachers and lecturers can order inspection copies quickly and simply via our website

www.worldsclassics.co.uk

American Literature

British and Irish Literature

Children's Literature

Classics and Ancient Literature

Colonial Literature

Eastern Literature

European Literature

Gothic Literature

History

Medieval Literature

Oxford English Drama

Philosophy

Poetry

Politics

Religion

The Oxford Shakespeare

A complete list of Oxford World's Classics, including Authors in Context, Oxford English Drama, and the Oxford Shakespeare, is available in the UK from the Marketing Services Department, Oxford University Press, Great Clarendon Street, Oxford OX2 6DP, or visit the website at www.oup.com/uk/worldsclassics.

In the USA, visit www.oup.com/us/owc for a complete title list.

Oxford World's Classics are available from all good bookshops. In case of difficulty, customers in the UK should contact Oxford University Press Bookshop, 116 High Street, Oxford OX1 4BR.

ALEXANDER POPE	Selected Poetry
ANN RADCLIFFE	The Italian The Mysteries of Udolpho The Romance of the Forest A Sicilian Romance
CLARA REEVE	The Old English Baron
SAMUEL RICHARDSON	Pamela
RICHARD BRINSLEY SHERIDAN	The School for Scandal and Other Plays
TOBIAS SMOLLETT	The Adventures of Roderick Random The Expedition of Humphry Clinker
LAURENCE STERNE	The Life and Opinions of Tristram Shandy, Gentleman A Sentimental Journey
JONATHAN SWIFT	Gulliver's Travels Major Works A Tale of a Tub and Other Works
JOHN VANBRUGH	The Relapse and Other Plays
HORACE WALPOLE	The Castle of Otranto
MARY WOLLSTONECRAFT	Mary and The Wrongs of Woman A Vindication of the Rights of Woman